PRAISE FOR SARAH J. DALEY

"With gloriously brutal worldbuilding, and the kinds of characters you can't help but root for, Wings of Steel and Fury *is a thrilling quest for survival, revenge, and redemption set against a vision of an imperfect heaven and an all-too-human hell. Weaving a story about the darkness and repercussions of war, as well as the importance of reckoning with our own angels and demons, this is a timely reminder of the strength and ingenuity of the masses when facing oppression by the powerful. The revolution is here."*
Dan Hanks, author of
Swashbucklers and The Way Up Is Death

"The hierarchy of humans and angels flipped? A fallen angel that fucks? Wings of Steel and Fury *is a live, pacy adventure with powerful twists that will keep your blood running hot!"*
Chris Panatier, author of
The Phlebotomist, Stringers and The Redemption of Morgan Bright

"A spellbinding tale of angels falling, worlds colliding, and the quest for vengeance. Daley always delivers."
Dan Koboldt, author of The Silver Queendom

"Daley's worldbuilding is deep and lived-in, and the protagonists' fight to reveal the truth of their world makes for a gripping read. Moments of beauty punctuate the darkness in a way that satisfies and feels truly magical."
Khan Wong, author of
The Circus Infinite and D

"Even in a world of angels and characters stands out. They're mess don't know whether to punch th
R.W.W. Greene, author of Mercury Rising

Sarah J. Daley

WINGS OF STEEL AND FURY

ANGRY ROBOT
An imprint of Watkins Media Ltd

Unit 11, Shepperton House
89-93 Shepperton Road
London N1 3DF
UK

angryrobotbooks.com
Lightning from Heaven

An Angry Robot paperback original, 2025

Copyright © Sarah J. Daley 2025

Edited by Simon Spanton Walker and Andrew Hook
Cover by Alice Claire Coleman
Set in Meridien

All rights reserved. Sarah J. Daley asserts the moral right to be identified as the author of this work. A catalogue record for this book is available from the British Library.

This novel is entirely a work of fiction. Names, characters, places, and incidents are the products of the author's imagination or are used fictitiously. Any resemblance to actual events, locales, organizations or persons, living or dead, is entirely coincidental.

Sales of this book without a front cover may be unauthorized. If this book is coverless, it may have been reported to the publisher as "unsold and destroyed" and neither the author nor the publisher may have received payment for it.

Angry Robot and the Angry Robot icon are registered trademarks of Watkins Media Ltd.

ISBN 978 1 91599 822 4
Ebook ISBN 978 1 91599 821 7

Printed and bound in the United Kingdom by CPI Group (UK) Ltd, Croydon CR0 4YY

The manufacturer's authorised representative in the EU for product safety is eucomply OÜ - Pärnu mnt 139b-14, 11317 Tallinn, Estonia, hello@eucompliancepartner.com; www.eucompliancepartner.com

9 8 7 6 5 4 3 2 1

For my husband Robert

CHAPTER ONE

The great dome of Upper Splendour stretched clear in all directions, save one. To the east, toward the Keeper's Archon, stood the thick purplish bank of a miles-deep nebula. The detritus of dead stars, the nebulae were the favored haunt of the creatures they'd come to harvest, and as Eleazar squinted toward the mountainous swirl of luminous clouds a glimmer of leviathans skipped into view. Blessed Sol set fire to their fine scales and dragonfly wings as they rose as one into the perfect-day blue of the heavens. His heart swelled at their beauty, and then abruptly sank to his toes. How could he bring himself to kill one of them?

The blast of a trumpet sliced through his skull – others had spotted the glimmer. Beneath his bare feet, the deck of the royal drachen thrummed as the Mithran-powered engines roared. Above him, the battened sails unfolded with a resounding snap to catch the wind and give pursuit. Excitement shivered through him despite his reticence, a primal response to the call of the hunt. His kind had been hunting the leviathans since the First Creation; their blood and bones, skin and flesh sustained the blessed world of Splendour. It was a hallowed communion.

Eleazar Starson knew this but the idea of plunging a lance through living flesh like a barbarian from the Below made his belly churn. It was savagery, this ritual, more symbolic than necessary since they farmed leviathans like cattle to fulfill their needs. These hunts were a cruel paean to the distant past.

It is a vanity. A game for callow youths, this barbaric hunt. Why not let these few wild beasts live in peace?

"Do you think they might have the minds of men?" Eleazar mused aloud to his shivering page. At the boy's peculiar look, he hastily added, "Not of Angelus, of course, but base thoughts and feelings like the Beasts of the Below? The barest sentience..."

The youth gawped at him. Eleazar cursed silently. He should have kept his thoughts to himself. His page's nonsense answer confirmed it: "The Flaying of the Blessed Leviathans formed the firmament of Splendour; they are Holy beyond measure, milord."

"Yes, that is so, good Verity."

His grave nod made the boy beam with pleasure, but he was still cursing himself. It was nerves prompting him to give voice to his soft-hearted flights of fancy, or so his brother would call his ponderings. Foolish, pointless, and entirely inappropriate, today of all days especially. Today, the heir to the Solaire Throne must prove himself in the Blessed Harvest or lose the respect of every Archon in Splendour. Even the pinioned might look upon him in disdain if he failed.

Resigned, Eleazar flung off his heavy cloak and let it slither to the deck. Instantly, his skin rose in gooseflesh as the chill air of Upper Splendour lashed him. He wore only a loincloth of deep purple and an elaborate harness across his chest and torso of matching leviathan skin which did little to shield him from the cold. But this was what the original Angelus wore to hunt the first leviathan. It was tradition, and, he had to admit, it exposed his bronzed skin in delightful fashion. After the hunt, he might just wear it to his favorite joint in Lower Splendour.

Imperiously, Eleazar threw his arm to the side and his page slapped an iron harpoon into his open palm. The slim boy gave him a grin and a cheeky wink, stepping back a mere instant before Eleazar spread his wings in a mighty whoosh of white and silver feathers. His wingless page went to his knees in adoration, his eyes boggling. Eleazar smirked. It never hurt to remind the pinioned of their place.

Almost immediately, he arranged his wings tight to his back, feeling a twinge of shame. Was he his brother, to torment a servant so? The boy was a good page. And as pretty as the sun. Which was why he forgave his cheek more often than not.

"Go to the hawk's nest for a good view, Verity," he said, giving the youth a benevolent smile. "Your prince becomes a king today."

Verity's eyes shone, and he scrambled to his feet. "Aye, milord! May the Luminous One bless you this day!"

"Bless the One makes this quick," Eleazar muttered to himself as his page skipped away. His heart full of thunder, he leapt to the railing of the drachen for his own good view. Spreading his wings against the fierce crosswinds, he grasped the rigging and leaned forward as far as he dared, the harpoon hanging in his grip. The drachen was over the vast nebula, closing the distance to the glimmer with ease. The leviathans were vulnerable when they skipped from cloud to cloud, seeking the freshest dust of the cosmos. The dense cloud banks provided good cover, but the open air of Splendour left them nowhere to hide.

In moments, the glimmer was beyond the deep cloudbank, the drachen in swift pursuit. Eleazar scanned the cluster of leviathans for a likely target. There would be no avoiding this unpleasant task; he might as well do it right. There. One smaller beast struggled to keep up, its tail curved beneath it like a hook and its four wings buzzing frantically. A juvenile, if he had to guess. Another far larger creature slowed to match its pace. The mother, unwilling to leave her child. His heart cracked. Her love would be her doom.

Just your bad luck to skip when a drachen is near. Poor beast, if it were my choice–

A sudden upthrust of wind nearly ripped him from his perch. The thick, braided line tore at his palm, but he kept his grip. Barely. His feet clenched the ornate railing hard enough to make his toes cramp, and he managed not to tumble over the side.

Unwillingly, his gaze dipped downward, drawn by a morbid curiosity and an atavistic fear. Far, far below him through layers of wispy clouds and open sky swirled a perpetual storm of black, charcoal grey and silver: The Black Silence, a gateway separating the world of Light from the world of Darkness. It shielded Splendour from the dismal world of Below. Only Mithran-armored drachens could survive the passage to that violent, dangerous place. That *human* place. They dared the maelstrom to collect the Hallow Tithe, as necessary to Splendour's survival as harvesting leviathans. The angels who crewed those ships were legends among Splendour's inhabitants. Heroes to be adored. But Eleazar envied them not at all. *Leave me to my books and my poems and my sweetest loves...*

Another updraft wrapped around him, tugging at his wings, ruffling his feathers in dramatic fashion. It pulled his gaze from the Silence, thankfully, and he tried to focus on the task at hand. *The fucking hunt, Lee. Do your stupid duty.*

Cries of worry and fear erupted behind him. His momentary falter had not gone unnoticed. The crew and captain reacted with decided alarm to see him perched so precariously. Winged though he was – as all the Angelus were – dangerous, unexpected gusts could potentially send him into an uncontrolled tumble. This far from the safety of any Archon Aerie, he'd be sucked into the Black Silence long before he found a perch. And his safety was their responsibility. They might all be hanged if he were lost.

"Oh! Be careful, my prince!"

Eleazar steadied himself against the buffeting winds then glanced over his shoulder to find the source of the high, feminine cry. His betrothed, the Lady Maurissa Chrystos, stood on the deck far back from the railing, dressed in warm, black hunting leathers which wrapped her from neck to wrists to ankles. Even her long, raven-black hair was contained beneath a scarf, only a few winding coils escaping. Her face and hands were the only bits of her alabaster skin exposed. Modest clothing for a modest woman. She carried a crossbow – a far more manageable weapon for her slim frame than a heavy harpoon – and looked entirely capable of using it. He met her wide, crystal-blue eyes and managed an awkward nod. Her wings, as black as her clothes and hair, were half-raised behind her as if she intended to take flight and grab him should he falter again.

And wouldn't that be peachy? To be snatched from danger like a naughty child? Eleazar gave her a stiff smile. But he dropped down from the railing. He was weary of fighting the wind, anyway. Once the drachen was close enough for him to launch, he'd need all his strength.

More hunters joined them on the foredeck of the drachen, led by Eleazar's half-brother, Duke Rastaphar Mikalson. Tall and broad-shouldered, his wings tinged rare and beautiful emerald, Rast was everything their mother wanted in a son: A warrior, a hunter, an ascetic, a monk, and the Queen Regent's most trusted adviser. He was also the son of her first husband, the late Duke of Arcadia, and not in line to take the Solaire Throne. There were whispers among the more devout Angelus that perhaps the Luminous One had made a mistake in the birth order of Queen Lucretia's sons. Eleazar could hardly blame them. Sometimes even he thought the Kosmos had made a mistake.

But. The Angelus who became the Great King of Honour, the One who Guarded the Gates to the Ten Worlds, the One who brought balance and peace to Splendour was part of an unbroken line stretching back to the First Creation. His father had reigned a thousand years before he'd broken his neck slipping on the steps outside the Hoary Frog. He'd been celebrating the birth of his first son. The entirety of Splendour had been mourning him for twenty-five years, the same amount of time Eleazar Starson had been disappointing them. On the bright side, as king, he might disappoint them for eons.

"You should know by now, Lady Maurissa," Rast said, with a reserved, proper smile for the slim woman. "Cautioning Prince Eleazar is a fool's errand."

Maurissa pursed her lips, but Eleazar caught the flash of her bright eyes slipping toward Rast then away just as quickly. A strange look from a strange woman. At least to him. Beautiful, yes, sharply intelligent, certainly, but as dogmatic as a Maiden of Light and as cold and inscrutable as the Crystal Cliffs with their shifting colors and fierce winds. He was as excited to marry her as he was to kill a leviathan nymph. One more unpleasant task on the path to the throne.

Still. He harbored a hope that perhaps she would reveal a secret fire on their wedding night. A hope as slim as a feather.

And maybe the Black Silence will swallow all of Splendour by morning...

It was a joke that his mother had chosen such a woman for him. Or perhaps a censure for his decadent ways. Saying she was disappointed in his enjoyment of all things sensual was a wild understatement. Well, the joke was on her. A frigid wife wouldn't keep him from the brothels and haunts in the Lower Firmament. Not even the Luminous One could turn him into a proper Elect. Leave the moral authority and judgement to men like Rast and his entourage of second sons and the wealthy children of mighty Archons. They spent their days preparing for the hunt, meditating, praying, and *supposedly* eschewing liquor and meat and sex.

Why live at all?

Rast, son of Mikalas, cocked his head and regarded him. He held a harpoon, one half as long as Eleazar's and made of sleek and deadly steel. Below-made, if Eleazar had to guess. Human-made. They were clever, those Beasts of the Below. Savage and homicidal, but clever, nonetheless. Eleazar wished his own harpoon was steel, but iron, just like his clothing, was traditional. Only a weak, ill-favored Angelus would demand an edge in the sacred hunt.

I suppose my father used his bare hands to bring down his first leviathan...

"You're awfully eager, brother," Rast said, the barest hint of mockery in his voice. "Are you going to fly into the firmament without the crew and before the ship can heave to?"

Eleazar tried a casual shrug but felt as though his shoulders squeezed his ears. Quickly, he straightened, unfurling his wings. He might be slender, perhaps even frail, compared to Rast, but his silver and white feathers were unmatched among the Angelus. They were his greatest pride, and he wasn't beneath flaunting them. Even among the highborn, plumaged as they were in a glorious range of colors, his glossy whites were unique and uniquely gorgeous. His gaze skipped beyond Rast, drawn to his raven-winged betrothed, wondering how much she was paying attention. Her eyes were upon him, studying his wings. His chest swelled. For a moment, he let himself admire her beauty. He supposed they made a handsome match, at the least.

Abruptly, the girl caught his scrutiny, and ducked her head, a spot of red on her pale cheek. Surprised, Eleazar wondered if he'd been wrong about her if she could blush like a normal girl.

"Oh, leave him be, Rast," spoke up one of Rast's entourage, a skinny fellow from a minor noble family with purple-dipped wings. Eleazar thought his name was Alexi but couldn't be sure. They didn't exactly frequent the same beerhalls or gin haunts or houses of ill-repute.

The one whose name was probably Alexi gave Eleazar an encouraging smile, and Eleazar deigned to return it though with a thin-lipped lack of graciousness. Alexi's smile faltered a bit, but he added in a hearty tone, "Don't you remember the first time you had a chance for a solo kill?"

Rast nodded, laughing. "I was ten years younger than this one. No wonder he's so eager."

Eleazar bristled as the rest of the entourage echoed Rast's laughter. Suddenly, the drachen lurched beneath them, picking up speed. Only Eleazar stumbled from the sudden shift, his brother catching his arm to steady him. The ship veered hard to starboard, the sails rippling in the constant winds. They all dashed to the railing. The mother leviathan and her flagging calf were within the sights of the drachen's colossal, mounted harpoons. Eleazar sucked in a breath. Would they take the beasts for him? He wasn't sure whether to be upset or relieved.

"They won't shoot," Rast said briskly, gripping his bicep encouragingly. He was grinning and Eleazar forgot his earlier mockery. After today, would Rast finally be proud of him? He found himself grinning back at his elder brother. "They won't shoot without my order," he continued breathlessly. "Take your position on the rail, and I'll tell you when to fly. You must time it well, brother. Aim for the nymph."

He urged Eleazar back onto the railing, who clambered into place, the harpoon heavy in his sweaty grip. A thin line lay curled in coils on the deck which tethered the harpoon to the ship. It was pure Mithran, the gods' metal, but it seemed a slim thread when compared with the wild vastness of Upper Splendour.

"Hold fast, Eleazar. Slow your breath and trust in your wings. Be ready to dive."

"Yes, brother." Breathless with excitement, his eyes locked on the struggling nymph and shrieking mother leviathan, Eleazar opened his wings wide to feel the currents. His harpoon suddenly felt light as a feather and his body snapped with energy and strength. Today, he would prove himself at last. The doubts in his heart were overwhelmed by adrenaline. His dive would be everything. If he missed the nymph, he failed.

"Get ready, brother! Soon. Wait until we are over them, and slightly ahead. Drive your spike into the young one's heart! It will be a good death – quick and clean!"

"Yes! I know!" Eleazar readied himself to jump, his muscles bunching and tightening. The ship tilted sharply; he found himself staring down at a green-backed leviathan nymph silhouetted against the deep blue sky, its wings shivering rapidly. Did it know what was about to happen? Did it know what was about to fall upon it? Sudden vertigo gripped him. What if he jumped and missed? Only the thin filament of Mithran attached to his harpoon kept him tethered to the drachen. The winds here were strong enough to tear him apart.

"Now, Eleazar! Dive now and take him!"

Rast's command compelled him off the railing. The wind buffeted him, straining his wings and shoulder muscles; he caught the updrafts and rode them clear of the ship. Then he folded his great white wings and dove.

The rush of air deafened him, but still he heard the shrieking fury of the beast's mother – like a teakettle left on the fire. There was nothing she could do to stop him, however. She moved too slowly to halt a diving Angelus. Eleazar snapped open his wings before he slammed into the hard, slick scales of the smaller beast, his harpoon hurtling forward with all the momentum of his dive. When it struck flesh, it was like stabbing solid rock. Pain lanced through his arm, into his shoulder. He cried out, clutching the quivering harpoon so he didn't slide off the beast. Its point held, thankfully. Vibrant violet blood poured from the wound and the nymph bugled in pain.

Gasping, Eleazar clung to his harpoon, dazed, his legs folded beneath him and his wings askew as blood splashed across his skin, onto his face, into his eyes. The creature was three times his size, much larger than he expected. He'd impaled the creature's spine, he realized through a fog of pain. It hadn't been a killing blow. Its heart still pumped ferociously, and his harpoon was lodged in leviathan bone – pure gods' metal.

The wild blasts from the mother suddenly changed in tone. The high shrill became a low bellow, a sound of pain and anger that battered his ears. He looked up, fighting wind and the nymph's desperate bucking – its attempt to dislodge him – and saw lines attaching the mother leviathan to the royal airship. Ah. They'd cast their harpoons. The mother was finished; she was already being drawn up to the drachen, leaving her child alone.

He braced his feet against the sleek back of his prey and stood. The beast gave a final, pleading squeak to its doomed parent – the sound slid into Eleazar like a knife. It shuddered and nearly tossed him off, but Eleazar held on with desperate strength.

Bright blood spewed from the deep wound, spraying into the air in shimmering ropes. He tried shifting to avoid it. It was so warm, almost hot, and it tingled on his skin. Most of it flew upward, floating as if in water, the creature's blood imbued with deep magic. He spat it from his mouth, horrified as it clung to him like a living thing. He looked up toward the airship, hoping for its great harpoon to do his work for him, but the royal drachen was occupied with the mother leviathan. He had to kill the calf himself.

How? With what?

The nymph hovered in the shadow of its mother, not even attempting to flee. The buzz of its wings had slowed dramatically and it was beginning to sink. The magic which kept its mother afloat was nascent in one so young. It needed her strength and that of their glimmer to protect it. Only the thin line of Mithran attached to his harpoon would keep it from falling into the void when its strength failed entirely.

Eleazar peered upward, his chest heaving. The crew crawled across the scaled surface of the mother, securing hooks and lines to tether the beast to the ship. He spotted Maurissa sliding down a rope to reach its underside, her wings tucked tight to her back. She waved at him, staring at him intensely as she hung from the harness. He returned the wave, puffing his chest and setting his jaw, hoping he looked like a conquering hero and not a fool. She had no interest in the butchering, only in him.

A rush of wind and the heavy beat of wings warned him others had taken an interest in his safety, as well. He knew it was Rast before he turned, shame filling him. Blood rushed to his cheeks and his palms grew wet where he gripped the wooden haft of the harpoon.

"Brother!" Eleazar cried, pretending he hadn't a care in the world. "I've severed its spine. Not quite a killing blow, but close enough." He gave his harpoon a twist which only ground splinters into his palm. "If you could finish him off, I'd be in your debt."

Rast stared at him, his face like stone. "You failed," he said simply. "You cannot sever a leviathan's spine with iron. It is pure Mithran."

"Yes, well, but the beast is dying. Surely. The blood…"

Rast interrupted him with a sigh, hefting his slim steel spike and walking across the nymph's back with practiced surety. His wings tight against his back to avoid the ever-violent updrafts swirling, Rast drew abreast of him and dealt the killing blow to the unfortunate animal. It gave a last shudder and its thrumming heart stilled. Eleazar blew out a breath.

"You never cease to disappoint me, Eleazar."

Eleazar started. "Pardon?" Their relationship had often been fraught, but Eleazar couldn't recall Rast ever speaking to him in such a manner. It was shocking. His shock turned to pique. He was sore and tired and covered in blood. And all for nothing. "I never wanted to participate in this barbarity from the start," he snapped. "It is a stupid way to prove one's worth."

"Stupid and barbaric? Our most sacred tradition?" Rast shook his head mournfully. He backed up a few feet, facing Eleazar. "This was your chance, brother, your last chance. It gives me no joy that you have failed yet again to live up to the memory of your blessed father. An Angelus I greatly admired. One who always treated me as a son."

Eleazar bared his teeth. "But you're not his son, Rast. I am!"

"And what do you do to honor him? What do you do to deserve the Solaire Throne?"

"Deserve? It is my destiny!" Eleazar gripped his locked harpoon. Above them, the mother leviathan was secured, and the butchering had begun in earnest. It had captured the attention of everyone on the ship, including those meant to guard him. A fine bloody mist clouded the air around her. A feeling of dread stirred in his belly as he faced his elder brother once more. "By fate and the will of the Luminous One!"

Rast narrowed his eyes. "You are a feckless cunt, Eleazar. You drink and dice with the pinioned as if they aren't less than the dust on our boots. You fuck humans, for the love of all things holy. You sleep through council meetings and let others govern in your place while you compose poems to whores and question the very foundations of our world. You are a prince by birth alone, and your ascension to the throne will be the doom of us all!"

Eleazar could hardly believe his ears; fury filled him at his brother's condemnation. "And spearing harmless leviathans and torturing human slaves makes you honorable? I may be feckless, I might even be Splendour's biggest cunt, but at least I'm not a sadistic fiend like you! And what harm is there in questions, Rast? Knowledge is not something to be feared! I would bring enlightenment to Splendour, not just stagnation cloaked in tradition." He sneered the last word, putting all his disdain into it.

Rast matched his sneer. "I am not alone in my opinion of you. Many of us feel the same."

"Who? The rabble who follows you like a pack of dogs?"

"There are others. Many you would never suspect." Rast looked up.

Suspicious, Eleazar followed his gaze. And found Maurissa above them still hanging from the belly of the mother leviathan, hidden in its shade. Her eyes were upon him, keen and calculating. She had her crossbow in her hands. Growing cold to the bone, Eleazar caught a flash of gold; she'd loaded it with bolts of Mithran. Bolts of iron and steel might sting an Angelus, but Mithran…

"Why?" he said softly. "What have I ever done to her?"

"You disgust her. She is pure and good. She wished to be a Maiden of Light, not the wife of a wastrel. Worthy of a better man than you!"

No one was watching her; no one was paying any attention to what was happening below the prize. Eleazar realized his danger too late. She raised the crossbow and loosed a bolt in one sudden swift motion, her eyes as cold as the clouds.

The Mithran bolt punched through his bastard wing, clipping bone. The blow sent him to his knees, his wing flailing uselessly. Pain blinded him; he'd never suffered anything worse than a hangover. He'd never had the stomach for fighting, except for trading wicked barbs. He screamed through clenched teeth, his vision darkening.

Rast. Where is Rast?

Eleazar struggled to right himself, hanging onto his harpoon – the only thing keeping him from slipping over the edge of the nymph. The scales, slick with blood, slithered away beneath his bare feet. His heart slammed erratically at his chest, and fear drove back some of the all-consuming pain.

His vision dark, he found Rast coming toward him. He flung himself backward, tried to bate his wings, to fly, but pain stopped him. Effortlessly, his brother kicked him square in the chest, his eyes stormy and dark, unreadable. Eleazar sprawled backward, his wings a tangle of crooked feathers. Helpless, he struggled to right himself before Rast could come at him again. But Rast made no move to attack. Instead, he stepped aside as if–

Maurissa. The crossbow. That treacherous bitch would have a clear shot!

No! He could not die this way. He'd rather–

Eleazar threw himself to the right, sliding desperately on his outspread wings. The slick back of the nymph sloped sharply, and he tumbled down its side, hitting its gossamer wing before bouncing off into the shrieking winds. Instinctively, he spread his own wings to catch the updrafts, but only one responded properly. The other screamed in protest and bent uselessly against the punishing wind. He gave his working wing one great downbeat, his face raised toward the drachen far, far above him. A drowning man trying to breach the ocean. It wasn't enough; his injured wing was a dead weight pulling him down.

And then he was falling, spinning, tossed about by screaming winds. Helpless in the void.

His last sight before a bank of thick clouds swallowed him was the half-butchered mother leviathan and her dead child beneath the silent bulk of the royal airship.

CHAPTER TWO

The river was swift and swollen from the recent rains, churning gray and white, murky and forbidding. But he needed the water. Desperately. His throat ached and his mouth was dust. How many days had he gone without water? Two now, probably. He didn't have another day in him.

And yet, he hesitated. Was it safe to leave the forest? The battlefield was far behind him. No man's land was a memory. A terrible, terrifying memory. A shattered stretch of mud and blood and death. Here, there would be no bullets singing at him from hidden snipers. No clouds of yellow smoke. Not here. Here, he was safe. Safe enough, anyway, so close to home.

Go on. Go to the river. Just do it. But it was hard to let go of the fear. Fear had been his best friend for so long. Fear had kept him alive these past months and fear had kept him moving these past few days despite hunger, and thirst, and the stinging and burning pain along his arms. His clothes and long canvas duster protected much of his skin, but the yellow smoke had seeped through in places. For too long, he'd let it linger on his skin. But removing his clothes during the mad dash for freedom, his stumbling passage from a warzone to the peace of distant woods, had been unthinkable without water nearby. The yellow smoke lingered long after exposure. The remnants would have contaminated his entire body, leading to rashes, intense pain, and scarring. Only a swift-running body of water would save him.

And now, at long last, he'd made it to the Stari river. Its waters would wash away the last of the contaminant and leave him safe. Angels willing...

Finally, he pushed the fear into his belly and stepped from the woods into the open.

No bullets zipped at him from the dense tree line or from across the wide river, and Private Diver Barrett-Cree slung his rifle over his shoulder and stumbled forward. The sound of his rasping breath echoed too loudly in the oiled canvas and rubber helmet that covered his head. A tube led from his mouth to the scrubber strapped to his chest, and glass lenses shielded his eyes. He didn't dare remove it until he'd washed away all traces of yellow smoke. The smallest amount could prove fatal if inhaled, and it was a horrid, agonizing death. Better to be shot in the head or blown to bits by artillery.

Better to run, he'd decided in the midst of that horrid, final attack as men screamed and died around him, clawing and trampling each other. Better to run, and live, rather than die shrieking like–

Diver stumbled on a hidden hummock and felt a surge of terror. Senseless but very, very real. Instead of hugging the earth, he forced himself onward to the river's edge. Running kept a man alive. His lungs pumped like bellows; it had taken everything in him to cross open ground. Shaking, he stood on a precipice, a steep, muddy bank his only obstacle to the precious water. It took him a moment to realize he knew this place, this spot. He was so close to home.

Home. I want to go home. Creator, help me, I want nothing else in all the world.

Diver cringed at the desperate thoughts. The last year had broken him in ways he'd never imagined. Full of purpose and pride, he had gone to war thinking it was for his country, for his people, but seeing his friends and fellows blown apart over a stretch of contested land even vultures avoided had changed his mind quicker than a wink. They were pawns. All of them.

Except maybe the commanders safe in their bunkers tap-tap-tapping out orders down the tele-net. No amount of land was worth the carnage he'd witnessed. And damn if he cared that their army was supposedly blessed by the Creator Eternal and His army of Angelus. They were bastards to bless such a hell.

"You fight in the name of the Creator Eternal, to fulfill our portion of the Hallow Tithe. For your faith and service, the Angelus will guide us to glory and victory so our bounty may nourish the Heavens and Heaven's bounty can nourish our souls! Blessed be the Koine."

Fucking lies.

The morning blessing had always grated on him, but he'd kept his feelings hidden. A heretic among the ranks would not have been tolerated. Even strong, tall, blond-haired Paul wouldn't have been able to protect his skinny ass.

For a moment, he let himself picture Paul's face, his broad shoulders and crooked grin. The lock of hair curled on his forehead. He longed to brush it aside, but before he could lift a hand the image crumbled, burned. Became the visage of a staring ghoul, devoid of flesh, showing bone through dried blood.

Diver squeezed his eyes shut, swaying on the edge of the riverbank. Guilt swirled uncomfortably in his belly. Guilt and grief and anger. Why was he alive when Paul – a man with more life in his little finger than Diver had in his whole, sorry body – wasn't? How had a coward survived what the strongest, bravest man he'd ever known hadn't? Where was the sense in any of it? Pain, a constant, distant ache, infused his being, overwhelming yet familiar. It was so much a part of him, he wondered what would be left of him if the pain ever vanished.

Diver opened his eyes. He was light-headed with thirst. He slid down the muddy riverbank on his heels, careful to keep his rifle and knapsack free of the muck. His boots sank into the wet earth, and he pulled them free with a sucking noise, clopping to the water's edge where a rocky sandbar provided better footing. A heron swept low across the water, hunting for fish. Diver stared at it, aware of his belly gnawing at his backbone. It would be an easy thing to shoot it. But he could not bring himself to raise his weapon. To kill something so beautiful...

Eager for fresh water, Diver shed his gloves, then shrugged out of his pack and divested himself of his oiled canvas duster. He moved quickly, but he was thorough with his gear. A vigorous shake of each item filled the air with clouds of dust and a fine, yellow powder.

He laid his clothes across a tangle of roots. His uniform tunic followed his jacket, and he dunked the grey broadcloth into the water, wringing it out thoroughly before placing it on the bank. It was a few sizes too big, but in excellent condition. He'd taken it off a fallen comrade who'd lasted a day in the trenches. The poor chap had been hit in the head, luckily, leaving his uniform spanking new. The man's blue cotton shirt followed the tunic, then Diver tugged off his own worn jackboots – the fellow had possessed remarkably tiny feet – and shimmied out of his stone-colored trousers. The shirt and trousers he soaked, as well, and he dipped his boots in the river a few times. He hated to have wet feet, but there was no avoiding it. In the trenches, wet feet sometimes led to slow and agonizing debilitation. And death. A soldier who couldn't walk or run didn't last long. If an enemy's gun didn't get him, he became easy pickings when the occasional wave of ghouls overran the frontlines. He shuddered; he'd seen it happen. Men ripped apart by those burnt devils hungry for human flesh. Akkadian or Koine, it didn't matter, all men tasted as sweet to the cursed creatures.

Naked but for his helmet and mask, Diver stepped into the water, the scrubber swinging against his chest. It was clear at the edge, though farther out it was gray and churning. He could see the rocks beneath his feet, and tiny fish nibbling at his toes. The cold instantly numbed his feet and set him to shivering, but the rush of water across his skin felt exquisite.

He plowed deeper into the river, slipping on the slick rocks as icy water swirled up his shins, around his knees, to his thighs and above. Bending at the waist, he reached deep into the frigid stream and let it wash the poison from his skin, the scrubber swinging. After days of running and hiding, he shook with relief. The river would wash him clean. Then he would be able to go home.

Home. How he longed to be home again so life could return to normal. He longed for the time before he'd joined the army. Why had he been so eager to run off to war? Fury had warned him it would change him, even if it didn't break him. And she'd been right. As usual...

Diver lifted his hands, now clean and numb, no longer itching, tingling or burning, but they seemed the hands of a stranger to him. The things he'd done with them. Terrible things. Slowly, he curled his hands into fists and fought down a rising urge to vomit. He swallowed convulsively.

He ducked beneath the water, letting it flow over him. Washing him thoroughly. Washing any lingering traces from his skin and helmet. When he broke the surface, he tore at the buckles of his helmet, wrenching the dreadful thing from his head. He took a long, deep breath, inhaling cold, clean air. After days of breathing his own dank, recycled breath, it stung with shocking deliciousness. Tossing his helmet to the bank with his other clothes, he went to his knees, sharp rocks biting his flesh, and drank from the river. Drank until he thought he would burst.

For a moment, he almost prayed. It did seem like a miracle that he'd survived, but he knew better than to believe in miracles.

Another face filled his head: His sister's. He'd often called her image to him when battle and fatigue and horror had threatened to overwhelm him. It seemed an age had passed since he'd last seen her. Would she even recognize her baby brother now? This soldier? He laughed bitterly, dragging his fingers through the chill water. What was a soldier but a killer? Had killing boys and girls like himself brought glory to his country as his old teacher-turned-recruiter promised it would? Where was the glory in gunning down a person, or slicing open their guts?

A shudder wracked him which had nothing to do with the frigid river. No matter what horrid things he'd done, it was time to go home.

Diver gave his skin a final wash and turned back toward shore.

A shimmer at the edge of his vision gave him pause. A flash of white. He froze, afraid an enemy had hidden himself in the reeds and roots. The white he'd seen remained unmoving on the muddy riverbank. Without the helmet to obscure his vision, he could see clearly what lay entwined inside a giant tree branch. It was not an enemy – no enemy wore armor made of giant feathers. But beneath those feathers was a man, half in and half out of the cold river.

With a shock, Diver realized the man wasn't lying beneath a pile of feathers. He had wings. He squeezed his eyes shut. *Finally, after everything, I have gone mad.*

Only one man-shaped thing bore the wings of a bird in all the great wide world of Avernus. They never deigned to touch the ground, staying aloft on their glorious wings even when they ventured from their airships for the Hallow Tithe. So, how could he believe this creature lying in the muck like an injured crane was one of *them?*

He ventured closer, cautious until he was certain. Until he *knew*.

On this day of days, his soul broken and his heart dead, standing naked in a river with poison swirling away from him in yellow streaks, Diver Barrett-Cree clapped eyes on a fallen Angelus and felt the world shift beneath his feet.

* * *

The skies had cleared. The glowering clouds broken and scattered. Azure sky peeked between the treetops, rich enough to diminish the high, distant Celestial Gate. Whereas somedays it was a swirling maelstrom of black and silver, today, it was only a dark smudge against the vivid blue. The gateway to Heaven, the portal was like the moon in its waxing and waning. It shifted across the sky on its path to the Hallow Tithing Grounds like a great, ominous eye.

For Fury Barrett-Cree, in her little village at the edge of a vast wood, the Celestial Gate might as well have been the moon for all the thought she gave it. Though she'd been taught to disdain the Angelus and their brutal Tithe, most days she couldn't care less about either. Feeding her belly was more important than feeding her soul. Or not feeding her soul, however you wanted to look at it.

Heartened by the warm sun and bright skies, Fury took to the woods with her bow and a full quiver, slipping through the wet bracken and between the dark, shaggy trunks of hickory trees. Her larder was bare but for a few stray apples and a canister of oats. Fresh meat would be a welcome addition. And if she was lucky enough to bag some rabbits, she could barter their fur for seeds and maybe even a few needles. Her last good needle had been bent beyond saving after she'd stitched her scarecrow back together. Again. Every so often, her neighbors' wretched children liked to tear it apart. Trying to make the half-Gullan girl think a ghoul was ravaging her garden, hunting for flesh. Their ridiculous howling never fooled her for a second. The little brats were lucky she didn't turn them into pincushions. A waste of good arrows.

I could spare a few rotten apples though. Fury cackled softly as she followed the narrow game trail threading between the tall trees, imagining the satisfying splat of an apple against someone's head.

There, a track. And another. The wide paw of a bobcat pressed into the soft, dark earth. Another hunter. Water filled it from the recent rains. Her boots and leg wrappings were already wet, but she trudged on.

The animosity of her neighbors was nothing new, but it had gotten worse with Diver gone. Her baby brother had run off to war, and his absence slammed home how isolated they had been in their little cottage. It had never bothered her before, but neither had her neighbors been so bold in their disdain. Attacking her scarecrow was the least of it. The village elders had taken her pony for the "war effort" only a week after Diver left, and derisive looks and comments followed her whenever she ventured into town. She was alone, now, and her strange ways were no longer tolerated. Against her nature, she found herself praying to the Creator to bring Diver home.

It didn't hurt to pray, she supposed, but it didn't help much either. Praying was just shouting to the void. She hadn't even prayed when her father lay dying. She scoffed. The lengths she would go for her little brother. *I kept that boy out of trouble his whole life, and he repaid me by running into bullets.*

Diver had always been a baby in her mind. Someone to be protected. Her father had not spoiled her as he had Diver: Rather, Grayson Barrett had taught Fury to stand on her own. He'd tasked Fury with the wellbeing of her baby brother the day their mother had vanished – never mind that she'd been a child, too.

"You were born strong, Fee," her Da had told her often. "Just like your mother. Just like me. Diver is sensitive; he needs you to protect him."

It hadn't been such a chore while her parents were alive. And then in a blink, they'd both gone. Her mother vanishing on the day of the Hallow Tithe so long ago, then their father soon after. Taken by the Scourge. Afterwards... the world had darkened. She became aware of evil lurking in every corner. The townspeople had shown them little sympathy, especially when she'd adamantly refused to take their portion of manna. Did they think she'd just forget all she'd been taught? Fools. Alone and seemingly helpless, they thought she'd be easily indoctrinated into Koine ways, but she was half-Gullan. She'd been taught the Manna the Angelus brought in return for the Tithe was not a blessing as most believed, but a curse. She would never touch it, or allow Diver to, either.

I imagine he has now. In the army...

Ironic, really. The army fought over land needed to produce the Hallow Tithe and were fueled by the Manna the Angelus exchanged for it – the "blessed gift". A vicious, unending cycle.

Fury paused near a sunlit glade, an arrow notched in her bow. She kept still, standing in the dappled shade, blending into the verge. Thick grass and broad patches of clover blanketed the clearing. The last of the dew sparkled across the green. A swath of disturbance was obvious through a section of the glade, too large to be made by a rabbit. What or who had passed this way? She set her jaw. She wasn't the only one who hunted these woods.

If Hugh or Lonnie show their faces, I'll put an arrow through them. Those two had always been trouble. They'd especially loved to torment Diver. In their schooldays, he had been small and slim compared to them. An easy target. Not his sister, though. As children, Fury had been able to beat them soundly a time or two. Age had stolen her advantage to some degree, though they still showed a marked reluctance to confront her directly. She'd never been shy about using her fists, or her height and reach to wallop a foe. Not so Diver. He was more likely to run from a fight. She suspected their abuse was part of the reason he'd joined the army.

Imagine, running from bullies straight into a war...

Sudden fear shivered over her skin. It came to her often, this fear, passing over her like a wave, or snatching her from sleep to lie in sweat-soaked blankets. What if her brother lay somewhere broken and dying? What if he'd fallen to a wandering ghoul? She should have joined the army with him. To keep him safe. She knew how to fire a gun. Her father had trained her with his lone pistol. She couldn't afford ammunition for it now, but surely the army would have provided it.

These worries weren't new; she forced her tumbling thoughts to still and scanned the edges of the glade. If she was lucky, some rabbits would come to graze. If she wasn't so lucky, she'd return home hungry. If she was well and truly unlucky, she'd run into some hostile soul.

A shadow moved beneath the trees across from her. Stealthily. It flitted behind the broad smooth trunk of a beech tree. Fury raised her bow, her heart thumping. She kept her breathing calm, slow, and sighted along her arrow. Waiting.

Show your face.

A whiff of woodsmoke tickled her nose. She was too far from the village for it to be coming from there. Someone had a camp nearby. Not a hunter. They wouldn't have a fire if they wanted to attract game. Her eyes narrowed and her bow was steady. She was patient. If someone meant her harm...

"Are you still a crack shot?"

There was laughter in the question, a humorous delight in a teasingly familiar voice. Fury's bow lurched in her suddenly numb grip and her arrow slithered away harmlessly to land among the bracken. She didn't care. Let the trees take it. That voice. It made her heart ache with a desperate joy. It couldn't be!

"Diver?" she said in a shrill squeak.

The shadow emerged slowly from behind the sheltering tree. It moved into the glade, became a person dressed only in breeches of drab stone denim with leg wraps around his calves. *A soldier's uniform.* His feet and chest were bare, his mop of curly black hair a tangled mess on his head. His cheeks were sharper than she remembered, his eyes deeper. Almost sunken. He looked too old to be her little brother. But it was him. It was Diver. He was grinning like a maniac. His teeth bright in his dark face.

She bolted across the clearing and into his outspread arms. Their laughter and sobs startled birds from the underbrush and set a squirrel chattering above them. Fury squeezed him tight;

he was thin but wiry. There was a strength in him which hadn't been there before. She noticed these things even as she cried in relief and held him as fiercely as she had when he'd been a child. If this was a dream, she didn't want to wake up.

"Thank the Angels!" she managed to say at last, her arms tightening around him. "You're alive! You're home!"

He grunted at her rough handling but chuckled low in his throat. "Of course. You didn't raise a fool, sister dear. I kept my head down and was the first to run from danger, just like you taught me."

Fury didn't let go, breathing in his scent, her heart quieting. "I did, I taught you exactly that, but you ran off to war anyway, didn't you? Maybe my prayers kept you safe."

Diver stepped back from her, disengaging her arms from him gently but firmly. "Suddenly you've gotten religious?" He scoffed. "Just when I stopped believing in miracles."

She frowned, studying his face in growing dismay. His eyes were terribly sunken. New muscles graced his chest and arms, and there wasn't a trace of softness left. "You're so thin. Didn't they feed you in the army?" She pinched his arm and poked him in the ribs. There wasn't any fat left on him anywhere, and he'd never been particularly stout to begin with.

He flinched and slapped her hands away. "Stop. I left the army to avoid torture!"

"You left the army? They let you go?"

Diver shrugged and swiped a hand through his thatch of unkempt hair, catching fingers in the tangles. "There weren't many left alive to notice."

Her heart sank. "We lost, then?"

"No. We didn't lose. We just didn't win. It's as it ever was – a stalemate. I thought we had them for a moment. The Akkadians nearly broke on our third charge. We threw everything we had at them. Guns, artillery, horses, men. We obliterated their barriers, tore apart their trenches. Men became little more than mud and blood and broken bone. But then they launched gas canisters to stop us. A desperate move. They lost almost as many as we did when the winds shifted. Only the ghouls gained advantage with that stupid act. And now a new stretch of the disputed territory is watered with poison and blood and useless to everyone."

He spoke matter-of-factly. Clinical and cold. But shadows haunted his eyes. Horror lurked deep within them, and Fury felt cold creep up her spine. His grey eyes grew distant, clouded and dark. Her heart broke to see the pain in her baby brother's once sweet and open gaze. War changed people. How many broken men now littered the village common, drunk or drugged or addled, shouting at unseen ghosts? Would it happen to him?

"You were right, Fury," he said grimly. "The war is an utter disaster. What is the point of any of it? I wanted glory and adventure, and I found only death and misery. What a mess. I fought–" His voice hitched in his chest a moment. "For my brothers, my friends. I fought for them, but they were still blown to bits or shot from afar or poisoned like dogs, or eaten–"

His lips pressed closed. He seemed lost, his eyes growing cloudier. Then he shook his head, and excitement transformed his expression. The boy she remembered. Or very nearly. She raised a hand to touch him, but he stepped out of reach.

"Why are you lurking out here?" she asked sternly, letting her hand fall to her side. Trying not to feel hurt. "Why didn't you come home?"

"I couldn't. Not yet. But I've been watching for you on the hunting trails. I knew you'd be along sooner or later." He hopped on his toes, grinning. "I have something to show you, something no one else can see. I couldn't move him far without help, and I couldn't leave him alone. Come nightfall, you and I should be able to take him home."

"Him? You have a person out here hidden away?" She couldn't think why he would have to keep someone hidden. "Wait. Is it a prisoner? An Akkadian? We should turn him into the authorities."

He shook his head. "Nothing like that. Just... come with me." He turned to lead her back into the woods, glancing over his shoulder to make sure she followed. "You remember that old tree we used to hide in? The one struck by lightning?"

Fury nodded, keeping on his heels. Of course she knew the tree. Burned out on the inside by errant lightning, the great, old bald cypress had made a perfect hiding spot for them. They had spent many carefree days playing there and avoiding chores. "Who is he then? Another deserter?"

She saw his shoulders hunch at the word. Damn. No wonder he was hiding in the woods.

"It's not another deserter," he said.

A sudden surge of protectiveness rose within her. The army would never have him back. "Don't worry," she said. "We'll deal with it. You understand? You're home now. Home for good."

He paused and turned to look back at her. "We'll see," he said enigmatically. The ecstatic grin split his face again. "This is big, Fury. Bigger than the army, the war. You won't believe me until you see for yourself. Come on."

The bole of the massive cypress was covered with moss; the hollow was between two great buttresses, deceptively small from the outside. Diver dropped to his knees and crawled inside, Fury following. His excitement was contagious, and curiosity and relief to have him home lifted her spirits higher than they'd been in months.

In the dim interior of the giant tree, Fury could only make out an impression of the "him" Diver wanted her to see. A great lump lay against the smooth wall of living tree, misshapen and covered in shreds of white cloth. She stood, her eyes adjusting to the low light cast by a smoldering fire at the center of the space, and she realized the shreds weren't cloth, but feathers. White feathers. They had an unearthly glow.

The man beneath the mound of feathers was slender and tall as far as she could tell and clothed in strange gear – strips of leather forming a harness of some sort around his torso, a loincloth of rich, purple fabric between his legs, and the feather... cape? over his back. His skin was a smooth, rich bronze, marred by dark streaks which sparkled softly in the firelight. He was alive at least, this stranger, but his clothes and looks were foreign to her. Not Koine, not Akkadian, not Naveen.

"Who is he?" she whispered. His narrow face was slack beneath a head of silky blond curls. He was young and uncommonly beautiful. A strong chin, smooth, high cheekbones and an aquiline nose. He wasn't rough-skinned or scarred by childhood disease or war. The hand lying alongside his slender body was soft, elegant. The fingers long and fine.

Still, he was dirty, and abrasions covered his bare skin. Blood trickled from several wounds, and his breathing was labored. The healer within her responded, and she stepped closer.

"Never mind who he is," Diver said impatiently. "Don't you see *what* he is?"

She frowned, concentrating on the man's wounds and bruises. What kind of hell had he been through? "He's a man, but not Koine or Akkadian. Not Naveen, certainly."

Diver made a noise of exasperation. "You're looking, but you're not seeing."

He knelt beside his prize and grasped the blanket of feathers draped across his back and side, lifting it. The man's face crumpled, and a low moan slipped from him.

"Diver, be careful," she hissed, reaching out a hand. "You're hurting his—"

Her lips clamped over the insanity she'd been about to say: "You're hurting his *wing*."

Madness. The world was madness.

But Diver held the sheath of feathers, pulling and stretching it out for her to see, no matter that the man groaned with every movement. Blood stained the bright feathers, oozing from a wound notched in what was clearly a joint in a massive wing.

She'd shot down enough birds to know exactly what she was looking at. Her head swam and she sat down abruptly, her legs turned to jelly.

"Now you see," Diver said quietly, triumphantly. "I brought us home our very own Angelus, sister. How's that for a prisoner of war?"

CHAPTER THREE

An angel. A real angel. One of the blessed Angelus, the Creator Eternal's Righteous Army. Not a mummer wearing wings made of paste and chicken feathers and wire, but a heavenly creature with wings attached by muscle and sinew and bone. A closer inspection convinced her entirely. His body was golden-skinned perfection, his face too beautiful to be human. And when she touched his downy-soft feathers with tentative fingertips, she felt a crackling energy reach through her skin and race up her arm. He was not of this world, but he was real.

And broken. And hurting. Possibly dying...

"Where did you find him?" she asked softly, her hand lingering on his wing. The strange dark streaks on his skin marred his feathers, as well. She touched one of them and the substance clung to her fingertips, almost seemed drawn to her like metal filings to a magnet. Grimacing, she wiped it off on her trousers, but a slight tingle remained.

"In the river." Diver knelt beside her. "Soaked and sodden like a drowned bird, freezing cold and blue-lipped. He would have died if I hadn't pulled him from the water." He scoffed. "Ma and Da were right; they aren't gods."

"How in the great green world did he end up there?"

Diver shrugged. "Don't know. Fell from the sky, maybe?"

He giggled, and she looked at him sharply. His eyes were too bright for her liking. Fury took her hand from the angel and put it to his forehead.

Wincing from her touch, Diver snapped, "Don't. I'm not sick."

"Are you sure? You feel warm, and you don't seem yourself at all."

"A lot has happened in the last year. I'm not a child anymore, Fury. I don't need you to fret about me."

"I always will. No matter how old you get." She looked away, frowning. "It hasn't exactly been easy for me since you left. I – I've had a hard time here alone."

"I know." His voice was heavy with guilt. "I can see, sister. You've lost weight, and you never would have let someone sneak up on you like I did. Not before. I'm sorry. I made a mistake."

Her throat grew thick, and Fury could only shake her head. Her loneliness and despair were not comparable to the horrors he'd faced, but it had affected her. There were times when she'd thought of falling asleep and never waking up.

"You didn't sneak up on me," she said at last, her voice rough. She cleared her throat. "You're home now. Everything will be fine."

Even as she said it her eyes fell on the unconscious creature, and she knew it was a lie. *Angelus.* An actual angel descended to earth, and he was nothing more than a broken-winged man. Nothing would be fine. This would change everything. She just wasn't sure how, yet.

"It will be," Diver lied with absolute conviction, and they looked at each other. He was the first to crack a wry smile. "I suppose we could believe such things if we weren't hiding in a tree with a fallen angel at our feet."

She giggled and clapped a hand over her mouth. Despite the insanity of the situation, she felt... happy. Her brother was home. He was alive. Together they could face anything. Even a soldier in the Creator Eternal's army. Growing sober, she pulled her hand away. Her lips tingled strangely, and she realized she'd transferred the strange substance on the angel's wing to her mouth. She wiped her lips across her shirtsleeve.

"So. What do we do now?" she asked.

"Well, first, we go home. And we take him with us."

They waited until full dark to steal their prize home.

Diver fashioned a crude sled from tree branches and rope from his pack while Fury stood watch over the angel. The creature had lain like a dead man for much of the day, only the occasional groan or whimper slipping from him. She'd soothed him a time or two with a gentle hand on his brow and low murmurs, wishing all the time to have him safely home. He needed attention. His wounds would fester in the dirt and wet.

Finally, after the sun dipped below the horizon and the stars winked awake in the velvet firmament, they wrestled him onto the sled, tossed Diver's long duster atop him, and started home.

It was slow going, dragging the primitive sledge between the tall, crowded trees, but the siblings knew the best paths through the woods, having spent their lives exploring this dark forest. As carefree, fearless children they'd turned over every rock and dead tree limb they came across, explored every stream and hidden pool, and climbed every tree with tempting branches. After life had knocked them around a bit, after their mother had disappeared and later their father died in the Scourge, they had turned to the forest for sustenance, hunting game along hidden paths, gathering nuts and seeds and roots among the great boles. Even those days, as hard as they'd been, had been good because they'd had each other.

There would be good days ahead. Her brother was home. She glanced back at the still form beneath Diver's duster, suddenly filled with doubt.

The forest thinned when they reached the edge of their small homestead, but it didn't entirely surrender.

Diver paused when they left the forest. Fury stumbled to a halt, nearly dropping her side of the sledge. Her hands were scraped from holding onto the rough branch. Exhaustion made her limbs shake, and she stifled a groan of annoyance. In the dim starlight, she could just see Diver's profile. His expression was raw, his lips parted and his eyes wide, as if he couldn't quite believe what he was seeing.

The trees sheltered their small cottage and edged a patch of cleared land. Fat pumpkins sat nestled beneath curling vines, looking almost black in the darkness, and a patch of tall corn stalks gleamed in the starlight. The branches of the two apple trees framing the door to their home swayed in the chill night breeze, leaves rustling. Crickets chirped steadily, but there were no other signs of life, human or otherwise.

"I never thought I'd make it home."

How often had she thought the same thing? She swallowed once, and again. "But you did, and you are. Creator willing, you won't ever have to leave again."

He turned to her, his face hidden in a shroud of shadows. "You believe that? Do you think the world will let me live here in peace?"

"I don't know about the world, but I'll keep you here whatever it takes."

She heard him sigh before he took up their load again. Slowly, he moved forward. "Everyone has to leave home at some point, Fury."

True to her name, she felt anger rise in her belly. "And what good does it ever do anyone?" she countered bitterly.

The sky had turned lavender by the time they settled their "guest" into their parents' long-empty room. Their wide bed was the only one big enough to accommodate his wings comfortably. It hadn't been an easy decision. The room had been kept like a shrine after their Da had died fighting an incursion of ghouls during the last Scourge. A decade ago. No... longer. Their possessions remained untouched, down to their father's coat tossed over their mother's rocking chair and their mother's dresses hanging in the wardrobe. It had only seemed right for Fury to sleep in the second bedroom she and Diver had once shared, while Diver had moved a cot into the main room at the front of the house. It was a small cottage. "Cozy", Ma had called it. Barely enough for a family of four, but more than enough when they had been whole and happy. It was beyond odd to have a stranger in her parents' bed, winged or not.

Fury went to the cast iron stove in the corner and set about lighting it. She was shivering from the wet and the cold and the exertion of dragging the sledge. The angel looked slim, but he weighed far more than his appearance warranted. Like his bones were made of gold. Which made her think perhaps he wasn't so "bird-like" after all. His wings were awkward to manage, too. Spread out around him like a cloak, they glowed with unearthly beauty. His injury was a hideous stain against the glorious white and silver feathers.

At least it isn't a featherbed, Fury thought perversely as they made the angel as comfortable as possible on the cotton-stuffed mattress.

"First time I've ever been glad we can't afford down mattresses," Diver said, echoing her thought.

Fury smiled; it was good to have him home. Their small house suddenly seemed larger with him there.

Soon, the squat stove emitted a steady warmth, driving the chill from the unused room. Fury tucked a blanket over the unconscious angel and gestured to Diver to follow her out. A short hallway took them into the front room. Broad windows opened onto a porch, curtains drawn tightly against casual observers.

A hearth took up one wall of the room, its mantelpiece holding pictures and family treasures – a pewter tea set and serving plate, a white ceramic vase painted with cornflowers, and their father's pipe which Diver had never tried to smoke. A large wooden larder sat against another wall, a larder pathetically short of food, beside a long, narrow table where Fury prepared meals. The center of the room held a table and chairs, an oil-burning lamp atop the table. There was one lumpy old couch and a stuffed chair near the hearth for reading. Diver's cot was curtained off from the main room in a corner. He went to it and tossed his pack behind the screen. He rifled through it a moment then brought out a few parcels. To Fury's delight, they held rations. Nothing special – just flatbread, cheese and a bag of dried beans – but to her it was an unexpected windfall.

He held back a wax packet clearly marked with holy symbols. Manna. Standard issue, no doubt. He tucked it into his jacket, avoiding her gaze. She didn't ask him if he'd eaten any. How could he have avoided it? At least he knew better than to offer it to her.

The oil lamp was the only source of light beside the glowing embers left in the fireplace, but Fury didn't light it. She only had so much oil and dawn had arrived. She stoked the fire in the hearth and hung a pot of water above it to heat then went to the larder to gather a basket of medical supplies. Pathetically few, but she'd always managed to heal their ills. Her mother and father both had trained her. She took stock of the small trove and added several clean rags, a sliver of soap, and her only bottle of rubbing alcohol. By now, the water was steaming, and motioning to Diver to follow, she returned to her parents' room.

Together, they stripped the angel of his strange harness, finding ties and fastenings unnecessary on a human but vital to a man bearing wings. Fury laid the item carefully to the side. Her thoughts had already turned to how she might modify her father's old clothes to fit him. Grayson had been a tall man, too.

By the Eternal, what am I thinking? It's not like he's some pathetic foundling to feed and clothe!

Fury focused on her patient. The cuts and abrasions were simple to clean and daub with alcohol. And most of the strange substances streaking his skin didn't seem to be his blood. It made her hands burn and tingle while she worked. She scrubbed them clean before tending to the worst wound. Something had cut right through his bastard wing and the joint within was severed. Clear fluid leaked from it. With Diver's help, she stretched out the injured wing, draping it across her lap like a blanket while she sat on her mother's rocking chair. Diver held the old chair steady for her, and she set to work.

With sunlight beginning to lighten the cozy room, she took to it with needle and thread. It was necessary to pluck away many of his feathers to clear the wound. Without them, the limb seemed thin and small. Like a naked chicken wing. The skin was different, though, more... human. She concentrated on her work, not on how strange it was to be doing what she was doing.

After she'd sutured his wing and surveyed her handiwork, she gave a satisfied nod. It looked like the wing of a wounded hawk she'd once nursed back to health. The hawk had tried to rip her fingers off on more than one occasion with its dangerous hooked beak. Not exactly a grateful patient. She hoped this one would be better. A giggle burst from her.

"What's so funny?" Diver asked wearily. He'd stood vigil far longer than she would have expected given all he'd been through. They had talked while she'd worked and she'd learned how far he'd come in a few short days. Fleeing death and destruction, starving and thirsty, locked in his helmet.

"Nothing. Never mind." She looked up and back at him. "You can go to sleep now, Diver. I'll watch after him."

He nodded, his cheeks sunken with exhaustion. He dragged himself toward the door. Without his heavy canvas duster, his strange helmet, and his boots, he looked more like her brother in his simple drab blue shirt and gray trousers. Soft and innocent. But he wasn't innocent and never would be again. Still, she could pretend.

Carefully, Fury folded the wounded wing against the angel's side, tucking it to his body, aligning the bones as she did so. A few strips of torn bedding held it in place. She tied them as tightly as she dared. Hopefully it would give the wing a chance to heal. But an injury like that in an actual bird would most likely never heal right.

Perhaps she jostled him too hard, or he had slept enough. Perhaps he possessed a superhuman ability to tolerate abuse, and had recovered from what he'd endured, whatever it had been. Regardless, suddenly the creature she'd thought on death's door had his hand around her throat, squeezing with incredible strength. She clawed at his iron fingers, unable to breathe, her eyes locked with his cold, angry gaze.

His eyes were the color of the sky on a clear autumn day – she'd never seen such eyes. Her brother's light eyes were unusual enough. But these – these were stunning.

She would have admired them more if she'd been able to breathe.

Despite her predicament, she forced herself to ignore the panic clawing up her chest. She gripped his arm gently, and stared into his mad eyes, pleading silently.

Please. I mean you no harm.

Her vision began to darken, and her mouth gaped like a landed fish's.

The iron fingers loosened abruptly, and those angry eyes closed. Fury collapsed onto his chest, gasping, and tried to roll away, but he pinned her to him with an arm over her back. And if his fingers had been iron, his arm was pure steel. She was no small girl to be easily manhandled, but she found herself unable to break free.

"Who are you?" he rasped. His chest rose and fell rapidly; his heart thundered in her ear. "Where am I? What's happened? Where is Rast and that treacherous bitch?" He shifted and let out a low cry of pain.

"Don't tear your stitches," she said, wondering why she gave a damn when he'd almost strangled her to death. "You're hurt, you're in my home, and I have no idea where or who Rast is, or any treacherous bitch you might know. Now let me up so I can see if you ruined my work. I've been at it all morning."

"Work? You? What..." He clutched her to him, groaning deeply. "I fell," he said, and his voice held terror like the cold dark depths of a cave. "Through the sky, through the Silence. The awful – all eternity–"

A sob hitched in his chest, and a shudder wracked his body. His arm became less imprisoning and more grasping.

She relaxed against him. He was hurting and damaged... and reacting as any human would. This, she understood. Something terrible had happened to him.

Fury sighed as he shivered and shuddered beneath her, patting him gently with the one hand she could move. The danger had passed. He hadn't exactly released her, but she didn't think he wanted to hurt her. Not anymore. Her instinct was to comfort him.

The sliding clack of metal against metal made her stiffen. Only one thing made a sound like that...

She craned her neck to find Diver standing over them, his bolt-action rifle aimed at the angel's head. When had he come into the room? Dear Creator, he was as silent as a wraith now. His face was blank, his eyes cold and deadly. Fear shivered up her spine even though the rifle wasn't aimed at *her* head.

"Release my sister," Diver said, his voice as cold, flat and deadly as his stare. "You have three seconds before we find out just how immortal you are."

The arm around Fury fell away and she slowly lifted herself. "It's all right. He wasn't hurting me. Put the gun down."

Diver ignored her, his entire focus on the angel. His eyes narrowed and his lips thinned into a bitter smile. The angel was as pale as the sheet upon which he lay. Slowly, a bead of sweat slid down his temple, and Diver's smile widened.

"You're afraid," he said, grim pleasure in his voice. "Why would an immortal fear a human weapon?"

"I am not afraid of you," the angel said, though the tremor in his voice belied his words. He attempted a snarl. "You are beasts! Lower than beasts."

Diver's smile tightened, as did his finger on the trigger. "Shall we see what a bullet can do to you?"

"Bullet? You – you should be on your knees." Confusion mixed with his anger. As if he couldn't quite believe what was happening. "How dare you point a weapon at me? Bow to me, you miserable cur! Worship me!"

"It's hard to feel worshipful towards a broken-winged jackass flat on his back in our spare bed," Fury snapped. She glared at Diver. Her whole body shook, but her voice was sharp and steady. "You've made your point, Diver. The great immortal being is afraid of you. Which means he's not immortal, he's not a god." Her lips pressed together; anger gave her courage. "If you would shoot a guest in my home, then you may as well shoot me, too!"

Before she had a chance to think, she grabbed the barrel of his rifle and yanked it toward her chest. Startled, Diver's eyes widened, his mouth agape.

"Are you crazy?" Diver tugged his rifle free of her grip and backpedaled, pointing the barrel at the floor. His face was suddenly as sallow as their captive angel's. "I could have killed you!"

"Then quit waving that gun around! I'd rather not spend a week cleaning blood and brains and feathers off the walls, thank you very much."

Without a loaded rifle pointed at her chest, Fury felt a bit calmer, though her heart slammed against her breastbone. *That was stupid, stupid, stupid.* She rearranged herself on the edge of the bed, putting herself deliberately between Diver and her patient. For his part, the angel lay stiff and wary beside her, wisely quiet. She folded her hands in her lap to still their trembling. She'd never been afraid of her brother, ever, but this man...?

"As for you, Angelus." She turned to him, speaking sternly. "We do not worship your kind – far from it. I'm afraid you've been rescued by perhaps the only atheists in all of Avernus. So, I suggest you keep your opinions about these two particular 'beasts' to yourself. Or I'll let you try your luck in the woods."

He glared back at her, but there were shadows in his blue eyes. A lurking fear. Good, fear might keep him compliant.

"Now," she continued briskly. "Let's be civilized and introduce ourselves." She laid a hand on her chest. "I am Fury. Fury Barrett-Cree. This is my home, outside Green Hollow,

Koine. You've met my brother, Diver. He's just returned from war, which explains why he's so quick to draw a weapon, but he did save your life by dragging you from a freezing river."

The angel's eyes jumped to Diver as if he found that hard to believe.

"So, now you know who we are. Who are you?"

Those bright blue eyes slid to hers and a frown bent his perfect lips. He didn't seem to want to answer, as if it was beneath him. Emotion twisted his features and his hands crumpled the quilt across his lap. Abruptly, his hands loosened and he sagged into his pillow. Defeated. "I am Eleazar Starson."

He said it like she should know the name, and be impressed by it, too. But she'd never heard of him. "Nice to meet you, Eleazar Starson. Welcome." She turned to her brother. "Diver? Can you welcome our guest?"

He stood frozen, staring at the angel, at Eleazar. The hatred and disgust had vanished from his expression. He no longer appeared cold and murderous, merely confused. And a little lost. This was her brother. She exhaled.

"Welcome," Diver said, his voice rough. He cleared his throat and made a show of slinging his rifle over his shoulder and holding his hands out to his sides. Fury watched him, sure he wasn't going to do anything crazy, but concerned, nonetheless. They both had been raised to think of the angels as oppressors, not gods, and had never questioned it. But perhaps there had always been a seed of doubt in their certainty. When they heard of "miracles" on the battlefield, or impossible cures brought about by the blessed manna. Now, though, the truth was lying before them. Hurt and angry and afraid. It was... disappointing and gratifying all at once.

"Are you hungry, Eleazar?" Fury asked soothingly. "We are about to break our fast."

He turned his gaze away, his face going blank, his expression closed. "Yes, I am... very hungry..."

"Fury. Please call me Fury."

"Fury," he echoed with a slight frown. As if the name tasted strange to him. And she supposed it would. Everyone thought her name strange. But she'd come into the world screaming, and her mother had anointed her "Fury", and she'd spent her life living up to the name.

She rose from the stranger's bedside, eager to be doing something. Even if it was as insignificant as making porridge. She dragged Diver back to the main room, ordering him to fetch bowls while she set about cooking. Her brother seemed properly chastised and not nearly as hostile. He fetched the bowls and cups for the table briskly, moving around the familiar cottage as if he'd never left.

As Fury heated more water over the hearth and stirred in the last of her dried oats for porridge, she was surprised to find her hands still shaking. How close had she come to witnessing a murder? How close had she come to getting shot by her own brother?

"I would never hurt you," Diver said quietly.

She turned and found him behind her, holding a bowl for the porridge. His eyes were beseeching beneath an errant curl of dark hair. "You must believe me. I haven't changed that much."

She wanted to believe him. Yet...

"You were ready to kill him."

"He had his hand around your throat. Of course I was ready to kill him." Sorrow and shame darkened his gaze. "I've killed to protect the men beside me. I've killed to protect myself. I will kill to protect you. You're all I have left in the world."

Heart breaking, she lifted a hand to his cheek. "I pray you never have to kill anyone again, Diver, even to save me."

A grim smile twisted his lips. "And who are you praying to, sister? Now that the gods are falling from the heavens?"

CHAPTER FOUR

The angel was dying.

The first night Eleazar had spent in their home, he'd been weak and injured, but otherwise aware and alert. He'd wolfed down the porridge Fury had offered him, though it had been a struggle just to prop him upright so he could eat. He was covered in sweat and panting by the time they'd wrestled him into position, his teeth clenched tight against cries of pain. His silky soft skin had felt warm beneath her hands, and his muscles were hard ropes under it, his body strong and fit. His hair shone like spun gold, and his wings were moon-bright and ethereal. How could he be sick? At the time, she'd wondered if maybe the Angelus merely ran warmer than humans.

It wasn't until the next day when his eyes grew glassy, and the warmth radiating from him turned into a raging fire that she knew for certain. Fever.

And it was no simple fever to be treated by yarrow and chamomile. Nothing she gave him made any difference. Face flushed, skin burning, Eleazar fell into a delirium by nightfall. It was impossible to get anything but a dribble of water down his throat, and for the next few days she soothed him with cool wet cloths, feeling helpless and terrified.

Unfortunately, she knew the cause of his illness. The wound she'd so diligently cleaned and mended had festered. Angry red lines traced a path down the flesh beneath his feathers, leading from a suppurating, pus-filled mess. The injury took on a terrible smell. When Diver caught a whiff, he'd announced callously, "Two-day old corpses smell better than him."

She couldn't disagree. She gagged on the smell herself and had to breathe shallowly. It had become a nightmare changing his bandages, but she persisted. Three times a day, she washed his wound and applied every tincture and salve she knew to stave off infection. But the healer in her knew medicine was futile. There was only one thing that might save Eleazar; she just couldn't bring herself to contemplate it. Not yet. Not until all hope was lost.

Exhausted, Fury tucked the blankets around a shivering Eleazar and joined Diver in the living room. Her brother had taken on the household chores without her even having to ask, which was a miracle all on its own. He cooked for them, kept the house tidy, and hunted and tended to her garden as well; vital with winter fast approaching. At first, he'd only emptied the traps she'd set, but he'd taken the rifle with him the last few times and returned with larger game. She hadn't questioned the streaks down his dirty cheeks, so much like the tracks of tears, grateful that he was bringing home food. She'd worried from the start how they would fill three mouths through the winter. Of course, now, with Eleazar so sick, she feared it might not be an issue.

It was a solemn meal they shared, seated at the table their father had built for their mother from a deadfall oak. Not hungry in the least, Fury traced a knot in the table while her greens and roast pigeon grew cold. The table was the finest piece of furniture they owned. Stained and polished and carved with vines and ferns and diving kingfishers around its edges, it was a thing of beauty, and memory. She could imagine her parents sitting here so clearly: Her father with his broad grin, sandy hair and deep brown eyes, telling tales and jokes, making her mother laugh. Tuilelaith had laughed so rarely; Fury was sure she remembered every single time she had. Only Grayson managed to draw any joy from her.

Solemn and fierce, Tuilelaith Cree had been more concerned with politics than her own children. Guilt followed the errant thought. As a Gullan woman, a refugee in Koine and an outcast, she had every right to be concerned with politics. Lore and scripture claimed her kind had been destroyed due to some unforgivable sin. Their Wrath had been terrible. Even a lone Gullan girl, lost and helpless, might bring that same Wrath upon Green Hollow. Tuilelaith, braver and prouder than wise perhaps, had scoffed at their fear.

Fury poked at her dinner. What would her mother think of Eleazar? An Angelus suffering and helpless? She snorted softly. It would have made her giddy. Even though the destruction of the Gullan had happened generations ago, she'd seemed to take it personally. She'd always claimed, rather loudly, that the Angelus were no better than humans. Worse, in some ways. Their Judgement was cruel, unforgiving. Those that shorted the Hallow Tithe or displeased them in some manner suffered the Angelic Curse: The Scourge. Humans transformed into monsters by a wash of black rain.

As for the Hallow Tithe itself, she'd called it a farce – a crime, even. Every human in Koine and Akkadia, in distant Veran and troubled Naveen, paid tribute to the angels. Grains and livestock, fruits and vegetables, iron and lumber. All the bounty of the great, wide world. And for what? Not just to avoid the Scourge but for the "blessed gift" of manna, too. Manna kept the people of Avernus fed. No matter how poor or destitute a soul, everyone received a portion. The terrible famines of the distant past were no more. Of course, the price was constant war for the land needed to fulfill each country's Tithe. Tuilelaith made sure Fury had understood this.

"The manna is a trick. A curse. We have all we need on Avernus." When she got in a dither, her mother would grip her by the chin, grey eyes sparking, her lovely face hard as rock. Fury had no choice but to listen. "Don't taint your soul with manna, my little angel, you are meant for grander things!"

And she'd taken that lesson to heart; she would sooner starve than eat manna. She'd come close a time or two these last few months, but with Diver home things were better.

But for the dying angel in their cozy cottage.

"Is he any better?" Diver asked softly. He was fiddling with his fork and staring at his roast pigeon. For once, he hadn't inhaled his plate.

Fury spared a glance toward her parents' room. The sick room, she thought of it now. She had just been in to check on Eleazar and there had been no improvement. With his wings tucked beneath him and his body covered by a thick quilt, he'd looked diminished. Weak. Even his bright, golden hair had faded. He was a shadow of what he'd been. It was cruel, pointless. Why had he fallen on their doorstep only to die in delirium? She'd thought it had been some sort of sign. A fallen angel. Found by two atheists, the only atheists in all of Koine, most likely.

Yet...it had to mean something. Since she'd touched his sparkling feathers, she'd been dreaming of Heaven. A Heaven filled with great, slim-winged creatures the color of rainbows. Their plaintive whistles and chirrs haunted her. Their giant, doleful eyes watched her expectantly...

Why did they call to her if they weren't real?

There are no gods, fool.

"He's dying," she said, and the words came out sharper than she'd intended. She winced at the coldness in her voice.

Diver went still. Horror lurked in the cool depths of his eyes. For all he'd put a gun to Eleazar's head, her brother had been obsessed with his wellbeing. Every moan or cry of pain from the angel seemed to slice through him. Fury knew he felt the same awe she did. Despite his obvious mortality, Eleazar was an unearthly being. Magical.

"No," Diver said at last. "I didn't pull him from the river just to watch him die! Please, there must be something you can do." He dropped his fork, his food forgotten, and tipped back in his chair. He ran his hands through his shock of curly hair, setting it on end. "Maybe you could try that tonic you gave me when I was a boy? When I had that awful fever. You remember? Can't you try that?"

"I have tried everything!" She squeezed her hand into a fist, fighting off an overwhelming feeling of helpless anger. She pinned him with a sharp look. "We should have taken him to the elders the moment we found him."

The legs of Diver's chair made a resounding thud. "You can't be serious? Take a wounded immortal to the town elders? They would have flayed him alive and denounced us as heretics. Not to mention they would have put a bullet in my head for desertion!"

"They wouldn't have known. Not yet. The tele-net is unreliable in Green Hollow. Besides, I could have taken him. Alone. Kept you out of danger."

"So only you would have been denounced as a heretic before they dumped Eleazar in the nearest swamp? That's so much better."

His tone made her cheeks burn. Worse, she knew he was right. One look at a broken-winged, sickly angel and the elders would have been on him like dogs on a wounded bear. The clerics would have been called in secret to poke and prod. Once they saw he bled like the rest of them... getting dumped in a swamp would be the least of it.

"I've tried everything," she repeated, her voice raspy. Desperate. She hunched over the table. She couldn't let him die, but the only option left filled her with terror. "Dr Jeffries was trained in Trin, at the Academy. He knows ways of healing I don't. Modern things. Real medicine. Not herbs and tonics. He has the equipment and the tools to save him!"

"What tools does he have that you don't?" Diver demanded. He pushed his chair back, the legs scraping across the floor, his face scrunched with anger. "What equipment? What can he do that you can't?"

Fury shook her head, tight-lipped. From down the hall, they could hear Eleazar moan and mutter. His delirium was growing worse despite everything she'd done.

Except the one thing that might save him.

She shook her head again, more vigorously. "I can't do it. I can't. It's too awful!"

"Do what? What can't you do?" Diver slapped his hands on the table to get her attention. Startled, she met his wide-eyed gaze. "Fury, please, do whatever you must. I'll help you any way I can."

"You don't understand. The cure might kill him, and if it doesn't, *he* might kill *us*!"

"If you can cure him then do it." His tone softened. "Please, I believe in you, Fury. Save him."

Her throat tightened and her belly churned. "His wing is infected," she said, swallowing bile. "The wound is poisoning his blood. The only way to save him now… I must… amputate."

The last word burst from her.

"Amputate?" Diver sat back in his chair abruptly as if his legs had given out. "Would it save him?"

Fury took a deep breath. Now that she'd said it out loud, she knew it was their only option. She also knew she was going to do it. The decision eased some of her terror. If she was going to do this, she had to be strong. "I believe it would, but I fear what his reaction will be when he wakes up to find himself maimed."

Diver grew thoughtful. "It won't be easy for him, no, but he'll be alive. I witnessed many soldiers who woke up with limbs missing. Some wished they had died instead, but only a few. Most were glad to be alive. And relieved to be going home."

"I don't know." She frowned. Even sick and pale and broken, Eleazar looked like a god come to earth. Could she cripple a god? "Losing an arm or a leg is one thing: losing the power to fly would be quite another, I imagine. And let's not forget; he's not a man. His strength is far beyond ours, his resilience. What if he wakes in a killing rage?"

"Our only other choice is he doesn't wake at all. Can you live with that?"

She shook her head.

"Then it's decided."

"Yes, I suppose it is." The tension across her shoulders gave way. She sat back in her chair, feeling stunned.

"Tell me what you need," Diver said, his voice firm and confident. Mature.

She stared at him until he raised an eyebrow.

"You sound so grown up," she explained, giving him a tentative smile. He didn't return it, merely waited for her to answer. He held himself with a deep stillness. That was new. "I need laudanum," she said, inexplicably sad for him. "You can't risk going into town, so you'll have to barter with Wren Pierson for it. Her husband has quite the habit. She'll be happy to steal some away from him and she knows how to keep her mouth shut. Take mother's scarf. She won't be able to resist it."

"Mother's scarf?" Diver said, incredulous. "No, Fury, we can't. She had it her whole life. It's the only thing left of her family and homeland. It's silk! And dyed with true indigo. It's valuable!"

"You think we can cut off an angel's wing without being killed? You know how strong he is, even sick and weakened. The pain will make him lose control. I have to put him under. I know the scarf is valuable, but Wren won't give us laudanum for deer hides and corn."

Diver dragged a hand through his hair, desperate to think of another option, but by the look on his face, she knew he was coming up empty.

"Please, Diver…"

He exhaled explosively. "Fine. I'll do it. But what else do we need? We should get more for Mother's treasured possessions than just a drug."

Fury winced at his accusing tone, but he was right. And there were other things she needed. "We need a saw. A steel saw with fine, sharp teeth. And stout cord, lengths of it…"

* * *

The next day, they began the preparations to remove Eleazar's infected wing. First, they moved him from the bed onto the floor where they had spread a sheet to catch blood and fluids and keep dirt from him. Fury removed all his bandages and left the wound open to the air. The flesh beneath was inflamed and oozing. The suppurating wound had turned black. The smell made her gag.

Eleazar's eyes fluttered open a time or two, staring at them in heart-wrenching confusion. Did a small part of him understand what was happening and why it was necessary? If he awoke crippled but healed and clear-headed, he might not kill them. Best to have Diver's rifle ready just in case.

In one of his moments of semi-lucidity, she held his face between her hands and looked deep into his strange blue eyes. "You're dying, Eleazar," she said slowly. "I can save you, but it will cost you. I must remove the infected wing. Do you understand?"

He blinked, his clear eyes growing cloudy. A grimace contorted his handsome face. "Please... stop the pain..."

His eyes rolled back, and a shudder tore his face from her hands. Her heart hurt at the tragedy of what she must do. If there were real gods up in the Heavens, they would never forgive her. She smoothed the hair from his clammy forehead and administered drops of the laudanum between his pale lips. Her eyes found Diver. He knelt on the other side of Eleazar; a knife, the saw, a flask of alcohol and a coil of cording laid out before him.

Once Eleazar grew limp, Fury nodded to her brother. Together, they rolled Eleazar onto his stomach and began to bind his undamaged wing with the cord; lashing it tight to him, in case he tried to flap free as any wounded bird might. She feared even the laudanum wouldn't be enough to keep him under. They stretched the broken wing across the floor and Diver laid his weight upon it to keep it still as Fury worked. The wing bones had never knit, and they poked through the infected flesh like broken teeth. With Diver in place, Fury tied a tourniquet on the wing as close to Eleazar's shoulder blade as possible. She didn't want to cut into the flesh of his muscular back; she would cut through the flesh and bone of the wing, leaving a small stub behind. It would be a hideous mutilation, but it couldn't be helped.

Fury took a deep breath and held out her hand to Diver. "The knife, please."

CHAPTER FIVE

The night had lightened by the time Fury released Diver from the horror in their small cottage. The cool air struck his sweaty face, chilling him instantly. He exhaled and stood shaking outside the door to his home, the heavy bundle in his arms a nearly impossible burden. Could he have prevented this? He'd dragged Eleazar through the woods like a prize boar, heedless of the risk. What if he'd gone to his sister right away? What if he'd gone to the village elders and demanded to see Dr Jeffries? Eleazar was an angel, revered and worshipped. The elders would have done what they could to save him–

No. They would have killed him. Named him a demon and burned him to ash and bones to protect their faith.

Diver stumbled away from his door, heading into the woods. Tears steamed on his cheeks. The last few hours had been terrible and incredible all at once. He'd always admired his sister's strength – she'd kept them both alive against all odds for years – but tonight she had seemed made of steel. She'd cut through the angel's flesh, undaunted by the difficulty of it. Sweat coated her face even before she managed to reach bone. The bone, so much stronger than human bone, took all her strength, forcing her up on her knees for leverage as she sawed relentlessly. A testament to human grit.

For his part, he had held Eleazar secure – even doused with laudanum, it was all Diver could do to hold him steady – and silently wept as he watched Fury work. The medics in the army had been like that – single-minded in their focus, fearless and determined. He'd barreled into live fire and killed men with his bare hands, but he'd felt like a coward next to them.

He grimaced. The endless grind of the saw through bone was forever etched in his memory.

He went deep into the woods, back to their old hideout. Safe inside the belly of the forest giant, he laid down his burden and began to dig at the soft earth with his hunting knife. It wasn't the knife Fury had used to sever the last bit of Eleazar's wing, but Diver had used it to slit a man's throat once. Because the man had been his enemy, and for no other reason. What had made him the enemy? Diver had asked himself the question every day since and had decided "because he had been told." And it wasn't a good enough reason.

In school, Diver had been taught the Akkadians were vermin, out to kill all the Koine. He'd heard countless stories about how they poisoned Koine wells, defiled Koine women, murdered Koine children, and coveted fertile Koine land. The Akkadians were ravaging locusts who needed to be wiped from the face of Avernus. And the Angelus encouraged this enmity, declaring Koine blessed and Akkadia cursed. The Akkadians did not keep to the Hallow Tithe, not like the Koine. They deserved annihilation.

But Diver had learned the Akkadians believed the same thing, that the Koine were the accursed ones. He'd always known the Angelus were not benefactors but oppressors. And he'd since learned the war was a lie, too. There would never be a winner, except for the angels and those humans in on the scheme – the kings and prime ministers, governors and Tithing Commissioners. The elite, the wealthy, those who didn't have to send *their* children to war. Each fruitless battle, each meaningless advance and retreat had left him even more disillusioned. There would always be fools lining up to fight for king and country, for glory and honor, while those in charge reaped unending reward from the Angelus. He'd witnessed it firsthand: not all of the Hallow Tithe went to the Angelus.

The Angelus steal our bounty and hand us manna as a sop. And we let them! They are the beasts. Far fouler than men, no better than the Burnt Ghouls.

He had to tell himself this as he dug the grave for Eleazar's wing. Otherwise, the heartbreak would kill him. Immortal being or a man with wings, either way, Diver had had a hand in destroying something magnificent.

The soil loosened beneath his long knife. He used his hands to scoop out great heaps of dirt, working methodically and mindlessly. It hurt too much to think about what was wrapped in his old blanket. He felt like they'd killed Eleazar, even though he knew Fury's actions had saved him. Already, his fever had broken. He was sleeping peacefully instead of fitfully. The laudanum would keep him in a pain-free haze. So long as it lasted. Diver had been tempted to take a few drops himself, but he'd seen what it could do to men and women who became dependent. He knew in his heart, after all he'd been through, he would fall down that well far too easily.

Without pain, what am I?

How would Eleazar react when the laudanum loosened its hold? Diver had seen men lose limbs in the war; they were never the same afterwards, no matter how hard they tried to adapt to the loss. Those men had to suffer two indignities: The pain and difficulty of the handicap, and the pity given to them by the able-bodied men around them. For many, it was a daily struggle. At least Eleazar was not among his own kind, being pitied, possibly shunned. Who knew with the cruel Angelus?

Although, what were the odds of him ever reaching his home again? An angel with one wing? There were the great drachen which collected the Hallow Tithe, flying ships descending from Heaven. They could take him home. But the closest Tithing Ground was in neutral Trin. Miles away through disputed territory.

Perhaps Eleazar might have to stay on Avernus forever...

A strange shiver passed through his belly. The earth was damp and cold beneath his fingers, but he could *feel* Eleazar's warm, silky skin. Even as he'd wept to see the angel mutilated, he'd marveled at the touch of his powerful body, the strength in his lean frame. It had stirred feelings in him he'd thought dead on the battlefield. A surge of protectiveness. A desperate desire to *save* him. It was stupid. Eleazar was disdainful of them. His beauty seemed his only redeeming quality, yet Diver still felt a strong urge to protect him. To keep him safe from those out to harm him.

An angel would just as soon as spit on me than accept my help for anything.

He told himself this, but he had seen true fear in those beautiful eyes, and he'd known much of Eleazar's bravado and condescension came from that fear. Lost, alone, injured, he'd reacted to Diver's threats with remarkable courage even if it was a courage marred by arrogance. Whether he would ever admit it, Eleazar needed their help. Now more than ever.

Diver sat back on his heels; the hole was big enough. With shaking hands, he unfurled the blanket, his nose wrinkling when the sweet, rank smell wafted to him. The feathers no longer held their faint luminescence. They seemed almost dirty now. Dead. He sighed and pressed the broken wing into the hole. His hand lingered on the impossibly soft feathers. Impulsively, he plucked one from the inner side of the wing, one which would have been tucked close to Eleazar's body, a small covert. Small enough to hide inside his shirt. It felt warm against his chilled skin. Swiftly, he covered the lost wing with dirt, packing it down as best he could. There. It was done.

Diver crawled back outside to a world bright with morning. It was autumn, and the air was chilly and damp, the trees a riot of yellow and red. He shivered, adjusted his hunting knife, and set off toward home. Fury shouldn't be alone with Eleazar. The laudanum might not hold him as well as a human and the winged man might lash out in righteous anger.

"Well, well, well. If it isn't little Divey home from the war."

Diver froze in the shadow of a rocky bluff. His heart raced and sweat popped out on his forehead. He knew that voice. Hugh Kantorek, his old school chum, if you could call a boy who used to hold you down and spit in your face a "chum". Slowly, he turned toward the voice, keeping his hand well away from his belt knife despite the urge to grasp it. There on the path lifting toward the village and snaking around the bluff stood a man a good head taller than him, stout where once he'd been trim. A broad grin was on his freckled face, and he had his arms crossed over his chest. He was dressed in an officer cadet's uniform, complete with bright brass buttons and twisted blue braid on his shoulder boards. A pistol rested at one hip and a shining saber at the other. Diver could tell in one glance he'd never used either.

Seeing him dressed like a cadet eased his nerves. Hugh wasn't an army officer. Diver outranked him despite being only a private. And Academy officers knew little of what went on at the battlefield. He felt a welling of disdain. Typical Hugh. He'd always been a man of flash, and very little substance. Choosing to remain behind and serve at the Academy rather than march off to war was very on mark for him.

Unfortunately, Hugh Kantorek didn't need to have substance. He already had everything else. His father was the mayor of Green Hollow and the Tithe Master. As an officer cadet, he'd never be called off to war while sending whole squadrons of boys to their doom. Inside, Diver seethed.

Another man stood in Hugh's shadow, a sneer on his vulpine face. Lonnie Baumer. Diver's heart stuttered and it was all he could do not to draw his knife. Where Hugh was arrogant and bombastic, Lonnie was sly and cunning. He was a dangerous man in different ways than Hugh. Another "chum" he knew all too well. He despised Hugh, but he hated Lonnie. Once, he'd thought Lonnie a true friend. Seeing him brought up memories both sweet and foul. For a time, he'd believed Lonnie might become a decent person if he didn't spend so much time with

Hugh. A stolen kiss behind the school and a misguided crush had convinced Diver Lonnie was only pretending to hate him, that if he tried hard enough, he could draw out the sweet boy hidden inside that cruel exterior.

But it was Diver who'd been fooling himself, not Lonnie. That stolen kiss had led to years of torture and abuse until he'd eventually fled to the army.

Let it be a lesson. Be careful who you try to save…

"Hugh," Diver said, giving him a nod. He spared the other man a sidelong glance, and a muttered, "Lonnie."

"Sloppy uniform, Divey," Hugh said, sauntering down the narrow trail, his hands dropping to clutch his leather belt with its buckle shaped like the Koine crest – a rampant eagle clutching a bundle of arrows and a swirling ribbon. He eyed him critically. "I see the army hasn't taught you much. I'd thrash any boy who showed up at revelry looking so slovenly. Your shirt tail's out."

So ingrained was his training, Diver nearly tucked in his shirt, but instead he smiled and shrugged. His palms were slick and his gut icy, but he wasn't going to let this fool get to him. He wasn't a scared little boy any longer, to be held down and abused. He was a man. Others had pissed their pants facing him in battle. Memory stiffened his spine; these two hadn't seen war. They were nothing.

"I'm on leave," he said, thanking the stars his voice didn't shake. He swung his arms and jumped up and down lightly. "Out for a bit of exercise this morning. Got to keep in fighting shape, after all. Might practice with my bayonet later." He lunged dramatically, miming a strike, and imagined Hugh's guts spilling to the ground. His smile grew genuine. "Skewer a few trees for practice. Though men are much softer targets."

Hugh laughed heartily. "You're hilarious, old sport. As if little Divey could hurt a fly." He nudged Lonnie in the ribs. The other man had slithered up beside Hugh, silent and watchful. Diver made sure to keep track of his every move. Hugh was loud, obnoxious and prone to pugilism. Lonnie, on the other hand…

"Remember when he cried over a dead cat?" Hugh asked his friend, shaking his head. "So pathetic."

"It was my cat, and you'd gutted it on my doorstep." Diver's lips lifted from his teeth. "I was five."

"I'd killed a dozen cats by the time I turned five," Lonnie said softly. His eyes flashed. "You were always a late bloomer."

"I'm just not a psychopath." Diver scoffed. "I see why the army rejected you."

The man's narrow face reddened. His father didn't have the influence Hugh's did, to land him a cushy post far from the frontlines. Nevertheless, he'd tried to enlist when his friend had joined the Academy only to be turned away after an initial evaluation. Even the army didn't want men like Lonnie.

"Now, now, Divey. Aren't you glad to see us? We always had such *fun* with you." Hugh gave him a nasty grin and closed the distance between them in a few long strides. He loomed over him, using his size to intimidate. Just like the old days. Meanwhile, Lonnie ambled lazily around them, circling like a jackal. Diver tried to be aware of him without turning to keep him in sight. He opened his senses, a technique he'd learned during long hours of combat among the trees and ditches. It was necessary for survival to keep track of your enemy in every way you could.

A familiar feeling was creeping up his legs and into his belly. A tension he thought he'd left in the trenches; a sensation that both excited and sickened him. His breath came a little harder.

"You made my life a living hell," Diver said flatly. He stood toe-to-toe with his old tormenter, though he had to look up to meet his gaze, refusing to take even a step backward. Memories made his heart pound and his blood rush in his ears. A fist to the gut, a razorblade at his throat. His face smashed into the ground, the smell of fresh cut grass and soil. Tearing cloth. Bile rose in his throat. "Step. Back."

"Careful, Hugh, he's a soldier now." Lonnie's voice was high and mocking. "Look at how angry he's getting; I think he might go for his knife."

Diver looked over his shoulder at Lonnie. "You'd better hope I don't," he said. He'd begun to shake, and not in fear. At least, not for fear of them. It was always this way when the rage came upon him. Where other men might grow still and cold, he shook like a leaf and felt almost on the verge of tears. Men had died assuming he was frightened. "What do you want from me, anyway?"

"Can't old friends say hello?" Hugh asked, his eyes wide and innocent. He licked his lips. "Lonnie spotted you this morning, wandering the woods on some secret mission. How could we pass on the opportunity to catch up? We've missed you since you ran away."

"I didn't run away. I fought for my country! And we were never friends." Standing so close, Diver could feel Hugh's breath on him. Hot and sour. His rage fought with old terrors. *Don't move, don't step back, don't show fear...*

"We weren't?" Lonnie said from behind him, his voice low and oily. He clucked his tongue. "I'm rather hurt. Didn't you like all the games we played together?"

"Like when we hung you by your heels off the stone bridge?" Hugh simpered at him hideously. "Or knocked you into the hog pen? How you thrashed and cried. It was marvelous fun!"

"Or the time we pulled your pants down in front of the whole class?" Lonnie cackled gleefully. "Even old Mr Hess laughed at you then."

Hugh's booming guffaw made Diver start, but the man was looking at Lonnie as he laughed. "Oh, yes, you particularly liked that, didn't you?"

"What? Why would you say that? I didn't – it was your idea!"

"And it was your idea to take him to the high meadow, wasn't it?"

The sly implication in Hugh's voice came through clearly, and Diver heard Lonnie sputtering denials. It was all distant to him. Inside, the rage was building like a fire, hot and fierce in his gut. One hand curled hard into a fist and the world took on the color of blood.

"You seemed eager enough at the time," Lonnie said nastily. He was standing too close at Diver's back. They had him trapped between them. Like old times.

"Let me go." Diver's voice was shaking, and he could barely make out Hugh's face through a sheen of red. He was trapped in the past as surely as he was trapped between these two men. His hand wrapped around the hilt of his blade, though he didn't draw. Yet. It took all his strength not to. *I am not a murderer. This is not the battlefield.*

"Relax," Lonnie snarled. "It's always better when you relax, Divey."

The world burned. Diver yanked his blade free and spun toward the sound of Lonnie's voice, seeing nothing, hearing nothing. He moved by instinct alone and would have gutted Lonnie from navel to breast if Lonnie hadn't been expecting his attack. Diver managed only to nick his ribs as Lonnie leapt clear, gasping. Diver moved in again, caught in a killing rage, screaming, "Let me go!" at the top of his lungs.

"Shoot him! Hugh! Shoot him!"

"I'm trying. He won't stand still!"

Swinging wildly, instinct and skill failing before his anger and terror, Diver pursued Lonnie, tripping over underbrush and deadfall while Lonnie nimbly kept his distance. In all his time during the war, he'd never lost such complete control of himself. He knew this in some dim recess of his mind. And knew just as assuredly it was going to get him killed, but he couldn't help himself. He'd buried his memories for too long. A flood of rage drove him.

The sharp retort of a gun rattled the woods, and Diver dropped to the ground, waiting for the pain of a bullet wound. He felt nothing, just bruises and scratches from landing on a pile of rocks and twigs. A bloodcurdling scream followed the echo of the single shot. Not a pistol shot, he realized belatedly. A rifle shot. The timbre was entirely different.

Diver rolled over and scrambled to his feet. Lonnie was

crouched nearby, looking shocked and frightened, and staring beyond Diver. Diver turned and found Hugh rolling on the sandy ground near the bluff, clutching his arm. Blood had soaked the sleeve of his uniform and was dripping through his fingers. A pistol lay on the ground next to him. How close had he come to shooting Diver in the back? Pain contorted the big man's face; his screams had diminished to panting sobs. Beyond him, emerging from the forest with Diver's rifle in her hands, was Fury. The look on her face made his blood run cold.

"Pick up your friend, Lonnie," Fury said, her voice calm and steady. She aimed the rifle at the skinny man. "Take him and leave our woods. Come back again and I'll shoot you between the eyes. You know I can, and you know I will." Her black eyes hard as diamond, she sighted down the rifle barrel, rocksteady. "Touch my brother again – no, *look* at my brother crosswise again, and I'll cut your fucking balls off."

Lonnie scrambled to Hugh and dragged him to his feet despite Hugh's cries of pain. He glared at Fury. "You'll regret this," he said, snarling. "Hugh is an officer. His father is the fucking mayor!" He held up his friend with some difficulty; Hugh was a bear compared to Lonnie, though he was sobbing like a child at the moment and hardly looked intimidating leaning on his much smaller friend. "The authorities will deal with you, just you wait."

"He's a stinking cadet, and his father is a cunt. I'm tired of your threats, you miserable sack of shit. Send the authorities if you will; I'll tell them what you two have been up to with some of the town's war widows."

He jerked, taken aback. "You can't prove anything!"

"I've treated their wounds, heard their stories. Every hideous detail. You do know what they do to rapists, don't you?"

His eyes widened. "Not one of them would dare accuse us in public!"

"Maybe." Fury lowered the gun slightly. "Would you stake your life on it? That *none* of them are willing to talk? Do you want to take that chance?"

Snarling incoherently, Lonnie backed off, taking the bleeding Hugh with him. Only when they were out of sight did Fury lower the rifle. She started shaking. "I wanted to try for some game," she said, her voice as shaky as the rest of her. "I heard their voices. They've only gotten bolder since you left. I was afraid–"

"Is it true?" He felt cold inside, numb. The rage had left him, draining away like blood. "Have they been... attacking people?"

It shocked him, even after all they'd done to him personally. He felt a sudden overwhelming guilt. If he'd said something all those years ago, could he have stopped them? Would they have been punished? Or sent away? *For what? For assaulting a half-Gullan orphan boy? Fat chance.* But the cynical thought brought him no comfort. He'd run away like a coward when he should have crowed for justice. He couldn't look at his sister. He focused on the moss-covered bole of a giant tree. "Have they?" he demanded again.

"Diver." She spoke gently. "It doesn't matter. Everyone knows about it, not just me. No one cares. No one has ever cared." She sighed. "I was just bluffing. But. I will shoot them if they come around again. They believed that much. It's all we have."

From out of nowhere, emotions overwhelmed him. His throat closed and his eyes caught fire. The forest spun around him.

Stop. Be still. Find your center...

The mantra came to him in a deep, beloved voice. Lost to him forever. He imagined arms around him, strong enough to contain all of him. Rapidly, he blinked his eyes clear. *Breathe. Breathe.* His gasps turned to long, gulping breaths. He closed his lips and forced the breath through his nose.

A hand settled on his shoulder, gave him a gentle squeeze. It took all his self-control not to plunge his knife through his sister's belly. His muscles twitched as he fought instincts honed by violent conflict. Unaware – how could she know? – her grip grew firmer. How could she know what caused him to shudder so? Not grief, but uncontrollable rage. A violent urge to kill.

"Don't touch me," he said. His voice sounded cold, distant. He felt her hand jerk away, and he heard her startled intake of breath.

"Diver..."

"It's not you. Please... just... leave me be for a bit."

"Alright," she said, sounding resigned. A moment later, he heard her move away from him.

Diver didn't look up until her footsteps had receded. He'd pushed his feelings back where they belonged – deep, deep inside of him. His eyes fell on Hugh's abandoned pistol. Without thinking, he stooped to retrieve it. He tucked it inside his shirt, his knuckles brushing the soft edge of a feather.

CHAPTER SIX

The sun never set on Splendour. Blessed Sol bathed the blue and crystal world with unending light. Only near the distant rim of the firmament did twilight shade the world of the Angelus. A lavender blush dusted with a riot of stars. But no one flew close to the firmament. Why leave the clear, bright light of Sol? Ten Aeries circled Sol – great, floating satellites blanketed with manicured lawns and pristine gardens spreading out from fairytale cities built of crystal and gold and pink marble, towers soaring impossibly high on the bones of dead leviathans millennia old. Every stone and plant and sparkling tree, every river and pool and shimmering fountain was nothing short of flawless. The Angelus tended to their world with a ruthless devotion to perfection. Even the haunts and gin joints of Lower Splendour retained an ethereal beauty and deep grace thanks to the diligence and servitude of the lesser folk, the pinioned – Angelus stripped of their wings.

As for the angels themselves, their glory rivaled the light of Blessed Sol. And their arrogance matched the vastness of the Kosmos. Children of the Luminous One, they were winged gods, denizens of Splendour and masters of the Below. That treacherous, chaotic world of darkness and despair. The Black Silence separated the glorious realm of Light from the hideous dungeon of Dark. The "Celestial Gate", as it was known to the Beasts of the Below. No Angelus dared traverse it except by armored drachen, all hatches battened, and Mithran shielded. No Angelus would be so foolhardy, so suicidal. Mothers told their children stories of fallen Angelus to keep them sweet and obedient. It was used as punishment for the worst offenders. Heretics and rabble-rousers. Those who dared disrupt the perfect balance of Splendour.

Eleazar Starson knew the stories well. Had cowered under his covers as his nursemaid regaled him with tales of wrath and woe. Angelus pinioned and tossed to their doom. Human spies daring to enter the sacred realm of Light, daring to think they could gaze upon their gods without consequence, cast out burned and cursed to wander the Below as frightful ghouls. Rightfully so. Righteously so. But always in his heart, hidden deep inside, Eleazar harbored a dreadful fear: Was he deserving of such a fate? Were his odd questions, his strange musings, bordering on heresy? Was he anathema to perfection? How could it be so, when his wings were purest white and silver, his skin smooth and unblemished, his face in ideal symmetry?

But, could it be, despite his beauty and grace, his very soul might be wrong?

These thoughts had troubled him his entire life. Until his own brother betrayed him and sent him tumbling into oblivion. A punishment...

The wail of the wind had awakened him. Awakened him to pain and confusion. His body was limp, his wings splayed uselessly, rippling in the rush of air cradling him, one throbbing with agony. His long hair had come loose from its queue and floated above him. Weightless in the shrieking wind.

Falling. I am falling...

Panic roared through him, blasting through the pain and confusion. He remembered sliding off the nymph, fighting to catch a thermal only to have his injured wing fail him. His brother's face. So satisfied. It was a fleeting image. He began to thrash, disoriented, mindless. His wings were a mess of crooked feathers and blood, the nymph's blood and his own. One responded as always, the other a burden now.

The Silence. How close?

He screamed through clenched teeth, a desperate mewling. His voice was whipped away in the rushing wind. He had to slow himself, he had to catch an updraft, ride a thermal, anything. If he could fly, he could survive. What Aerie was closest? He had only to reach the lowest spire...

I must reveal Rast's treachery. See him pinioned!

He tried to call up rage, to give himself the strength to fight, but hysteria crowded out all other emotions. He'd been cast out. Cast into the Black Silence. As he'd always feared. His greatest terror. The scream of the wind was deafening, drowning out even his own pounding heart. It roared like a thousand angry beasts. He tried to right himself, drawing his wings close so he could turn facedown. But again, his injured wing thwarted him; he could not move it without blinding pain.

Do it! Damn you! Ignore the pain. You are a god!

He didn't feel very godlike, trapped in pain and falling like a stone. A whimper slipped from him, panic rising like a fist in his throat. But he fought it and tried again to draw his wing closed. Fire raged along the bone and tendons; blood pounded in his head and limbs; his vision grew dim. Slowly, the wing folded, but he could only close it part way. At least his uninjured wing was flush to his back. It would have to be enough.

More streamlined, his wings no longer at risk of being torn to shreds in the violent airstreams, he rolled into a dive, headfirst, arms tight to his sides, and his legs held together though the wind fought to drag them apart. The sight which met his eyes nearly burst his heart. The Black Silence, vast and churning below him, spreading in all directions in inky horror.

Death. Despair. Destruction.

Desperately, he opened his wings, pushing against the rushing wind. Sweat popped out on his skin; he clenched his teeth, muscle and bone strained to the breaking point. Inch by inch, his great wings spread wider. He felt himself slowing; relief and hope flooded him, and he pushed harder, forcing past the torment of his injury through sheer will.

Yes! Yes. Thank the Luminous–

The snap startled him, so loud and sudden. There was a moment of stunned disbelief before fresh agony tore through his wing, down his back and into his belly. He tumbled into a spin, torn in a spiral, his wing bent backward, broken and fluttering uselessly. One wing could not hold him, but he flapped it uselessly, only to increase his spin. The world was a confusing up and down of blue, black, blue, black. His heart threatened to burst from him, his muscles screamed, his stomach leapt into his mouth.

Blue, black, blue–

Black.

Everywhere was blackness. *Reaching* for him. He felt a power grip him, inexorable. Pulling him down, down, down into...

Silence.

Nothingness surrounded him, no wind, no sound but for the rush of his own blood in his ears, the thunder of his heartbeat. He was still falling, he had to be, but there was no up, no down. Only blackness.

I'm dead. I am dead, and this is hell.

He couldn't see. His ears seemed muffled. Assaulted by silence so intense it was a living thing. The air vanished from his lungs. His mouth gaped, desperate for breath. His eyes spun madly, but the black was unrelenting. He wasn't being tossed about like a leaf in a raging river, but it brought him no comfort. He longed for the wind. He waved his arms and legs and felt no resistance. Cold crept across his skin, entered his bones. Would he freeze? Would he float here forever? Spots appeared before his eyes. His chest burned from the lack of air. He would suffocate long before he froze...

Was there a bottom to this Silence? He knew in his soul there was; where did the airships go when they breached the Black Silence? There was a world below him. Somewhere.

Suddenly, he very much wanted to reach the Below, even if it meant darkness and chaos and beastly humans.

Time slowed and stretched around him, and he continued to fall through the black. The thunder of his heartbeat lessened, his blood ceased its wild rushing. His mind was cotton. Fatigue settled deep into his strained and torn muscles; the pain from his broken wing grew faint. A distant fatalism replaced his fear and horror. It would all be over soon. Without air, he would die in this darkness and cold. Die swiftly...

Light. Light and sound and substance. Eleazar gasped, his starved lungs drinking in warm, soft air. Never had he been so relieved to feel the wind rushing around him. He was falling backward; he did not know when he had turned over again. Above him swirled a churning black storm, swiftly receding. He had passed through the Black Silence, and he was still alive! A miracle. What else explained it?

Perhaps he truly was a god.

He twisted away from the Silence, fighting pain and his own broken wing to right himself. On his back, he was helpless.

A stunning sight met him. Not darkness, not chaos. A color. Green. A green world. No. This was too simple to describe the world below him. Green and purple and brown, red and rust and yellow. Details leapt at him. The sky here was blue beneath the swirling maelstrom, a storm that seemed almost benign from this side. White and gray clouds marred this world's sky, and mist hung heavy around the vegetation that he was hurtling toward. Trees, he realized. Trees beyond counting. Wild, tangled and unkempt. Not like the manicured landscapes of the castle grounds. Not like the crystal-leaved sacred trees of Splendour. Their flaring tops spread toward the sky, each seeming to fight for its own space, reaching.

Reaching for him.

Fast.

Panic returned. Had he survived the Black Silence just to shatter against the earth? Desperate, he grasped his injured wing with his hand, using his arm to hold it open, though his muscles screamed in protest. It didn't matter. Fear lent him strength: fear and the certainty he was not meant to die today. He spread his uninjured wing to its full length, catching the air. The action slowed him to a more reasonable speed, though he was still falling, not flying.

The great green limbs of the impossibly tall trees leapt up and grabbed him. The branches whipped him mercilessly as he crashed through them. The snapping reminded him sickeningly of his broken wing and he pulled his precious appendages as close as he could. He tumbled through slender branches and hit thicker and thicker limbs. Each one slowed his plummet but cost him pain and blood.

And then he was through the punishing trees and into another free fall. The wind no longer rushed through his ears and feathers. The air was heavy and wet, dragging him down. He couldn't lift his wings to stop his fall, let alone fly. Had he slowed enough to live? The ground had to be close–

He hit cold, cold water in a great splash. It sucked him down and under and carried him along. He fought to rise, but the weight of his sodden wings hampered him. With a desperate thrust of his legs, he breached the surface, thrashing wildly. He heaved in deep breaths, afraid he would be pulled down again. His wings dragged at him. Heavy as stones. But he kept his head above water, drawing in the precious air.

He was alive. Alive! Nothing else mattered…

"Alive."

The word rasped from him, pulling apart parched lips. His eyes were closed, weighed down by weariness. He lay upon a cloud, thick and substantial, embracing him in softness. The agony which had plagued him for days, weeks, eternity perhaps, had receded. A crashing wave on a distant shore. He felt light as a feather. And dry as dust. "Water," he begged.

"Eleazar?" A voice heavy with sleep. The woman. The fiend. He tried to turn his head to twist away from her, but the cool rim of a cup touched his lips and he settled. Blessed water slipped into his mouth, down his throat. He swallowed convulsively. A fit of coughing wracked him. He braced for a rush of pain but felt only mild discomfort. His limbs, his wings, were wooden. Feebly, he struggled against this violent lethargy.

"Be still," the voice admonished. "We have you restrained. For your own safety, mind you. If you could wait..."

All Eleazar heard was "restrained". He redoubled his efforts to rise, dragging at his closed eyelids with every fiber of will. Eyelids as heavy as the thick draperies in his private chambers. Many-layered, designed to block the everlasting light of Sol, for even gods must sleep at times, it took five pinioned servants to draw those drapes. Eleazar longed for those servants now as it seemed just as difficult to open his eyes. Panic alone gave him the strength.

Strange shadows rewarded his efforts. Unfamiliar shapes loomed in the gloom. A figure, its warm breath washing his shivering skin, moved over him and he felt a loosening along his limbs. Suddenly, he could raise his arm. In a flurry of movement, he struck out at his tormentor, his hand a claw. The fiend cried out. A hand grasped his wrist, but he had already unleashed his wings, and a great sheath of white feathers knocked his enemy away. He heard the fiend, the woman, land with a thud. He himself was flung in the opposite direction, his flapping wing pushing him out of the bed.

Falling...

His heart thundered wildly in his chest, his nerves afire. He nearly choked on his terror before the solid floor reached up to catch him, knocking the breath from him. He hugged the slick wooden boards, grateful and spent. He'd had one burst of violence in him. One. And it was finished now. His right wing twitched, sprawled as it was across the bed above him. Carefully, he pulled it closed, dragging it to its proper place nestled tightly against his back. It was a painstaking effort which further exhausted him.

"Eleazar! Did you hurt yourself?"

"Careful, Fury. He's gone mad!"

"Nonsense. He's disoriented. Help me get him back into bed."

"Let me get my rifle first…" This second voice trailed off with deliberate footsteps. They vibrated through Eleazar. Receding.

"Don't be ridicu – Diver!" The first voice fell into incomprehensible mutters. "I'm going to help you rise, angel." Her tone was firm and chiding, like a nursemaid with an unruly child. "Keep your wing sheathed, will you?"

Wing. My wing…

A hole opened within him, as black and enormous as the Silence. He let the woman help him up, moving in a fog. His legs shook, barely held him, and he tumbled face-first back into the soft embrace of the mattress. Soon, the woman had him arranged on his back again, cautious with his wing and the thick bandages which encased his back and left shoulder – his *empty* shoulder. She tucked the blankets to his chin.

"There. Right as ruin. Let's have a touch of tonic, yeah?"

Her face hovered above him, teeth bright in the dim room. Was she smiling, or snarling at him? These were beasts, after all. All he could do was stare at her. She had high, broad cheeks, a long nose and a mane of wild hair sprouting from her head. Coarse and lowly features. Her dark eyes held sympathy, but not a little exasperation. She wedged a spoon between his numb lips. He swallowed a bitter draught.

"That's a good lad," she murmured, fussing about with his blankets like a mother cat arranging her kittens. "You've been through quite a bit. Rest now, and we'll talk come morning."

As she turned to leave him, euphoria settled through his veins. (What was in that glorious "tonic"?) But he had to know, had to know for certain. "It's…it is gone, isn't it?"

The words were low, rasping, barely more than a scratch of sound. Still, she heard him. Her broad shoulders went rigid, her back straight. She turned her head toward him, offering him her cheek and a sliver of eye. "Yes, Angelus. It was the only way to save you."

A shriek built within him only to die beneath a soporific wave. He felt no pain. He felt nothing.

"You should have let me die."

He might have said it – he wasn't sure. Maybe he only thought it. Those heavy draperies had five pinioned dragging them closed, leaving him in blessed darkness.

CHAPTER SEVEN

In the early, terrible days of Eleazar's recovery, laudanum became Fury Barret-Cree's best friend. Perhaps she leaned on it too heavily – she feared she might regret it when all was said and done. Laudanum dependency was an ugly business – but keeping the Angelus in a tranquil state seemed a wise course of action. Especially as he regained his strength. A phenomenal strength. She'd learned the hard way when he'd tossed her across the room with a flick of his wing. Her ribs still hurt when she took a deep breath. She respected his otherworldly strength as she would the strength of a raging bull. And as she couldn't keep her distance from Eleazar as she could a penned bull, instead she kept him doped and docile. Besides which, she preferred his glassy-eyed gaze to the piercing rage and hatred he usually skewered her with.

"Miserable creature," he would mutter as she brought him trays of food, his gaze full of malice. He would snatch the tray when it was barely in reach, then complain at the poor quality and quantity of the meal while she watched their meager larder disappear day by day.

Diver spent his days hunting, wearing himself to the bone to provide meat for their household. Meanwhile, she was tethered to the cottage, tending to the ungrateful Eleazar and her ripening garden. The corn and winter squash and pumpkins were almost ready to be harvested. She'd already gathered the last of the pole beans and greens. Another year, she might have been pleased at what her small plot had yielded. Not this year.

When they'd brought Eleazar home, she'd fretted about filling three bellies through the hard winter months. But Eleazar's hunger seemed bottomless, like feeding wood into a blazing bonfire. It seemed one lone angel might eat them out of house and home. They'd be lucky to make it to winter at this rate.

Still, it was gratifying to see him mend so swiftly. The infected wing had indeed been the cause of his troubles. Free of the diseased appendage, his skin regained its healthy bronze glow, as if he'd soaked in warm sunlight his entire life, and his lone wing gleamed with the ethereal luminescence which had captivated her so much. Despite his cruelty toward her, she was glad to see him improving. Diver was, too, not that he would admit it or even get close to the Angelus except to peer at him through the doorway, curious and pensive. For his part, Eleazar ignored Diver completely. So completely, it was a palpable thing.

Fury sighed, watching Eleazar inhale the "thoroughly repugnant slop" she'd given him, her own belly shrunken and aching. It was all she could do not to snatch the bowl of porridge from his wretched hands. Sprinkled with cinnamon and topped with chopped apples and walnuts, she'd made it with care and attention Eleazar hardly deserved. Nothing pleased him, and she hated him. Hated his nasty sneer and disdainful sniffs. His supercilious manner toward their humble home and "primitive" living conditions. You'd think they lived in a cave, the way he acted, shoeless and filthy.

Yes, she hated him as she hated the snooty townspeople who'd always looked down their noses at her family, at her. Hated his pretty face and perfect body, and the way he measured her own tall, bulky frame with a dismissive, disgusted flick of his bright eyes.

And when she thought her hate would boil over into sharp words and cruel insults, Eleazar would get a look on his face as the laudanum took hold and the bright day waned. A lost look, devoid of guile, almost childlike in its innocence and bald fear. He would gaze toward the window, the descending sun aflame beyond it, lighting the world in reds and golds. For some reason, sunsets horrified him, and he would sink down into his blankets, hugging them to his chin as if he could hide behind them.

"How do you stand the dark?" he asked her one night, deep in a good dose of laudanum. "It makes your world a terror."

Fury frowned at his question, busy lighting the sconces in his room, knowing he couldn't sleep in total darkness. Not that she cared. His night terrors tended to keep her awake. It wasn't for *his* comfort. "You don't have night in your world?"

He shook his head. He hadn't revealed much of where he'd come from, only that it was miles and miles beyond their awful world in grace and beauty and wisdom. "Sol never sets on Splendour. Even with my curtains drawn I knew Blessed Sol warmed me still. No wonder this place is such a misery." A shudder wracked him. His eyes grew unfocused. His face relaxed. "It is pretty, though. Some of it. What I've seen beyond my window anyway. Like the trees have been painted by the finest artist. Such color, such unbelievable colors. Reds and yellows, purple even. I've read the scholarly texts, all of them in fact, but I think they might be lies. They say the Below is always dark, always savage and ugly. But, even you, as hideous as you are, you aren't really savage. The other one, even he has been gentle in his strange way." A chuckle rumbled through him. "He hasn't tried to shoot me again. There's that."

He blinked at her languidly. She held still, holding the glass of the last sconce in one hand and a lit match in the other. He'd never spoken so long without being nasty. Was this the true Eleazar, or was it the arrogant beast she'd come to expect? "You're a scholar?" she asked carefully.

He lifted his shoulders and made a noise. "Not according to the Keeper's Archon. They only let me read the scrolls because I'm the prince." Another soft chuckle. "Was the prince. I'm nothing now, I suppose." He focused on her. "Do you have scholars here?"

"We do. All sorts. Trin has a university."

"A what?"

Fury hissed as the match burnt her fingertips and she waved it out briskly. "A place of study," she explained. "It's full of scholars. Full of books. Scrolls, too, I suppose."

His eyes shone. "How many? How many books?"

"I don't know. I've never been there–"

"Thousands." Diver stood in the doorway, half in and half out of the shadows. "There are thousands of books. The library at Trin is the largest in the world."

"Fascinating." Eleazar's eyes drifted shut and he sank into his pillows, his mouth going slack, his chest rising and falling in a deep, hypnotic rhythm. Diver stared at him intently, his face unreadable. Fury sighed. Eleazar was a beautiful enigma, she decided, replacing the sconce at last. And trouble.

Such moments of vulnerability were few and far apart, but Eleazar's open contempt eventually faded to irascibility and mild condescension. Even with one wing, he considered himself a superior being. The day he "let" Fury help him navigate the small cabin to the front porch was a tiny victory which left her with a healer's satisfaction at a patient on the mend and a sore jaw from gritting her teeth hard enough to crack walnuts. It had not been an easy journey. Having a single wing left Eleazar off-balance and clumsy, but he adamantly refused to admit to any handicap. He'd knocked over her mother's rocking chair and smashed a wall sconce before he'd finally allowed her to duck under his arm and help him.

"You are a giant of a woman," he said thoughtlessly, his elegant arm slung across her broad shoulders and hers braced around his slim waist. Her strength balanced him, replacing the weight and mass of his missing wing. "We are almost of the same height. You must tower over your own kind."

"Aren't there tall women in heaven?" she snapped, moving in sync with him, and resisting the urge to let him tumble to the floor.

"Of course, but female Angelus are delicate creatures. Elegant and lovely. As are all my people. Beautiful beyond compare."

His lofty tone had her cracking walnuts again. By now, she knew some of the circumstances which had landed him on their doorstep, and she couldn't hold her tongue. "Was the 'treacherous bitch' who shot you lovely and delicate?"

He caught his toe on the doorframe as she helped him to the porch, so she wasn't sure if his oath was for her comment or his pain. Either way, it brought a smile to her face. He cursed like a soldier. Hard to feel awed by a foul-mouthed invalid.

She was panting by the time she'd settled him into a cleverly made chair of willow branches curved and molded into shape, a worn cushion on its latticed seat. It was the only chair large enough to hold Eleazar and his wing. Grayson Barrett had often spent his evenings there, smoking his pipe and surveying his small kingdom. Fury's garden sat lush and verdant at the base of the steps, taking up most of their yard. A split rail fence separated it from the surrounding woods, but the trees loomed dark and mysterious. Eleazar curled his toes against the floorboards, his gaze on the trees. He wore only a pair of her father's trousers, his upper body bare to the chill air. She rubbed her goose-pimpled arms, but he seemed unbothered by the cold. His bronze skin gleamed.

"It's so... wild here," he said suddenly. The edge of conceit in his voice had vanished. Her ears perked. "So vast and uncultivated. How do you make sense of it all?"

"Don't you have forests in Heaven?" She took a seat in the matching chair beside his, a smaller version which had been her mother's. Diver usually sat in it while she preferred their father's chair. It was a tight squeeze for her as she took after her large-framed father. The slim branches bit into her hips and she hoped the chair would hold her.

I am a giant of a woman. Eleazar hadn't been the first person to comment on her size, but it stung more than she'd expected. It was hard not to feel ugly and awkward beside a real-life angel.

"We have gardens. Magnificent gardens. All in their place. Ordered and sublime. This" – he waved a hand – "this is chaos."

"I have a garden. It grows food, not magnificence. We have orchards and vineyards, too. Bounty you all seem to love, by the way. And these woods might seem chaotic, but they are ordered in their own way. Balanced." She did her best imitation of his pompous tone. "You are a stranger here, of course, so I can forgive your ignorance. Perhaps if your kind deigned to be in our world rather than leech off it, you would understand it a bit better."

Brooding silence met her comment. She risked a look at him and saw that he'd dozed off, his head lolling against the back of the chair. She sighed and shifted into a more comfortable position. Perhaps it was time to ease off on the laudanum...

A breeze rattled the leaves of the apple trees, now stripped of every cherry-red piece of fruit. Her stomach growled, reminding her she hadn't eaten yet. And wouldn't until evening. It didn't matter. She was growing used to the ache of hunger. Besides, there was still work to be done in the garden. Pumpkins to pick and weeds to pull. Beds to ready for winter to ease her spring planting. An urgency entered her, a sudden need to be doing something. Anything. She couldn't sit here all day on the porch. So much needed to be done if they were to survive the coming winter.

Eleazar's soft snores drifted to her, drawing a smile on her face. He was an arrogant jackass and a drain on their resources, a one-winged timebomb dropped in her home. He was the reason she dreaded the winter. Not even Diver's haunted eyes and moody silences occupied as much of her mind. And yet. Sometimes when she thought he couldn't be more alien, more awful, he showed a deep vulnerability. She would wake him from his night terrors and soothe him as he sobbed. He would reach for her in the depths of his misery, then punish her for it the next day, but she couldn't leave him to suffer alone. Deep in the throes of laudanum, he would be self-deprecating and modest, thankful and kind. He would be... human.

Those moments made it easier to tolerate his horridness. Besides, as unpleasant as he could be at times, there was something magical about his presence. His broad white wing, furled tight to his back, glowed softly in the dim light, brightening their miserable hovel in ways a lamp never could. He was beauty and light and magic...

And petulance and misery and ugliness.

He was trouble. For her, for Diver. They couldn't keep him hidden here forever. What would happen when he was strong and ready to leave? What if someone found him before he'd regained his full strength? Had he survived a fall from Heaven only to die in a dark and strange world?

A cloud passed over the sun and the breeze picked up. Even Eleazar wrapped his arms around himself against the chill, murmuring in his sleep, his smooth brow furrowing. She held still, watching him until he settled, wondering what dreams haunted him. His brother's betrayal? (Unimaginable to her.) His fall from *actual* Heaven? The terror he'd endured, the trauma. He and Diver had that in common; if only they would speak of their pain, they *might* become friends.

She scoffed at the idea, feeling foolish. Eleazar had nowhere to go, not crippled as he was. He was trapped with them. He hadn't *chosen* their small cottage for refuge. It was an accident of fate. Once he was strong enough, he would leave, and gladly. Most likely, he would demand that the elders take him to the nearest Tithing Ground. Perhaps in Trin, or somewhere else. Somewhere he would be treated like royalty. Like the prince he was in truth.

That he would leave was inevitable, and good riddance. To have her simple life back would be a relief. Just her and Diver as it had always been. Eleazar would be just as glad, no doubt, to be away from them. Especially her, the "fiend" who took his wing. They were even, after all. Diver had saved his life, and Fury had crippled him. The debt was paid. Soon, it would be as if this time in her life had been a dream.

The thought brought a strange hollow feeling in her chest.

Across the yard, Diver emerged from the shadowy wood. The carcass of a deer was slung over his shoulders. She extricated herself from her chair and slipped past Eleazar, careful not to wake him. Grinning, her stomach grumbling loudly at the thought of backstrap for supper, she skipped down the steps and strode through her garden to meet him. He lifted his head as she neared and the look on his face stopped her cold. His eyes slipped toward Eleazar asleep on the porch and his features hardened with steely determination.

"What is it?" Fury demanded.

Diver answered with one, ominous word: "Trouble."

CHAPTER EIGHT

The shot was true. The young buck dropped like a stone to lie twitching among the ferns. Yet Diver felt his heart squeeze and the sting of tears as he lowered his rifle. It was foolish, these feelings. He had to hunt, to provide meat; they couldn't live on roots and nuts and mushrooms, not through a long, cold winter. Fury was depending on him, trapped as she was in the cottage, tending to an invalid. It wasn't as if they could trade places, either. Eleazar hated him, feared him, and it was Diver's own damnable fault.

I just... I couldn't control myself. When the rage comes on me... I don't think. I act.

He wanted to apologize to the angel, to tell him he'd meant no harm. That he would never hurt him. Not now, not after watching him suffer, his eyes full of pain and confusion. There was a good soul behind his arrogance. A lost soul, perhaps. And Eleazar was so, so beautiful...

The tears dried on his cheeks as he set to work field dressing his kill. The smell was the worst part. It invoked unpleasant memories of gutshot men, spilled intestines, and trenches full of shit. Few men died as cleanly as this buck had. A headshot was the best way, an easy death. Alive one second, dead the next. Neat and tidy.

When he was cleaning the blood from his knife, he heard them. He froze, his ears open to catch the sound: Voices. Men. He was in a small gully, having chased the buck down a narrow game trail, and the main path to Green Hollow was high above him on the limestone bluffs. The thick trees shielded him from sight, and shielded the approaching men from him, too. But he could hear them talking; sound traveled strangely in the woods. He recognized the high, needling tone of Hugh Kantorek, his voice raised in complaint. Finally, they had come for him. Brought reinforcements, too, by the sound of it.

Quickly, Diver collected his deer, hoisting it across his shoulders. He wasn't about to lose such a good kill. The meat would feed them for weeks. A sense of urgency filled his slim frame, giving him uncommon strength; the carcass seemed light as a feather. Fear for himself, fear for Fury, and yes, even fear for Eleazar drove him into a steady trot. He would reach home well before those men arrived. What he would do once he got there was less clear.

"They've come for me, no doubt," he blurted once he'd warned Fury of the trouble descending. Carelessly, he dropped the still-warm deer carcass in the middle of Fury's garden, ignoring her dark look as it crushed a patch of tomatoes. He was blowing like a winded horse. "Even Hugh would have figured out I'm a deserter by now," he panted. His mind raced. He had to protect her. "I'll head them off, turn myself in. Take the blame for shooting him."

Fury made a rude noise. "Nonsense. I'll admit to it. Proudly. The bastard would have killed you. He's lucky I only winged him."

He shook his head. Eleazar looked to be rousing from his nap and Diver dragged Fury with him toward the porch. They had to get the angel out of sight. "Take Eleazar inside," he ordered his sister. He pushed her toward Eleazar, who was blinking at them drowsily, sunk boneless in his father's chair. "Let me deal with them as best I can. If you must, run out the back and hide in the woods."

"Wait, if they're here for you, it doesn't make sense for you to try and talk to them. They'll arrest you on sight!"

"I'm not going to talk to them." He checked his rifle, made sure he had a cartridge chambered and tried to remember how many remained in the magazine. At least six. He hoped. He met Fury's wide-eyed gaze. "Get in the house, Fury, and stay silent."

Her jaw set stubbornly. "The hell I will."

"What is all the ruckus?" Eleazar had pushed himself to his feet and was leaning with one hand braced against the porch railing. Diver had forgotten how tall he was; his blond head nearly brushed the low ceiling of the porch. Even disoriented and swaying slightly, he was an impressive specimen. Broad-shouldered, slim-hipped, skin so bronze it gleamed. His blue eyes had sharpened and there were lines of pain around his full lips. The laudanum must be wearing off. "Quit squawking like a couple of pinioned," he growled peevishly.

"Take the angel into the house, Fury," Diver said, fixing Eleazar with a hard stare. Inside, his heart fluttered. The men coming would find him frightening. Alien. Worse, they would see a wounded animal, a dangerous animal. They would tear him apart in an instant. He was sure of it.

"You take him into the house," she countered, pushing open the front door and gesturing inside as if she were encouraging a recalcitrant cat. "I'll deal with this, I swear it." She softened her tone. "I've kept us safe all these years. I won't fail now." She stepped closer to him. "And you have to keep *him* safe," she whispered, her eyes cutting toward a frowning Eleazar. "It's him I fear for, more than either of us. He's not human. He's injured and he's alone. He needs you more than I do right now."

If she'd appealed to him in any other manner, or demanded he hide to save himself, Diver would have refused. But his sister knew him better than anyone. Her steady gaze, knowing and wise, made his cheeks burn. He slung his rifle over his shoulder and jerked his chin. "You're with me, Angelus," he said gruffly. "Come inside before they get here. And keep your mouth shut."

"Who are they? And who are you to order me around like a child?"

"'They' are men. Dangerous men, and it's best we get out of sight." Diver approached him, intending to take him by the arm. With a low growl, Eleazar pushed off from the railing, staggering only slightly before he steadied himself, his wing tight to his back, the long flight feathers brushing the floor.

"I do not fear your kind," he said haughtily. The laudanum had definitely worn off. "No more than I fear dogs. I refuse to hide like a frightened mouse. These men will worship me as is proper."

"Like *we* worship you?" Fury scoffed.

Diver could hear Eleazar grinding his teeth. "I had the misfortune to be rescued by the only atheists in all of the Below," he muttered. "Other men, godly men, will see me for what I am. A true Angelus. A god."

"They'll see a broken god doused with laudanum," Diver said cruelly. "And they'll rip that golden hide from your bones."

Eleazar's bright eyes grew round, though his jaw was rigid. Doubtful.

"Please, Eleazar, go inside," Fury pleaded, trying a more tactful approach. "We don't know how these men will react to seeing you."

Frowning, he turned his fierce gaze on her. "Or you're just trying to hide me from those who would give me proper obeisance."

"Their 'proper obeisance' could be several bullets to your head." Diver shrugged as if he didn't care one way or the other, but his heart was thudding as he calculated how close Hugh and the others would be by now. "I'm going in the house, and I'm staying out of sight. You may follow if you wish or take your chances with 'godly' men."

Turning his back on the angel, Diver entered their cottage. A moment later, a heavy tread followed him, and it was all he could do not to grin. Given the dire circumstances, it felt strange to feel such a surge of happiness at so simple a thing. For now, Eleazar had chosen to trust him. It was gratifying. He turned back as Fury closed the door behind them, catching his sister's dark eyes briefly before the door shut. Calm, clear pools. If she was afraid, she gave no sign of it.

With a fervent wish for her brother and Eleazar to stay safe, and most of all *quiet*, Fury shut the door firmly, spun and dashed off the porch, flying down the steps in a panicked clatter. Who knew how close the village men were? She had to be ready. A plan had begun to form in her head the minute she convinced Diver to take Eleazar and hide. It was a slim plan, barely a plan at all, but it was all she had. The entire town thought she was half mad for her strange, elusive ways. Her reputation to hit first and talk later, too. So, if they wanted a crazy, unpredictable Fury, by the Eternal, they'd get one.

The deer carcass provided a welcome prop for her impromptu tableau. She slid to her knees beside it, careless of the mud, and ripped off the tie binding her wild mane of curly black hair, recalling with a cringe how Eleazar had scornfully compared her "rat's nest" with the silken locks of the Angelus. He was strangely obsessed with her hair. She could only describe it as fascinated disgust. Now, she was glad for her wayward curls, raking her hands through them to further stand them on end. Next, she pulled her belt knife and set about butchering the fresh carcass. Soon her arms were crimson to the elbows, and she had a goodly pile of backstrap cooling in the thin, autumn sunlight.

By the time she heard rustling in the forest underbrush and felt the thump of steps through the damp ground beneath her knees, she was ready. For a final touch, she dipped two fingers in the deer's blood and drew lines down each cheek. There. The blasphemous, half-Gullan girl was ready for them. Blood-mad and dangerous. Let them tread lightly.

For good measure, she had her father's pistol tucked at her back, hidden beneath the tail of her loose shirt. She'd started carrying it after their run-in with Diver's old chums. It was cleaned and loaded for the first time in years. Diver had brought home more ammunition than he had weapons to load, thankfully. She didn't know if she had the guts to use it, but she felt reassured by its presence.

"Fury Barrett-Cree!" The strident call made her jump, but she hid it by sawing at the carcass. They hadn't come to play nicely, it seemed. So be it. The copper tang of blood stained the air and made her want to gag. She kept her eyes on the kill.

"Citizen Barrett-Cree, put down your knife and stand at attention," the voice continued, growing closer. Other, quieter voices followed the first, full of nerves and suspicion. She smiled grimly. Let them believe her mad as a loon.

A shadow dropped across her. Finally, she paused in her work and blew out an impatient breath. She kept the knife firmly in her grip and looked up at the man accosting her. The sun was behind him, obscuring his face. But she knew him by his shaved head and impressive bulk. Constable Fritz, Green Hollow's most reprehensible citizen. He took his role as town peacekeeper to extreme measures, sending pickpockets to the gallows and terrorizing even the most straitlaced townspeople. No, they definitely weren't here to play nicely.

"Constable," she said pleasantly, licking her lips and switching her gaze back and forth as if she didn't quite know where she was or what she was doing. "How nice of you to come calling."

The shadows creased with a dark frown. He moved to the left so the sun fell in her eyes, momentarily blinding her. She raised the hand with the knife to shield her gaze.

It was as if she'd pointed a gun at his face. The next instant, he had her by the arm, twisting hard, wrenching her across the deer carcass. The knife fell from nerveless fingers. She barely registered her shock before she had a mouthful of dirt, a knee on her back and her arm bent awkwardly. She struggled for all she was worth, kicking and growling like a trapped beast.

I suppose I am...

The click of a chambered round and a cocked hammer took the wind out of her faster than a blow to the skull. She froze. Something cold and hard pressed against the back of her head. The barrel of Constable Fritz's revolver.

"If you wish to behave like a monster, I will treat you like one." His voice was as cold as the steel of his gun. "Now. Do I have your attention?"

He eased up on the revolver enough for her to raise her face from the muck. She spat out a mouthful of dead grass and mud. "Yes," she gasped. So much for her plan to play the addled madwoman...

"Good." His knee dug deeper into her spine. She gritted her teeth, refusing to cry out as he so obviously wished her to. Her arm was going numb, which somehow hurt worse than the twisting of it. She had to endure it. She couldn't shout or scream. Diver would come running like a fool if she did.

"Where is Diver, you useless whore? Tell him to come out of hiding!"

Lonnie. She recognized his shrill voice instantly. Constable Fritz made a noise of consternation. "I told you to stay silent, Baumer!" he snapped. "You are only along as a courtesy."

Disgruntled silence answered him, but Fury had no time to revel in Lonnie's humiliation. Fritz gave her arm a quick twist and her vision darkened with a wave of pain. "Answer him."

"He's – I sent him away." The words ground from her. She let true bitterness color her tone. "He betrayed all my family stood for. He's become a true citizen. A *patriot*."

"She lies," muttered Lonnie.

"Shut. Up." Constable Fritz leaned over her, his hot breath ruffling her hair. "Are you lying, woman? Are you protecting a deserter?"

His words drove a stake of fear through her. Did they know? Really know? Or were they just speculating? Deserters were shot on sight.

Mustering all her indignation at being so roughly treated, she spat her answer: "No, I am not!" Then she went on for good measure, hoping she sounded convincing. "I wish he was a deserter. Then I could at least respect him. But, no, he's more than willing to die for Koine. Blessed Koine, he calls this land. As if you've ever accepted us among you."

"Yes, yes, you're so put upon as you leech off our land." He released her arm and took her by the back of her shirt, hoisting her to her feet. Constable Fritz was one of the few men who could manhandle her so easily. He grabbed her arm and shook her like a ragdoll. "Tell us where he is so we may get on to other business."

Other business? What business? She found Lonnie standing stiffly among a group of men, all volunteer constables – the "home guard", though they were little more than bullies – but for one. This man stood out like a sore thumb, her neighbor, Mister Pierson. Disheveled, unshaven, his clothes threadbare and dirty, he looked miserable. His eyes were red and small, his face bloated. His hands were shaking, and he refused to look at her.

"Well?" Fritz urged when she'd stayed silent for too long.

Fury drew herself up with a dignified lift of her chin. "The fool returned to the front, back where he belongs. And good riddance."

The constable peered at her, narrow-eyed. "If he has, then praise the Creator. May he bring glory to Koine. If not," and he shrugged, the implication clear. He released her abruptly, smiling viciously as she staggered. He holstered his revolver, too. She would hardly seem a threat surrounded as she was. Fury marked every man around her, certain they were more likely to shoot each other than her if the bullets started to fly. First, she would find out what they wanted from her. If it was about shooting Hugh, she was ready with her defense, and she would spill her accusations about him for all these important men to hear. She'd spill all the damn tea and hope they drowned in it.

The only thing that gave her pause was Mister Pierson. Why was he here? Did they know about the laudanum, the saw? Were they suspicious of her need for such items? Laudanum was legal. She couldn't even guess as to why they would care if she acquired it. Still, not knowing set her nerves on end.

Finally, Constable Fritz put her out of her misery. He pulled a bundle of cloth from his jacket. It shimmered in the sunlight, a rainbow of color dominated by dark blue. No, by pure indigo. It slithered from his fingers to dangle above the ground, flowing like water, eerily beautiful. A scarf. Her mother's scarf.

"Care to explain this?" he asked.

"It's a scarf. It belonged to my mother. I traded it. What of it? Is that a crime?"

"Indeed." A cruel smile curled his lips. "It is contraband, my dear. A holy relic stolen from the angels themselves. Only heretics and apostates would have such a thing. If we'd known your mother possessed it, why, we would have shipped her off in the Hallow Tithe years sooner than we did!"

CHAPTER NINE

The sweet elixir keeping him sane had worn off, leaving Eleazar on needles. They pricked his skin, everywhere all at once. Stinging, stinging. His missing wing throbbed wretchedly, his shoulder burning and strangely heavy as if the wing still hung there. Sweat coated his skin. It was all he could do to stay on his feet beside the awful boy with the rifle. If not for the danger of the moment, he would have returned to his lumpy bed and the bottle of elixir on the rickety table near it. A good dollop would put him out for hours, and he yearned for that soft haze of existence. It was far better than the hard reality in which he found himself.

The need for vengeance burned like acid in his belly whenever the medicine faded in his veins. A useless longing, worse than any he'd ever experienced. Worse than his longing for the laudanum. The rage made his teeth ache, his muscles throb, his gut tore up with it. The urge to fly was overwhelming, leaving him weak and spent after it took over his body and soul with no outlet but bitter grief. Lying in pools of sweat, miserable and frightened, his desire to return home and throttle his brother, and put a spike through Maurissa for good measure, reduced to wishful dreams and unfulfilled fancy. Eleazar hid his helplessness in nasty words and harsh arrogance. He couldn't let these fiends know how much he depended on them, how much he needed them. It wasn't fear for Fury which now turned his stomach into knots, but fear of being alone.

"What is happening?" he asked in an agitated whisper. The boy stood at the curtains, peering outside, careful to keep himself back from the slim opening between the thick drapes. A knife's edge of light slashed the floor at his feet, but he was in shadows. Darkness befitting his dark soul. Eleazar wanted to shout at him, to demand an answer. It was frustrating to be ignored by one so far beneath him.

I am at the mercy of violent beasts.

The "beast" emitted a low sound – distress – and stiffened. His rifle appeared in his hands, rising to his shoulder with whipcrack speed, the barrel pointed at the window. His entire lean frame became still as stone; his eyes narrowed at a target. His finger was poised on the trigger of his weapon. He didn't fire, not yet, but primitive fear coursed through Eleazar. He didn't know how many men were out there, or what kind of weapons they possessed. If they harmed Fury, he had no doubt Diver would exact revenge no matter the danger to himself. There was no love lost between them, but the two siblings were the only creatures he knew in this awful place. This place of darkness and chaos. He'd rather keep the devils he knew than face the hostile unknown. With only one wing, he was at a terrible disadvantage against human-made weapons.

"Wait," Eleazar hissed. "You'll get us all killed if you act rashly."

Diver's pale eyes cut to him. "I don't like the way they're crowding her. And that bastard Lonnie has always hated her. If they harm one hair…"

"Yes, yes, you'll blast them all to bits, I'm sure. You're quite terrifying." He'd intended for it to come out sarcastically, but the honesty in the words shone clearly. The coldness in Diver's eyes eased for a moment. If Eleazar didn't know better, he'd think the boy almost… ashamed. But then the freezing stare returned.

"If you're frightened of them then leave out the back." He jerked his head dismissively toward the rear of the house. "Hide in the woods until one of us comes for you."

"And if neither of you comes?"

"Then I guess you'll be rid of us to make your way in this world as you will." He gave him a nasty smile. "I'd avoid men since I know you aren't bulletproof."

Eleazar sniffed. He knew *theoretically* what it took to kill him, but reality was a far more frightening beast. That he wasn't lying helpless and injured gave him some confidence, but would his strength and speed and one lone wing be enough to keep him safe against several determined foes? He knew without a doubt Diver's rifle wasn't enough to keep any of them safe.

He could run as the boy had so mockingly suggested. Take his chances in this wide, wild world. Alone…

He ground his teeth in frustration. *Better the devils I know.* "Perhaps there is another way to see us all safely through this."

"What way is there besides violence?" Diver scoffed, his gaze tracking back to the window.

"Have they hurt her?" he asked. If they had, he doubted Diver would be so calm. Here was a brother who *loved* his sibling.

"Not yet." He growled in frustration, distracted by whatever was happening outside. "What are they doing? Why does the constable have *that?*"

"Your kind worships mine," Eleazar continued urgently, seeing Diver's body grow tense. "Let me show myself. They will see me as the superior being I am."

Diver snorted. "You really think they'll fall at your feet dressed as you are in my father's torn trousers?"

Bristling, Eleazar pulled himself up to his full height, feeling his blood pulse like a river in flood, determined to make the little brat eat his words. They were not indestructible, the Angelus, but they possessed an innate magic, a supernatural bent they'd used to subjugate the foul humans for eons. It took strength and focus, but he assumed terror would work just as well in this instance. And so, despite his weakened state, he drew on his Charisma, letting it shine through his crystal blue eyes, his golden skin and white wing. The dim hovel brightened. Diver's skeptical gaze took on a burnished glow, eyes growing wide, his lips parting.

Pleased, Eleazar turned his ancestral charms to full strength, flicking his broad wing wide, unfurling it like a banner, though he remained keenly aware of his deformity. The missing wing was a searing emptiness at his left shoulder. Still, he knew his own beauty. The glory of it. The lesser creatures that populated Splendour, the pinioned and the human slaves, turned to gibbering sycophants when subjected to the full Charisma of an Angelus.

Diver blinked slowly, his eyes unreadable, and his expression not nearly as adoring as Eleazar might have wished even if his dark cheeks seemed flushed. "Neat trick," he murmured. "It explains all the iconography in the temples. All the glowing heads and bright halos. Still. Are you sure you want to risk yourself? You leave this house, and I can't guarantee your safety."

Eleazar lifted a brow. That was rich, coming from the man who'd put a gun to his head. Perhaps Diver recognized the absurdity of his statement for his flush deepened and his eyes cut away. "It's your skin," he muttered. "You'll be a distraction, at least. Just... get out of the way when the shooting starts."

"That's what I am trying to avoid," Eleazar said, shaking his wing vigorously. Even filled to the brim with Angelic Charisma, he felt off-balance. Unsure. He hated it, and he hated the way his heart pounded erratically in his chest. Could he bluff his way through this? Humans were far cleverer than he'd ever thought.

A voice reached them from outside. Shrill and strident. "What do you mean? What did you do to my mother?"

Eleazar jerked, startled. The woman. Fury. Diver cursed, his rifle hard against his shoulder. "Go," he said, low and urgent. "Go now or I start shooting!"

Mustering all the courage he had, drawing on the needles of fire shuddering across his skin to stoke his ire, Eleazar burst through the front door and unleashed a roar, the sound reverberating like thunder. It achieved its intended purpose. The men surrounding Fury startled and turned as one to stare at him. He stood tall, gleaming bright in the shade of the porch. Slowly, he stepped down the stairs, raising his wing as he went, letting it catch the sun and sparkle. Slack jaws met this miracle.

Only Fury stared at him without awe, her face in an ugly grimace. She and one of the men seemed to be joined by a slim length of cloth, like two children playing tug-o-war. Taking advantage of Eleazar's stunning appearance, she wrenched the cloth away from him, holding it to her chest like she'd rescued a baby from some ravenous fiend.

"Who dares accost my holy acolyte?" Eleazar demanded, his voice booming.

Shocked silence answered him. One of the men, a dirty, disheveled sort of human, fell prostrate. Eleazar expected the others to follow suit, but instead they remained standing. The large man near Fury hardly looked impressed. His gaze slid over the Angelus, stopping at his empty shoulder, narrowing. Judging. He was armed, but only with a pistol. Nothing of concern. Not at this range. None of the men carried long rifles, thankfully. A barrage at this distance might not kill him, but it would do damage. He'd seen pinioned torn apart in some of Rast's "experiments" with human-made carbines and rifles. It was one of the reasons Rast found the humans such a potential threat. The Angelus had turned a blind eye to the advancement of their chattel, ignoring their wars except as a means to keep them from uniting in purpose against their true oppressors. Their weapons had grown fearsome, even to the powerful Angelus.

They worship us, they fear us. He told himself this as he approached the group of men, moving deliberately, serenely. It gave him confidence to know Diver watched keenly from inside the cottage, his rifle aimed and ready. How good a shot was he?

Eleazar stopped a goodly distance from them. He raised a hand and crooked a finger to Fury. "Come, disciple, attend me."

Wisely, Fury attempted to dart toward him, but the large, suspicious man latched onto her arm, dragging her back. "Not so fast, missy. What in the blessed heavens is going on here? I'll not be fooled by some mummer's farce!"

"A farce? How dare you doubt me!" Eleazar didn't have to fake the rage in his voice. He lifted his wing dramatically, presenting the glory of his feathers spread like an exotic fan above his head. Like a swan in full display. He poured on Charisma and took a menacing step forward. Three more of them dropped to their knees in the garden, overwhelmed. The obnoxious doubter and two others remained standing, a stout fellow with his arm in a sling and a scrawny man with a pinched nose. Something dark lurked in that one's eyes.

"Ridiculous," the thin man scoffed, unafraid. "He's probably another deserter. Like Diver. Put a bullet through his so-called wing and see if he bleeds."

"Don't!" Fury cried, quick to back Eleazar's ploy. "Do not harm the Angelus. You will bring the wrath of the heavens upon us."

The man holding her snarled. "Since when does an apostate fear the gods?"

She glared at him, her scarf tangled around her raised fists. "The angel appeared to us, Constable Fritz, hurt and helpless. To us, seeming atheists by your narrow definition. We knew immediately it was a test sent from the Creator Eternal. As the Sacrum tells us, the most holy Angelus will come to us as a simple beggar in great need. Only the purest of souls will recognize Them despite Their base appearance!"

Base appearance? It was all Eleazar could do to maintain his beatific expression. It wouldn't do to scowl with displeasure.

"Now it is you who are being tested. And you are failing miserably. Creator have mercy on your souls!"

Moans from the prostrate men filled the air and doubt wrinkled the constable's face. His grip on Fury had eased, he'd made no move to reach for his pistol as the unpleasant one had suggested. Fury held still though Eleazar suspected she could easily break free. Her eyes jumped to him.

"Dear Angelus," she said. "Please forgive these poor souls. They know not what they do."

Now she was really pouring it on thick. Tilting his head magnanimously, he pulled his wing closed, tucking it to his back with a neat flip. Exhaustion was stealing his glory. The needles were stinging fiercely, and the sweet tonic was calling. "Fear not, good daughter," he said in dulcet tones. "I have not come to sow discord, but to bring a message of peace and joy to your land."

"Have you come to end the war?" the stout boy in the sling exclaimed excitedly. His eyes shone as he looked upon Eleazar, thoroughly convinced.

Eleazar waved a hand, stalling. "My message is only for those ready to receive it."

"Bull*shit*!" The other one, the scrawny fellow with crawling eyes spat the harsh curse. "Fury is a worse performer than even you! *Angelus*." He sneered the word just before he snatched the pistol from the constable's belt and pointed it at Eleazar.

"Lonnie, don't–" sling-boy shouted.

The crack of the gun was an explosion in the still air, the bullet speeding toward Eleazar. But Eleazar was faster. He felt the bullet zip past his ear as he closed with his enemy, and it only added to his anger. How dare this *man* shoot at a blessed angel? In an instant, he had him by the throat. It took hardly any effort at all to lift him into the air.

With their companion dangling in his grip, suddenly every man there fell to groveling at his feet. The man in the sling begged for mercy while the others fell into desperate prayers. Even Fury seemed stunned by his speed and strength. His eyes met hers and it was gratifying to see astonishment reflected within their dark depths. (So rich, her eyes, a deep gleaming brown. How had he not noticed?) He looked away, to the man dangling in his grip. It had been so long since he'd felt powerful; he reveled in the feeling. He could crush this boy's throat like a grape. Like he wanted to crush Rast's throat. The desire to kill roiled through him. Intoxicating. Exhilarating.

Sickening...

He released the boy abruptly, letting him drop to the earth. The exhilaration of the moment left him in a rush, leaving him shaking. He had never killed anything in his life, let alone a person. Even his lone attempt to kill a leviathan had gone awry, and he wasn't sorry for it. The memory of the poor creature's mournful cries, its violet blood hot on his flesh, haunted his nightmares. Reeling backward, he nearly fell, thrown off-balance as he whipped open only one wing when there should have been two. Luckily, Fury was there, hard against his side.

"Pray your sacrilege does not bring destruction upon all of Green Hollow," she said stridently, forcing him to stand tall, her hip braced against his, her arm around his back. He knew they were still vulnerable; he couldn't show weakness. Not now. He used all his remaining strength to extend his wing and glower at them, hoping there remained within him some vestige of Charisma.

"Take yourselves away until you can show proper obeisance to a holy Angelus!" he said. "Do not tempt my wrath again."

They gathered themselves to leave, bowing and scraping like proper supplicants, scrambling toward the woods, their problems with Fury and her brother forgotten. The constable touched his fingers to his forehead in homage after retrieving his stolen weapon, his eyes slipping to Fury only briefly before he made his exit. The stout boy in the sling dragged his friend away with him. The scrawny man shot Eleazar a final look. Black as this world's infernal night.

They waited several minutes after the men had left, Fury the only thing keeping Eleazar on his feet. "They'll be back," she said, finally relaxing. "But I think they'll be a bit more respectful next time."

"We can only hope." Eleazar's limbs were trembling, and his stomach was starting to cramp. "Get me inside."

She sighed. "As you wish, most holy Angelus."

She took more of his weight and helped him turn toward the cottage. The shimmering scarf in her hand touched his bare torso. It felt like silk, but it wasn't silk. It was something not of the human world at all. He recognized it immediately and stumbled in shock.

"Easy, Eleazar," she murmured, her arm tightening around his waist. His stumble had dragged her off-balance and they both would have fallen if Diver hadn't appeared to help prop him up.

"Creator's balls," Diver said, grinning. "I can't believe that worked. Were they looking for me? Why did they bring back Mother's scarf? Wren Pierson must be furious."

Fury scoffed. "The constable said it was contraband. Diver, he said something else. About Mother…"

"You should have killed that bastard," he added, speaking to Eleazar and running over whatever Fury had been trying to say. "He won't forget this, and he won't forgive."

Eleazar was well aware he'd made an enemy, but he couldn't explain his reluctance to kill. He hardly understood it himself. A weakness, Rast would have called it, but it wasn't that. He feared letting himself go. Feared what he could do. Unleashed.

It didn't matter, not right now. What concerned him was their complete ignorance of what Fury held.

"You don't even know what you have, do you?" Eleazar asked, incredulous.

"What are you talking about?" Fury still had the scarf pressed securely against him and the feel of it was both soothing and appalling. It was so unexpected to find such a thing in the Below, it shook him to the core. How had it come to be here of all places?

Eleazar shook his head, too tired and sore and desperate for his tonic to measure his words. "How in the name of the Luminous One do you possess leviathan skin?"

CHAPTER TEN

The bonfire crackled pleasantly against the night's chill, sending sparks and smoke drifting skyward. The sun had set long ago, and the night was growing colder, but neither Diver nor Fury moved from their log-seats around their old stone-lined firepit. It had been an age since they'd done anything relaxing. Most nights since Diver's return, they'd dropped into bed as soon as the light bled from the day expecting to be woken by Eleazar's night terrors at least once or twice before dawn. But things had taken a remarkable turn for the better since Eleazar had been revealed. The village elders, the clerics, and the mayor himself had come calling, bearing greetings and gifts for the blessed Angelus. And questions. Those curious inquiries were met with patronizing smiles and meaningless drivel.

The common folk had come to gawk, as well, some bold enough to whisper fervent prayers to Eleazar who would listen solemnly and prattle some nonsense about worthiness and piety.

"All will be revealed, my blessed children. Once you have proven yourselves, all will be revealed..."

After being the town pariahs for so long, it was both gratifying and insulting to suddenly be considered some sort of holy acolytes. On the one hand, they were being shown respect for the first time ever, even if it was insincere. But, how easily the villagers accepted that their lifelong convictions had been mere camouflage to pass some religious test. Not that they weren't enjoying the profound shift, especially since it meant plentiful food laid at their doorstep and heaps of coal to see them through winter. Even Diver's desertion, for it had been near impossible to keep his presence hidden with so many people coming and going to pay homage, had been forgiven. In one of Eleazar's more lucid moments, his Angelic charm at full strength as the laudanum wore thin but before he was reduced to a gibbering mass of pain and anxiety, he announced it had been he who had prevented Diver from returning to the army. Fury's claim that she'd sent him away, her bald-faced lie, he'd merely dismissed as a necessary evil.

"I direct my acolytes in all they do," he'd claimed superciliously when confronting the officer who'd come for Diver. "To serve a higher purpose. I wouldn't expect a human to understand what plans a god must wrought to bring justice to this world. One soldier in your army is meaningless to victory. A soldier in my army, however…"

He'd let the implications hang in silence, allowing the man to infer his own meaning.

Shifting a log deeper into the hot coals with the toe of his shiny new boot, Diver couldn't help smiling as he recalled Eleazar's audacious fibs. Were all the Angelus just brilliant cons? It should have infuriated him but watching Eleazar work his magic on the town rubes only made him strangely proud. As if he had created this beautiful, obnoxious fraud from feathers he'd collected off the forest floor.

The shifted log sent up a shower of sparks into the black and gusty sky, drawing a protest from Fury who sat nearby with Mother's scarf across her lap. Her hand flew, busily wiping away tiny motes of flame from its shimmering surface. Not that fire could hurt it. Nothing could damage that mysterious length of fabric their mother had worn wrapped around her on special occasions. Strange holidays only her people had celebrated, accompanied by equally strange rituals Diver barely recalled. Fury remembered more. Since Eleazar had told them what it truly was that they possessed, she'd been obsessed by the scarf.

Leviathan skin.

"What in the name of the Creator is a leviathan?" Diver had demanded once they'd returned to the safety of their cottage and gotten Eleazar into bed with a goodly dollop of laudanum down his gullet. Fury had remained silent, the scarf still wrapped around her hands and clutched to her chest. It was strange because Fury had always eschewed their mother's things, out of anger or grief Diver had never really figured out. He believed their mother had been lost through no fault of her own for the world was a large and dangerous place for a lone Gullan woman. But Fury thought differently. Their mother had often been strange and distant, her gaze fixed on something only she could see. Something far away from them. Maybe, just maybe, Tuilelaith Cree had left to go and find it. Left them.

Now, suddenly, Fury held tight to one of mother's most precious heirlooms as if it were some dear blanket she'd kept in her crib. Diver peered at her, wondering. What had she learned about their mother from Constable Fritz? In the chaos after the confrontation, she'd started to say something.

"Leviathans are enormous, majestic beasts which inhabit Splendour," Eleazar said, sprawled across their parents' bed in euphoric bliss. He lifted a hand, undulating it through the air. "They fly on gossamer wings, their skin shimmering in rainbow scales which deepen to indigo upon maturity. It takes a thousand years or more to produce such a color as you have there in your scarf. They are vast, some as long as a drachen, with great mouths full of shining baleen meant to scoop up cosmic dust. Their eyes are large and luminous, so deep and calm. Full of wisdom, I think, though others call me a fool. They are the holiest of creatures, but we treat them like dumb beasts." He emitted a small, humorless laugh, spots of red high on his cheeks and his eyes small from the drug coursing through him. "We slaughter them like cattle for their meat and skin and bones. Their bones…"

His voice trailed off, his brow furrowed as if he were contemplating the mysteries of the universe. A shake of his head. "The flesh of the leviathans is for you human beasts. To feed your soul. A sacred covenant."

"Manna," Fury whispered. Her lips were pinched and bloodless. "Manna is leviathan meat."

Eleazar nodded weakly. "To us, it is poison. So, we give it to you." He pointed at the scarf in Fury's clutches. "But leviathan skin is useful. Powerful. We use it to make the sails of our drachen ships and as sacred raiment. We bestow it upon those favored of the Luminous One, blessed of the Angelus. It is only meant for the worthy. A gift, a rare gift for the best of you."

Again, he laughed. Short and sad, and so bitter it left a taste in Diver's mouth. He looked at Fury, but her eyes were on the angel. They had both been stunned into silence as Eleazar spoke, knowing if he were sober he might not have spoken so freely. No, most certainly he would have bided his words. In a few minutes they had learned more about the Angelus and their "Heaven" than any human in the whole of Avernus, including the High Cleric, no doubt. Certainly, more than any army chaplain knew, a thought which gave Diver no little satisfaction.

Eleazar's eyes began to drift closed and at this Fury jerked forward. "Wait! Tell us more," she said. "Do you take humans in the Hallow Tithe? What happens to them in your world? Please, Eleazar..."

"Forget it, Fury," Diver said. "He's out. He probably won't remember a fucking thing when he wakes."

"Watch your language," she said absently, staring down at Eleazar as if she wished to shake him awake.

Diver bit his tongue. This from the girl who'd threatened to cut off Lonnie's "fucking balls"? "Leave him be, for now. You said something about Mother earlier. What was it Fritz said to you?"

And what she'd told him had been at least as shocking and disturbing as what they'd learned from Eleazar. Diver contemplated the orange and red depths of the bonfire, feeling a matching burn in his heart. He had been right all along. Their mother hadn't gone of her own accord: She'd been taken to Trin for the Hallow Tithe.

"They take *people* for the Tithe?" he'd asked his sister, appalled by the implications. War had taught him humans knew no bounds for cruelty, but this? Shipping people up to Heaven (no, Splendour. There was no such thing as Heaven). Why? To what end?

Fury had shaken her head at his question. "I don't know, but I know they took Mother and sent her off to Trin with the rest of Green Hollow's Tithe."

The days which had followed this revelation had been full and busy, their world suddenly upended. They'd barely had time to take a deep breath, let alone process all they'd learned or have a conversation about it. Eleazar did indeed forget most of what he'd said to them, except to reiterate that their mother's scarf was a sacred relic and they had to treat it with care. Otherwise, the angel kept himself busy consuming the fine food and even finer liquors the villagers brought him daily. Diver watched him eat enough for five men, astonished the angel's physique remained as sleek and perfect as ever. His health was improving quickly; Fury had removed the bandages from his back just the other day. There remained a stump of a wing rising from his scapula, covered in soft, new feathers. Eleazar looked at it once in their mother's full-length stand mirror and broke down, weeping horribly. The sound of his tears had torn through Diver, leaving an ache in his belly for days. Fury had disappeared into the woods, returning only when the sun had set, her eyes hooded and her expression grim. Eleazar had chased his laudanum with an entire bottle of brandy that day.

"How do you suppose Mother got it?" Diver asked, gesturing toward the scarf across his sister's lap. "Or her family, I guess. She always said it was an heirloom."

Fury ran her hand across the fabric, creating ripples of light.

Now that he knew more about it, that it was a creature's skin and not silk or linen, Diver realized what he'd thought was intricate beadwork was most likely *scales*.

"It is more than an heirloom," she said. "Mother told me its purpose years ago, but I never really understood. I was young and cared more about the woods than family history. Or Gullan traditions. I never got the chance to learn more."

"You know more than I do. So, what is it for, if not for high fashion?"

"It is a talisman. You remember how she wore it? It's for protection, good luck. Also," and she hesitated a moment. "It is a weapon. Of sorts."

"A weapon? How is a scarf a weapon?"

"The Gullan women had their own way of fighting. Mother tried to teach me, but I – I had no patience, no discipline. I stopped practicing the techniques the moment she disappeared. I was so angry, thinking she'd abandoned us."

"Mother taught you how to fight?" Diver said, astounded.

Fury nodded. "I'd always thought Father was the strong one, the fighter, until I watched them spar. She flowed like water and balanced like a dancer. So much grace, and such power! Father couldn't touch her, and she would disarm him and send him flying. With this, with a strip of cloth."

It was hard for Diver to imagine his mother fighting. He barely remembered Tuilelaith Cree beyond her soft, dark skin and gentle touch. All his life he'd been told he took after her in appearance, small and slim and lovely whereas Fury had the height and broad shoulders of their father. He looked at his sister. Perhaps she'd gotten their mother's warrior spirit, too. He certainly hadn't been born with one if his youth was any testament. He could fight now, but by the Creator, his skills had been forged in the hottest crucible imaginable.

"If you didn't want to learn, you could have taught me." Her reveal felt like betrayal. "Maybe, maybe if I'd been able to defend myself, I never would have run away."

"Maybe," she admitted, looking uncomfortable. "I just couldn't, Diver. I couldn't bear thinking about her. I thought—" she sighed, stroking the leviathan skin. "But now we know what happened to her. Now we know what must be done if we ever want to see her again."

"See her? You think she's still alive?" Was it possible? The burning anger in his chest turned to something else, something far more dangerous. Hope.

"There's only one way to know for sure." Her dark eyes found him, the light from the fire flickering across her face, washing her skin in shifting shadows.

He didn't need to ask. He knew his sister. It didn't surprise him at all that it had come to this. When he'd first clapped eyes on Eleazar he'd felt the world shift beneath him. Excitement made him shiver. "We go to Trin," he said. "To the Tithing Field."

She nodded slowly, her eyes hooded. Was she excited or terrified? He scoffed. Fury was afraid of nothing.

"It won't be hard to convince Eleazar," she said. "It's his only chance to return home."

"They might want him dead, those who betrayed him and cast him out."

"I think he'll still take the chance. He's miserable here even with the villagers worshipping him. And it won't last forever. They'll get tired of catering to his needs. I've seen the looks pass between elders, and among the clerics, too. It won't take much for them to turn on him. He keeps telling them 'all will be revealed' and yet has nothing to show them."

Diver tried to recall any dark glances, but he couldn't. He'd probably been too busy staring at Eleazar. He didn't doubt her, though. She'd always been the more observant, and especially keen about their neighbor's poor opinions of them. "Then we go to Trin," he said firmly. "All of us."

Their eyes met. "We go to Trin," she agreed.

* * *

Eleazar stood at the front window, peering into the night, watching his "acolytes" at their fire, full of dread for the oppressive darkness beyond the tiny cottage. But for the soft lamplight on the table behind him and the flickering bonfire in the yard outside everything was dark. The sky had vanished, become a black void filled with riotous stars. How were there so many stars? He'd only ever seen a sparse scattering in the gloaming firmament, yet they were numberless here in the human world. As were the trees and the blades of grass and the shrieking insects which tormented him when he was trying to sleep. It was pure chaos, this place, and he missed the order of Splendour.

They'd asked him to join them, but he had been too frightened. Night was a terrible thing. The cabin was small and primitive and drab, but it was safe.

For how long? How long?

A dreadful ache began to pound at his shoulder. He rolled it, trying to will away the pain. The tonic and brandy hardly helped anymore. Yet he tried mightily to give them an even shot.

"What are they plotting?" he muttered to himself, taking a deep whiff from his snifter before downing the contents. It was a fine brandy, he had to admit, better than he would have expected in this remote region of Avernus, far from the vast, modern cities he'd heard so much about but had yet to see. It wasn't as fine as he was used to, of course, but he couldn't complain. But for better food and drink, his situation hadn't changed. He was still crippled, still lost in the Below, still banished from his home. His only allies were two barely grown atheists he didn't dare trust. Who was to say they wouldn't turn on him, too, when the townsfolk did?

Which, unfortunately, was inevitable. He had seen the doubt start to creep into the cleric's eyes, the constable's too. The suspicion. They had accepted his broken body, helped him all they could – they liked to remind him of this often when they came calling – so, when would he reveal his true, Angelic form in all its perfect glory?

This is it. This is my true form. A one-winged Angelus drowning in terror, dwelling in muck. Half an angel. His hand tightened on the curtain, wanting to yank it shut and block out the night. The horrible, terrible darkness.

Eleazar escaped to his room. *It is not my room. It is my prison.* He resisted the urge to throw himself face down on the bed like a child and instead went to the side table for the vial of laudanum. They had a steady supply of it, now, thank the Luminous One, and no one had questioned his need for it. Apparently, plenty of the village elders enjoyed its euphoric effects. The small, brown glass bottles had become dear to him. He clutched this one, frowning fiercely, his thoughts riotous.

The only way home was through a Celestial Gate. He would have to catch a Tithing ship, yet he had no idea where or when one was due. Trying to navigate his way through this dark and dismal world terrified him as much as the Silence. He could ask the men who'd been providing him sustenance to escort him, but he did not trust their beneficence to last. Even now, their groveling had grown performative. Alone with them, they would bear witness to his weakness, his pain and fear. They would soon learn he perspired and bled and shit like them. He would not be able to hide it.

"And if I go alone?" he asked the flowered paper adorning the walls of the cozy room. "To a Tithing Ground? How would I find one? How would I get there? This world is a horrid maze. An unsolvable puzzle. No, by the Luminous One, I cannot do this alone."

"And why would you have to, Angelus?"

The voice was soft, but it startled him, nonetheless. He spun toward the door to find his "acolytes" gazing at him, side by side. United. Fury had adorned herself with the leviathan skin and he knew it should have offended him. Instead, he stared at her in wonder. She looked ready for battle, like an ancient priestess from one of the historic scrolls. A memory tugged at him, not his own, something almost... atavistic. A collective memory. Of humans, dark-skinned, defiant, dressed in similar raiment. He shook it away.

Beside Fury, Diver stood grinning, a light in his eyes which made Eleazar's stomach tighten. It was Diver who had spoken. He gave Eleazar a cheeky wink.

Fury for her part was serious. Deadly so. "We will take you to Trin, Eleazar," she announced, and the relief he felt nearly sent him to his knees. "There are answers we seek which only your people can provide. Be assured. For now, our goals align."

CHAPTER ELEVEN

Fury slipped in the mud and landed hard on her hip. Cold slush soaked into her pants faster than she could struggle back to her numb feet, hampered by the scarf wrapped around her hands. The leviathan skin, so seemingly impervious to fire and knives, was streaked with black gunk. An angry flick sent the detritus flying. Mostly into her face. She sputtered, growling every curse she knew and wiped her face with the silky cloth, smearing it once again with muck.

"Well, that was genius," she muttered, frowning at the filthy scarf. The mud squelched beneath her feet, oozing upward between her toes. Like worms. She squished back to the grassy part of her "training" ring, nearly slipping on a lingering patch of ice before she reached the dead-brown clumps. She laid the scarf across the wood stump to dry. A pile of freshly split logs sat beside it, damp from the recent rains. Her aching shoulders bore testament to the hard work.

It wasn't as if they needed the wood. They had plenty of coal. She'd done it to strengthen her muscles. To prepare.

Rolling her shoulders, she peered up at the sky. Thin lines of white clouds skittered across a deep blue backdrop. Not rain clouds, thankfully. Finally. Three days of torrential downpours had left the earth a rutted mess, frozen at dawn but a sucking slush as soon as the sun touched it. Not so unusual this early in the winter, but it was damn inconvenient. The rains had kept the villagers away for days, too.

Or perhaps they'd finally grown tired of catering to Eleazar's every whim? She didn't like to think their sudden absence was ominous, but it was peculiar.

She clutched the grass with her feet, trying to clear the mud from her toes and scrape her soles clean. The sweat steamed on her skin, her muscles loose and warm from her activity. She had to get inside before she took a chill.

I can't get sick now. Not now. The weather is turning. It will be frigid come morning.

And it would stay that way for days to come. Long enough for them to make it to the rail lines without having to slog through knee-deep mud. If the trains were running on time, they could be in Trin long before the season's Hallow Tithe. These thoughts rattled swiftly through her head. So simple and perfunctory; as if they did this all the time: A quick little trip to one of the biggest cities on the continent. A city of tall buildings and taller chimneys. People stacked atop each other, living in filth and misery. Ash-black walls and shit-clogged streets—

Her stomach flipped and her skin grew suddenly icy. She rubbed her clammy arms, shivering. The forest around her loomed dark and silent and she felt small. Vulnerable. The wide world stretched beyond her little yard, huge and terrifying, and unavoidable.

It had been her idea to leave, though Diver and Eleazar had eagerly agreed. But she'd made the decision on a whim, out of anger and hope. And now she could no longer hide from the sinking despair threatening to suck her into the mud. Soon, she would be exposed. Fury the warrior, the fighter, so strong and confident. Ha. How hard was it to be strong facing people and places she'd known her entire life? This was her home, no matter that she sometimes hated it. It was familiar. Safe. And soon, too soon, she would have to leave it and then both Eleazar and Diver would see her for what she was: A fraud. For Fury Barrett-Cree wasn't full of rage, or confidence, or strength, but fear.

I can't do this. She took in her small yard, her home and the dense forest, nostalgia nearly making her sick. *I can't leave.*

Yes, you can, little angel. You were meant for grander things.

Her gaze landed on her mother's scarf, the imaginary voice echoing in her head. The long strip of skin gleamed in the bright afternoon light, no trace of mud on its glistening surface. She'd always thought it magical, and now she knew it truly was. A talisman. Protection. The churning in her belly eased. A bit.

Just fake it, she told herself. *Like you always have.*

Weary and sore, she gathered up her strange, new weapon with a long sigh. She was getting better with it, she had to admit. Faster and more effective. Especially so when she had Diver to spar with. She'd tossed him to the mud a time or two and disarmed him with quick throws and twists. The way of it was almost a dance, intricate and beautiful. She was working her way up to deadly. More than once, Eleazar had been a silent observer, and she had the satisfaction of watching his doubt and disdain morph into something close to approval. Dare she say… admiration, even?

Tossing the scarf around her shoulders, she gave a most unladylike snort. Eleazar admired nothing but his own reflection.

When she entered the cottage, Diver and Eleazar were in the kitchen, hovering over a map spread on the table. She willed her heart not to sink. Diver had felt the change in the weather, too. The cold might make for rough camping, but nothing they couldn't handle. There was no good reason to delay once the ground was firm. If they waited for the sake of waiting, like she wanted, they would miss the Hallow Tithe altogether.

Fake it, Fury.

"Did you get the ammunition you needed?" she asked casually, padding across the floor in her bare feet. She'd gotten most of the mud off them and the warm wood felt lovely against her soles. Diver nodded, his eyes never leaving the map. Eleazar tossed her a look, grimacing slightly at her appearance. She set her teeth, but she also felt a twisted gratitude. It was easy to fake confidence with a bellyful of anger.

Only when her shadow fell across the map did Diver look up at her. "I acquired a few necessities. Warm bedrolls and thick socks. A few firestarters. Nothing terribly suspicious, or expensive, but I got some looks." His brow furrowed and his eyes darkened. "There's some grumbling." His eyes cut toward Eleazar. "Angels are expensive. They want their promised reward."

Fury grimaced. "I was afraid of this. Luckily, the weather is turning. We can leave within a couple days–"

"Tomorrow," he said, cutting her off. She bit her tongue; there would be no arguing with him. "We leave tomorrow at first light."

To her credit, Fury didn't flinch. "Tomorrow then," she agreed. A strange relief filled her. It was done; they were leaving. Now, she could move on to something new to fret about.

"Finally," Eleazar added peevishly, his blue eyes rolling. "I thought I was going to have to go alone after all, the way you two were dithering."

Fury glared at him. He'd been prickly lately, and last night had been particularly rough. The terrors had come upon him for the first time in days. As if their decision to leave the cabin and seek Trin – seek a way home for him – had unleashed all his barely contained fears. She could sympathize, but if she had to fake being brave, he could at least try and fake being nice.

The Angelus stood hunched over the table, wrapped in a quilt and holding a steaming cup of tea beneath his chin. The vapors bathed his face, leaving his skin dewy. Or was he sweating? She knew for a fact that he'd foregone his morning laudanum. It concerned her. Withdrawal was no joke, but perhaps an Angelus would have an easier time of it? She sighed. At least she'd found something new to fret about.

Eleazar waved a hand at Diver's map. "And can someone explain to me what in the name of the Luminous One I'm looking at? Is this a map or a child's scratching?"

"It's a topographic map," Diver explained with far more grace than Fury would have shown. Eleazar's tone made her want to hiss like an angry cat. "Here we are, and this is Trin. See the darker outlines for the cities and towns? And you see these lines, see how they're close together? They demarcate a hill. Steep terrain. These wider spaced ones indicate flatter land."

Eleazar followed the path of Diver's finger as he gestured from one point to the next, frowning fiercely. "It's gibberish. Gives me a headache trying to imagine the shape of your world. How do you find anything in this upside-down mess?"

"How do you find your way in your world?" Diver asked, still maintaining his pleasant demeanor, though Fury could see the flash in his eyes. He didn't like Eleazar's tone any better than she did. "Don't you have maps in mighty Splendour?"

Eleazar sniffed. "Every Angelus is born knowing their place in Splendour. We know every cloud and Aerie like we know our own limbs, our own fingers and toes. Even when we hunt the leviathans, it is instinct we follow, not maps. We *always* know where we are."

Diver seemed uncertain how to reply. He gazed at Eleazar, his brows dipping toward his nose. "No wonder you barely step foot outside the door," he murmured. "It must be strange to feel lost for the first time."

Eleazar started. "It is," he said, his voice strangled. The cup in his hand shook and he set it quickly on the table.

"It was like that for me when I first left home. The world is vast and terrible." Diver held Eleazar's wide-eyed gaze. "It helps to have friends."

The angel's gaze cut away quickly and a shiver rolled through him. He recovered himself instantly. Shrugging off the quilt as if divesting royal robes, he stepped closer to the table and stabbed an imperious finger at an area of the map covered in hash marks and red Xs. "What is this, map-reader?" he demanded.

Diver's eyes followed his finger, his brow darkened. "That... is the front."

His flat reply seemingly meant nothing to Eleazar. Fury, on the other hand, went cold and she stared at the thick band of benign ink snaking its way through the right side of the map. The front. What an innocuous way to describe a living hell. It was far closer than she'd realized. Or, at least, it seemed so. But then she checked the scale of the map. The front was at least a few days by foot. Close enough by her measure. Far more alarming than its proximity was the fact that it bordered part of the road to Trin, and in some places, bulged across it.

"The battlefield," Diver expounded when Eleazar's face screwed up with confusion. "The armies of Koine and Akkadia face each other across a shattered stretch of bloody land, making the occasional incursions, the daring charge or ill-fated advance."

Eleazar studied the map, his eyes shifting from the red-inked lines of the front to the outline of Trin far to the east. The great city sat upon a vast lake; its harbor was immensely important to the war effort of both countries, and Trin maintained a "neutral" status due to the presence of a Tithing Ground. Fury watched understanding begin to dawn on the angel's handsome face.

"We must cross the battlefield to reach our destination," he said quietly. His wing lifted from his shoulder as if he might take flight if he could. With a quick shake, he settled it once more upon his back and fixed Diver with a narrowed glare. "If it as horrible as you've said, it's impossible."

"On foot, yes. Which is why we're catching the train."

"Even on the train, won't it be dangerous?" Fury asked.

"As long as Koine still holds the rail lines, we'll be fine. It's a narrow corridor, but it's solid and safe. We probably won't even see any fighting."

Diver's breezy answer was hardly reassuring. But he was right. They had to catch a train, or they would never reach Trin in time. It would take them weeks to walk that far.

Eleazar was still frowning fiercely. "I don't understand," he said.

"We catch the train here," Diver explained, pointing toward a spot just outside the embattled region. A station a few days west of Green Hollow in the town of Streeter. Their parents had gone there once on holiday and had always spoken of it in fond breathlessness. To Fury, it had seemed like an exotic, faraway place. Green Hollow wasn't important enough to be on a rail line. Diver slid his finger along the double line marking the train tracks, following it through the disputed area. Hatch marks on either side of it indicated friendly territory. It was a relatively short stretch. The rest of the journey to Trin would be through open countryside. Farmland and fields. Settled land.

"What don't you understand?" Fury asked.

Eleazar looked at her and his eyes were wide. "What's a train?"

Her laugh died in her throat at the look on his face. Finding her own fear mirrored there was comforting. She softened towards him. A bit. "You'll see," she said cryptically. "It's a truly modern invention. One of the wonders of our world."

Diver opened his mouth, and she could tell he was about to say something snarky, but the faint sound of bells stopped him. They all fell silent, listening. It was the wrong time of day for the bells to sound. It wasn't a day of worship, either. Was there trouble in town? Was it a warning? Without a word, Fury went to the front door and stepped out on the porch so she could listen, Diver at her heels. The pattern was repeating, a series of long and short clangs. It was familiar...

Diver understood before she did. He looked at her grimly. "Someone's died," he said ominously. "Someone important."

"Who?" she said, but he could only shrug. She shook her head. "This doesn't have anything to do with us."

Diver's lips thinned. They listened for a moment longer, until even the echo of the bells faded. In the grim silence which followed, Diver announced, "We'd better finish packing."

CHAPTER TWELVE

The temperature was dropping like a stone when Diver placed the last over-stuffed pack in the lean-to shed pressed against the back of their cottage. Twilight had brought the shift with sharp winds and a cloud-scudded sky. By morning, the ground would be well and truly frozen. Good for traveling. They wouldn't leave any footprints, either. An added bonus. He'd warned his sister and Eleazar they had to be up and gone before dawn, but Diver doubted any of them would sleep. Well, maybe Eleazar. The angel was intent on finishing the last of their brandy.

The clear weather had not brought any villagers to their door, causing Eleazar to grumble about "ingrates" and "heathens" while Fury had grown pensive and watchful. Diver understood. He was feeling the same way, especially after the portentous sounding of the bells. Something had changed: leaving in darkness seemed the best idea. He didn't think anyone was watching the paths to and from their home, but he couldn't be absolutely sure. Being extra cautious had saved his life and that of his fellows more than once.

But every caution in the world can't save you once your time is up...
It was a bleak thought, and a familiar one. Soldiers were a macabre bunch. It was a survival mechanism. The ones who took things too seriously didn't last long. He'd been like that, at first. Grim and closed off. Just keeping his head down...

"Give sweet death a smile now and again, Barrett," Paul had teased, pinching at his cheeks until Diver slapped his hands away, grinning even as he cursed. Paul's laughter rang in his memory. "See? I knew you had it in you!" A wink and a crooked smile and a look he gave only to him.

The memory was a warmth in his chest. A flush on his cheeks. Diver readjusted the closures on Fury's pack, half lost in another place, another lifetime. Behind him, inside the house and down the hall, he could hear Eleazar and Fury talking, Fury so obviously speaking through clenched teeth in response to some imperious demand of Eleazar's. She was making adjustments to the clothes he would be wearing tomorrow, making sure their father's modified sweater didn't impede his wing. The cloak she insisted he must wear was one of the sticking points. He absolutely hated it, felt "crippled" by it.

"I may be one-winged, a pathetic half-angel, but I'm not a fucking pinioned!" he'd shouted at her when she'd shown him how it fit over his brilliant white appendage, completely concealing his nature. To her credit, Fury hadn't slapped him, though he'd gotten right in her face, only reminded him that his wing would attract the wrong kind of attention on the road. A bottle of brandy had pacified him after his initial outburst and Fury had continued her work. She'd finished Eleazar's final outfit and the cloak in a frenzy of activity that afternoon while Diver had packed all their gear. He knew she'd been dragging her feet about leaving; it hadn't been just the rain. But, as always, once the decision was made, there was no stopping her.

From the living room, Eleazar's voice rose in a needling whine and Fury answered angrily, "You drank it all, mighty Angelus! Give over and let me finish, Creator take you."

Diver winced. *Hope he doesn't have a sore head come morning.* Though, Eleazar had a supernatural ability to avoid a hangover. Only the laudanum, or lack of it, seemed to bother him. Which was why Diver had stuffed two extra bottles of the stuff in his own pack and another in Fury's. Just in case. The angel had been weaning himself off it for the last week or so, and had been almost as unpleasant as he'd been those first awful days after Fury amputated his wing.

The warmth left his chest. Leaving him hollow. He was eager to be gone, eager to be *doing something*, but fear for Eleazar and Fury ate at him. The world beyond Green Hollow was an awful, awful place. And it was a long way to Trin. Anything could happen.

Could it be any worse than what you've already endured? he asked himself. *Or what Eleazar has endured?* He turned to go back in the house, unwilling to answer either question because he knew there were worse things in Avernus than even what he'd seen. But. It was growing late. If he intended to be up before dawn, he should at least try to sleep.

As he turned, a flash of orange in the small, glass-paned window of the lean-to caught his eye. The window faced west, so he thought for a moment it might be the last dying light of the sun. But, no, the sun was well set by now. He stepped back into the lean-to and went to the window, pushing aside Fury's gardening tools to reach it. It was high in the wall, and he had to stand on tip toe, his fingers gripping the sill, to see outside. There. A flicker of orange, another. A line of flames tracking through the dark woods.

Torches. Diver tensed, trying to count how many men there might be out there among the trees, heading straight for them. The villagers had come at last. This was not going to be a friendly visit.

The creak of a door hinge made him turn, thinking Fury might be coming out to find him. But the door to the hallway remained half-open and empty. A shiver rose up his scalp but before he could turn to check the outside door something struck the back of his head. Hard enough to knock him to his knees. Pain split his skull and his eyes went blurry. Instinct made him twist aside, lunging for the brightly lit hallway. Too late. Something heavy landed atop him, and he was rolling and grappling with a man, fighting to keep a knife from his face. In spite of his pounding head, adrenaline burned through him, sharpened his focus. A face loomed above his, liquor-soaked breath making him gag.

"He's dead!" hissed his attacker. "Your cunt of a sister killed him."

Lonnie. Attacking him. Wild with anger and grief. Red-eyed, snarling. Did he mean—

"Hugh," Diver tried to say, but his throat was dry and aching with the effort just to breathe. Now he understood the bells. The mayor's son had died. Because of Fury? *Shit.* Even a minor gunshot wound could lead to blood poisoning.

The man on him seemed impossibly strong. Had him pinned. Diver clutched Lonnie's knife hand by the wrist, and it was all he could do to keep the sharp blade from impaling him. "Don't!" he gasped.

"First you, then your fucking sister!" Lonnie heaved back, yanking his hand free of Diver's grip. The knife gleamed in the light from the hall, bright and lethal.

Fury tossed her father's old cloak – now the ungrateful Eleazar's – on the kitchen table, spreading it out to finish a few final stitches. The angel stood in the center of their living room where she'd left him, adjusting his new clothes and grumbling because he had no more brandy. Fury ignored him, hiding her own small glass of brandy on the chair beside her. She hadn't exactly lied – Eleazar had finished *his* brandy. There was still one bottle she'd kept for herself. She wasn't one to judge another for their drinking habits, but Eleazar had had enough for a dozen men already. A dozen men's *lifetimes*.

She snuck a glance at him. Despite her irritation, she couldn't help but admire the snug fit of his denim trousers. And the dark blue sweater she'd refitted for him set off the bright blond of his hair and showed off his tapering waist. Damn, it just wasn't fair how beautiful he was. Made it hard to hate him. It wasn't like she wasn't trying, either.

"You should go to sleep," she suggested, more so she could drink her brandy in peace than with the hope that he might actually rest. As anxious as she and Diver were, Eleazar was like a live wire tripping about and setting off sparks. Creator protect whoever came into contact with him like this.

"I'll sleep when I'm dead," he murmured, then chuckled to himself. He tugged at the rolled cuffs of his wool sweater and smoothed the sleeves, frowning. All the clothes she'd provided seemed to confound him. He was, after all, used to silk and fine linen and the softest of lace. Or so he told her every chance he got.

"Creator pray that won't be for eons, mighty Angelus," she intoned dramatically, batting her eyelashes at him and doing her best to simper. She'd gotten quite good at playing the worshipful acolyte. Instead of being pleased at her act, it always seemed to make Eleazar angry. Which was probably why she did it.

"We are alone, foul woman." He strode toward her, frowning darkly. "Don't pretend with me. I can't stand it when people pretend to love me."

Something in his voice stopped her from continuing the game when normally it would take more than a peevish retort to make her cease. "I meant it, though," she said gently. "You should try and sleep, Eleazar."

"Lee," he said absently, his gaze distant as he ran a hand over the cloak. "You can call me 'Lee' if you want. My friends – some people call me Lee. Back home. In Splendour."

Fury held herself still as if some stray movement might startle him. And she didn't want to scare him away, not this Eleazar. This... Lee? "If you wish. Lee."

He relaxed, a smile brightening his face. Brightening the room. The world. She stopped breathing.

Then his head tilted, the smile vanished as his eyes cut away. Toward the front door. Toward the windows looking out upon the night.

A flurry of white feathers, a thunder of gunfire. Shattering glass.

Fury had time to let loose a startled shriek then Eleazar's wing enveloped her, brought her down to the floor tight against his powerful frame. She felt the thud of bullets shiver against his feathers, and she screamed, but none of the hot metal projectiles made it through to her. The barrage stopped and she heard the angry shouts of men. More glass breaking. Wood splintering. They were breaking into her home!

Panting, on her knees, she looked up to find Eleazar crouched over her. She was in the shelter of his great, white wing, hidden from their attackers. He appeared unharmed. At least, the only expression on his face was pure, unadulterated rage. No fear, no pain. Just... rage.

"When I open my wing," he whispered urgently. "Run. Don't look back. Run down the hall. Find Diver and go."

"But–"

"Do not disobey me, acolyte!"

Shaking, stunned, she could only nod. A tension shuddered through him. He was readying himself. He met her gaze one final time, returned her nod, and stepped back, his wing opening wide. The way was clear to the hall, and she took off in a sprint, staying low. A rattle of gunfire followed her, a roar of anger made her cringe, but she scrabbled down the hallway, unharmed, though bullets shattered the wall sconces, plunging the hall into darkness.

Diver. Diver was in the lean-to. With his rifle...

She raced past her parents' room expecting a bullet to hit her at any moment and burst through the half-open lean-to door at the end of the hall – right into two men struggling on the floor. The glimpse of a knife was all that registered as she slammed into the combatants. It was the threat; she wasn't even sure who held it, but she grabbed for it anyway. Her fingers closed around the blade, holding fast as momentum carried her beyond the tangle of limbs and torsos. She felt no pain as the knife bit into her fingers – she had it, that was all that mattered. Tumbling to a stop against the far wall, she struggled upright, screaming for her brother.

Hers weren't the only screams. Beyond the lean-to, deep in the house, the screaming was horrific. She blocked it out, forcing herself to focus on the skinny, narrow-faced man lunging for her, his face so screwed up with anger and madness she barely recognized him. He was crawling away from her groaning brother. She could see dark blood pooling beneath Diver's head, but his desperate gaze found her. "Fury," he gasped. "He's–"

"*You killed him! You killed him!*"

Lonnie's screams reverberated through her bones. The words made no sense to her. Nothing made sense but the sight of Diver on the ground, blood seeping from his head. Hurt. Someone had hurt her brother.

Something within her exploded. There was no other word for it. She became *incandescent*. The man scrabbling toward her was no more than a cockroach. Something to be crushed. Annihilated.

She felt no pain, yet she *burned*.

With a flick of her wrist, she had the knife by the hilt. Lonnie clawed at her, unafraid, intent on tearing her apart. She let him crawl up her legs, reach her torso, lunge for her neck, keeping the knife low near her thigh. His hands circled her throat, fingers tightening. Their eyes met and she sneered at him. Right as she plunged the knife into his groin.

Shock painted his face. She twisted the knife and the color seeped from his cheeks. His jaw grew slack, his eyes wide. She held his gaze, twisting deeper.

"I. *Fucking*. Warned. You!"

She yanked the knife free. Hot blood rushed across her legs, soaking her. Lonnie slumped across her. Limp. Not dead. Not yet. He was groaning. She pushed him off her, letting him roll onto his back. He stared at the ceiling, breathing shallowly, as he bled out onto the dirt floor.

Beyond him, Diver staggered to his feet. His mouth was twisted in disgust as he stared down at Lonnie. A terror deep and foul crossed his face, followed swiftly by a shaking, staggering anger. His hands bunched into fists, his back hunched, and he let loose a scream that broke Fury's heart.

When it finally died on his lips, Diver fell to his knees and wept.

And into this blood-soaked mess, this storm of pain and chaos, strode Eleazar. Crimson streaked his hands and arms to the elbows, but his glorious white wing rose like a lantern in the dark, shabby lean-to. He was resplendent. His blue eyes rested briefly on Diver, and he laid a hand on his quivering head, then those bright eyes found Fury.

"It is done," he said.

And in that moment, Fury Barrett-Cree almost, *almost*, believed there might be gods in this world after all.

CHAPTER THIRTEEN

The rhythmic rocking of the wooden floor lulled Eleazar into a fitful doze. He fought it, dragging open his eyes and shifting against the crate he was using as a backrest, struggling to stay awake. Which wasn't easy given how far they'd traveled through the snow and woods. Eleazar had been forced to carry Diver or Fury when they flagged, only his strength and resilience keeping them moving. But someone had to keep watch for danger. Out here in the wide world, danger was everywhere, and for days now, he'd been the one standing in its way.

Since leaving Fury and Diver's cottage behind, burning fiercely in the dark, he'd been filled with strength and confidence. His fear had left him, shed as easily as blood. It had been a strange and invigorating feeling. For once, he'd been the one others depended on and he had reveled in the new role.

But now, since they'd sneaked aboard this dreadful, fantastical contraption, the fright he'd kept at bay was sneaking closer with every frosted breath he released into the enclosed car. Fury had called it a "wonder," this train. But it was a shaking, stinking, *noisy* beast of iron and steel and wooden planks. It seemed alive, ready to consume him if he failed to remain vigilant. To Fury and Diver, it was normal. Unfamiliar, maybe – Fury had never been on one, she'd admitted easily with a dismissive shrug – but it was part of their world. A *known*. To Eleazar, it was a living nightmare.

Faint light bled into the train car from a moon-bright night beyond the frigid metal walls (he'd already learned the hard way not to touch the freezing iron with damp fingers). Diver had kept the sliding door open a crack for Eleazar's sake. Embarrassingly, Eleazar had panicked like an untrained falcon when the door slammed shut the first time. He'd knocked Fury into a pile of feed bags and nearly reopened Diver's head wound beating his wing in uncontrolled terror, instinct telling him to flee, to fly! Not until Diver dragged the heavy door open to let light and fresh air in did Eleazar relax.

But he couldn't forget he was being carried along by a smoke-belching monster, grinding and creaking at impossible speeds along tracks of solid iron.

A machine, just a machine. Not a living thing. It won't *eat me...*

As much as he'd dreaded the thought of traveling through the open wilderness of this world, the woods, stark and snow-choked and serene, had been easy to endure. He'd only ever read about the many different trees and strange plants, nothing like the sterile gardens of home. And the creatures inhabiting the woods had all been wonders come to life. It was like being dropped into a favorite book. A cold, dark, frightening book, of course.

Unfortunately, he had never read anything about trains. The history of Avernus was spotty, at best. The Angelus, even the scholars, had little interest in the human world beyond what they collected in the Hallow Tithe and a few mentions of war and "violent tendencies." The Keepers seemed to revel in their dismissive ignorance, choosing to pen long narratives about heroic Angelus instead. To them, humans were little more than talking beasts.

Better to make them all slaves, Rast had been fond of saying, since humans could barely govern their most primitive, base natures.

How primitive is murder, brother?

Eleazar grimaced, the thought sparking an anger he stoked. Anything to stave off the looming fear. And a looming horror just as terrible. Horror for his own actions in their escape. He'd managed to stave it off this long, why not forever? His companions lay in oblivion, stretched along either side of him, basking in his unearthly warmth. Despite the icy iron walls, it was as warm as they'd been since leaving the cottage and they slept apart from him rather than pressed tight to his body. It was lonelier in his opinion, but humans were strangely prudish about certain things. Sleeping in a tangle of bodies made them uncomfortable.

Not that first awful night. Not after they'd struggled through the treacherous woods, injured and traumatized. Then they had sought Eleazar's warmth gladly, sealing to him like his most loyal human slaves in Splendour.

Of course, freezing to death had been their only other option.

After escaping the men come to kill them, they had fled into the woods. The icy air had solidified the black mud between the tall, forbidding trees as expected, but the way had been anything but easy. The steep, narrow trails took them to the top of a stretch of rocky bluffs, a void looming to their right just beyond a raggedy screen of trees. Eleazar could hear the violent roar of water in the still night, a rushing river far below them. Once, it would have seemed a good place to launch. Now, crippled as he was, the fear of falling nearly incapacitated him.

Well, it would have, if he hadn't been so busy keeping his companions going. Going where, he had no clue, but as long as it was away from where they'd been, it was the right way. Nominally, it was Fury leading them, but it was Eleazar's urging and occasional assistance which kept her moving. An unconscious Diver had been a dead weight in his arms, but Eleazar's otherworldly strength found him a light burden.

They'd set fire to the cabin before abandoning it. Hopefully, by the time the villagers sorted through the ashes and counted the bodies and realized the three of them were not among the dead, it would be too late for them to give close pursuit. Fury had vehemently resisted the idea, her injured hand bound firmly in the leviathan skin and tucked close to her chest, but her brother, his eyes cold and glassy, had spilled lamp oil throughout the house, soaking the dead most thoroughly, and lit the conflagration himself. The flames had brightened the path into the woods for a time, but the thick trees had blocked their view soon enough, plunging them into darkness. Not even the light from this world's so-called "moon" had penetrated the leafless canopy of tangled black branches.

Eleazar *should* have been terrified. He'd been dreading this journey for days, his heart constricting and his skin growing clammy whenever he thought about leaving the safety of the cabin and entering the wild world.

But now, on the run in the dead black of night, surrounded by immense, living trees where untold numbers of beasts lurked, accompanied by two barely functional human guides, Eleazar felt no fear. He had no time for it. First, Diver had fallen, delirious and weakened by blood loss. His skull wasn't cracked beneath the terrible wound, but he'd bled profusely before Eleazar had sewn his skin back together with Fury's guidance. Head wounds were worrisome, Fury had confessed to him (for what did an Angelic prince know of wounds, head or otherwise?) They had no choice but to continue, though, so Eleazar had volunteered to carry him. Soon after, Fury had begun to stumble, and it was all he could do to keep her going.

No, Eleazar felt no fear. He felt something he'd never felt before. He felt... competent. His companions *needed* him. His skin was tingling, his heart thundering, his senses more alert than he could ever recall, but strength coursed through his limbs and his feet were sure. With his remaining wing tucked tight against his back, the hated cloak pinning it in place, he was properly balanced for the first time since waking up a cripple, a – a half-angel. Fury had done something to the cloak, weighted it along his empty shoulder, and he moved as if he had two wings. It was a relief, though he knew it was a temporary solution.

In his arms, Diver shifted, muttering. His eyelids fluttered as if he fought to wake from a nightmare and Eleazar made soft noises to soothe him. Just as he had soothed his pet humans, once, when they'd been abused by some Angelus in the high halls of the Honour's Archon, his home. The thought made him cringe. *They are not pets. They are people.* It was getting easier to think of them that way, as unnatural as it seemed. After all, it would bother him if Diver didn't recover from his injuries.

"Bother" might be the wrong word as the stray thought made his heart seize unexpectedly. What if the boy did die? Would Fury abandon him or take him to Trin as promised? Did she even know the way? Diver was the one with the maps and the worldly knowledge. His grip tightened ever so slightly on his burden. He really hoped the boy wouldn't die. For purely selfish reasons, of course.

Humans are so fragile.

Breaking glass, a hail of bullets, cracking bones, screams cut short–

Eleazar cringed. No, he couldn't think about all of that. Not now. He pushed such thoughts aside and concentrated on putting one foot in front of the other, all the while keeping an eye on Fury ahead of him and Diver in his arms. There was no time to be afraid when others depended on you. No time to worry about anything other than making it through to dawn. When the sun returned, he would be able to think again. He knew his excitement would fade, the blood pumping through his veins would calm. Then he would have to face what he'd done.

The searing spray of blood, the stench of loosened bowels, soft organs bursting–

So. He couldn't keep it out of his head entirely. Humans were indeed fragile. Soft creatures easily torn apart. He'd known this, he'd seen his Angelic brethren treat humans like chattel, disposable and replaceable. They lived such brief lives with barely a spark of sentience. Or so the Angelus told themselves as they crushed them to bloody pulp or tossed them into the ether or turned them into ambulatory blackened corpses. "Ghouls," the humans called them.

All his life, Eleazar had shied away from such violence. It was sickening to him. But, back there in the cabin, bullets slamming into his wing, Fury's terrified face turned up to him, he'd felt something take hold. An atavistic response to a threat. There had been nothing reasonable in his reaction. He had become the "beast" then and torn those humans limb from limb. Even Diver, battle-hardened, a soldier who'd seen untold death and destruction, had paled upon seeing what Eleazar had done. The look on his face lingered in Eleazar's memory. Through his excitement, his surge of elation, he could feel the horror creeping at his edges. When this euphoria passed, he would have to reckon with what he'd done.

Better to keep moving, keep running. Never let it catch me...

It was then that Fury collapsed. She crumpled to the forest floor without a word, landing between the snaking roots of an indifferent forest giant. Eleazar caught up with her, climbing over a scattering of sandstone slabs slick with ice. She'd pulled herself to her knees, but she was wheezing and shaking, her injured hand hard against her chest. Something dark stained the front of her jacket. Blood. His nostrils flared as he settled Diver gently to the ground before reaching for her wounded hand.

"Let me see," he said, unsure what he could do. In Splendour, one did not "heal" humans.

She recoiled from his touch, jerking to the side. "No. Let it be. There's nothing to be done about it. Just hurts like the devil."

He dropped his hand. "We've been walking for hours. Surely, we've put enough distance between us and any likely pursuers. We should rest."

She looked ready to argue, her chin set stubbornly, but exhaustion and pain lined her sallow face. Weariness won. She slumped, nodding. "We can't stay on the trail," she said. "Get us into the trees. Somewhere sheltered. It's cold." Her shivering intensified as if she'd only now noticed the temperature. "We can't start a fire, not yet."

"That won't be a problem," Eleazar assured her, helping her to her feet before lifting Diver from the ground. "Find us a suitable place to sleep and I promise I won't let you freeze to death."

She eyed him skeptically, but was too exhausted to argue, thankfully. It took some effort to leave the trail and enter the forest. The underbrush was a tangle in some places, tearing at them and snagging their feet. But Fury seemed to know where she was going, and what she was looking for.

Soon a massive deadfall tree loomed in the dark and Fury led them to it. A blanket of thick brown needles lay on the ground here and the trees were farther apart, tall and straight-trunked, their lowest branches some distance above their heads. The dead tree provided shelter from the steady wind and Fury started gathering fallen branches to lay against it for a makeshift shelter. Eleazar helped her as best he could after propping Diver against the rotting trunk. They weren't at it long before Fury tumbled to the ground again. With a sigh, Eleazar gathered her up and took her to lay near Diver.

"We need more branches," she protested, teeth chattering. "Blankets won't be enough. It's f–f–f–freezing."

"Hush." Eleazar shed his cloak and crawled in between them. He tucked Fury beside him, opening his wing to embrace her in soft feathers then he laid the weighted garment over Diver, fussing with each of them until he was satisfied they were sheltered from the cold. Bracing against the trunk, he pulled them both close. A soft murmur rose from the insensate Diver, and he snuggled deeper against Eleazar's side. Fury drew back a moment, gazing up at him blearily. "You're so warm," she said. "Like a sun-soaked rock on a summer day."

"Sleep, woman. I told you; you won't freeze tonight." He shifted his wing, moving her closer. "We'll resume our trek when the sun returns."

Soon both siblings were sound asleep. Eleazar sat in stillness, letting warmth radiate from him. He focused on their steady breathing, or tried to, and not the forest grand and dark and silent around him. It had grown lighter as they'd struggled through the underbrush, a strange brightness in the clouds above. The air was crisp, shiveringly cold, even to one used to the frigid heights of Splendour.

A fleck of ash landed on the heavy cloak spread over Diver and himself. Eleazar stared at it, confused, watching it slowly vanish. Then another took its place. And another. More landed on his head, dusted his shoulders. It was cold, this ash. He wrestled a hand free from the cocoon he'd fashioned for his acolytes and turned it to catch the falling substance. White. Delicate. Ephemeral. Bits of it settled in his palm, melting rapidly against his warm skin, but he could see the structure of it before it vanished. Crystalline. Beautiful beyond measure.

"What is this?" he breathed out loud, full of awe and not a little fear. It was falling steadily, covering the ground in a thin layer of white. "Is this... is this the end of the world?"

"It's only snow," came a muffled voice from beneath his wing. He felt Fury shift against him, her frigid arm snaking across his chest. "The world will be here when we wake, Angelus."

Snow. He stared in amazement as the night grew brighter and brighter around them. It wasn't daylight. The snowfall reflected the ambient light in a strange, wonderful manner. He had read about snow in the Keeper's scrolls but had never been able to imagine it. He watched it build layer upon layer, thinking he'd never seen anything so beautiful. It felt like he'd discovered something new. He watched until his eyes began to ache, and only then did he close them. Sleep followed swiftly, and he dreamt of clean, white drifts splattered with blood.

Since that night, they'd slept together as a unit. *For the humans' sake*, Eleazar told himself, but deep down he knew he'd needed it more. Somehow, having them as bulwarks kept his dreams manageable. And the days of endless trudging through snow growing ever deeper, and the air growing ever colder, made him focus on one foot in front of the other and little else. They'd been forced to hunt to add to their larder, even though Eleazar had tempered his appetite to the point of starvation. At least in his opinion. And his empty belly distracted him from the fear and the horror waiting for him. In that, it was a blessing.

For the first time since escaping the cottage, here on this strange contraption, surrounded by constant noise and motion, Eleazar felt suddenly alone. He wanted to reach out and gather his companions to him, but he feared how they would react. If they shrank from him or responded with irritation, he knew it would ruin the tenuous relationship they had built in their shared hardship. No, he had to endure the night on his own–

The pain struck like lightning, searing into his empty shoulder so hard it bent him in half. A groan escaped his clenched teeth as hard as he tried to remain silent. His lost wing always ached abominably, but he had ignored it just as he'd ignored the horror of his memories. Now, both slammed him at once. A trembling gripped him to rival the shuddering train and his breath came in short, hard gasps. Great Throne of Honour, no, he could not endure this! Not on his own. And an urge filled him, sudden and undeniable. Moving carefully, quietly, he leaned forward to reach Diver's pack tucked near his feet, glancing at his companion worriedly. But the boy slept on, his mouth open, his chest rising and falling gently, his shock of dark hair strewn across his smooth forehead.

Eleazar eased the bottle of laudanum from the tangle of Diver's spare clothes and wax-wrapped rations. The glass was cool and smooth beneath his fingers, and he felt a certain relief even before he brought the precious tonic to his lips. He drained half the bottle before replacing the cork and tucking it away in his cloak. For later, but only if he needed it. It was the train, he decided. The strange, alien train was making all this extremely difficult. The laudanum would take the edge off and drop him back into that most pleasant fog he remembered.

Euphoria drifted through him, and he eased back against the crate, hoping sleep would take him now. What exactly was he standing guard against anyway? Best to rest while he could. After all, it was only a matter of time before another new horror found him. This world was a waking nightmare. As his eyes drifted closed, he laid a hand over the bottle lying hard against his chest, clutching it like a treasured friend.

CHAPTER FOURTEEN

The metallic squeal of the brakes reverberated in the enclosed train car and Diver was jolted awake by the sudden lurching. Instinctively, he braced for impact as he fought against the forward momentum from the train slowing dramatically. He slammed into Eleazar, who grunted. The Angelus was wedged against a crate and held him steady. Fury wasn't so lucky, and her angry screech rivaled the brakes as she was jolted from sleep by an uncontrolled slide into the boxes and crates.

A sudden jerk shook through the car, throwing them in the opposite direction as the train resumed its forward momentum, though far slower than before. Diver scrambled to his feet. The freight train, heavy with railcars full of cattle, feed, goods, and iron ingots bound for Trin, would normally have run fast and dark through the front. Koine controlled most of the rail lines, but the run was dangerous and sometimes uncertain. A reality he'd kept hidden from the others. He'd hoped for an uneventful trip.

I should have fucking known better!

"What's happened?" Fury demanded, nursing bruises and her injured hand as she extricated herself from a tangle of feed bags. "Why are we slowing down?"

"Have we reached the city?" Eleazar asked hopefully. Eleazar skipped from arrogant to vulnerable at the drop of a cap. Diver felt bad to have to disappoint him.

"No," Diver said as he stumbled to the door which had slammed shut in the unexpected braking. He cranked at its latch and heaved it back open. Frigid wind crashed over him, and he looked out upon a stretch of muddy earth blasted beyond recognition. Bloated mounds and odd bulging drifts marked untold death. Men and horses left to rot. Scraggly remnants of once-flourishing trees stuck up from the ground, blackened and broken. Blown to hell, he knew, by nonstop artillery barrages.

A few stray vultures perched ominously on the shattered trees, waiting for dawn to feed. The actual fighting had moved on, rolling over this territory with more power than the train now carrying him through it. Had the front shifted again? Had they slowed because of the fighting? Or worse? "I don't know what this is, but we're nowhere near Trin. Not yet."

"Is it a trap?" Fury asked, joining him. She leaned out the open door, looking ahead. It was difficult to see even with the bright moon, but it appeared as if the train had barreled into a low hill. A cloud of debris had created a nimbus around the engine. The rest of the train was creaking through it at a lumbering pace. What in the name of the Creator had they hit?

He caught a flicker of movement beyond the train in the blasted fields. The earth itself seemed to heave and ripple towards them. His mouth went dry. "Get my rifle!" he shouted. "And Papa's pistol! Ah, eternal fucking hell! They're trying to swarm the train!"

The train whistle began to shriek, incessant and random. Diver imagined the panicked engineer desperately trying to warn the brakemen and guards stationed all along the train. The railcar shuddered beneath them, swaying as the train attempted greater speed. But it would take time to reach full speed again, and in the meantime they were vulnerable.

"Who's they?" Fury screeched, but she lunged for her pack and his rifle. "Is it the enemy?"

"Worse," Diver said. The sound of heavy gunfire erupted in the night. Good. The train was armed, at least. He thought he'd seen gun turrets atop it. Well, he'd do what he could to help even if it meant exposing their location. He'd worry about that later. Right now, they had a wave of Burnt Ghouls to fight. Against such a foe, all humans were on the same side.

"It's a ghoul zone," he explained. "Fuck my luck."

He turned to his sister and Fury tossed him the rifle. Her lips were pinched with fear but she joined him, pistol drawn. Diver dropped to a knee and braced himself against the doorframe, focusing his sights on the approaching wave of creatures. They weren't any faster than people, but were running full tilt at the train. They'd slowed it with a barricade of bodies and hungry ghouls, a common tactic when enough of the creatures gathered together. And a corpse-filled battleground attracted hordes.

Burnt, blackened flesh glistened in the moonlight, streaked with the red of exposed muscle and organs. An ominous howling rose above the noise of the train wheels and the spattering of machine gun fire.

"What is happening?" Eleazar demanded. He was staring at them, huddled inside his cloak, his face a white mask. The powerful Angelus from the woods had vanished, leaving an exhausted wreck in its place. Diver wondered how long he'd been hovering on a breakdown while he and Fury had needed him so badly. Unfortunately, there was no time to coddle him. Right now, they needed a god.

"Brace yourself," Diver spat at him, hoping to goad him into action. "The Burnt Ghouls have come for our flesh. We must fight or be devoured!"

Impossibly, Eleazar grew even paler. "*'Those that dare to touch the heavens shall be accursed. For having so offended the Angelus, they are burnt and scattered as ash upon the wind.'*"

"Yes, we know the scripture." Fury's reply was calm and cool, her entire focus on checking her weapon's chamber and bringing it to bear on the masses rolling toward them. The train's guns had already cut down a great swath, but there were so many of them! She began to pick off the ones getting too close for comfort. A few had reached the train cars ahead of them. Shouldering his rifle, Diver leaned out and shot those clinging to the ladders two cars away. Others were falling beneath the grinding wheels which did nothing to deter the rest.

They moved like a wave or a flock of blackbirds, shifting and swirling. Did one mind direct them? Did any mind direct them? No one really understood what powered these walking corpses other than an Angelic curse. *The righteous need not fear the Burnt Ghouls.* Or so they were told, but Diver knew better. He'd seen men torn apart and devoured before his eyes. Slow men, injured men. Their screams haunted him.

The wave surged closer, the ghouls seeming to leap atop each other, rising ever closer in their mad desire for what the train held. Cattle or humans, flesh was flesh to a ghoul. Diver tamped down a welling terror, focusing only on firing his rifle even as he calculated his remaining ammunition in his head. He'd close the car door when the attack became overwhelming and hope for the best. Could the Burnt Ghouls manage the simple lever of the latch? There was no way to lock their car – he'd broken the lock getting into it.

Fury shouted suddenly, waving her pistol forward. "Look there, ahead of us!"

Diver paused in his shooting to follow her gesture. A flash of flame. No, an eruption! Suddenly, an entire section of the encroaching ghouls vanished in a sweep of fire. The train was easing along a broad turn, its engine and forward cars nearly covered by clinging ghouls. Streaming flames burst through the writhing figures. Diver let loose a triumphant shout. The train had flamethrowers along with the gun turrets. Maybe his luck wasn't so bad after all?

"Burn those bastards!" he shouted, leaning out to get a better view, thrilled and elated to see the miserable creatures burst into flame. Blood roared in his ears, his heart thundered.

Memories clawed at him, threatening to send him to a place he had no desire to ever return. He forgot the weapon in his hands and screamed vile curses into the night.

"*Die! Fucking monsters! Burn!*"

"Diver!" Fury cried, aghast. She pulled him back from the edge, targeting a ghoul practically at his feet, taking it clean in the head with her pistol. "Get hold of yourself!" She fired again. A second ghoul dropped to her weapon, tumbling away to shatter against the earth. The train was picking up speed at last, the ground outside rolling by faster and faster. Soon, they would be moving too fast for the ghouls to keep up, but the danger was the creatures who'd already managed to climb onto the train cars. Diver shook himself, feeling like he was in a dream. It all felt so surreal. Past memories juxtaposed with the current horror. He had to focus! There were at least a dozen of the creatures crawling on their car, creeping toward the open door.

"Fuck!"

Blackened hands reached for his rifle, grasping blindly from outside the car. From everywhere! He backpedaled, firing haphazardly, barely avoiding Fury in the process. She threw herself to the side, away from him, and a gap opened in their defense, soon filled by a snarling, howling ghoul. And another. Crawling up from below like demons from the Abyss!

Diver froze, horror and panic overwhelming him. The roaring in his ears became deafening. Even Fury's desperate screams for help sounded distant. This was his worst nightmare, come back to take him!

A hard shove knocked him onto the bags of feed, now shivering violently as the train accelerated. A cloud of dust choked him and he didn't even try to rise. The tumble of feed bags seemed as good a place to die as anywhere else.

A cloaked man, tall and powerful, blond hair gleaming against his shoulders, began to attack the ravenous ghouls. Breaking them apart like dolls, dolls blackened and charred and bloodied. For a moment, Diver thought it might be Paul.

Come back to life to save him. (But why would Paul save him after Diver had let him die?) Then he realized the man wasn't coming to his aid, he was tearing through the ghouls in a desperate attempt to reach Fury.

"Lee!" she screamed, bashing at the ghouls clawing at her legs with the butt of her pistol. "*Leeee*!!!"

Eleazar. It was Eleazar. Roaring as loudly as the entirety of the ghoul horde. The creatures hissed and shrank before his onslaught, falling back out the open doors and taking their unholy brethren with them. He reached Fury and hauled her to her feet. The two of them moved in concert, dashing to each door panel and sliding them closed. The heavy metal doors smashed through a few ghoul arms as they clanged together, leaving disembodied hands crawling on the planks. Still roaring, Eleazar stomped on them as if they were cockroaches.

By now, the steady rocking of the train had resumed. It was once again at full speed. A whistle blew long and loud. Then again. Once more, and then only the clackity-clack of the iron wheels filled the darkened rail car.

The wild rush of blood in Diver's ears faded, but not his trembling. The feed bags suddenly weren't so comfortable a resting place. He sat up and had to use his rifle to get to his feet; his legs were shaking uncontrollably. "I'm sorry," he said, nearly choking on the words. Hysteria rose in his throat. He teetered on the edge of a cliff. He'd failed them all with his cowardice! "I'm sorry!"

"Gods, Diver." Fury. Sounding exhausted and stunned. "It's alright. By the Creator, how did you ever survive?"

A sob hitched in his chest. One. He held in the rest, his entire body shaking with the effort. After a moment, there was a grinding of metal and the doors opened a crack. The moonlight flooded in, illuminating Eleazar's face. He looked ragged. And nearly as shaken as Diver felt.

"We did this," Eleazar said.

The Angelus opened the door further, revealing a flat and empty land beyond. Desolate and shattered. Clouds had gathered in the distance, low and ominous. Lit from below by the unearthly fire of heavy artillery. Raining death on terrified soldiers too dumb to know they were already dead. They were passing it at a safe distance, but even this glimpse of no man's land made Diver want to vomit.

"Humans did this," Fury countered bitterly, staring at the ruined landscape.

Eleazar shook his head. "The Angelus have no regard for your world, except for what we can take from it, and even less regard for its people. I am so sorry. I never... I never *knew*."

At his soft denial, something within Diver cracked. "You never *knew*?" he cried, his voice shrill. He let his rifle fall and advanced on Eleazar with clenched fists. "We fight and die for you! For the blessed Angelus. And you say you never knew!" His bunched hands struck Eleazar's chest but his blows had no strength. "Why? Why do you do this to us? You're the monsters. You are!"

"I know." Eleazar ignored his weak pummeling and gathered him close. Diver didn't resist. His words had dissolved into bitter sobs. He clung to the Angelus desperately. "I know now, my good acolyte. I know now..."

CHAPTER FIFTEEN

The sun rose on pristine fields of snow. Glittering and serene, untouched but for animal tracks and fence lines. They stretched to the horizon, these rolling swells. This was the great breadbasket of Avernus. Beneath the thick blanket of white rested rows of winter wheat. Quiescent until the spring. It was an important crop, the first to be harvested for the Hallow Tithe. Celebrations surrounded the event, lasting days. All to see a third of the bounty delivered to their overlords. It was difficult not to feel bitter about it. Others might believe it the holiest of communions, the Hallow Tithe, but to Fury Barrett-Cree it was a crime.

A road cut through the fields, churned to mud by the passage of feet. Wrapped in her mother's scarf, Fury trudged along beside Eleazar, shoes stiff with muck and sore beyond measure. It was hard going, but it was the quickest way into the city and the view was pleasant enough, the air crisp and clear. Much better than where they'd been.

Her gaze cut to the glistening snow, half expecting a boiling knot of monsters to rise from beneath it. The Burnt Ghouls haunted her dreams. She shivered and tugged the scarf tighter around her shoulders, though Eleazar's ambient heat kept her warm. It wasn't cold making her shudder.

Lately, all my dreams are haunted...

A great, doleful eye peering at her from a field of stars. A keening song.

Lamentations...

They'd abandoned the train the day before, not wishing to push their luck with the brakemen. Once they were beyond the danger of war and ghouls, human fellowship lost its shine. Here, in a place of relative peace, everyone had to fend for themselves. It was still a million times better than the warzone.

Seeing the front, the utter destruction and desolation, had forced her to confront the reality of what her brother had gone through. She had tried hard not to think about it, to fool herself into believing Diver had come through unscathed, that maybe it hadn't been so bad for *him*. She no longer suffered under that delusion, not after seeing him break down so completely. It was guilt, a lot of it. For surviving, and for killing. She couldn't imagine having the deaths of dozens, hundreds, on her hands. She'd only killed one man – well, technically, two – and that had been horrible enough. That rush of hot blood across her skin, soaking into her trousers, the look of shock and confusion on Lonnie's face. It had brought a flash of memory of the boy she'd known before he'd chosen to make Diver the target of his cruelty and hate.

He deserved it. He was going to kill my brother.

Well. No one *deserved* to get stabbed in the balls and bleed out like a stuck pig. No one deserved to die of sepsis from a bullet wound, either, but people rarely got what they deserved. Hugh's death didn't haunt her as Lonnie's did, but there were times she wished she could take back that one shot. She could have shot *at* him and achieved the same effect. Maybe. She wished–

If wishes were gold, we'd all have full purses.

Her mother's brisk voice rang in her head. Ever sensible, Tuilelaith Cree, except when she was raving against the Angelus. She had always shied away from memories of her mother but with recent revelations the vanished woman was always close to the surface of her mind. It was hard to let go of the anger she'd felt at being abandoned. She knew her mother hadn't left them voluntarily, but she still couldn't entirely give up her hard feelings. Being outspoken had made her mother a target – an outspoken *Gullan* especially. The entire race of Gullan people had been decimated and scattered for their sinful ways, their blasphemy and heresy against the Angelus, and Tuilelaith Cree made a point of being an unapologetic atheist. A rabble-rouser in a land of faithful adherents. Was it any surprise she'd been taken into custody and handed over to the Angelus?

Did you ever once think of us, Mother, and not your crusade?

Sometimes she wished her mother had allowed them to eat the manna. Like everyone else. It had made them outcasts, not accepting the gift of the Angelus. It all seemed so pointless now. Especially with her stomach gnawing at her backbone. Other travelers had passed them by and offered slabs of manna – the one food everyone had in abundance, seemingly. It had been a struggle to turn it down, but even Diver had refused it so what could she do?

"We'll have plenty to eat when we get to Trin," he'd insisted with forced cheer, suddenly full of cockeyed optimism. The closer they got to the city, the happier he seemed. Not her. All she felt was dread.

Trin. She honestly never thought she'd go anywhere near that fabled city. She'd certainly never wanted to. But there it lay ahead of them in all its glory. A cluster of impossibly tall buildings rising from the flat plain like a strange, dense forest. Smoke smudged the sky above it, smoke from hundreds of foundries and factories and mills. From thousands of coal-heated homes as well as from the cookfires of the refugee camps spreading out from the edges of the city. Those whose homes had been lost in a hail of bombs or the grind of artillery all came to Trin to seek sanctuary. The great city was neutral with their own guard force to keep the peace, and a haven of industry which cared not who paid the bills.

Fury shuddered. So many buildings, so many people.

"Are you alright?" Eleazar asked, sounding more peevish than concerned. "You shouldn't be that cold."

"I'm not. Sorry. It's just… I don't like cities."

"Oh, don't be so provincial, Fury," Diver said breezily. He strode along on the other side of Eleazar, his steps eager. He'd concealed his rifle under his long duster, but his clothes were very obviously of a military nature. Soldiers had passed them a time or two and given him hard looks, Koine and Akkadian and the occasional Naveen. He'd removed any insignia and his uniform had faded to an indeterminate drab, and he'd returned their stares with a grin and a jaunty wave. Eager to reach the delights neutral Trin offered, none of them took the time to question him. Luckily.

"I can't help it," she snapped. "I *am* provincial."

"It'll be fine. I promise. Just keep your wits about you."

Sooner than she would have liked, they reached the city limits. It wasn't an abrupt change. The fields grew cluttered with cottages and smaller settlements until there were no fields left at all. Civilization replaced the bucolic scenery, crowded and noisy and smoky. They funneled into the teeming streets, joining the masses, skimming along like leaves caught in a river. The heat from Eleazar grew to near uncomfortable levels, but Fury kept close to him. Afraid to lose him in the crowds. The Angelus had run out of laudanum days ago – she'd seen the empty bottles rolling around in the train car – and he was sweating profusely. He had to be in withdrawal by now. It would only get worse.

Even at the outskirts, the sprawl of structures was overwhelming. Half-timbered buildings stacked crookedly, threatening to topple, the sky reduced to a mere strip of cobalt, greasy with smoke. Forced to a crawl among the mass of humanity, Fury could feel the tension in Eleazar. The smells and the mud and the noise had to bother him as much as her. People knocked into him as they made their way down the sidewalks – little more than planks thrown atop the muck – and cursed him: Fury feared he might lash out.

"This city is a miserable place full of miserable people," Eleazar grumbled. He twitched his shoulders aside as another person barreled past him. He stopped abruptly, forcing the flow of people to part around them. "I'm starving," he announced. "And weary. And this street stinks. Surely, there must be a place to rest, or a better neighborhood, at least. Where are all the haunts?"

"Haunts?" Fury echoed, keeping as near to him as possible even though *she* was starting to sweat now, too.

"Places for food," he explained. "For drink. For enjoyment. You do have places like that, don't you?"

"Of course," Diver said. The noise and the crowds seemed to have punched a hole in his good humor. He was frowning and casting furtive glances in all directions.

"I need to rest. And eat. And a brandy would be nice."

"Not here."

"Why? What harm would it do to rest a moment here? One of these flats must offer refreshment." He peered at the buildings along their side of the street, little shops and storefronts and plain brick facades. Some places did seem to be offering food and drink.

"We can't eat here," Diver said, keeping his voice low. "This is the Akkadian ghetto. We need to reach the city center before we try and eat or rest. Everyone is welcome there. We won't be welcome in these establishments. Haven't you noticed how people are looking at us?"

Fury started. She'd seen the dark looks but had written them off as the general dismal demeanor of city folk. Suddenly, the hard expressions on people's faces took on ominous undertones.

"What do we do?" she asked pensively. She inched closer to Eleazar. If there was any trouble, he'd be forced to reveal himself. She didn't like that idea one bit. Who knew how the rabble would react to him?

Or how he would react to them…

"Nothing. I think they just want us out of their territory." Diver laid a hand on Eleazar's arm and spoke soothingly. "Once we reach the gates, and find someone of authority, you can charm your way into their good graces. Yeah?"

"Yes, yes, of course," he mumbled, drawing his cloak closer. "I will do what must be done. I must return home. I will have my vengeance."

Diver squeezed his arm, his expression grim. "You'll have it. I promise."

"Can we get somewhere safer first?" Fury interjected, feeling irrationally angry. What was Diver even promising? Angelic vengeance was the least of their worries.

"Alright. Follow me. I think it's up this way, around the corner…"

"You don't know?" she demanded. The idea of getting trapped here in this throng of hostile Akkadians set her teeth on edge.

"I've only been here once," he said. "Give me a minute to get my bearings – Ah! That's what I was hoping for. Look. That wagon coming down the street! Do you see it?"

Fury spotted it immediately. It was hard to miss: An ornate covered wagon painted a bright purple with gold stars and stylized wings adorning its tall, wooden sides. A traveling show. One had come to Green Hollow a long time ago. She'd liked the jugglers and the acrobats. Diver had been far more interested in the men performing feats of strength. The driver was bundled in a thick velvet coat embroidered with stars to match the wagon. A woman sat beside him, concealed by a heavy dark cloak. Fury could only see the lower half of her face beneath her cowl. Her lips were painted ruby red.

"So what?" she grumbled. "You want to see a sword swallower again?"

Spots of color rose on his cheeks and he scowled. "No. But I do want to follow them. Most shows try to set up in Hero's Square. They'll need entrance to the city center."

***

Diver's hunch proved correct, but there was a queue when they reached the gates to the city center. They took their place among the rabble. Some were refugees from the fighting, carrying battered, overstuffed suitcases and odd items like a vase or heavy quilt or framed portraits. Family heirlooms, precious possessions. Others were workers in overalls, trudging home from the factories on the outskirts of town. Those too poor to take the trams.

A few large lorries inched along slowly with the pedestrian queue, and Fury and Eleazar stared at them in amazement. To Diver, they weren't so impressive. The army moved on those things almost as much as horses and wagons. They broke down too often for him to think much of them. Better to have a horse or your own two feet than be stuck on one of those when fleeing the enemy. He'd seen entire companies torched on broken-down lorries.

They ended up directly behind the purple wagon. A collection of men and women in Akkadian uniforms were its strange honor guard, making him think it might be a military show. Those were always good for propaganda purposes. He spotted a few dark-skinned Naveen among them, too. Looking out of place in Akkadian forest green. Shockingly so. Right before his desertion, he'd heard rumors Akkadia had annexed Naveen, but he still couldn't believe such bitter enemies were now allied. How could the Naveen fight for Akkadia after all the things those bastards had done to them?

Worse than what the Koine has done to them?

Diver grimaced. There were no innocents in this conflict. But what would it mean for the greater picture? What would it mean for Koine to have those two nations aligned against them? Diver tried hard not to think about it. He'd abandoned his post, hadn't he? He was done with the war.

Funny thing about war, though, it was never done with you...

"I bet they've got a dozen people crammed inside that contraption," Diver murmured, stamping mud from his boots. This line was interminable. "It'll slow up the line even more, unfortunately. The regulators will have to search it."

Fury peered at the wagon. "Search it for what?"

"Contraband. Illegal weapons. Medicine. Illicit drugs. There's a thriving black market in Trin for just about everything under the sun. War breeds scarcity."

"We all must do our part," Fury chimed in, quoting a popular propaganda poster. "It is our joyful sacrifice!"

She made a face and Diver giggled, full of nervous energy. The closer they got to the gate and the grim, black-coated regulators patting down visitors, the closer they were to reaching the Tithing Ground. It was exciting and frightening. He glanced at Eleazar, wondering what the angel might be feeling, but the golden-haired "god" seemed lost in his own, private misery. Head down, jaw rigid, sweating like a blacksmith. Diver grimaced. Coming off laudanum wasn't pretty. He sidled closer to him. "Only a little while longer. You're almost home... Lee."

Eleazar threw him a look, his expression agonized. A breath snagged in Diver's chest as he met the angel's bright blue eyes. Hope lay deep within them, a small spark, but the fear was wide and terrible.

Diver looked away. And found one of the Akkadian soldiers staring directly at him. The man was leaning against the back of the wagon smoking a cigarette. A tall, broad-shouldered Naveen woman stood near him, her braids and mahogany skin a stark contrast to the soldier's pale face and flame-red hair. She peered at him suspiciously but the man grinned and waggled his eyebrows, not terribly upset to have been caught looking. "Hey, kid," he called boldly. "Care for a smoke?"

The Naveen woman elbowed him in the side, eliciting laughter from some of their companions. "We aren't here for strays, Weaver," she said.

He shrugged, rubbing at his ribs, then pushed off from the wagon and sauntered toward them. "Doesn't hurt to talk, Ellis."

She sighed and trailed him, her eyes passing over the three of them, assessing. Casually, her hand settled on the pistol at her belt as her bright gaze landed on Diver. She smiled. A warning. Not *quite* a threat.

Both Eleazar and Fury tensed at their approach, but Diver stayed relaxed. They wouldn't cause any trouble so close to the gates and the city regulators. Such nonsense was not tolerated in Trin. Here, divisions and conflicts were set aside. Everyone was one big happy family. Or at least not actively trying to kill one another.

The redhead, Weaver, stopped in front of Diver, lit a second cigarette in his mouth and handed it over with a shit-eating grin. Despite his uniform, he looked no more soldierly than Eleazar. His hair hung in a disheveled mop and red stubble stood on his fair cheeks. He had nice eyes, though. Sea green. A bit bloodshot. Diver took the offered cigarette.

"Thanks." After taking a drag, he waved it toward the queue. "Long line, isn't it?"

Weaver shrugged. "Always is." His eyes narrowed and swept him from head to toe. "Are you Koine, soldier boy?" he asked, not sounding convinced. "Or did you take that uniform off a corpse?"

Diver bristled. "It's mine." He spilled his rank in a fierce burst. "Private First Class Diver Barrett-Cree, Koine army infantry." He'd had to say it so many times during his service, it was an automatic response. He scowled, annoyed that he'd been so easily insulted.

And so easily tricked...

The man's grin widened. "Well, well, you're quite the proud deserter, aren't you?"

Shit...

CHAPTER SIXTEEN

Shit...

"He's on leave," Fury blurted, shoving her way in front of him, acting the protective sister. Again.

"Calm down, sweetheart," the Naveen said, seeming genuinely amused by Fury's, well, fury. Her teeth flashed white in her dark face. "I suspect none of us are military police, right?"

Flustered, Fury subsided. "We don't want any trouble."

"You won't get any from us. We're all *former* soldiers here, despite how it looks." The man, Weaver, tugged at the scarf around his neck, grinning even more broadly. The motion revealed the insignia on his stand collar and Diver recoiled in shock. And not a little disgust.

"You're Iron Corps? The *fuck*?" The Iron Corps was the most notorious division in the Akkadian army. They were responsible for more massacres and war crimes than any other military body. The Iron Corps struck fear in the heart of any reasonable Koine soldier. Akkadian, too, honestly. And here one stood, casually puffing on a cigarette! "You've got to be fucking kidding me!"

The Naveen woman hissed at his reaction. "Mind your tongue!"

Weaver raised a hand. "It's fine, Ellis. I know what I am. What I was. Captain Joseph Weaver of the Akkadian Iron Corps. Murderer, sadist, monster." He readjusted his scarf, hiding the distinctive crimson cross. He fixed Diver with a serious gaze.

"But war makes monsters of us all. Some more than others, maybe. But we do what we're told, right? Until we just can't do it anymore." He ran a gloved hand through his hair, his eyes cutting toward the wagon behind them. "Then we end up on the run, seeking something better. Something worth fighting for. Know what I mean?"

Diver wasn't quite sure, really. But while Ellis nodded in encouragement, Diver couldn't help but look at Eleazar. The Angelus was hunched in his cloak, watching the exchange with deep apprehension. He was lost, a stranger in a strange world. In great danger from the humans who should worship him. Diver felt a surge of protectiveness. Of purpose. Reluctantly, he nodded, too. "The Abyss can take the army. I'm done with all of that."

"Same with us," Weaver said, spreading his hands. "But the fight continues, yeah?"

"Not for us," Fury declared. "We aren't looking for a fight."

"You're looking for something, though. I can tell." Weaver kept his attention on Diver. Did he think he was the weak link? Diver frowned. "Be honest, soldier boy. It's not so easy to walk away. Soldiers fight."

"I'm not a soldier, not anymore." His eyes slid toward Eleazar once again. "And I've already found something worth fighting for."

Weaver sneered, following his glance to the glowering Eleazar. The Iron Corps captain didn't seem nearly as enamored of him as Diver would expect. By now, the painted wagon had pulled ahead and reached the city regulators. Ellis tapped Weaver's arm and gestured toward it. Weaver nodded, dropping his cigarette and grinding it beneath his heel. He gave Diver one last lingering look, his lips quirked, before he and Ellis started back to their post. "See you around, soldier boy," he called back.

"Not likely," Diver muttered, but not loud enough for Weaver to hear.

"What was that all about?" Fury wondered. "Were they trying to recruit us, or something? For what?"

He shrugged. Weaver and Ellis disappeared behind the wagon, avoiding the black-jacketed guards. Smart. He suspected the whole traveling show might be part of some underground movement. There were always rumbles about rebellion in certain sectors. Approaching deserters to recruit into their crusade was probably a safe bet. "Collecting strays", Ellis had said. Her statement made more sense now.

"It's not our problem," he said, and Fury nodded.

The regulators began their search. A sharp knock on the wagon's door and a shouted command resulted in people pouring from the vehicle like ants from a disturbed nest. Some costumed, some half naked, men, women, children and others of less discernable genders and age. The regulators had their hands full trying to organize and search the group. A few blackcoats jumped into the wagon, sending it rocking on its wheels. The crowd of mummers laughed and sang and milled about, hardly concerned by the intrusion into their space.

Diver watched closely, grinning at their antics. If they were part of some underground resistance, they certainly hid it well.

A gasp rose among the crowd as the performers made way for one of their own, forming a circle around a tall woman in a dark green Akkadian uniform resplendent with gold braid and medals, a formal style reserved for parades and ceremonies. Her hair was golden, pulled into a tidy bun beneath her military cap. Her lips were painted a bright ruby red. One of her compatriots tossed a wooden box at her feet and she stepped on top of it, giving the crowd a wave and a jaunty salute. Immediately, cheers lifted from the mostly Akkadian onlookers.

"Come one, come all to our performance this evening at the Hero's Square!" The master of ceremonies stood on the seat of his wagon, his arms outspread as if to embrace the onlookers. He waved toward the preening woman. "See the Night Witch herself take out the eye of a crow at a hundred yards! Come early and have a chance for an autograph. You can tell your children you shook the hand of the Heroine herself. The woman whose lone rifle turned the tide at Radene's Crossing. Akkadia's own Colonel Star Fletcher!"

The woman, Star, waved and blew kisses, basking in the adulation of the crowd. People started chanting her name. She was well known, seemingly, some sort of hero though Diver had never heard of her.

Scowling, one of the regulators approached her. "None of that here, missy," he growled, grabbing her by one slender wrist and yanking her from her box. "You are subject to a search just like anyone. Trin is neutral. Don't think you're special!"

And with that harsh statement, he began to grope her. The woman for her part endured it, her chin lifted and her expression brave.

"I have borne worse at the hands of our enemies," she exclaimed loudly as she was manhandled. She gasped as the regulator pulled at the belt on her jacket and angry grumbles erupted from the crowd. The mood turned ugly. A tidal shift toward violence.

Diver clenched his fists, resisting the urge to unwrap his rifle from the bindings he'd used to conceal it, knowing he'd only get a knock on the head if he interfered. Or worse. Where was that damnable Iron Corps captain and his Naveen partner? Weren't they serving as guards for this so-called traveling show? But they were nowhere to be seen.

Suddenly, the regulator laughed and, shockingly, tore open the front of the woman's coat. She screamed at the affront and jerked her arms across her body, trying to conceal her undergarment. She wore a corset under her jacket, oddly enough, one made of... gold? It glittered like sunlight on water as she desperately tried to wrap her jacket closed. The regulator growled something foul at her and wrenched her arm behind her back.

Diver took a step forward, aghast.

A roar erupted from behind him. A terrible, awe-inspiring shriek of pure rage. It rattled through him, setting his bones to aching and turning his bowels to water. He dropped to his knees on the cobblestones, his hands clapped over his ears.

Frightened screams rose from the crowd and the people moved as one in a widening ripple. Falling to their knees. Diver was dimly aware of Fury crouched beside him. He managed to glance up and was nearly blinded by a shimmering figure moving toward the captive woman, toward the war hero in the golden girdle.

Eleazar.

His wing rose above him, glowing like the sun. His whole body was encased in light. It pulsed around him. A halo of pure radiance. Diver's mouth went dry, and it was all he could do not to fall on his face and grovel. The only thing that stopped him was that he'd seen Eleazar do this once before.

"I am Eleazar Starson," he said, his voice like thunder. "Here to bless your pitiful city, to edify your pathetic souls. To bring righteousness to your sinful world! You *WILL* worship me!"

He strode slowly toward the woman now abandoned by the regulator who'd been molesting her. She stood alone in the center of the street, her jacket hanging open and the golden corset shining. She shrank from the Angelus but did not fall to her knees as the others had. Her arms were tight around her midsection, hands futilely trying to cover her shimmering corset, her wide eyes pinned on Eleazar. Diver held his breath. What was he going to do to her?

Eleazar stood over her, bright and shining. The only thing which gleamed as brightly was the metal corset spanning the woman's waist.

"Where did you acquire the Mithran?" His voice turned low and dangerous. The light pouring from him lessened a fraction but none among the kneeling crowd dared lift their faces. Only Diver, the woman and Fury seemed able to resist his Charisma.

His sister was still on her feet, but even she seemed reluctant to approach Eleazar. "I will spare your life if you answer truthfully."

The woman's eyes widened and shifted from side to side, seeking escape and finding none. "I cannot say," she said, her voice shaking. "I will not say."

"Very well." Eleazar reached down and took her by the neck. A moment later she was high above the ground, her hands around his wrist and her feet kicking uselessly. Her cap fell off and her hair came loose. She hammered at Eleazar with her fists, but he was unaffected.

"Eleazar! No!" Fury rushed to him and grabbed his arm, tugging uselessly. "Don't kill her! Please!"

He looked down at Fury, his nostrils flared and his eyes burning. "What she wears is blasphemous. No human hand may touch it. It is not for this world. It is not for your kind! I must know how she stole it."

Fury pulled harder. "You didn't kill me for the leviathan skin," she argued. "Why murder this poor soul over a bit of metal?"

"It is the gods' metal!" he roared, his hand squeezing the woman's throat until her face purpled. "The very foundation of our world! I must know which Angelus betrayed the entirety of Splendour to deliver it to this – this hell!"

"Kill her and you'll never know," Fury said. "Lee. Please. You don't want more blood on your hands. I *know* you don't."

A shudder rolled through the Angelus. Fury reached up to take him by his golden hair, pulling it to force him to look at her. Shockingly, it worked when Diver half-expected Eleazar to flick her away like a bothersome flea. His gleaming eyes settled on Fury, and his shining light receded to a tolerable glow. He blinked as if waking from a dream. With another, longer shudder, he released the woman to drop to the road. She rolled about at his feet, coughing and sputtering, heaving for breath as she clawed at her red-marked neck.

"You!" Eleazar pointed at a prostrate regulator. The man started but leapt to his feet at Lee's imperious gesture. "Arrest this woman and deliver her to the proper authorities. She has violated divine law! My acolytes and I will accompany you. Who is lord of this domain?"

"G – G – G – Governor Vogel, most worthy Angelus. I will take you at once, blessed one!"

"Good, my child." Eleazar nodded, looking pleased. A benevolent god. The man grabbed up the woman. The other regulators formed around them in an impromptu honor guard. The tension and fear eased from the crowd and cries arose in a fanatical wave that carried them through the gateway and into the city center: "Angelus! Angelus! Angelus!"

CHAPTER SEVENTEEN

The governor's mansion was a sprawling edifice of white marble and soft yellow bricks. It shone in the winter sun, a jewel atop a hill. Built for beauty and not defense, its façade held tall glass-paned windows framed by white columns in the imperial style of Akkadia. The roof was bright terra-cotta tiles manufactured by Veran artisans. The Koine influence was obvious in the decorative frieze beneath the overhanging eaves. The grand double doors at its entrance were made of ironwood from the forests of Naveen. All in all, it was a most impressive, multicultural palace in the heart of the greatest city on the continent. Trin even tried to stay neutral in its architecture. Or, at least, equitable. But for it being a nest of vipers, Diver was almost able to relax and enjoy himself.

"Don't drop your guard," he whispered to Fury as they were escorted down the broad, carpeted hallways, through corridors extravagantly painted with murals and gold trim and hung with some of the world's finest artwork. He recognized a few pieces which had once hung in Koine museums before they fell to war and ruin. It was hardly surprising to see that Trin profited off more than just the sale of weapons. "The governor owes loyalty to Trin and Trin alone. I doubt a one-winged angel is worth much to him."

Ahead of them, striding along as if he owned the place, Eleazar twitched and cast him a brief side eye. Diver winced; he'd forgotten how good the Angelus's hearing was.

"Do you think I'm daft?" Fury whispered back. She cast a dark look at the four gaudily dressed palace guards escorting them, all striped jackets, gold trim and feathered helmets. None seemed particularly bothered, impressed or even curious to have an Angelus in the governor's mansion. It was hardly the reception they'd imagined.

Not that Eleazar seemed to notice. He held himself as if the guards existed merely to make him look good. He'd folded their father's repurposed cloak over his forearm, the Mithran corset he'd taken from the smuggler – before she was carted away – hidden beneath it, and kept his one wing slightly open rather than trim to his back. He moved as if his plain workman's clothes were the finest raiment, and to Diver's chagrin, he and Fury followed him exactly as if they were his underlings.

At least they let us keep our weapons. He touched the strap of his rifle snug against his chest. It was barrel down across his back, but a quick twist would have it in his hands in a second. Their escorts carried tasseled halberds which were obviously ornamental. He doubted they would give him much trouble if things took a violent turn.

They marched down another corridor, this one smaller and more intimate if no less fancy. Diver had never seen so much gilt and velvet wallcoverings in his life. Was this how all the rich lived? Eleazar certainly seemed more at home here than in their small cottage back in Green Hollow. It was beginning to dawn on him why the Angelus had felt so out of place if this was the kind of opulence he was used to.

It should have made Diver embarrassed, but instead he felt a gnawing discomfort. A sense of unease that bordered on disgust.

We bleed and die for this, we common folk. Relegated to the darkness of war while Trin basks in the favor of the Angelus.

Diver felt a hatred unfurl in his heart. When he glanced at his sister, he saw the same feeling mirrored on her face. She clutched one end of the leviathan skin draped around her neck, her eyes darting about the hallway, drinking in the extravagance and excess, the corners of her lips hard in a downward turn.

And still they marched deeper into the palace, down lovely hallway after lovely hallway, passing a gawking servant every so often. By the fifth turning, Diver was lost, and he grew more and more convinced they were being taken through a maze with the sole purpose of keeping them prisoner without being obvious about it.

"This was a mistake," he whispered to himself, too softly for even Lee's sharp ears. But it was too late now. They had reached the governor's office.

The palace guards slammed the butt ends of their halberds against the tiled floor and pulled open another set of heavy ironwood doors, ushering them inside a far less opulent room than the palace hallways. Full of dark wood, desks and book-lined shelves, lit by gargantuan bowed windows overlooking a winter-wrapped garden, bustling with scribes and uniformed staff, it was most definitely a working office and not one for show.

"Greetings, most holy Angelus!" said a man seated behind the biggest desk. It stood supreme beneath the windows, bathed in dusty light. He rose from his over-stuffed leather chair, shuffling papers aside as if he'd been hard at work. "We've been expecting you! Do pardon the mess. Getting ready for the Winter Tithe and all. Well, I guess you would know all about that, wouldn't you?" He laughed as if he'd made a terrific joke then suddenly clapped his hands together. "Here, now, why hasn't anyone sent for refreshments?"

The nearest person, a bespectacled youth in civilian trousers and ink-stained shirt laid down his burden of files on the man's desk and gave a sketchy bow. "Right away, Excellency." He exited through a door secreted among the bookshelves.

"Please, come, sit," he said to them, gesturing toward chairs arranged before his desk, each word delivered as a separate command. As if to a dog. And then, before they even took another step inside the office, he barked at his staff, "Clear the room! All of you."

The entirety of the room vanished in a rustle of paper and a swish of tweed. A few curious or pensive glances were thrown in their direction. The governor (who else could it be?) settled back into his chair, watching them with a bland smile on his broad face. He looked far more youthful than Diver had expected. Smooth-cheeked and dark-haired. It was hard to place his nationality, his skin a dusky hue and his features unremarkable, and he wore a suit far older than current fashion though it was of exceptional quality. Diver had glimpsed enough nobility and fine lords to recognize good taste. This was a man who wielded power, a man of exceptional wealth. Generational wealth. He had nothing to prove by following the latest trends.

"Please, sit," he urged, more gently this time.

Eleazar took a hesitant step toward the proffered chairs, seemingly flustered by the brusqueness of the greeting. Perhaps he'd expected a bit more pomp and ceremony? Considering how the common folk responded to him, Diver could hardly blame him for such an expectation. He gave Fury a glance and understanding passed between them. They flanked the Angelus and ushered him forward, playing the dutiful acolytes with respectful bows and grand gestures. It snapped Lee out of his bemusement, and he approached the governor's desk in his usual nose-in-the-air manner. He even waited for one of them to pull out his chair for him. Fury, eyes downcast and her cheeks dark with annoyance, beat Diver to it.

"This is hardly the greeting I expected from the Master of the Hallow Tithe," Eleazar said the moment he'd settled into his chair. Or, perched on it, as it was far too small for him, his primaries lay against the floor like the tail end of a cloak. All three of the chairs facing the governor's desk were small and delicate, forcing their occupants to be careful how they sat and moved. A silly power play.

"My apologies, Angelus." No more "most holy". "Your story is rather remarkable. It isn't every day one of your kind *literally* falls from the sky and arrives to my city unannounced."

"I very much did not intend to fall from the sky," Eleazar said. "I was betrayed. Egregiously so. It is nothing less than an attempted coup which lands me in your city. My half-brother hoped to send me to my death and claim the Solaire Throne as his own. As you can see, he failed."

Vogel's eyes widened. "Most extraordinary. What travails you must have endured, Lord Eleazar."

Diver couldn't tell if the governor was being sincere or not, but Eleazar bowed his head in appreciation. "You have no idea, good sir. If not for my blessed acolytes, I might have died a dozen times over. You must treat them with all the respect due me."

"Why, of course, dear Angelus. Anything for the Starson heir. I knew your father, after all. A most blessed and glorious king. I am honored to be aiding his only son." He bowed his head gracefully.

Eleazar relaxed, mollified by his sudden deference. Diver watched him puff his chest and grimaced. A little flattery went a long way with Eleazar. Never mind that Governor Vogel was watching him with a grim and calculating look in his eye while the fingers of his left hand beat out a steady rhythm on his massive desk. Like a man weighing the odds in his head.

"You'll stay here, of course," Vogel continued. "As my honored guests until the winter drachen arrives. It will be several days before we can communicate with the ship via our orb." And he gestured toward a dark corner of the office, to a pedestal draped with a velvet cloth of deepest blue. "Our tele-net doesn't reach your world, unfortunately, so we must wait."

"*Your world*"? Diver stiffened. Not Heaven? How many men of authority knew the truth of the Angelus?

All those who benefit from hiding it.

Eleazar was nodding, oblivious to what Vogel had just revealed. It explained why none of the folk who dealt directly with the Angelus and the Tithing ships showed the expected obeisance to him. Diver felt like the butt of a joke everyone else was in on. Eleazar, on the other hand, seemed distracted and uncomfortable. He shifted on his tiny chair, the thing creaking alarmingly beneath him. Diver noticed his hands were trembling. Knees, too. Sweat glistened on his bronze skin.

"I thank you for any help you can give me," he said. "It has been a long, hard road–"

Eleazar swayed in his seat, his face turning the color of ash. Diver leapt to his feet, but Fury was beside him instantly, on her knees and taking his weight on her shoulder lest he tumble to the floor. Diver exchanged a worried glance with her. She bit her lip, color on her cheeks. She almost looked... ashamed.

"Governor Vogel," she said, turning to the man. "My lord," she continued, more firmly, even as Eleazar's head dipped toward his chest. "The blessed Angelus requires medicine for his dire injury. Please, if you could provide the necessary tonic, he would be most grateful."

Governor Vogel frowned at her, leaning forward across his desk. Though he seemed more annoyed than concerned. "What are you on about, girl?" he said. His eyes narrowed at the incapacitated Angelus, and Diver could see the disgust in his eyes as plain as the stars. "Spit it out, would you? What's wrong with him? What does the Angelus need so urgently?"

The word came out strangled. "Laudanum."

Eleazar made a noise, lowing like an injured bull. A desperate sound that cut to Diver's core. There were tears in Fury's eyes. Shame. Regret. Fear.

"He needs laudanum, my lord."

* * *

They were hustled from the governor's private office as quickly as his staff had vanished. No palace guards this time, but nurses in white dresses and headwraps and a lab-coated physician. The laudanum was administered only when they reached a private suite of rooms. Copious amounts. Fury argued with Dr Rhiner, nearly coming to blows with the supercilious professional before Diver felt it necessary to intervene.

"I'm warning you now," the man snapped as Diver ushered him from the room. "His tolerance is high, too high. He will need something stronger just to function."

"He is an Angelus," Diver countered, pushing him out the door. "He's not like us. He'll be fine as soon as the laudanum takes effect."

The man dug in his heels, frowning hard. "He isn't the first Angelus I've treated, son. You and your... friend would do well to heed my advice. Nothing short of morphine, administered directly into his veins, will ease his suffering. Trust me."

"I'd sooner trust an Akkadian gunner!" Diver snarled, giving him a last shove before slamming the door in his face.

"He's burning up," Fury said anxiously. She hovered over Eleazar who lay sprawled on a chaise lounge before an elaborate hearth with a crackling fire. "Feel him. I don't like it. It's as if the laudanum has done nothing for his withdrawal symptoms!"

She was kneeling beside him, her hand on his forehead. His skin looked taut across his sculpted cheekbones. Fury chewed on her lower lip, casting wide, worried eyes at him. "I don't like any of this. I don't trust that so-called governor. He's put us up in a tower like some fairytale princess. There's no way out."

"We could be in a cell, Fury, along with that smuggler. I think we're well set here." He waved at their opulent surroundings.

"Why was he so angry?" she asked, more to herself than to him.

"I don't know." Diver frowned. Eleazar had refused to explain anything to them about the so-called gods' metal. The Mithran. Just that it was holy beyond measure and the very foundation of Splendour. It was not for humans. And yet, humans were smuggling the precious substance. A commonly known "secret" apparently. City folks were *consuming* it. Somehow. Were they melting the damn stuff? Treating it like a drug, according to the regulators who'd brought them to the palace. They'd been eager to answer the questions of the "blessed Angelus". "I don't really care, either. We are where we need to be if we have any chance of reaching Splendour."

Diver crossed the honeyed floorboards to the chaise. As he neared Eleazar, he could feel the heat radiating from the prone angel. His own worry spiked. Had that doctor actually been right? "Let's get him away from the fireplace. Maybe he just needs a chance to cool down and let the laudanum work? We don't want him dosed with morphine, do we?"

"The laudanum was a bad idea." She shook her head, her lips pinched. "I only wanted to make it easy for us. At the beginning, I mean. He was so *angry*. And so strong. It was dose him or have him tear the damn house apart. But look what it's done to him. I turned him into an addict."

"Don't. Eleazar was hurting. We did what was necessary. We, not just you."

"I shouldn't have relied on it so heavily. I did this to him. It's all my fault." Her voice grew ragged, and her head dropped.

"Nonsense." A slim, pale hand settled on Fury's bowed head. Eleazar's blue eyes were open, though nearly black from his dilated pupils. Color stained his cheeks. Fever-bright. "I would have killed you both if you hadn't found a way to ease my agony. This is not your fault, Fury."

"Then whose fault is it?" she demanded. Despite her tone, she was trembling. Diver chewed his lip. Fury hated to show weakness. He was surprised she hadn't knocked Eleazar's hand away. Seeing the look in her eyes, maybe he wasn't that surprised. With a soft sigh, he settled on the opposite side of the chaise and gazed up at Eleazar like a proper acolyte. Worshipful and attentive. The angel's pain made his chest ache.

"Mine," Eleazar said. "I was done with it. My pain was tolerable. But I took it to chase away the nightmares." He squeezed his eyes shut, baring his teeth in a pained grimace. "The blood and the screams. I couldn't close my eyes without seeing–"

He choked on the words, a most uncharacteristic sob bursting from him. Diver blinked. How had he not seen it? He stared at Eleazar far more than necessity dictated and he hadn't seen any signs of shellshock. *Or I just didn't want to see it.*

"Lee," Fury whispered. "Oh, Lee..."

She reached up to grasp his hand, but he pulled it back. He covered his face, sobs wracking his lean frame. Guttural, wrenching, pain so deep it was hardly comprehensible rolled off him.

It was too much for Diver. He pushed his way onto the chaise beside Eleazar and gathered the angel into his arms. The stump of Eleazar's missing wing ground into his chest, but he ignored it. No, he welcomed the sharp pain of it, holding the angel as tightly as he could. Fury looked stunned, her lips parted, but then a determined expression crossed her face, and she took up position on Lee's other side, ducking beneath his remaining wing, her arms wrapping around his waist and her head on his chest.

"Let it out," she said firmly. "Let it all out, Lee. We're here."

"We will always be here," Diver murmured, his lips brushing Eleazar's nape. The angel still burned, but Diver didn't loosen his grasp. He held on like his life depended on it.

CHAPTER EIGHTEEN

In the deepest dark of night, Eleazar extricated himself from the exhausted siblings. Carefully. He did not want to wake them. They had held him together during his drug-induced collapse. Skin to skin, even though he knew his feverish flesh had to have seared their frail human bodies. They had held on despite the pain, comforting him in his agony and keeping the nightmares at bay. The laudanum had certainly helped once it worked its magic, but he had no doubt his companions could take more of the credit for easing his spirit. Fury had been a rock, a solid presence holding him firm. Diver had been a whisper in his ear, talking of all he'd done as a soldier, the trauma and horror of it. He understood. The trauma of what Eleazar had done, however necessary it might have been, was not so easily dismissed.

I am no killer. He couldn't help the thought which followed: *Rast was right. I am weak. A spineless coward.*

He made his shaky way to the balcony of the grand suite. A suitable place for an Angelus. And yet, he felt insulted to the very core of his being. Governor Vogel's attitude toward him had been dismissive and falsely deferential. If not for the agony of withdrawal erupting in his bones he would have put the man in his place. He was a prince of the Angelus no matter his current circumstances, the heir to the Solaire Throne, future Great King of Honour. Yet it meant nothing in these human halls.

Falling to Avernus had stripped the blinders from his eyes. Yes, the vast majority of humans worshipped them, paid homage to them, fed and sustained them to avoid Angelic wrath, but the few that mattered viewed the Angelus as... as...

Parasites.

He winced. Of course, they were useful parasites for the most part, judging from the wealth of Vogel's domain.

The freezing air outside his too-hot room cooled his burning skin, and he stepped onto the snow-covered balcony gratefully. The white drifts sizzled around his bare feet. Soft clouds of steam rose into the night with every step he took. He wore trousers still, but at some point Fury or Diver had stripped off his shirt. The cold air felt delicious on his naked flesh. It reminded him of the upper heights of Splendour even though he was surrounded by darkness.

No, not exactly. Above him hung a ball of light in a star-spangled field of black. The moon. He'd grown familiar with its many faces over the past weeks. It changed with each passing day. So unlike the eternal countenance of bright Sol. A pang of homesickness made his stomach roil and he stared at the perfect sphere of the moon until his eyes blurred.

I will feel His light again. I swear it...

Blinking the water from his eyes, he lowered his gaze to the vast, white field far below. The Tithing Ground of Trin. A perfect flat circle at the exact center of the city. A landing site for broad-keeled drachen ships. Soon this field would contain the Hallow Tithe of the Fourth Season. Winter to the humans. For the Angelus, it was a turning of the firmament, significant only for their need of Avernus' bounty.

At the far curve of the field, distant smokestacks reached into the sky. Frail spires from this distance. Around this remarkable industry lived a vast population. Humans crammed together in a warren of buildings and twisting streets.

They seemed to like it, these odd creatures. In Splendour, the Angelus had learned their human pets survived longer if allowed to live in communal barracks rather than kept scattered amongst the grand palaces. A twinge of unease filled him. He never mentioned the practice of keeping humans as slaves, not to Fury or Diver. He felt... ashamed now. A truly unusual feeling for a Prince of Splendour. How many times had he dismissed their suffering because he thought them no better than animals? Their place was understood, their purpose: To serve the Angelus. And be grateful for the honor.

But if they were no better than animals, why did the Angelus depend on them to create art and music, fine wines and spirits, silk and woven cloth, poetry and intricate jewelry? All the "menial" tasks the Angelus eschewed. Eleazar grimaced. His people floated through life reaping the benefits of others' labor. Blind to the advancement of humans. Blind to their cleverness and industry.

And now the humans had Mithran. The most precious of things. The most powerful of magic. The bones of the sacred leviathans, far more important than their skin, their flesh or blood. Mithran was the very foundation of Splendour. Of all Creation, according to the Keepers Archon. In an unstable form only the most talented of Angelic alchemists could achieve, it was used to blast apart mountains. The same form imprisoned in vast orbs powered their ships. How and why did his people allow the smuggling? The discovery had shocked him, enraged him. But the Angelus were as base and greedy as the humans, it seemed. Certain items were forbidden in Splendour, but some Angelus had been trading Mithran to humans to acquire the contraband. It explained how he'd come across such items in the haunts and brothels. Weapons and inventions and drugs not allowed to sully perfect Splendour. He had ignored it, ignored anything real, focusing instead on philosophical ponderings.

But to allow Mithran into human hands. It was mind-boggling. Even if they seemed unable to work with it, to make anything useful from the holy substance but some sort of drug. Nevertheless, if they were *ingesting* it as the regulators had claimed...

As his ancestors had once ingested it long, long ago...

We became gods by eating the bones of the dead.

Eleazar shuddered. He grasped the freezing balcony rail, his thoughts unsettled. He had always questioned the way of things. Always sought truth and knowledge. But the more he learned, the more he was filled with doubt. Was Splendour a place of gods and beauty? Were the Angelus holy and blessed of the Luminous One? Or was it a rotten, sterile world built on death, the Angelus no better than parasites?

It is the laudanum muddling my mind. But no. He was shaking with want in the moment, his head achingly clear. How had the laudanum worn off so quickly? His hands gripped the iron balustrade and his fingers left dents in the cold metal. He felt the urge to squeeze harder, to rip the railing apart. To rip the whole mansion apart brick by brick. To destroy this world which felt more real than his own. To wreak havoc like a vengeful god–

"Lee?"

Fury's soft query was like a shock of frigid water through his veins. He jerked upright, his wing snapping open, a great, white flag caught in a violent wind. He whipped around, his teeth bared as if she were a tiger attacking from the brush. His reaction made her brown eyes widen, but she remained motionless otherwise, standing in the snow in front of the balcony doors dressed in her trousers and linen blouse, her arms crossed over her chest, hugging herself in the cold. Her wiry hair was loose and coiling about her shoulders, the wind tugging at it, tossing it into further disarray.

"Sorry," she murmured. "Didn't mean to startle you."

Her calm demeanor, the humor in her dark, shining eyes, *enraged* him. She was the reason for his doubts. She was the cause.

"Can't I have a moment to myself, for the love of the Luminous One?" Pain lanced through his shoulder, and he grimaced, falling into a stoop like a broken old man. Fire roared across his skin. "I need peace!"

She jerked. "Well. You're back to your usual lovely self. I assume the laudanum has worn off?" She dropped her arms, her hands curling into fists. Her eyes cut to the side, but not before he saw the hurt within them. "Really, Eleazar. I thought we were past all this."

She was trembling. With cold, with anger, with hurt... he couldn't tell. He was trembling, too. His skin was burning, itching. "We will never be past anything," he said. "Not until I'm out of this hellish place and back among my own kind. Where I belong!"

Her gaze stabbed him. Sharp and cold. "You are where you belong. Down here in the muck with the rest of us. Desperate for your fix. Weak and broken and *wanting*." A shaky laugh burst from her. "And here I was feeling sorry for you."

"Keep your pity for yourself, you hateful woman." The words burst from him even as he regretted everything he'd said to her. He couldn't help it. Emotions gripped him, too wild and complex to sort. "You have no idea what I want, or what I need."

He stalked towards her. She was tall, but he loomed over her, his wing wide and bright in the moonlight. His proximity forced her to look up at him, and he could tell by the gleam in her eyes that she hated having to do it. Nevertheless, there was something more in her gaze. Deep and wide, drawing him in, wanting him close. The gap between them became a finger's width.

Breath fast and hard, he stared at her, studying every line and curve of her face, his belly tight.

"Lee," she said, uncertainty clouding her expression as his silent scrutiny stretched uncomfortably long.

"I hate you," he said gently, and her lips parted. There was no fear in her dark eyes. They were wide, caught in his gaze, a deep and beautiful brown. He felt a need rise in his center, hot and urgent. He reached up and grasped her by the back of the neck, his hand tangling in her hair. The gap between them vanished.

"Lee..."

"I hate everything about you." There was an ache in his throat, a shuddering fire rolling up and down his limbs. He moved his hand, tilting her face closer to him. "I hate your eyes... so dark and deep and angry. Always seeing straight into my soul. Daring me to be better." He brushed his lips against her eyelashes, feeling them flutter like trapped moths. Her hands were flat against his chest, warm and soft. He moved his face over hers, nuzzling her cheeks as he made his way to her lips. "I hate your need to see goodness in me. I am not good."

His hand tightened in her hair, pulling hard enough that she had to tilt her head still farther back to ease the strain. A tiny whimper slipped from her, sending a lightning bolt through his belly, knowing it was neither fear nor pain which caused it.

"I hate your mouth," he murmured against her smooth skin, his lips drawing a line across her cheek. "Always full of bitter words, when it was made to speak of sweet things. Made to give and receive joy." He took her bottom lip in his teeth, nipping gently. Her breath was hot and quick, her eyes closed. She was shaking. It set his body afire with a deep, sweet ache.

He pulled back suddenly, and her eyes flew open. He stared into their dark, beautiful depths, seeing his desire echoed, amplified. A feeling of lightness entered him. His pain was a memory. "You speak of my want, Fury. But you are the one full of longing."

"Lee," she gasped. She lunged at him, her hands twining into his hair, pulling fiercely to bring him to her eager mouth.

There was nothing soft in their kiss, or in their searching hands as desperate need gripped them both. Cloth ripped beneath seeking fingers. Flesh pressed to flesh. The heat in Eleazar's body did not deter Fury. She wriggled out of her torn shirt and molded herself to him, grasping and groping every inch of his exposed skin while he tried to do the same. A confident, knowing hand slid beneath his waistband and found him ready, fingers encircling him, making him gasp. His own hands tore at her belt, shoving her trousers down over her hips. Gooseflesh covered her skin, and he was aware in some distant part of his mind that she must be very cold. But his fingers found her hot and silky, and she bit his shoulder to stifle deep, guttural cries.

"We can go inside," he started to suggest, worried at her violent trembling and desperately wanting to throw her to the ground. Only the freezing wet snow stopped him.

"No," she said, her lips never stopping their exploration of his neck and shoulders, somehow both violent and gentle against his skin. And her hand, dear Luminous One, her hand was driving him to impossible heights. "Diver's there. Here. Now."

Abruptly, she disengaged, but only to shimmy out of her pants before she leapt at him, her arms encircling his broad shoulders. Needing no encouragement, he took her by the waist, lifting her with ease. Her round thighs gripped his hips and he slipped into her, sealing them together in one smooth motion. Buried deep in her welcoming warmth, he released a long, low groan and felt her teeth clamp down on his shoulder. It sent a shiver down his spine, and he held her close and still for an endless moment, their hearts thundering together. And then a rhythm gripped them, fast and urgent and undeniable, fear and doubt and pain abandoned.

He knew the moment she reached shuddering completion though she remained stubbornly silent, her body like a living lightning bolt, every nerve and muscle alive and snapping, only his arms keeping her from tearing apart. Unable to hold back, he followed her to the pinnacle. The pleasure in the release enough to stagger him. He kept her clasped to him even as he crashed to his knees in the churned and freezing slush, his body pulsing until he was drained.

"Lee, oh, Lee," she breathed into his ear, her fingers tangling in his hair, moving gently. Lovingly–

Agony like a knife slashed through his midsection. His muscles seized and cramped. Passion and lust, the sweetest agony, had kept it at bay, but in the aftermath he had nothing. No burning desire, no laudanum. The wrath of withdrawal doubled him. Bile rose in his throat, his stomach clenched, and he pushed Fury away and scrambled for the balcony's railing. Cold iron dug into his belly as he leaned over the balustrade, vomit spewing from him. He retched until there was nothing left, and yet he still heaved helplessly.

Finally, the sickness passed, leaving him trembling. He blinked away hot tears and pushed away from the railing. Needles rolled across his skin, pricking deep. His muscles continued to seize, so hard he thought his bones might break. His legs wouldn't hold him. He found himself on his hands and knees, snow melting beneath him in an expanding pool. Fighting through the agony, he looked up to find Fury standing forlorn, shivering, her cheeks sallow and her eyes wide, her clothes hanging from her hands as if she didn't know quite what to do with them.

As another fearsome cramp tangled his bowels, he managed to gasp, "The doctor. Call the doctor."

"That should do it. There now, aren't we all better?"

Eleazar nodded, a blissful expression on his face as the liquid dripped from the glass bottle and into the tube snaking down to his arm. The doctor shot Fury a triumphant look over his insensate patient laid out on the broad, silk-sheeted bed, as clear of an "I told you so" as a person could get without screaming it. She regarded him blankly, not able to muster even the barest annoyance. Her skin still tingled from Eleazar's touch, and her body ached in all the right places, but the aftermath of their encounter had her in a daze. This supercilious man was the least of her worries, and she was glad when Diver ushered him and his nurses out the door after promising to administer the drug at regular intervals.

"They want him docile," Diver muttered angrily.

"Withdrawal is painful, violent," Fury said dully. "His seems far worse than a human's. I – I should have listened to the doctor…"

Diver ignored her. He moved around the room like a restless cat, checking the door, checking the windows, checking the balcony only to return to his rifle propped against a chair near the hearth. He was avoiding her and avoiding Eleazar, though his eyes darted to the prone angel again and again. Confused, angry… stricken.

Her screams had brought him out to the balcony less than an hour ago (had it been only an hour since she'd been in his arms?) as she'd struggled to bring Eleazar inside. The angel had been shaking and retching. An absolute mess she was too stunned to deal with alone. And she would have, given Diver's obvious feelings for Lee, if not for the confusion and agony rolling through her, too.

Their mouths locked, their bodies one. Him a shaft of heat inside her, clasping her to him effortlessly. His strength boundless, her desire all-consuming. In that moment. That eternal moment…

She'd managed to drag on her own clothes, at least, before she'd screamed for Diver. But Eleazar had been left in all his glory and it was obvious what they'd been doing. As bad as Eleazar's abrupt vomiting fit had been, the look on Diver's face had been worse. Never in a thousand years would she have expected to hurt her baby brother this badly.

"I didn't mean for it to happen," she said quietly, hovering near Eleazar's sickbed, one hand holding her torn shirt closed.

Diver ceased his restless movement. He'd gotten up from his chair, his rifle slung over his shoulder and was making another round. His back was to her as he looked out the floor-to-ceiling windows once again. She watched him grow rigid. It made her heart hurt.

"I didn't want to..." She trailed off before she could utter another complete lie. She might not have meant for it to happen right then and right there, but she'd wanted it to happen. Lying pressed against him night after night on the road had been sweet agony.

"What, Fury?" He showed her his cheek and the rigid set of his jaw. "You didn't want to what? Fuck him?"

His crude response shocked her, and a spark of anger bloomed in her heart. "I didn't plan it, is what I meant. Yes, I wanted him. And *he* wanted me. I'm sorry if it—"

"Are you sure about that?" He turned just enough so she could see a lifted brow. "He wasn't exactly in his right mind, was he?"

She jerked and all her doubts flooded back. It had seemed so right, so easy. An irresistible encounter. But the sound of his violent retching rang in her ears. Had she forced the moment? Had she taken advantage of his raw, desperate state? Offered him a tempting distraction from the pain of withdrawal? Cold nausea seeped into her belly. She looked at Eleazar, so wan and limp. Had it meant something different to him?

"It doesn't matter," she said woodenly. "We're here to find out about Mother. What happened... it was a stupid mistake. A moment of weakness. It's over." She clenched her teeth, fighting a wave of impossible sadness. Eyes blurring, she glared at her stiff-backed brother. "Happy?"

He faced the window once more. "It's better this way," he said. "He'll be back in his own world soon enough. He's not meant for either of us, Fury. Remember that."

CHAPTER NINETEEN

Days passed. But for the nurses keeping Eleazar in his euphoric stupor, and various servants tending to their needs, they encountered no one else in Vogel's sprawling palace. Nor were they allowed to wander far, Diver discovered to his annoyance after a harmless trip down the hall led to an interaction with the foppish house guards and ended with an obdurate escort back to his room.

Days of boredom and silence thawed Diver toward his sister. Despite the shock and hurt he felt at her and Eleazar's... encounter (he couldn't bring himself to name it, think too long on it, or Creator forbid, picture it), Fury was all he had. All he had in the whole of Avernus. Besides, it could just as easily have been him who'd ended up in Eleazar's arms if he'd gone onto the balcony.

Or at least that's what he told himself when he finally decided to forgive his sister.

"How are we going to find out anything about Mother stuck here like this?" he seethed after another wonderful breakfast of flaky rolls and soft butter, fresh fruit and thick slices of bacon. Slim, crisp slices of manna, too, slathered in honey, which he and Fury avoided like poison. He'd eaten *some* manna in the army – unavoidable at times – but it hadn't been like this fancy offering. It had been tasteless stuff, though filling and nutritious.

Fury brushed crumbs from her fingers, her brows raised slightly. Surprised that he was talking to her, probably. "I've been watching them prepare the Hallow Tithe. The time draws near. When the drachen arrives, I – I believe we'll find some answers. Or at least find the people we need to *ask*."

"And what if we don't? What if the drachen arrives, swoops up Eleazar and leaves us to Vogel's mercies? I doubt the governor of Trin wants two Koine refugees lurking about telling tales about fallen angels and heavenly power struggles. They're supposed to be infallible gods, remember?"

"Then we'd better be ready for anything," she returned with a bit of her usual fire. She picked apart a piece of the manna as if furious with it. "I won't let them take off with Lee. Not until I know–"

The doors to their suite burst open, flying inward with a startling clatter. On edge as it was, Diver leapt to his feet, a butter knife clutched in his fist, and dropped immediately into a triangle stance. He heard Fury's chair squeak across the tiles and the jangle of cutlery and knew she'd reached for her own weapon. Their reaction proved needless, as the guards who'd knocked the doors open stood at attention and made no further move into the room. Instead, it was a glowering Governor Vogel who entered their dubious sanctuary, the white-coated physician who'd been dosing Eleazar at his elbow and a flock of nurses milling nervously behind them. Ignoring both siblings, Vogel crossed to Eleazar's sickbed, his face scrunched with a look of distaste.

"How much have you been giving him?" he demanded, throwing the words over his shoulder at the pale-faced doctor. With an impatient snarl, he yanked the blankets away from Eleazar's prone body and the angel barely twitched.

Diver tensed at the rough treatment, and behind him, Fury let out a low growl. He made a placating gesture; he didn't think Vogel meant Eleazar any harm. Part of him was glad to see someone in authority acting on the angel's behalf. Neither he nor Fury had approved of this course of treatment, but they'd had no say in stopping it.

Unfortunately, Vogel's next words revealed the stark reality of their situation and proved how little Vogel cared about his Angelic guest.

"I told you to keep him docile and compliant, not turn him into a drooling vegetable. Cut off the dosage and give him whatever it takes to make him coherent, you miserable incompetent. The drachen has passed through the Celestial Gate and will be in communication range by nightfall, and I want this mess off my plate. The Hallow Tithe must proceed as usual to maintain order. Do you understand, Dr Rhiner? Since you failed to understand the most basic instructions once already!"

"Y – y – yes, Governor Vogel. Right away, Excellency."

The governor turned his back on the doctor, and the man began snapping instructions at his nurses, berating them as viciously as Vogel had him. They swarmed Eleazar's bed, wielding shining metal trays topped with syringes and swabs and bottles. For his part, Vogel ignored the activity behind him as he strode to the doorway, certain in his authority that his orders would be followed precisely.

"What are you giving him?" Fury demanded, her voice nearly a screech. To a one, but for a young, wide-eyed nurse who threw her a startled glance, the medical professionals ignored her.

She started to sweep toward them, and Diver grabbed her arm, dragging her to a stop. Her savage glare nearly made him let go. A look like that would have sent him scrambling as a kid. But he'd faced artillery shells since then, so she wasn't *quite* as frightening.

"Let them work," Diver urged. "Don't you want him back?"

She recoiled. Luckily, though, his words reached her, and she subsided. She was trembling when he let go of her arm: All her senses, her entire body, focused on Eleazar.

"It will be alright," he said, more to convince himself than Fury. A sudden nervous excitement filled him and turned his skin clammy. He felt lightheaded and breathless, and regretted eating as much breakfast as he had. "The drachen, Fury," he murmured. "It's here. In our world. The Angelus have arrived."

Golden light bathed the fine halls of Vogel's mansion, pouring in through tall, stained-glass windows depicting scenes from scripture: the Founding of Avernus, the Fall, the Great Scourge. Diver's skin crawled as they passed the three-window, life-size pictorial of the destruction and scattering of his ancestors. The bestial depictions of the lost Gullan people were grotesque. Inhuman. No wonder everyone in Avernus thought they deserved it: Half turned to Burnt Ghouls, another quarter slaughtered, the rest cast upon the wind. It had happened long before even his mother had been born, yet she'd acted like it had happened to her personally. Such an attitude had cost her everything.

Is she even alive?

They took a few more twists and turns through increasingly familiar halls to finally arrive at the governor's study. Fury was focused on Eleazar, who'd woken from his drug-induced coma befuddled and cranky, acting as his nursemaid. It mollified Diver's envy to see her interact with him like a caretaker rather than a lover.

Whatever Dr Rhiner had given Eleazar to bring him around didn't seem to be working as he'd hoped, given the layer of moisture on his brow and beneath his nose. Every so often, he would whisper to Fury, imploring her to let him administer another shot before they reached Vogel's study, but her dark glare and rigid shoulders – far more impressive in breadth than poor Dr Rhiner's – kept him from pressing too hard.

Eleazar's voice rose in a petulant whine. "Why are we in these skyless halls? We were bound for Lucien's haunt, weren't we? To sample the Fourth Season ale? I've a terrible thirst today." Eleazar was gripping Fury's arm, stumbling along like a drunk, speaking of places and things which had her brow furrowed with worry.

"After we speak with the drachen captain, perhaps," Fury murmured. Again. "This is very important, Eleazar. You must speak with the Tithing ship, remember?"

"A Tithing ship? I don't care for the Tithing ships. They only ever go to the Below. Why would I have any interest in that terrible place?"

"Eleazar... Lee. You are in the Below. Remember?"

The Angelus frowned and threw her a look as if she were mad. Then his expression slowly changed. Grew disturbed. "My head is all muddled today. What was your name again? You're new. My mother... My mother must be so worried."

"Yes, yes, Lee." Diver caught a hint of excited hope in Fury's voice. "She has to be very worried. She'll want you home. The ship will take you back to Splendour."

Eleazar's face crumpled. To Diver's shock, he began to weep. "I want to go home. Dear Luminous One, deliver me from this Abyss!" And in the next second, he shook himself and straightened. "No. No, I mustn't appear weak in front of a Tithing captain. He'll pounce on me like a hawk on a titmouse."

"Then stand strong, Angelus."

Eleazar stopped and the two locked eyes. Diver felt his heart crack a bit. Eleazar's elegant fingers gripped Fury's forearm as if he sought to draw strength from her.

"Remember who you are, Eleazar Starson," she said firmly.

Her command seemed to break through to him. Suddenly, his feathers gleamed and his expression cleared. A shudder passed through his body. He gave her arm a final squeeze then released her.

"I remember," he said softly. "Thank you. I feel... I feel more myself now."

Fury searched his face then gave a nod. She stepped back, taking her place as his faithful acolyte alongside Diver. The Angelus started forward again, his steps grown steady, his golden head held high.

With Fury out of his way, Dr Rhiner sidled close to the Angelus. "I can give you something for your head, Angelus. Something to keep you steady–"

The doctor slammed into the wall of the narrow hallway as if tossed by a bull. Diver watched him crumple senseless to the floor. Eleazar lowered his stiffened arm and continued down the hall without a backward glance. "You won't touch me again with your foul concoctions, apothecarist. I'd rather suffer."

Eleazar's shoulders were rigid, his back straight. A god once more.

He stumbled only once as the guards flung open the ornate doors, catching his toe on the thick carpet. Diver had to fight every instinct within him not to help the Angelus recover. It was the right move. Eleazar covered his slip with an elegant snap of his bright wing, entering the dim study with a flourish.

The flurry of activity within the office slowed but did not cease. Eleazar frowned darkly. "Governor Vogel!" he boomed. "Attend me!"

The man himself looked up from a report he was perusing. He'd startled at Eleazar's abrasive demand. And he seemed rather put out by it. His eyes narrowed and his nostrils flared before his expression cleared, replaced by a vapid smile.

"Ah, Angelus, I am so glad to see you well again! Dr Rhiner has certainly worked magic." His brow furrowed. "Where is the good doctor?"

"Dismissed," Eleazar said with menace. "His concoctions are no longer necessary."

"Well, very good, I heartily agree. You look as well as can be expected after your ordeals." He flashed a toothy grin. Like a dog showing its canines. He foisted the files in his hands onto a flustered secretary and gestured for Eleazar to come closer.

"The crystal is primed and ready. We were merely waiting for the drachen to make contact. And for you, of course." Another flashy smile, this one thrown over his shoulder as he strode toward the shrouded pedestal in a dark corner of the study. His eyes were flat as a snake's.

Eleazar followed him after a brief hesitation. As much as he might wish to put Governor Vogel in his place, the desire to speak to his people had to outweigh everything else. His wing practically vibrated with eagerness as he went to the hidden crystal.

Without preamble, Vogel whipped the velvet covering away, revealing a milky white orb held aloft by elaborate coils of metal, scaled like strange serpents in a range of colors from green to light blue to deep indigo. Almost instantly, as if removing the covering had activated it, the interior of the globe began to swirl with clouds of black and silver, turning slowly.

Eleazar stiffened, leaning away from it as if repulsed, perhaps recalling his passage through the Celestial Gate. *The Black Silence*, he'd called it. A horrid, lightless, soundless, airless void between the two maelstroms which connected their worlds.

A glow appeared deep within the slowly churning maelstrom. Eleazar made a sound, somewhere between a sob and a gasp. The glow expanded until the entire crystal gleamed with blue light. A hard, hawkish visage appeared within the globe, above a set of broad shoulders clad in a deep blue suit of a rather martial appearance. Gleaming buttons on a double-breasted jacket, gold braid dripping from the shoulders and across the chest. Strange insignia marked the jacket's right breast, a ten-pointed star. Black and brown mottled wings rose above those shoulders in graceful curves. The wings of a raptor, not a swan like Eleazar's. Everything about this Angelus screamed "predator."

"Captain Pace!" Eleazar cried, sounding relieved and eager. The man in the globe winced, and Eleazar modulated his tone. "Captain Pace," he repeated in a more dignified manner. "Thank the Luminous One you are here at last. I have been eagerly awaiting your arrival."

Captain Pace's dark brow screwed tight with confusion over his impressive nose. His eyes danced over Eleazar, jumping from his face to his hair and chest, and finally settling on the lone wing peaking above his right shoulder. The horror shone clear in his eyes a moment before he suppressed it. "Prince Eleazar? Is it truly you, or is this some terrible trick?"

"No trick. It is I. Your prince. Alive and well, though others thought to see me dead." He drew himself up to his full height, even as he tucked his wing closer to his back. As if to hide his infirmity. Had he caught that look of horror in Pace's eyes, too?

"What? What are you saying, my prince? The report from the royal drachen was that you'd slipped from the back of your first kill and were lost to the Black Silence. Prince Rastaphar himself delivered the terrible news. He searched for you for days! There was no other conclusion to be made." Pace's gaze passed over him again, almost suspiciously. "Are you trying to tell me it wasn't an accident? Did someone take you through the Silence?"

"I was betrayed, Captain. And by the grace of the Luminous One and my own sheer will, I survived the attempt on my life. No one 'took' me through the Silence. I fell, by all the gods and monsters, fell straight through the Silence and into the Below. Injured, poisoned, broken!" His voice cracked on the word, but he continued, growing louder and angrier, spitting out his story like *it* was poison. "And it still wasn't enough to kill me. I lost more than you can ever fathom, faced death and pestilence and destruction worse than any nightmare your mind could conjure. Not all the Beasts of the Below worship us as gods, Pace. A rare few showed proper obeisance, and those few shall be rewarded grandly, but those who stood in my way will pay dearly."

On the other side of the raging Angelus, Vogel squirmed at his comment. Diver threw Fury a glance and her lips tightened with a smirk before she wiped it away. They were the "rare few", no doubt.

"When you tell my mother of my miraculous survival," Eleazar continued. "Be sure to tell her everything. Tell her what the 'pampered princeling' endured. Tell her that he survived the Black Silence without a drachen to take him through it. And now, now I am back to reclaim what is mine! And when you tell her, also inform her that her eldest is to blame for all of it! Tell her, Prince Rastaphar Mikalson is a traitor to Splendour!"

"Prince Rastaphar?" Shock painted the captain's features, and his great, mottled wings opened in response, flaring wide. "That is a severe accusation, Eleazar. How can you be certain? Do you have proof?"

"My word is proof! He attacked me on the back of that unfortunate leviathan nymph, but it was the cowardly bolt cast by Princess Maurissa, my betrothed, which sent me helpless into the void. Because of her... because–" and a shudder rolled through him, sending Fury a step closer to him. Diver remained still, watching Pace. And not liking what he was seeing. At. All.

"Yes," Pace murmured slowly, his eyes narrowing. "I see what their betrayal cost you."

"The wound festered. Poisoned my blood." Eleazar struggled to produce words, shame and anger and hurt warring in his voice. Disgust clouded Pace's features and Diver wanted to reach through the globe and strangle him. "My wing was... sacrificed... to save my life."

Fury slowly closed her eyes, her face sallow in the light from the orb. Diver took her hand.

"Tell my mother, Captain. Tell my mother everything and you will be well rewarded for your loyal service when I ascend to my rightful place on the Solaire Throne."

"I will give her my report immediately." Captain Pace bowed deeply, his face hidden. "Await us on the Tithing Field. You will be returned to your rightful place. I swear it." Before Eleazar could reply, the crystal went dark. He blinked rapidly, frowning, but then his face cleared. "Well," he said with painfully false cheer. "There. It is done. Tomorrow all will be set right."

Diver looked at Fury, grim-faced and doubtful. She gave him a slight nod. All might be set right tomorrow, but they would damn sure be ready if everything went wrong instead.

CHAPTER TWENTY

The procession which made its way to the Tithing Ground was a strange one. Like something out of the past. Horses, not motorcars, pulled the important dignitaries in ornate carriages. A mounted honor guard of Vogel's men in plumed helmets seemed a show of strength, except they wore scimitars and carried tasseled halberds. Halberds! Useless against anyone with a gun. Laughably pathetic against Angelic superpowers. For all the pomp and ceremony, the obvious display of extravagant wealth, the rows of soldiers might as well be made of tin.

The only modern weapon among the troops, the only obvious one anyway, was the rifle slung over Diver's shoulder. And it had taken Eleazar's rage-filled Charisma to convince Vogel to let him carry it. Diver couldn't help remembering the last time he'd carried a rifle near a Tithing Ground, back when he'd been on Tithing duty for the Koine army. He and a few friends, drunk on whiskey and ale, had thought it would be a great adventure to disobey orders and watch the Angelic drachen receive the Tithe. It had landed him in the stockade for a week. Soldiers were not allowed on the Tithing Field.

Both he and Fury carried pistols, as well, tucked out of sight but within easy reach. They wore the clothes they'd arrived in – washed and repaired, of course. Fury had wrapped their mother's scarf around her like some sort of primitive armor. The indigo scales shone in the thin winter sun, sparkling prettily. Eleazar, resplendent in a black velvet coat, rode atop a horse as white as his feathers, the two siblings flanking him on matching blood bays. Another concession they had demanded. None of them wished to be locked inside a closed carriage despite Eleazar's insistence that all would be well.

Diver wore his own "armor" under his drab, faded Koine uniform. The girdle of Mithran graced his torso, cold against his skin but surprisingly supple. He'd expected the strange metal to be warm like Eleazar, but it had its own odd properties. The chill of it on his flesh was almost invigorating. It gave him a sense of imperviousness. The so-called gods' metal.

They'd never learned where that woman Star had gotten it. Their requests to interrogate her had been met with stony silence, and Eleazar had hardly been in a position to insist.

The Tithing Ground held the Hallow Tithe in all its immensity. Towers of crates, pyramids of bales, produce, livestock, lumber, great pallets of iron ingots. A veritable city of resources laid out for their overlords. How many drachen would arrive to carry it all away?

It was disturbing to see it all. Here was food, shelter, the hard labor of thousands of humans. And in exchange the Angelus would leave behind barrel after barrel of holy manna. It had been this way for centuries. By now, most humans were convinced they would face another "Great Famine" like the one that killed half the world if they didn't receive the manna. Some grumbled at the imbalance of the exchange, but those voices were quickly silenced. No one wished to call down a Scourge upon the world. The Angelic Curse had wreaked havoc before on "ungrateful" populations.

The Tithing Commission took their share of the manna, of course, plus a cut of the Tithe itself, and they also received their "fee": All the gold and jewels collected from the population remained with the commissioners. The Angelus had no need for such frivolous things.

Their streets are paved with gold.

Diver shifted in his saddle, glad for the fine beast he rode, and threw Fury a look. The same thoughts had to be going through her head because she was already looking his way, her brow cloudy. They shared a grim smile.

"All the riches of our world," she said, sitting easy in her saddle. She'd always been the better rider. "It makes me sick to think about it."

"A few grow fat while the rest of us starve."

"You exaggerate," Eleazar interjected somewhat petulantly. His cheeks were bright in the chill air, perhaps with excitement. Or nerves. "Our manna feeds your world."

"I didn't mean it literally," Diver said. "The manna keeps us alive, yes, keeps us fed, but it's hardly worth what we give you for it."

"Your kind can't even eat it," Fury countered. "You might as well be giving us your trash."

His head snapped toward her. The color in his cheeks had deepened, but he said nothing. An uncomfortable shifting in his saddle and he was looking forward again. Unlike the two of them, he had never been on a horse, but his mount seemed docile enough. Luckily. "I'm beginning to regret refusing the carriage," he grumbled. "These creatures smell."

Diver chuckled. "You might be happy to have a fleet-footed creature when the time comes."

And it was his turn to get a sharp look from Eleazar. "Don't be absurd. Everything will be well. I swear it. Captain Pace takes orders from my mother. The queen herself! So, he serves me, too." He looked ahead, holding his reins in a stiff grip. "All will be well."

Ahead of them, Governor Vogel and the other members of the Tithing Commission had reached the landing site. Myriad attendants rushed to serve them as they disembarked. The servants were professional, dutiful, impeccable. The members of the commission, on the other hand – Vogel included – looked cold and uneasy, as if they'd rather be anywhere else than where they were. This exchange with the Angelus must be trying for them. To have to bow and scrape to creatures you know aren't gods, yet you must maintain the farce at all costs. The Angelus were powerful enough to smite a crowd of humans, especially ones armed with mere ceremonial weapons. By the Abyss, Eleazar had slaughtered several men armed with pistols and shotguns. Effortlessly...

Diver's trusty rifle was a reassuring weight upon his back, but would it be any use against an Angelus? Especially one as impressive as this Captain Pace they were about to meet. But, by the Creator, he would be ready. His own speed and instincts had been honed by battle. No one would take him by surprise today. The Angelus would most likely underestimate him, too. Small, slight, unremarkable. In Eleazar's significant shadow, he would attract little attention.

They reached the edge of the landing site, a broad sward of dead grass swept clean of snow with strange contraptions ringing it, which Diver finally parsed were movable ramps. Directly overhead, the swirling clouds of the Celestial Gate dominated the sky. A silent storm in the clear blue. Flashes of lightning illuminated the boiling vapors, adding to the Gate's general ominousness. Beside him, Eleazar sat stiffly astride his mount, staring wide-eyed at the menacing clouds. His wing was half spread, as if he might take flight. Which, of course, he couldn't. And the agony of that knowledge was clear in every line of his taut frame.

On the other side of the Angelus, Fury was scanning their surroundings, marking everyone and everything around them. Exactly what he should be doing. Some soldier...

Liveried grooms arrived to hold their horses. They dismounted, Diver and Fury somewhat reluctantly, but Eleazar with alacrity. He strode forward, staring up at the clouds intently. Expectantly.

"Stand here and wait," Fury ordered the grooms, gesturing imperiously. "The holy Angelus may have need of his horse. Do not fail him!"

At her strident tone and menacing scowl, the head groom stammered an affirmative. "As his most holy Angelus wills it."

Fury shot Diver a look, her eyes wide as if she was surprised that had worked. He was glad she'd done it; he didn't want the horses out of reach.

Vogel and his people cast the occasional pensive glance skyward, partaking freely of provided refreshments. Not a single servant was being sent their way, and all the dignitaries were keeping their distance from the lone Angelus among them. Diver grimaced. The governor was done with them apparently, and gladly. He supposed they were Splendour's problem now.

Fine with me. How could Heaven be any worse than here?

Eleazar stood alone on the field, head tipped back like a stargazing child. Diver and Fury stood near him but not beside him. They were his acolytes, after all. Not his equals. It seemed more important than ever to maintain this façade. Eleazar's people wouldn't understand their relationship, not at first. They would need time to adjust, but Eleazar was their king. Or soon to be king. Surely, he was allowed eccentricities…?

The maelstrom above suddenly billowed fiercely, and a red light shaded the clouds the color of blood. Diver sucked in a breath, and everyone standing there echoed him, all but Eleazar. He was calm and still.

The light grew brighter, harsher, the clouds boiled, and then a golden hull split the maelstrom. It descended ponderously. More ships broke the clouds behind it, smaller but no less beautiful. They looked like sailing vessels from a century ago but for being fashioned from metal, seemingly. *Mithran.* The word whispered in Diver's head, and he touched his midsection briefly, aware of the same metal strapped around him. Battened sails of deep crimson rose above them like shark fins, and more sails jutted from the sides of the ships like glorious wings. The planks of the airships… sparkled. Flashes of gold rippled along the enormous keel of the main ship.

Diver didn't remember such details from before, and he found himself gawping in amazement. Of course, he'd been dead drunk and bleeding from the head the last time. These "drachen" were far more impressive and daunting with a clear head.

The smaller ships moved away from the main drachen, and the army of workers watching over the Tithe moved into action, rolling the ramps to different points around the landing site, lining them up with the arrivals. The large ship – Eleazar had said Pace captained the royal flagship, and this had to be it – descended at the center of the Tithing Ground, close to where Vogel and his fellows had set up their banquet tables. The Tithing Commission no longer looked bored. A few of the foppish guards gripped their halberds or sword hilts as if they were real weapons. Diver's hands itched to shoulder his weapon.

Instead, he moved it into better reach. A simple shrug of his shoulder and it would be in his hands. He glanced toward their horses. The grooms had heeded Fury's order and hadn't moved. Good.

His eyes returned to Eleazar. A look of steely determination rested on the angel's face. He'd closed his wing, holding it tight and smooth against his back. The longest primaries brushed the grass at his heels, a slight tremble the only sign of his trepidation.

Even Fury was staring at the ship now. Her eyes wide and her lips parted. The wind had picked up from the ship's descent; it whipped her hair around her face until she was forced to hold it back with one hand. Diver winced as dust struck his face. He lifted a hand to shield his eyes. A great gust of wind nearly knocked them all over as the ship slowed to a halt well above them.

Heart pounding, blinking grit from his eyes, Diver looked up to see a row of angels along the ship's railing. One stood out among them, taller and broader with great dark wings. Captain Pace. He spread those wings wide, stepped up onto the railing and launched. His wings caught the wind and he rode it, spiraling lazily to the ground. Two more angels followed him, one golden and the other an amazing bright blue. Like a jaybird. Even his skin had a faintly blue cast to it.

Despite all he believed, all he knew, Diver felt awe at their graceful flight, their unearthly beauty. The impressive Captain Pace settled to the earth before them, landing in the shadow of the drachen. The two others landed to either side of him and slightly behind. He was dressed in dark leather studded with iron and carried a curved saber at his hip. He looked far more martial than he had in the crystal. Governor Vogel, standing some distance away with his fellows, was forced to scramble to greet him. Irritation was writ clear on his face, but he quickly schooled his features into proper obeisance as he scurried to them. He might have little respect for his Angelic overlords, but he was no fool. He would never outright disrespect the captain of a Tithing ship. There were always other men to take his place.

"Greetings, Captain. We have arranged refreshments for you and your crew," he stated, stiffly formal. He turned and waved impatiently to his servants who'd set up a smaller table with wine and bread some distance away. They scrambled to move it closer, lifting and carrying it across the dead grass. "Please, honor us by breaking bread and sharing wine. Our eternal agreement is a blessing to us and your holy presence only–"

"Silence." Captain Pace raised a hand covered in a leather gauntlet, not even bothering to look at the annoyed governor. His eyes were on Eleazar. "Wait, man. This does not concern you."

Vogel sputtered into silence, and his lips sealed into a line.

"Eleazar Starson. I bring a message from the queen. Your mother grieves deeply for the fate which has befallen you."

Eleazar nodded, his shoulders relaxing at Pace's words. "Thank you, Captain. I look forward to speaking with her myself. Hopefully, my return will ease her sorrow–"

"You do not understand, Eleazar."

Diver stiffened at Pace's words. Where was the respectful "your highness"? And why hadn't they moved one of the ramps to the ship as they had the others? He eased his rifle into a better position. Slowly, calmly. The blue-winged angel on Pace's right stared at him sharply, and Diver gave him a vapid grin.

"What don't I understand?" Eleazar was asking Pace. "Why don't we discuss this aboard the drachen? Whatever I'm misunderstanding, I'm sure it can be resolved by speaking with my mother directly. I am eager to return to Splendour, after all. It has been a trying–"

"Your mother grieves. She grieves her lost son, whereas before she'd harbored hope you may one day return to her."

"But – but I have returned. I'm right here, you fool. Take me to the ship! I can't exactly fly there on my own."

"Precisely."

The word dropped hard and cruel. Eleazar's face crumpled. He took a step as if he would go around Pace to try to reach the ship. Pace raised a gauntleted hand and shoved him back. Eleazar stumbled, his wing flaring out for balance. It had taken him a long time to learn how to balance and move with one wing, but he'd gotten very good at it. He stabilized himself quickly, his hands raised in fists.

"How dare you! I am your prince!"

"You are no one. Man."

Eleazar jerked as if struck. His face went white. His voice shook as he shouted, "I am your future king! I'll see you pinioned for this!"

"By order of Queen Regent Lucretia, you are banished."

Pace's voice boomed in the cold, still air. The word echoed ominously. Eleazar made a noise, deep and guttural. His wing flared wide, and Diver braced himself for violence. Pace drew his saber in a swift, ringing movement and Diver dropped his shoulder, his rifle falling into his hands.

The curved blade flashed in the light of the rising sun.

Fury shouted, lunging toward the towering Angelus captain. Diver feared she meant to throw herself in front of his blade. But even in his rage, Eleazar shielded his companions, putting himself firmly between Pace and his acolytes. His white wing was a wall between Fury and the captain.

"Do not harm—"

But Pace had not been aiming at Fury, nor Diver, nor even to kill, and Eleazar presented himself exactly how he wanted — wing wide open, stretched out like a sacrifice.

The golden blade of Pace's saber sliced through the gleaming white feathers of Eleazar's wing, shearing through muscle, feather and bone. A blood-curdling shriek tore from his throat, and he fell back, parted from his lone wing. A spray of bright blood erupted from the severed stump. Eleazar collapsed to the ground.

With a wild screech, Fury leapt at the huge angel, her hand striking upward toward his belly. Diver caught the flash of their father's knife before it found a joint in Pace's leather armor. The Angelus grunted as her blade struck home, looking down at her in shock. To him, she must seem a bug.

Instincts in overdrive, his rifle at his hip, Diver aimed not at Pace but at the Angelus to his right, the blue devil. He fired two quick rounds, taking him squarely in the chest. The angel's bright eyes flew open in shock as he was flung backwards. Whirling, Diver fired at the second Angelus to Pace's left, blasting him in the face. He crumpled without a sound, his golden wings splattered with red.

Bulletproof wings, he thought wildly. *Face and chest, not so much.*

By this time, Pace had Fury by the arm, wrenching her off her feet. Rage darkened his face and he hardly seemed slowed by the wound she'd inflicted. Dangling in his grip, her knife still in Pace's gut, Fury reached behind her and whipped the pistol from her waistband. She fired with cool precision, taking him in the neck. Blood fountained. He staggered, dropping her and clapped a hand to the pumping wound.

"Eleazar!" Fury screamed, racing to where he lay writhing in a pool of blood. Chaos had erupted among the dignitaries and servants. The honor guard waved their useless halberds and swords, unsure who to attack. Fury pointed her pistol at the rioting commission and their cowering servants, many of whom had fled at the first shot from Diver's rifle. Only Governor Vogel remained close, crouched and glaring at them, somewhere between shock and anger.

"Stay back!" Fury ordered.

"What have you done?" he shrieked at her, but she was already gathering up Eleazar and running for the horses. Despite his grievous wound, Eleazar stumbled along on his own legs and managed to pull himself up on one of the blood bays, Fury mounting behind him. Blood from Eleazar's severed wing soaked her shirt front. Diver leapt on his own horse, firing his rifle over the heads of the terrified commission. They screamed and ran in all directions. Chaos erupted.

Fury slapped Eleazar's horse on the rump, driving it into a gallop. She wheeled her mount and kicked it fiercely. "Make for the city!"

Diver glanced up, his horse dancing in a circle. Dark shapes milled at the railing of the drachen. Did they understand what was happening? All they would see was panicked humans racing in all directions. Pace was on the ground on one knee, hand to his neck to staunch the bleeding, but dark blood coated his side. Diver thought about shooting him. Instead, he urged his horse after Fury. They made for the maze of the Tithe, leaving chaos behind them.

By the time any of the Angelus winged their way off the drachen, they had lost themselves in the labyrinthine streets of Trin.

CHAPTER TWENTY-ONE

A strange sight filled the skies above Trin: angels. Their broad wings – not only the bright white described in holy doctrine but in colors as varied as the multitude of birds in the fields – darkened the air. Any man or woman with sense knew to run when those shadows passed over them. Not all were fast enough or clever enough to escape. Those unfortunates were lighted on and subjected to questioning which left them moaning and bleeding on the hard streets. Many were taken away, never to be seen again.

Citizens flocked to the temples, praying and weeping. What sin had brought this punishment upon them?

At the pubs and taverns, there were more complaints than prayers. Resentment rose like so much dust.

And then, one day, as abruptly as they had arrived, the Angelus vanished. The city exhaled. The celebration of the Winter Tithe had turned to suffering, and now the darkest days of winter proceeded unrelentingly.

Hunched beneath Eleazar's cloak, Fury trudged home from the market in ankle-deep snow. The sun didn't reach the narrow streets between the brick tenements and factories with their massive smokestacks and ghostly workers: "Ash men" to Fury. Grey and grim and silent as they trundled to and from work, called and dismissed by shrieking whistles. Many were women, she'd realized after a week or so – they wore boiler suits for the hard, heavy work in the factories – but she couldn't drop the moniker. Clanking trollies constantly carried coal from the edge of the city to the interior, spewing smoke which coated everything and everyone in a gray film.

Not everything was misery in Trin, she had to admit. The market was a bustling place of community, as well as the public houses tucked on every street corner. There were places of worship, too, temples to the Angelus. Many found comfort and welcome within their gilded walls. Fury avoided them like the plague.

She carried a canvas sack beneath her cloak, heavy with day-old chunks of bread, dried lentils and meat ends. It was all they could afford. They'd released the horses once they'd found their way deep into the city, not daring to sell the branded animals. Instead, they had sold her father's pistol. They couldn't leave Trin, not while Vogel monitored every way in and out of the city, and they had to eat. No one would be showering Eleazar with gifts and luxuries anytime soon, or ever again.

The Angelus had broadcast an image of Eleazar across the clouds and dubbed him "Eleazar the Fallen". He and his companions, two treasonous, blasphemous atheist scum, were wanted for the attempted theft of a portion of the Hallow Tithe. She supposed they couldn't accuse them of murder. How would a human murder an immortal Angelus?

Fury turned down a narrow alley between two dark-faced buildings, stepping carefully. She pulled her cloak tight, grateful for its warmth. She'd had it stowed behind her horse's saddle when they'd gone to the Tithing Ground, and a lucky thing. Eleazar had no wings now, but the unsightly stumps were a dead giveaway.

Not that he was venturing out much. Only she and Diver had dared leave their hiding place – a basement dwelling in an abandoned tenement. It had running water, at least, a marvel, though it was barely a dribble and tasted of rust. Dirty and grim, filled with broken scraps of furniture, the dreary place nevertheless provided perfect concealment. The angels hadn't considered going "under" the city to find their missing prince, though the city regulators had done a cursory search.

By some miracle, given the filthiness of their surroundings, Eleazar's wound had not festered and was healing swiftly. Nevertheless, his phenomenal appetite had vanished, and he'd dropped into a state of lethargy. The one glimmer of hope had been that it seemed his dependency on laudanum was done. Perhaps he was suffering in silence, but he'd made no demands for the drug. No demands for anything, really, which was in and of itself disturbing given his nature.

Fury passed a few men and tucked the bag of pitiful groceries closer to her. It had taken being robbed only once for her to learn to conceal anything she wanted to keep. A bloody lip and a bruised ego were the worse she'd taken from the encounter, but it was a lesson hard learned. It hadn't been a total loss. For a moment, her puffy face and split lip had roused Eleazar from his despondency. He had looked stricken and touched her cheek, a brief flicker of rage in his eyes. Then that distant stare was back...

At night, curled on her lumpy pallet, she wept remembering the glory of his lost wings, silently, tragically. He hadn't seemed diminished even when he'd possessed only one. Now, though, he looked smaller, paler, weaker. He lay on his stomach since his wing stump was still tender and he rose only to use the ancient privy they'd uncovered in their hidey-hole. Each day, he grew weaker and more withdrawn. He didn't even sleep; he merely stared, seeing something only he could see, eyes moving, searching, his lips twitching, muttering silently.

Did thoughts of revenge obsess him still? He had no wings; they had no drachen, no allies, no chance. It would take all their resources – she had to laugh at that – and all their cunning to leave Trin alive. Vengeance was as out of reach as Splendour.

Fury ducked down another narrow alleyway. Midway down, the trim buildings gave way to older, ramshackle tenements, most abandoned since the newer factories blocked the light and spewed smoke and ash into the sky. She paused, glancing around to make sure no one was watching, then she squatted near a window level with the street, shoved her bag of groceries through it and swung herself down after it.

She landed with a thump. Neither Diver nor Eleazar reacted to her entrance; the bag of food had given away surprise of course, but she'd still been expecting at least a greeting. Eleazar was staring off into the distance as always, his arms hanging off the narrow cot, the backs of his hands resting on the floor. *Like a dead man*, she thought half in horror and half in irritation, wishing she could break him out of his despondency.

Frowning, Fury snatched up her satchel. What could she do, starve him? Kick him in the rear end, or dump him out of the cot and force him to lie on the hard, dirty floor? No. She'd keep taking care of him as she would anyone who needed her. She'd be patient. Patient as the day is long...

It's winter, Fury, the days are short.

Light flickered weakly from a bare bulb hanging over their one rickety table. She and Diver had reclaimed it from a trash heap and fixed its broken leg to make it serviceable. *City dwellers,* she'd thought derisively upon seeing the mound of garbage. *Everything is trash to them.* Diver sat at the table on a moth-eaten chair, his shoulders hunched, all his attention focused on what lay before him.

Fury dumped her meager groceries on the washboard beside the sink. The Mithran was the most valuable thing in their possession, but they couldn't sell it, not without attracting unwelcome attention. Not that Diver *would* consider selling it. He was obsessed with it.

"Why are you so infatuated with that useless pile of scrap?" she snapped, divvying up their meager supplies into the small, metal bins she used for storage. The bins were dented and rusted on the outside, but she'd scrubbed the insides clean. They were depressingly empty, and the new groceries barely filled them halfway.

"It's valuable," he murmured, running his fingers along the slim golden laths of the strange girdle. It... rippled. Mesmerizing. It possessed its own light, like the leviathan skin she wore beneath her clothes. Her shield against the world. She longed to reach out and stroke the Mithran. It drew her as strongly as it drew Diver, but she fought the pull. It repulsed her as much as it tempted her.

Her gaze lingered on the Mithran. It wasn't all loathing which kept her from touching it. It was fear. Her mother's scarf was legacy, protection. *Talisman.* The Mithran was something else.

Power. Transcendence. Change...

"We should get rid of it," she said knowing Diver would just as soon get rid of her than the Mithran. She tried an old argument. "What if the Angelus can sense it? What if it draws them to us?"

"They would have found us then, right?" Diver made a frustrated noise. "I can't get it apart. Even the wires holding it together are unbreakable. I can't cut them. I can't melt them. Not even a hammer puts a dent in it. It's indestructible!"

"It can't be indestructible," Fury countered despite her reluctance to encourage his obsession. "The regulators told Eleazar it's being used as a drug. How? If people are ingesting the stuff, there must be some way to break it down."

"Well, if there is, I don't see how. There must be some way to work with it! Some way to... to melt it, maybe. Maybe a forge would do it? If we can find any of those smugglers who got away, maybe we'll understand better." He paused, stroking the shimmering corset. "If we could find those two soldiers again..."

It wasn't the first time he'd suggested hunting down Weaver and Ellis. Those two had managed to escape the regulators, unlike their friends. Not exactly loyal soldiers.

"I wish we *could* eat the damn stuff." She tore her eyes from the Mithran and retrieved a battered tin pot from beneath the sink. Bleary-eyed, she poured in a measure of lentils, and added a few slices of the meat ends, as well. Her hands shook as she worked. She couldn't take much more of this. Surrounded by hundreds of people in a stinking, crowded city, being hunted by supernatural beings who would kill them all if they were discovered, stuck in a dark pit with two men who only made her feel more alone every day–

"Blast it! It's useless!"

Diver's angry outburst startled her. She scattered some of the precious legumes and her misery turned to anger. "Look what you made me do! We're already starving. We can't afford to waste food."

"Just pick them up," he suggested reasonably, and had to duck a thrown chunk of bread for his remark. "Damn it, Fury. Now who's wasting food?"

Fury's hands curled into fists. "You think the Mithran is useless? It's no more useless than you! How often have you gone out for supplies? When was the last time you tended the fire? Have you ever even once cooked food for us, or done anything other than play with that miserable pile of garbage?"

"You don't get it." Diver grasped the Mithran in his fist; it looked insubstantial, but it was strong as steel. Stronger. "This is what Heaven is made of – literally. Discovering its secrets is everything. It is magic, Fury, not 'garbage'!"

"Magic." She put all her disdain and frustration and anger into the word as she filled her pot with water from the rusty tap. It sputtered and stalled before resuming its thin, sad trickle. "More like madness. We should be focusing on how we're going to get home, not putting all our hopes into so-called magic."

"It is magic."

The smooth, dulcet tones had been ravaged by grief and pain, but it was Eleazar's voice. Fury turned to find him on his feet. He was trembling and white-faced. A stiff breeze could have sent him sprawling. Nevertheless, relief welled within Fury to see him standing. Not whole, not strong, but on his own two feet without encouragement or help from anyone. A miracle.

"Eleazar." Diver stood. "You're up. Are you…?"

"I am as well as I can be." Slowly, Eleazar crossed the room, setting each bare foot carefully ahead of the other. He stumbled only once, and Fury swallowed a gasp and gripped the edge of the sink behind her so she wouldn't jump to help him. Diver stared, stricken, but made no move to help him either, though his entire body seemed to strain toward the struggling Angelus.

"The Mithran." Diver held it out to him. "Can you help us? Do you know how to work the gods' metal?"

Eleazar reached the small table and took a seat. The rickety stool creaked under him, threatening to buckle. He leaned heavily on the table and gestured to Diver to lay out the Mithran. Eagerly, Diver spread it out. It nearly covered the nicked surface in coppery glory. It was a corset by all appearances. Considering how strong and resilient the material was, Fury wondered how it had been created. Even the wire binding it was Mithran. Only the laces at the edge were made of anything human. Bronze-colored silk.

"I wore it under my clothes for days," Diver said. "It improved my figure, I guess, but I didn't feel anything but discomfort. So why did someone go to all the trouble of turning it into a garment? And how did they do it? Maybe if I had a true forge, I could have melted it down. I don't know."

"Without an Angelus to work the bellows, the fires needed to melt Mithran would have to be very hot indeed," Eleazar said. He ran a hand across the material, and a wave of light followed its passing. "No, this was crafted by an Angelus. A gift for a lover, perhaps. It is a common practice. I–" and he paused, lost in a memory. "I had something like it commissioned for my betrothed. It was meant to grace her slender figure on our wedding day."

A flicker of jealousy roiled Fury's belly. Ridiculous, really, but she couldn't help herself. She imagined Eleazar's betrothed was a stunning beauty. Slim, graceful, feminine.

And a traitorous bitch. The wave of jealousy settled.

"Mithran is not truly metal," Eleazar continued, his tone casual as he spilled his people's secrets. "It is bone. Leviathan bone. Sacred, magical, powerful. And it is as much a part of the Angelus as it is the leviathans."

Bone. Fury covered her mouth with her hand, feeling ill. She dreamt about those creatures, the leviathans. Great, beautiful beasts moving peacefully through the cosmos with ponderous grace. They called to her in those dreams. In lamentations...

His eyes reflected the light as Eleazar picked up the edge of the corset and plucked one of the slats free. The fine wire unraveled at his touch; the Mithran practically leapt into his hand. Diver made a sound deep in his throat. How many hours had he spent trying to break off a piece of the stuff?

Eleazar manipulated the long, slender piece of golden material, turning it over in his hands. Light oozed from his palms, his face. His Charisma. Fury exhaled, relieved. Even without his wings, he still possessed it, though it seemed far weaker. The Mithran softened, grew pliable. He played with it as if it were clay.

"We can work the Mithran, make it suitable for the forge, for molding and crafting. It is the only thing Angelic artisans can do better than the humans. Humans have poor success with it, you see, though we've forced them to try. Just to be sure, you know. And yet, somehow, your kind has managed to put it to use."

"As a drug," Fury interjected disparagingly, recalling the stories she'd overheard on the streets. "One which maims and kills."

A soft chuckle rumbled from him. The Mithran in his hands had become a soft, bronze-colored ball the size of a walnut lit from within by unearthly light. "Yes. When I found out how humans were utilizing Mithran, it was all I could do to keep still. How could the Beasts of the Below be so close to understanding?"

"Understanding?"

Abruptly, Eleazar tossed the ball of Mithran into his mouth and swallowed. The light washed down his throat and passed into his chest, then down into his gut, dissipating and vanishing. Fury's eyes widened, and she glanced at Diver whose expression mirrored hers.

"Why did you do that?" Diver asked softly.

But why became apparent a moment later when color rose in Eleazar's cheeks. A spasm crossed his features, and he bent over the table, groaning.

"It isn't easy, ingesting the gift of the Luminous One," he said between pants. "In Splendour, it is consumed only at the most holy of ceremonies. For enlightenment. For healing. But. It is well worth the suffering. I suppose, even for us, it can be a drug of sorts."

His freshly mutilated wing shivered, knocking away the bandages Fury had placed over it. A sheath of feathers still clung to the stump, and they gleamed with sudden vigor. The remnant looked weeks-healed instead of days.

Diver murmured a soft, awed expletive. "Why didn't you do that earlier? When you were suffering from drug withdrawal? Maybe you wouldn't have been so desperate. Maybe you wouldn't have–"

He stopped himself, but Fury knew what he'd been about to say. Her cheeks burned. She lifted her chin stubbornly, not about to let him shame her, and went to stand near Eleazar. Her hands twitched, eager to touch him. Eleazar took a shuddering breath and straightened. He looked almost whole again. He picked up the Mithran and rolled it into a tight bundle.

"I didn't want to risk it, trapped as we were inside Vogel's mansion. I didn't want to reveal all our secrets. And my people were coming for me," he added ruefully. "I had only to manage until my rescue. But now I have no choice. I am abandoned. Banished."

The pain in his voice was palpable. Fury laid a gentle hand on his shoulder. He felt hard and cold, like a marble statue, but there was a glimmer of his usual heat.

"Will it... will it return your wings to you?" Diver asked tentatively.

Eleazar shook his head sadly. "Not in the way you may think, but I have a plan. Maybe 'plan' is too strong a word. Let's say I have an *idea*. But it is my hope to seek a transformation. It is why I lay in repose for as long as I did. I wasn't – it wasn't due to... hopelessness." His voice grew thick though he gave them both a weak smile and even went so far to lay his hand atop Fury's. The simple touch sent a cascading shock through her. She swallowed.

"I will never be the Angelus I was," he continued, resigned. "I have spent the past few days ruminating on my fate. I survived the fall from Splendour. I survived betrayal, not once, but twice. I am trapped in your world, unable to reclaim what is mine, but I refuse to slink away as Rast wishes. I refuse to be a – a 'feckless cunt' as he called me. I was a prince, destined to be king, and though now I am no better than a pinioned, no better than a man, I will bring down my enemies. I will bring them *crashing* down to me." His hand tightened around the Mithran corset. "I only need enough Mithran. And I need human minds, human hands. Human ingenuity."

"For what, Lee?" Fury asked when he fell silent. "What do you need?"

"Wings."

CHAPTER TWENTY-TWO

For days, Eleazar had lain in a stupor, his thoughts scrambled and confused. Depression, rage, grief, and hatred whirled inside his head like angry crows. He'd ached for laudanum, for the euphoric release of it, but it had been too much to even ask for it. Eventually, that need had lessened. It had been a relief. Finally, he was clear-headed. Himself again as laughable as it seemed with both his wings gone. Then, the golden light of the Mithran had been his focus, whispering promises. Of flight, of freedom, of vengeance.

All Angelus revered the bones of the leviathans. Mithran was a gift from the Luminous One. Eons ago, consuming it had granted the Angelus their wings, made them gods. They had torn entire continents from Avernus and risen to the skies. Among the clouds, it became even easier to hunt and kill the leviathans. The skin of the leviathans created the firmament. The blood of the leviathans created the Black Silence, a gateway separating them from the human world. As was right. And upon the bones of the leviathans, they had built their Aeries. They had created paradise: Splendour.

Except Splendour, for all its beauty, was a harsh place to live. Beneath the shining perfection was sterility. Their beautiful, floating islands struggled to grow anything edible. Crystal and gold and marble sprouted instead, along with flowering vines and perfectly manicured shrubbery which fit into their ideal of perfection but provided little sustenance. The ugliness of cultivation and animal husbandry had no place in Splendour, even if the land could have supported it. So they found their way back to Avernus and took what they needed.

In return for this bounty, they gave the humans the flesh of the leviathans. Manna. The Angelus could not consume manna. Ingesting their bones brought great power, but ingesting their flesh brought only suffering. They had tried, of course. But the manna caused deformities among their children, forcing them to cast entire generations from the islands and into the Black Silence. A dark and terrible time.

The Mithran had given his ancestors their wings, but it had taken generations and included other, more invasive breeding programs. The process and history of this evolution was shadowy, incomplete. Shrouded in myth and legend. Eating the Mithran would not grant Eleazar wings, but if he found a clever enough human, perhaps that human could build him a new set of wings. Their trains, their cunning weapons, their clever vehicles and their industry had built an amazing world. Trin was an ugly, smoke-filled place, but it was a miracle in its own right. Human-made.

With the Celestial Gate closed for now, and the Angelus back in Splendour, Eleazar felt free to act. He hoped to be ready when Pace returned.

That Pace had survived, he'd learned by chance. The captain's distinctive wings had been easy to spot among the searchers. It hadn't been difficult to hide from him. Angelic arrogance had worked in their favor. His heart had stammered to see him alive, though. It had been his profound hope Fury's knife and bullet had taken him down, but there was no denying his toughness and strength of will. Pace was his mother's most trusted and rewarded general for a reason.

Eleazar was not foolish enough to think Pace had given up hunting for the two humans who'd humiliated him. Only the closing of the Celestial Gate had stopped him this time. On the next occasion, he would be prepared to scour the city. He would bring reinforcements, no doubt. And if he threatened Vogel and his regulators enough, they would stop at nothing to find them.

"I will be ready," he said aloud to the empty apartment. He had been alone all day, pacing endlessly. Fury and Diver were out searching for the Mithran smugglers. Cautiously, carefully.

"They were trying to recruit me," Diver had reminded them when they'd been discussing a plan of action. "Weaver and Ellis. They're part of the smuggling ring, part of something even bigger, maybe. They need soldiers like me. They can help us."

In the end, they decided to make inquiries among the black-market traders, the criminals and thieves. To Eleazar, it had seemed fitting. This was the bottom, there was no going lower.

The sound of shuffling at the window made Eleazar stiffen. Without his wings, even the one, he felt vulnerable. His strength and speed was unmatched among the humans, his golden skin tough, resilient, but he was hardly bulletproof.

Luckily, it was a familiar pair of legs which slid into the apartment amidst a shower of snowflakes. It had been snowing for an entire week, and drifts constantly threatened to bury their lone window. Despite the inconvenience, the snowfall which had so captivated Eleazar in the woods proved equally magical as it covered the rough edges of the city. Not so much for Fury and Diver, who had nowhere near the tolerance for cold as he did.

A layer of snow covered Fury's head and clung to her coat. She untwined the thick scarf from around her face – stolen from a careless washer woman – and dashed the ice and snow from her curly hair as she stamped her feet. Her toes went numb in the cold.

"Blasted snow," she muttered, stripping off her insufficient coat – Diver had the good cloak today, having vowed to hunt the streets all night to find the two deserters. Fury had been to the market, carefully making inquiries about "golden pearls" as the Mithran drug was called here. She'd wanted to appear poor and desperate, which hadn't been difficult since they were poor and desperate. "Makes walking anywhere twice as difficult. Keeps people shuttered in their homes, too, even drug seekers, apparently."

"No luck, then?" he asked, moving to help her. "Here, give me those. You must be freezing!" Eleazar took her coat and hung it on a hook then turned back to her with the idea of wrapping his arms around her, but she was already slipping past him to go to their meager stove in the corner. He followed, frowning. He was far warmer than the sad little stove.

"Not even the residue of luck," she said grimly, then a moment later, "You let the fire go out!" With a growl of annoyance, she opened the grate then gathered up some of the piled trash beside it. "Did you forget we pathetic humans get cold?"

"It stinks," he said, watching her stuff trash and broken bits of wood into the opening. "And it hardly warms one corner of this miserable hole. Why bother with it?" He removed his shirt, the white silk a bleak grey by now. "Come here, Fury."

She didn't leave her task. If anything, she seemed even more determined to light the little stove. Kneeling on the hard floor, she took a match from its box, intending to strike it, but her hands were shaking terribly as she held it above the strip. He could almost read her mind: *Don't waste a match. There are so few left...*

"Fury," he urged. He rubbed his hands together to generate warmth. "Please. Come here. You're freezing."

Her shoulders slumped and she returned the match to its box, slowly, reluctantly. Even more slowly, she rose to her feet. He could almost hear her teeth chattering. She turned to him, her face downcast. "I – it's n – n – not a g – g – good idea."

"Nonsense." He approached her, moving as slowly and as carefully as she had. Since their one night together, he'd been reluctant to touch her, fearing she would shun him. Their last night together at Vogel's palace, she had avoided him, choosing a cold, empty bed over even sleeping in the same room with him. And then, there had been only horror and pain for days after that. Now, she stood stiffly, refusing to look at him, shaking almost convulsively with cold, rather than seek his embrace.

Did she hate him? Had he hurt her that night and ruined everything they'd built over the last months? But, no, he didn't believe that. The way she had screamed when Pace–

"Fury," he whispered. He laid his hands on her frigid cheeks. She shuddered violently. He moved down her neck to her shoulders, slipping his fingers beneath her thin shirt to massage her cold flesh. "Let me warm you, please." He kept one hand on her clavicle and plucked at her buttons with the other. "Will you allow me…?" he asked softly.

Reluctantly, she nodded and let him remove her shirt, leaving her only in an undershirt. It was thinner than her blouse and her shivering increased. Eleazar drew her close, pressing her against him. Her trembling didn't cease, but he felt her relaxing against him. A soft sigh slipped from her. He ran his hot hands down her back. She should have worn the leviathan skin beneath her clothes, but she'd been reluctant to be caught with it. Eleazar cursed himself. He should have insisted.

Her shivering stopped but she didn't move away from him. Nor did she wrap her arms around him, either. He didn't want to let her go. He wanted…

Desire flared within him, a fierce lance of heat. Deliciously painful. His sudden lust couldn't have been more obvious in their close embrace, but Fury didn't recoil as he'd half expected. And yet, she still did not embrace him.

"I'm sorry about… the balcony," he said. He rested his cheek on her hair, though he ached to do so much more. He ached to feel her legs around him again, to bury himself in her forever, but guilt nagged like meat caught in his teeth. "I was out of my mind. Half mad from the laudanum. I didn't mean to… to do what I did."

She stiffened. "So, you didn't really want me, then? That night?" Her voice was small. Suddenly, she seemed to hunch into herself. "Diver said I took advantage of you. Was he right?"

"What?" The agony in her voice astounded him. He'd been thinking only of his own part in that night, his own guilt. But how had she felt when he'd leaped from her arms so dramatically? His cheeks burned at the recollection of his violent retching. A moment before it had happened, she'd been stroking his hair, whispering his name…

"Oh, Fury, Fury." He took her face in his hands, forcing her to look at him. It wasn't easy. She was stiff, her face scrunched with pain, her eyes wounded. "That's not what I meant. I wanted you more than air that night. I thought I forced *you*. Humans do not say 'no' to an Angelus."

"Or perhaps no one can say no to you, Eleazar," she whispered, her gaze softening.

At last, she reached for him, her hands settling lightly on his waist, fingers spread wide as if to touch as much of him as she could. They were icy cold. Her thumbs pressed into the bones of his hip, sharper now after days of deprivation. "You've gotten skinny," she remarked, somewhat breathlessly. She wasn't pulling away now. Memories of their last encounter sent waves of want through him.

Eleazar groaned, pressing his forehead to her brow. "You vex me so, woman," he murmured. "And I must have you again. I *will* have you if you allow it. But–"

"Yes, Lee." She tipped her chin up, lips parted, begging to be kissed. Her nails dug into his flesh playfully, and she tugged him closer. "Yes," she said and nibbled at the sharp line of his jaw. "How many times must I say it?"

It was hard to speak with the flames coursing through him. She continued to tease him with her hands and mouth, and his breath grew hoarse in his throat. "Fury, please, I'm trying to tell you something. You must – know – Dear Luminous One!" The invective burst from him as she went to her knees before him, her hands busy at his belt. "Please!" he cried, catching at her persistent fingers. She stared up at him, her eyes bright with lust. He called himself every kind of fool as he stopped her with her full lips so close to him, but guilt raged along with his passion. He couldn't let her continue, not before she knew everything.

"Humans do not last long in Splendour," he managed to say. "I should have said so sooner, and I don't know why I'm telling you now, to be honest. I just don't want this lying like a – a field of ghouls between us." He had her by the wrists, holding her from him. "You should know everything before you give yourself to me. I am an Angelus, Fury, even without my wings. Cruel, selfish, wanton. It made me sad to see a slave die, but it was as if I lost a pet. I – I know I am different now, but I cannot change what I was. All the Angelus are like me, like I was. And Splendour is a cold and terrible place for humans. If – if your mother was taken to Splendour all those years ago, by now she must be dead."

He hated himself for telling her such an awful truth, and he hated himself for being an enabler of such an awful truth. If she hated him now, he wouldn't blame her…

Her dark eyes gleamed, inscrutable as she stared up at him. Slowly, she lowered her gaze then slowly stood. He ached to take back what he'd said and kept his hold on her wrists, afraid to let go lest he lose her forever. But she pulled free of his grasp. For a moment, she stood rigidly, staring at the floor between them. Eleazar trembled, wishing desperately to be in her arms once more, tempted to clasp her to him and beg forgiveness.

Finally, her eyes shot up at him, sharp and bright. "You don't know my mother," she said firmly. She reached up and took fistfuls of his hair, yanking him down to her for a hard, fervent kiss. With dizzying abruptness, she broke away. "If anyone can survive the impossible, it is Tuilelaith Cree. And that is the last we will say on it." Her hands returned to his belt, and she dropped once again to the hard, dirty floor. Eleazar managed a strangled moan and hoped his knees would hold.

***

It wasn't until much, much later, while she lay wrapped in Eleazar's arms, the taste of him on her lips, both of them sated, warm and limp with exhaustion that worry reared its ugly head and startled Fury awake. Eyes open, heart thudding, she stared at nothing, the worry nagging at her. Beside her, Eleazar purred in a deep, contented sleep, the only sound she could discern. It was dark. A deep, still darkness. The dead of night. Soon, the dark would tip toward dawn...

Diver had said he would search all night. But truly? She'd expected him home late, of course, but she'd expected him home long before morning. Where was he?

Even before she'd given Eleazar her breathless "yes", she had intended to be dressed and huddled on her own sad, lonely pallet by the time Diver returned. For Diver's sake, she would go on pretending there was nothing between her and Lee. Unfortunately, the entire Koine army couldn't have dragged her away from the Angelus after they'd collapsed together in a tangle of limbs and sweat and salt. If Diver came home before she could cover her crimes, then so be it.

And that was all the thought she'd given her brother. Her *missing* brother. It landed like a punch to her stomach. A cold sweat covered her. Dear Creator, where was he?

"Lee," she whispered. She elbowed him in his abdomen. "Lee. Wake up."

He growled low in his throat and engulfed her, his arms and legs pinning her securely. If not for the worry churning in her gut she would have let him bury her in his embrace. The touch of his skin against hers sent electric shocks deep inside her. She'd only *thought* she was satiated–

"Diver," she gasped, struggling to free herself, albeit without much conviction.

"Hmmm? Is he back?"

"No. He's not. I don't like it." She extricated herself from his arms and sat up. The chill in the air was even worse when compared to Eleazar's warmth. She shivered. "Something's happened to him. I know it."

The certainty in her voice brooked no argument. She felt him sit up beside her. "What should we do?"

"Find him," she said flatly. "Get dressed, Angelus."

CHAPTER TWENTY-THREE

The acrid smell of burned air, tortured metal and sweat filled Diver's nostrils, but it still wasn't enough to mask the absinthe-and-lavender scent of the man beside him. He tried to filter the different aromas and ignore how his stomach flipped every time he breathed in his captor's scent.

Perhaps "captor" wasn't accurate, but he was blindfolded with his hands bound before him, so…

He hadn't been kidnapped – he was a willing prisoner – and this was what he'd sought: Entry into the smugglers' inner circle. Access to the humans and their Mithran source. Eleazar's need was now his need, too. Nevertheless, he was tense and on edge, and hyper-aware of the risk he was taking. The rope around his wrists was a formality rather than a restraint. It wouldn't take much to break free.

The sudden, intense heat, rhythmic clanging of hammer on steel and the sizzle of showering sparks (even through his blindfold he could see the flashes of light) coupled with the distinct smells revealed he'd been brought to a foundry. A firm grip on his arm guided him through the noisy, smelly place, away from the heat source, thankfully. He heard a door slam shut, and the noise lessened significantly. A moment later, the blindfold was whisked from his eyes, revealing once again a familiar face and a familiar grin.

"Hello again, soldier boy."

He'd hated being called that back in the queue. The dismissive condescension had rankled. But in this more intimate setting, with its undercurrent of peril, the nickname sent a little tingle through him.

When he'd heard it whispered in his ear earlier that night at a crowded underground club, it had elicited an unexpected level of excitement. The club catered to a very specific clientele. A place of crystal sconces, velvet wallpaper, dark leather couches and finely dressed gentlemen. Diver stood out in his drab, mended clothing. His obvious lack of funds didn't work against him, though. He'd been fending off advances from tipsy patrons, watching for one particular man.

"Why, hello, soldier boy..."

At the sultry greeting, a hot caress of air tickling his ear, Diver had grown lightheaded from the electric thrill which rocketed through him. A thoroughly unexpected reaction, but nonetheless enjoyable. He took a sip of the green fairy to gather himself, one hand gripping the brass railing of the bar. Weaver invaded his space with bold indifference, grinning cheekily as he bellied up alongside him. He'd lost his uniform and wore the fine clothes of a dandy, down to a lace cravat at his throat. His fiery red hair was slicked to his scalp but for a curl across his forehead. He was clean-shaven and smelled like flowers. A very different man from the one he remembered.

Slim, well put together, tall and confident. *Damn*. Just his type. Diver's face burned and he hoped the dim lighting hid it, though he should have known better. Weaver was a sharp observer, and he'd had his eye on Diver from the beginning.

"Yeah," the lean man said, squeezing so close he jostled Diver's elbow. "I've missed you, too."

"It's about time," Diver said, settling his drink on the varnished bar. "I've been waiting for you. Figured you'd find your way into one of these places eventually."

"'These places?'" He scoffed. "Seems you're pretty comfortable here yourself. And quite popular to boot," he added somewhat petulantly.

Diver's lips quirked. Was he jealous? Of Diver, or of the men seeking his attention? "Lots of men like the look of me." He shrugged.

"It's not hard to get attention with a face like yours." He sidled closer, sneaking a hand toward Diver's drink. He flicked the crystal coupe with a manicured nail, making it ring. "Fancy another?"

"This isn't a social call. I'm here on business. Captain."

Weaver pushed his face close to Diver's. "No need for insults," he said. "I'm trying to be friendly, kid."

Diver bristled, though his heart was pounding. He turned a cold shoulder, slamming back his drink in one go. "I have enough friends, thank you. This is business."

"Friends." The sneer in his voice was loud and clear. "What friends? That big, angry girl with the fancy scarf? Or the golden-haired crippled angel who got my friends arrested? I don't see either one of them here to watch your back."

"Does my back need watching?" Diver asked, though Weaver's remark about Eleazar made his blood boil. "Are you planning on stabbing me?"

"I should." He poked him in the ribs, hard, making Diver wince and whirl to face him. It took everything he had not to go for the knife in his jacket. Weaver got in his face, trying to stare him down from his greater height. "You've been stirring the pot quite a bit lately, you little bumpkin," he said in a low, hot voice. "Asking questions that shouldn't be asked. Drawing attention you do not want, believe me. Just be glad I found you first."

"I was looking for *you*–"

"I *know* what you were looking for, and I know who is looking for you, *atheist scum*."

This last he said in a harsh whisper. Suddenly aware of the bustling crowd all around them, Diver moved closer. His chin nearly touched the shoulder of Weaver's velvet jacket. To outside observers, they would look like two canoodling lovers.

The smell of lavender threatened to overwhelm Diver's good sense, along with an intoxicating musk that was Weaver's alone. His eyes fixed on the throbbing pulse point beneath the pale skin of his neck.

"Then you know what I've risked searching for you. We need your help. Joseph."

The man jerked slightly. Hiding a smile, Diver pretended to nuzzle Weaver's neck, blowing gently just to tease him. Not to be outdone, the redhead trailed his fingers down Diver's chest and chuckled, low and throaty. "Why, Diver?" Ah, so now they were on a first-name basis. "Why take such a risk for that... that *creature*?"

The disgust was clear in his voice, but it didn't anger Diver this time. He'd once felt the same. "You wouldn't understand unless you'd been through what we've been through together."

"Oh, really? And what have you been through together? You and your broken god?"

Jealousy again. Diver's lips twitched. "Perhaps I'll tell you. One day. For now, know that I need your help. He needs your help. And all of us together might have a mutual goal."

Weaver played with the collar of Diver's shirt then chucked him under the chin, forcing Diver's gaze up to his. "And what goal is that?" he asked, though he seemed poised for a kiss. He had a very kissable mouth. Diver swallowed, telling himself it was the tension of the moment fueling his attraction.

"Why," and it took everything not to stammer, "to storm the gates of Heaven, of course."

After that, Weaver had agreed to take him to his people. Eventually, of course. First, he'd taken him on a circuitous route through the underbelly of the city: Dance clubs, illicit fighting rings, opium dens, plying him with liquor to muddle his mind, no doubt. Diver had enjoyed it despite his eagerness to find the smugglers. A bit sharp-tongued, Weaver was nevertheless witty and playful and seemed to be on friendly terms with almost every prostitute they encountered, male and female.

Finally, Weaver took him into an alley, arm-in-arm and singing loudly. Just two drunken idiots out for a good time. Once in the concealing dark, he'd wheeled Diver, put his back against a brick wall and pulled out a length of black silk.

"I think we've already played about quite enough tonight," Diver said upon seeing it. "Either take me to your lair or let me on my way."

"It's not for play." He grew suddenly serious, and remarkably sober given the amount of absinthe he'd consumed. "I tried to get you good and lost, but I still can't let you see the way to our compound."

"Compound? Are you serious?"

Weaver sighed and folded the piece of silk lengthwise into a long strip. A blindfold.

"As serious as a heart attack, kid." He ran the cloth through his fingers. "This is your last chance to turn back. Once we let you in, we can't ever let you go, you understand? Not just you, but all of you. You join us and there's no changing your mind and opting out. What we do is far too important to risk ne'er-do-wells and malingerers among us."

"There is no 'opting out' for us," Diver said with a fatalistic shrug. "There is nowhere safe on Avernus to run. Not until we destroy that which threatens us. If your cause aligns with ours, we will willingly join you."

"Do you speak for the others? The Angelus and your sister? Does he want to wage war against his own?"

"Eleazar the Fallen will be the greatest weapon in your arsenal. I swear it."

And finally, Weaver had led him here, to this room inside a foundry, and they were no longer alone.

"So," spoke a voice from behind Weaver. A male voice. Deep and rough. "This is the man who killed an Angelus?"

The man sounded doubtful. Weaver gave him a wink and stepped aside, revealing his compatriot. The man, dressed in workman's clothing, a cap over his straw-colored hair, was burly and squat and missing his left eye. A twisted scar ran through it and down half his cheek. Diver's gut tightened in empathy. That must have hurt. They were in an office of sorts, though the wooden filing cabinets were broken, and papers were scattered haphazardly about. The man was sitting on the edge of a battered desk, appraising Diver.

"Two, actually," Diver said coolly. "And who are you, sir?"

"Sir," he drawled, smiling. "I like that. You sound like Weaver when he first got here. All soldierly and whatnot."

"I was trained to respect authority," Weaver said, grinning. "You certainly broke me of that habit, boss."

The man's eye fixed on Diver, icy blue. "Call me Conrad," he said. His expression hardened. "You've been making a lot of noise lately. You and your... sister? I can see the resemblance. You're both Gullan anyway. Well, half-Gullan, I suspect."

Shrewd man, this Conrad. "Does it bother you? Some think my people cursed."

"It bothers me to see a Gullan in league with an Angelus. They cursed your people. It's in all the scripture, right? Way to turn on your own."

"You're Koine and you are in league with an Akkadian," Diver countered. "And a Naveen, too. You seem open to many different allies. Why should my choice of companion bother you?"

"Because the Angelus are the enemy of us all, boy," he growled. He crossed his arms over his barrel chest and leaned back, regarding him. "Koine, Akkadian, Naveen, Gullan. We are *human*. The same no matter what country we call home. The Angelus are monsters."

"Not Eleazar," Diver said sharply. "He is a better man than most humans, I can guarantee."

"'Eleazar,'" Conrad mocked in a sing-song voice, rolling his single eye. "I heard his name shouted across the city: Eleazar the Fallen! And now suddenly he wants my Mithran. Has his little minions searching the city for me. I don't like it. Not one bit."

"He wants to take vengeance against those who cast him from Splendour. He needs Mithran to achieve it. That's all. It isn't some trick to lure you out!"

"Sure. Even if all you say is true, what's in it for me? For my people? Why should I give anything to an Angelus, even one out for revenge against his own kind? Once he gets what he wants, what's to prevent him from destroying my entire operation out of pique?"

"He wouldn't do that!"

Weaver laughed. "How can a hardened soldier be so naïve?" he said to Conrad.

Diver bristled, his bound hands bunching into fists. Suddenly, Weaver was far less attractive to him, what with the ugly sneer on his face. He suppressed his inexplicable need to defend Eleazar. It wouldn't get him anywhere with these two. They had to see a measurable value in an alliance with him.

"What is it you are hoping to accomplish here?" he asked. "You've managed only to transform the sacred Mithran into a drug, at best. Though from what I've heard, it maims and kills humans more than it harms the Angelus. Why do you think they let you have it at all? Even with all your effort, the Mithran remains useless to you!"

"You have no idea what we've built here," Weaver snapped angrily. "The things we've–"

"Shut up, Weaver."

The redhead subsided immediately, deferring to Conrad with surprising meekness. Conrad regarded Diver with his bright eye. He raised a hand to touch the scar on his cheek. A shimmer of gold rippled through the twisted seam. "We've made remarkable progress working with Mithran. The engineers and craftsmen we have gathered are the best and brightest in all of Trin. Perhaps in all of Avernus. But we haven't found a way yet to touch the Angelus in their flying ships. To bring down those monsters. And, believe me, we have tried."

"Having just had my own encounter with them, I imagine it ended quite badly for you," Diver said. "We at least got close with Eleazar by our side."

"That advantage is lost to you, if I'm to believe he's been banished."

"Believe it. They took his wings, called him 'man'. Eleazar is no longer one of them." Diver leaned forward excitedly. "And he burns for vengeance. Enough that he will share his talents with you, his abilities."

"What talent?" Conrad scoffed. "The Angelus don't do anything but oppress and threaten."

"I watched him mold Mithran like clay. It responds to the Angelus. Imagine the possibilities with him here to help you. The gods' metal. Their whole world is built upon it. It's *fueled* by it."

A spark lit Conrad's eye. He and Weaver exchanged another inscrutable glance.

"Let me bring him here," Diver pleaded. "You must want to at least meet with him."

"We'd very much like to meet your Angelus, actually," Weaver interjected. "It's why you're here, after all." A small, rueful grin. "But we'll be meeting with him on our terms, not yours."

Diver made a frustrated noise, twisting his hands in his bonds. "Then what did you need me for?"

His grin widened. "Bait."

CHAPTER TWENTY-FOUR

They didn't dare leave the Mithran behind, nor anything else of importance. Eleazar felt a profound shift when he crawled out the window on Fury's heels. The air outside was crystalline. His breath fogged in great clouds, but to him the cold was exhilarating. The snow had ended sometime during the night and the narrow aspect of sky above them was clear. Fading stars announced imminent dawn. He cast a final look at the place they'd exited and knew deep in his bones they would not be returning.

Fear tempered the nervous excitement coursing through him. He was keenly aware of the loss of his wings, and he felt more vulnerable than he had since he'd first awoken in Fury's little house, injured and alone in an alien world. Trin was far worse, far stranger. Far more dangerous. He tugged the blanket he had draped around his shoulders a bit tighter. The Mithran girded his torso, a much tighter fit on him than on Diver, but it gave him a semblance of his previous invulnerability. The leviathan skin was draped loosely about Fury's neck, and she carried their remaining weapons strategically hidden on her person. With Eleazar beside her, her thin coat was sufficient to stave off the winter chill so long as she kept close to him. Hunched forward against a cold he didn't feel, wrapped in a tattered blanket, a knitted cap hiding his glorious hair and the stolen scarf covering his face, Eleazar turned to Fury.

"Where do we start?" he asked, his voice muffled by the scarf.

"I know where he's been looking for that Akkadian captain. We'll begin there."

The streets of Trin were white and silent beneath a blanket of snow. But as the sun rose, people emerged from their tenements. Soon, muddy slush clung to Eleazar's fine boots and soaked his pants nearly to the knees. Fury led the way as they dodged grumbling citizens, threading their way upriver in the flow. She took them down street after street until Eleazar was certain they'd never find their way back home even if they had planned on returning.

Finally, they found the street she wanted. Here, dens of ill repute had clientele stumbling into the sunlight with blinking, pained expressions. Fury's gaze traveled over the thin stream of stragglers, her fingers digging into his elbow, worried but not frantic. He scanned the area, too; his eyes were far sharper than hers. There was no sign of Diver and they broadened their search as the pale sun lifted higher and higher. Eleazar followed Fury's lead, overwhelmed by the number of people. Everyone looked the same to him, all these humans–

A glimpse of dark braids and broad shoulders tickled his memory. Eleazar grabbed Fury's arm and dragged her to a halt. "Look there." He pointed across the muddy street. "Isn't that...?"

A beeping lorry blocked their view for a moment, but then the target was revealed. The tall, dark-skinned figure was unmistakable. Any doubts vanished when Ellis looked over her shoulder and grinned at them. Before Eleazar could stop her, Fury started across the street, dodging traffic and leaping puddles. With a low curse, he chased after her.

"Ellis!" she shouted, forced to pull up short when a gaggle of chimney sweeps skipped past her. She cursed the little urchins and one of them stuck out his tongue, calling her "old maid!" while his compatriots howled with laughter. By the time they got across, Ellis had vanished.

"She slipped down an alley," Fury said, pulling him down the sidewalk.

"Don't lose her!"

"I won't."

They nearly caught up with the ex-soldier a few times only to lose her when she took a sudden turn down a side street or slipped into a shop. It was a game. She was leading them, taunting them. Infuriating. Using their concern for Diver to lure them. To lure him. Did she think to trap him? She would be sorely disabused of that notion.

They caught Ellis at last down a blind alley. Faced with an ice-shrouded wall, she put her back to it and waited for them, unconcerned. She *appeared* unarmed.

Fury dragged Eleazar to a halt a body length from her. "Where is he?" Her voice was shrill with anger. She grasped the ends of her scarf and whipped it free from her neck. Slowly, she wound the ends of it around her fists, creating a short, stiff length of cloth like a shield in front of her.

Ellis's eyes narrowed at her move. "Safe," she said. "Patiently waiting for you."

"You're holding him captive!" Fury scowled at Ellis' dismissive shrug. "We've been searching everywhere for you. For days! Why do this? We could have met like civilized people!"

Another shrug. "It's how we operate. My mates are not the trusting sorts." She gave Eleazar a pointed look. "And we don't like the company you keep. With or without wings, an Angelus is not to be trusted!"

"I have found most humans to be less than trustworthy, as well," Eleazar countered blandly. Slowly, he unwound the scarf from around his face. He removed his knit cap and shook his golden locks, aware of how they caught the light. Without his wings, his Charisma was weaker but not gone. He let it fill him. The power gave him confidence. Ellis moved closer to him, irresistibly drawn. Even she was susceptible to Angelic charm. Ellis's expression grew slack, her lips parting.

"But I would like to trust you, my lady," he continued in a low, seductive voice. "After all, we have a mutual enemy. Together, we may be able to achieve the impossible." He took a step toward her. "Take us to our companion and we can–"

A fine mesh net dropped onto him from above. Startled, Eleazar grasped it. It seemed insubstantial, certainly nothing an Angelus couldn't tear apart. A poor attempt to ensnare him. Almost laughable. Beside him, Fury reached out with a scarf-wrapped hand.

"Don't touch it!" Ellis shouted, lunging to grab her, suddenly bright-eyed and alert despite Eleazar's Charisma.

Fury used the length of scarf stretched between her fists to turn Ellis's arm aside, knocking her off-balance. In a flash, she had the woman from behind, the scarf wrapped around her neck. The ex-soldier dropped to a knee, attempting to throw her attacker, but a yank of Fury's fists had her under control. Growling, his Charisma disrupted, Eleazar took hold of the net, intending to tear it apart.

The only warning was a low hum, and then a fierce shock blasted through him. It froze him in place, muscles spasming, teeth locked, waves of pain immobilizing him. Fury was shouting. Calling for him. He couldn't move. The shock went on and on, an eternity of agony.

Then it vanished. He staggered. His skin steamed. He tried to tear through the netting, but he had no strength. The hard, slick cobblestones leapt up to slam him. Meltwater soaked through his clothes, and for the first time since he'd fallen to Avernus, he felt *cold*.

"Eleazar!" Fury screamed. Distantly, her voice muffled by a fierce ringing. The vibrations of booted feet rose up through the ground and into his bones, the sensations amplified by whatever had been done to him.

"Well, well, well." A stranger's voice stretched out in a slow drawl, full of conceit. "The mighty Angelus caught like a fly in a spider's web."

"I told you it would work!" Another voice, this one vaguely familiar. More stomping feet, scuffling, and Fury's angry screeching. He knew when bodies hit the ground, felt it like a blow to his stomach. A thin, high mewling was the only protest he could manage.

"Creator damn you all, get her under control!"

"I'm trying, Conrad!"

Another flurry of movement, then abrupt stillness. Eleazar fought to move, terrified for Fury, but his bones were trembling, his muscles melted into wax.

"You didn't need to do that!"

"She had you in a chokehold—"

"Fucking dunce!"

The voices descended into incoherent squabbling. Eleazar felt a tear slide across his nose. The stones were freezing beneath his cheek. Someone rolled him onto his back, and he blinked against sudden brightness. A shadow blocked the sun. A face. It came closer. A leering eye. A hideous scar. Teeth bared in a malicious smile.

Eleazar's mouth worked. "Kill... you..."

"No doubt you wish to. Don't worry. Your girl is fine. She might have a headache later, but she'll be good as new in a day or so."

Relief gave way to anger. A muddled sort of anger given the circumstances. "Why?" he said, the word high and wheedling. Pathetic. "I need... help."

"Are you begging, Angelus?"

Eleazar struggled to lift a hand and managed to flop it onto his chest. His fingers wouldn't work properly. He scrabbled at his shirt. The man seemed to understand and pulled it open for him. The Mithran illuminated the man's scarred face. His eyes narrowed.

"You brought a gift," he cried mockingly. His tone hardened and he thumped Eleazar's chest. "Do you think we're stupid? Do you think we'd trust one of your kind?" He scoffed. "You ask me 'why?' after my comrades witnessed your betrayal?

Star is a true hero, and you threw her to the wolves! You don't make the rules here, Angelus. This is a human place. You get our help on our terms."

If he hadn't been so incapacitated, Eleazar would have killed this man without regret. Instead, he swallowed every scrap of pride he'd ever possessed. "What... terms?"

"Depends on how useful you are. Then maybe we can negotiate."

If he was lying about Fury, or if any harm had befallen Diver, Eleazar would unleash hell upon him. Once he got the chance.

His eyes must have betrayed his rage because the man smirked down at him and waved a languid hand. "Tully," he said. "Make him reasonable."

He felt the vibration of footsteps, then something pinched the side of his neck. It was beyond him even to jerk away from the sensation. A flood of warmth followed the pinch, and all coherent thought vanished.

"Fury! Fury, please, for the love of all, wake up!"

The urgent demands drew her from the fog. Fury blinked open gritty eyes and was met with water-stained plaster. She took stock of her battered body, momentarily ignoring the voice pecking at her insistently. *Diver*. She knew this and felt a numb relief, but she also knew her arms were wrenched behind her, her wrists tightly bound. Maybe her ankles, too, but the pounding in her head was the worst.

Someone had clubbed her. The wretched pain in her skull throbbed. She remembered multiple attackers. Remembered Ellis breaking loose, though the woman had tried to defend her despite Fury putting her in a chokehold. Tried to keep the others at bay. Fury had fought like a wild cat, tossing off attackers, disarming some, striking others in the face with the whip of her scarf. But there had been too many of them. One of them–

Weaver. He'd been the only one with a bludgeon. *Bastard.*

"Fury. Please wake up!"

"Stop shouting," she moaned.

A hitching sob answered her. "I'm sorry. I thought they'd killed you!"

With painstaking effort, she rolled away from the wall and was forced to lurch like a landed fish to face him. Her brother sat tied to a chair in the center of a stark, four-walled windowless room. A single bare lightbulb hung from the ceiling, flickering.

Her stomach roiled. That web... Eleazar. She'd never imagined he could be brought down so quickly and efficiently. Not him. Dear Creator, how huge a blunder had they made?

"Where have they taken Lee?" She struggled into a sitting position. They hadn't bound her ankles, but she didn't think she could stand quite yet. Panic broke through her like cracking ice. "They *electrocuted* him. I don't even know if he's alive!"

"He's alive. They want to use him to work the Mithran. They have a whole cabal of engineers and craftsmen and artisans here. Slavering like dogs to learn how to use the gods' metal."

"He would have done it willingly." Her eyes burned. "They didn't need to do this."

"I know, I tried to explain it to them. No one would listen, no one would believe me. Imagine a room full of Mothers. The hate and distrust toward any and all Angelus is insane."

Fury curled over her knees. "What will they do to him?"

Diver shook his head, twisting at his bonds in frustration. They'd tied his feet to the legs of the sturdy chair, but Fury could see he'd managed to work one foot free. Not that it would do him much good. He settled back into the chair, practically growling. "I swore our loyalty to them, Fury. Like a great, blind idiot. I swore Eleazar wanted the same thing as they do – to bring down the Angelus, to change the world! And this is how they treat us. When I get out of here, I'll tear them all apart!"

The door to their cell swung open.

"Don't be so hasty, kid," spoke a grinning Joseph Weaver, a tray of food balanced on one hand.

His amused expression slackened to one of shock as Diver half stood, chair still firmly attached to him, and lunged for the doorway. The tray went flying in a clatter of ceramic dishes and an arc of spilled milk. Weaver barely got his hands up before Diver barreled into him. Both vanished from the room. Between Diver's roaring and Weaver's screeching came the sound of cracking wood.

Suddenly, Fury found the strength to scramble to her feet. She raced after her brother, eager to join the mayhem, never mind her bound hands, driven by pure rage.

She found the two men grappling on the floor, Diver's ropes loose and the chair shattered. He had Weaver pinned, an arm free and ready with a fist. Snarling, Weaver yanked his head aside. Diver's blow glanced off his cheek. Fury aimed a foot at the Akkadian's skull. "Hold him still!" she ordered.

Weaver rolled frantically, taking him and Diver out of her reach, though she managed to land a kick on the man's back. He spewed a vile curse at her, slammed Diver against the floor with one hand and tried to grab her leg with the other. She danced back and hit a solid wall of flesh. Whoever had her held her in a headlock before she could bounce free. It was Ellis: Fury shifted her feet to throw the woman. Chuckling, Ellis manhandled her back into place.

"Calm down," she said, putting pressure on her neck. Fury's vision dimmed and she went limp. The pressure eased.

"Stop this at once!" demanded a high, clear voice. The two men rolling on the floor ignored this newcomer's order, flailing at each other more like schoolboys than trained soldiers. Ellis muttered in Fury's ear, "Idiots."

This new person was short-statured, slight of build with close-cropped silver hair and thick goggles. Dressed in a boiler suit, it was hard to guess their gender. Their disdain, however, was crystal clear. "So many children in this place," they complained. With an aggrieved sigh, they pulled a pistol from the holster at their belt. Fury tensed. Would this odd person shoot Diver?

No, not Diver. The stranger pressed the barrel against *Fury's* temple.

"Stop playing or the girl gets it!"

Instantly, Diver froze. Weaver took the opportunity to clock him one last time. Blood spurted from Diver's nose, and he swore viciously, clapping his hands to his face. His ill-conceived escape plan fizzled to a halt.

"Right. Better." The gun went back in its holster and the person dusted off their hands in satisfaction. "Now. Which one of you is the healer?" Thick lenses turned toward Fury, the eyes behind ludicrously magnified. "Is it you, girl? You look competent."

"B – b – both," Fury stammered. "We're both healers!"

The stranger looked doubtful. They rubbed their pointed chin, contemplating.

"They are siblings, Master Tully," Ellis said. She'd loosened her hold, and Fury knew she could easily break free. She didn't even try. "Similarly trained, no doubt. We might need both of them."

Tully hesitated a moment longer then nodded decisively. "Yes, both will do. The Angelus needs all the help he can get. For a creature who supposedly fell from Splendour, he's awfully fragile."

CHAPTER TWENTY-FIVE

Eleazar screamed, his teeth crunching through the wooden dowel in his mouth. Pain roared through his shoulder blades, hot and terrible. He smelled burning flesh as another bolt speared him. Spread-eagled on a steel rack, shackled firmly in place, arms and legs and torso immobilized by canvas straps, Eleazar was at the mercy of these so-called engineers.

What were they doing to him? There had been only a moment of discussion, hurried and whispered, before he was readied for the rack. He was bare to the waist in the brutal heat from the forge – a massive contraption of steel and molten metal, noisy and vile, like a demon from the Abyss. Sweat poured down his flanks. Perhaps blood, too. He tried not to think about it. He was desperate for this torture to end, and desperate for it to continue. But his Charisma was nearly exhausted. How much longer *could* he go on?

Eleazar spat the splintered dowel from his mouth. "Stop," he ordered hoarsely.

Too late. Another lance of fire tore through the tattered remnant of his right wing. This time, his scream rivaled the thumping boom of the forge. His tormentors exclaimed in alarm, and a wash of cool water sluiced over him.

"Alright, that's enough, give him a chance to breathe."

Conrad. His harsh voice was unmistakable. He wasn't one of the engineers, but he was the mastermind behind this whole operation. Eleazar couldn't help the surge of hatred at the sound of his voice. He'd admitted he was holding Fury and Diver as collateral until Eleazar proved his unwavering commitment. It was entirely unnecessary. Eleazar had already capitulated. Completely, irrevocably. Fury might be disappointed in him for how easily he had caved, especially after they had been so brutally attacked. But... she hadn't seen the drawings.

They'd dragged him here, half conscious, nearly paralyzed, and propped him at a table covered in great sheets of paper. Surrounded by men armed with long sticks which hummed at one end, Eleazar didn't even attempt to fight. Not even his fear for his friends could give him the necessary strength. Besides all that, he needed to know if what he desired was possible. So, he sat in meek compliance and studied the papers before him.

Someone named Tully shuffled them about eagerly, explaining the different designs, the ideas and inspirations they dreamt of developing. With Eleazar's help, of course. "I never thought to see an Angelus among us," they'd exclaimed more than once, seemingly flabbergasted at Eleazar's presence. "Do you understand what we might achieve if we can produce an alloy with Mithran? To actually tap into the Angelus's greatest magic? I – I can hardly contain myself!"

"What might you achieve?" Eleazar had asked, slowly, painfully. His teeth hurt. "And how might it help me?"

Tully had smiled at his question, full of smug triumph. Then another drawing had been revealed. This one an elaborate sketch with various elements drafted out in painstaking detail. Eleazar froze, riveted by what he was seeing.

Wings. Fashioned from steel and Mithran. The two metals merged into one. An alloy, Tully called it. Something new, something glorious.

Theoretically, these mechanical wings might allow him to fly again. Tully had been sure to emphasize "theoretically", but Eleazar had agreed to the experiment without hesitation. Perhaps the sedative they'd dosed him with had made him more compliant; he didn't care. When he'd laid eyes on those drawings... not even the Luminous One could have convinced him not to at least try.

How quickly he'd given himself over to these monsters for the chance to fly again...

The canvas straps bit into his arms as Eleazar sagged in his restraints, gasping desperately. He hadn't expected Conrad to show any mercy, but he was pathetically grateful for the chance to catch his breath. Tully, on the other hand, seemed put out by the suggestion.

"Now? We almost have the framework in place," they said. "By the Luminous One, I've never been able to manipulate Mithran so easily. Soft as bronze, I tell you! It's like sculpting a masterpiece. We can't stop now."

"I don't know. He's not as... as 'glowy' as he was before," said one of the other engineers, a bear of a man with an impressive beard and massive hands. He was also one of the gentler of his tormentors. "I think we've drained him."

"For the Creator's sake, Rory, he's not a damned battery."

"Right, boss," came Rory's meek reply. Then he added somewhat challengingly, "He's a person, though, isn't he?"

Someone scoffed. "He's an Angelus."

Tully again. The genius behind the drawings, and the idea to merge Mithran and steel. Man or woman, Eleazar couldn't tell, but they had absolutely no sympathy for his pain.

Eleazar gripped the steel frame beneath him, listening to his new "allies" debate his wellbeing while he desperately tried to catch his breath. Agony had tempered his desperation for new wings, but the desire still raged. It wasn't enough to merely *dream* about flying. He would endure anything to be whole again.

"I need a new bit, please," he said, his head spinning. He would continue if it killed him. He felt his Charisma pulsing weakly, reduced to a wisp. "I can continue..."

The spinning turned to stars, and all the strength drained from him. His head lolled to the side, too heavy to hold up.

"Eh – fuck! Angelus. Angelus!"

A rough shake of his shoulder, and the last thing he heard before darkness took him was Conrad's frantic order, "Get the atheists, Tully. Quick…"

They didn't bother with restraints this time. Ellis, Weaver and the newcomer, Tully, marched them down cramped, windowless corridors that felt more like tunnels than hallways. Diver had a suspicion as to where they'd taken the Angelus, so he wasn't surprised when the temperature began to rise and the smell of the forge seared his aching nostrils. He poked gingerly at his injured nose. Was it broken? At least it had stopped bleeding, though it still burned abominably.

Beside him, Fury walked so fast she was clipping Tully's heels. Ellis had her by the arm, but it was Fury dragging the other woman along.

Diver probed an aching cheek. Fucking Weaver. His stomach ached with worry for Eleazar, but his blood boiled.

"Ass," he muttered, touching his battered nose again.

"I didn't break it," Weaver said in a low, sullen voice. He had Diver by the arm, too, unnecessarily.

"Feels like it," Diver said, scowling. "So much for my pretty face, yeah?"

"It doesn't look so bad." His grip on Diver's arm tightened momentarily, almost like a reassuring squeeze. "I could get you some ice…"

"I want nothing from you."

There was a frustrated growl beside him, then: "You *attacked* me."

"Oh? Are we listing offenses? Because I think I'll win." He spoke out of the side of his mouth in a low, angry whisper. "You tricked me, used me as bait, ambushed my friends – my own sister! – and tied me to a fucking chair. Be glad I only tackled you, you rotten scoundrel."

"Scoundrel?" He sounded amused, though Diver failed to see the humor in this situation. "Scoundrel... how quaint."

Seething, Diver fell silent. He should have known better than to trust a former Akkadian soldier, especially one belonging to the infamous Iron Corps. No better than rabid murderers, that bunch. He'd witnessed one of their "operations" firsthand. He still had nightmares about that mass, shallow grave. The tiny hands poking up through the bloody soil...

Diver shuddered.

"Hey now," Weaver said. "You alright?"

He bit down on his first, brutal response and was shocked at the surge of emotion the gentle question evoked. Tears stung his eyes and he blinked rapidly, turning his face away from Weaver so he wouldn't see.

Luckily, they had entered another, wider hallway built of brick and timbers and their destination lay ahead, so Diver didn't need to hide his face for long.

"We're here," Tully announced, stopping at a set of wide, sliding wooden doors at the end of the broad tunnel. The clanking boom and metallic thumps of a factory forge seeped through them. Tully dragged one door open. Beyond, the room was shadowed and smoky, the air acrid. The surreal glow from the molten metals and forge fires lit the vast space, the edges lost in shadows. Only part of the forge seemed in operation. Giant metal crucibles hung from the raftered ceiling in an ominous row, silent and cold. Shadowy figures moved against the backdrop of the working forge.

Diver suppressed the urge to cough. Beside him, Fury gasped in horror and bolted forward abruptly. A group of people were gathered around a table near the brightly burning forge, heads bent and murmuring. One had a bucket of water and a dripping sponge. A man lay on the table.

"Eleazar!" Diver cried and dashed after his sister.

"Get away from him!" Fury shrieked as she shoved her way to the table. A big, burly man moved aside without hesitation, his eyes wide. Another man wearing a long, leather apron, his mouth covered by a kerchief against the fumes, tried to restrain her and received an elbow to the throat for his trouble. He choked and sputtered, wheeling away and two more of the workmen tried to grab her.

"Leave her be," came a gruff order.

Conrad. Diver found the one-eyed man on the opposite side of the table. He fixed his lone blue eye on Diver, his face as pale as his straw-colored hair. The others backed away. One of them, a bright-haired Koine with a soot-smeared face except where he'd been wearing goggles, peered at him, his thick mustache quivering. "We've done what we could. He's in a bad way, though."

Eleazar lay on his stomach on the long, narrow worktable. Diver sucked in a breath at the blood oozing down his back and staining the surface. He was naked from the waist up, his arms hanging to either side, and his slack face turned toward him. Someone had attached long, thin pieces of metal to the bones of his mutilated wings. Part Mithran, he could tell by the angry red-gold gleam tracing through them. It shimmered and pulsed like living veins through the framework of steel. There were bolts through the metal where it met the bone of his severed wings. Broken feathers stuck to his sweating skin. Eleazar's stumps were swollen, inflamed, and dark blood seeped from around the bolts.

Fury was bent over him, examining the wounds, her brow furrowed, her lips pinched. All emotion was wiped from her face as she looked over her patient. Diver wished he could be so detached. Bile had risen in his throat, and he swallowed anxiously. It would lessen his credibility as a healer if he vomited. He went to Eleazar and brushed golden hair from his feverish brow, murmuring soothing sounds while Fury worked.

Carefully, Fury probed at the bolts embedded in his wing remnants. Anger etched her face suddenly, and she glared at the men crowded around the table. "Take this off him. You've pierced blood vessels, you fools. He'll bleed to death now or die from infection later."

"No," Conrad said. "The bolts stay. This is only the first step; I can't let you ruin our work. Stop the bleeding, healer. That's why you're here. If you can't do it, I'll kill you and your brother and find someone else."

She scowled. "Go ahead and kill us. Eleazar will bleed to death before you track down another healer."

"I don't wish to kill you." His eye bored into her. "So, you'd best save him."

"Then I have to remove the bolts!"

"No." Eleazar said. His face was flushed, his eyes feverish, but he spoke clearly. "Do not remove the metal bones. Please. Find another way..."

Fury stroked his face. "Is it worth it?" she asked. "All this pain. This suffering! You don't have to do this, Eleazar. You are more than your wings."

His face crumpled. "I must fly again, Fury. Please! Please, do whatever it takes to preserve the work we've done. Please..."

Shudders shook through him, and the metal attached to his back seemed to pulse in response to his desperate plea. A hardness settled over Fury's expression. She touched his cheek one last time then straightened. Diver held his breath, watching her as she poked and prodded at Eleazar's nascent wings. At last, muttering to herself, she turned to Diver.

"Mithran," she said. "We need the Mithran. It can heal him, like before."

"But aren't those 'bones' made of Mithran?" he countered, frowning.

"Partly," Tully interjected, sounding more fascinated than concerned. They moved closer to the table but kept their distance from Eleazar, peering at his makeshift bones through their oversized goggles. "It is an alloy of steel and Mithran. A miraculous combination, a fount of potential. If the Angelus lives long enough to benefit from the magical properties, of course."

"I need pure Mithran. You must have some. You can't have put all of it into the alloy!"

"You must have some in an ingestible form," Diver added, keeping a protective hand on Eleazar's nape. "You use it as a drug, right?"

"We don't," Conrad said sharply. "That is a lie we propagated. A myth to hide our true purpose." He lifted a hand to touch his scar. It glittered in the ambient light. "We thought we'd inherit Angelic properties by consuming it. Ancient texts claim Mithran grants the eater transformative power, unnatural strength, and advanced healing ability. Everything which makes the angels seem divine." He scowled, his hand curling into a fist as he lowered it. His scar pulsed angrily. "It did nothing but sicken us, maim us, kill us. So, we had to find another way to make use of it."

"It is not for you..." Eleazar's voice was weak. "The gods' metal is not meant for humans. That is why you failed."

"Ah, the Angelus speaks, but his tongue is forked," Tully hissed. "It is the manna which prevents us from utilizing the Mithran, not our humanity. But we are fed that poison practically from birth, so who among us can ever truly realize the power of Mithran?"

Diver stared at Tully, a strange shiver rolling up his spine. Something about them tugged at his memory, a recognition he couldn't quite fathom. Their words rang with familiarity, and he realized abruptly that Tully was echoing his mother. They could be Gullan, he decided, given their dusky skin and small stature. That had to be what was so familiar. Were all Gullan as mad as his mother? And was it really the manna which kept humans from using Mithran like the Angelus? It might explain why his mother had been so against it.

A scowl marred Tully's dark face, but their magnified gaze shifted to Fury who was waiting expectantly. "Please," she said. "It will heal him."

"Get it, Tully," Conrad ordered.

The engineer jerked then went to one of the workbenches near the forge. They pulled open a drawer, and retrieved a small, velvet bag. For a moment, they held it in one hand, as if weighing options, bouncing it against their palm. Finally, they returned to Eleazar's sick table.

"Here." They settled it in Fury's eager hand. "It's pure. I promise. And easily ingested in this form. It's one of the few things we managed to accomplish without Angelic help."

Fury opened the bag and upended it. Several small, golden pearls dropped into her cupped hand, clinking musically. She brought them to Diver and between the two of them, they managed to get one of the metal balls into the angel's mouth. Eleazar swallowed convulsively.

Almost immediately, golden light rolled through him. The metal bones attached to his wings shuddered. The blood oozing from him grew bright, shimmering like sunlit water, then vanished. With a long, low moan, Eleazar shifted, drawing his new wing "bones" tight to his back. Another shudder passed through him, then he relaxed, his skin gleaming with good health.

"It works for the Angelus," Conrad said bitterly, once again touching his scar. "Maybe he was right. It's not meant for us."

"Bollocks. They spurn the manna is why," Tully exclaimed. "They've cursed us with it."

Fury was checking on Eleazar, examining his wings and the now-healed bolt wounds. Diver held the remainder of the pure Mithran beads clutched in his hand. He lifted his palm, studying them. They lay innocuously against his skin, giving no sign of their unearthly aspect. Would they work for a human who'd never touched manna?

But you have, Diver. In the army. Remember?

Did that count, though, really? After a lifetime of avoiding it? Diver plucked one of the pearls from his hand, lifting it, rolling it between his fingers. Such a small thing. Inconsequential. It wouldn't hurt him. He'd been raised right.

"My mother never let us eat the manna," he said aloud. The others turned to look at him.

"Diver," Fury said, drawing out his name. A warning. She'd always been able to read his mind. "Don't–"

He grinned at her and tossed the pearl of Mithran into his mouth.

CHAPTER TWENTY-SIX

Stunned silence followed Diver's rash act. Fury stared, frozen, one hand lifted toward her brother. A glimmer of gold moved down his throat. He was smiling, his eyes bright, excited, only a wrinkle in his brow expressing any shade of doubt. The wrinkle deepened, became a grimace.

"*NO!*" someone shouted. It was Weaver. He'd abandoned the game he and Ellis had been playing in a scattering of coins and cards and was staggering toward Diver in a stumbling half run, his face white. The gobsmacked engineers and artisans moved out of his way – all but Tully, who blocked him.

"Wait," Tully hissed, holding the struggling soldier with relative ease despite being half his size. "Let's see what happens." They peered at Diver over their shoulder, excitement written on their goggle-shrouded face. "If what he said... someone not raised on manna! Let's see!"

"We know what will happen," growled Conrad, in a towering rage. He grabbed Diver by the arm and wrenched him around. "You damn bloody fool! Men twice your size have died in agony from that poison. Cough it up if you want to live!"

"No! I'm fine–"

Conrad's fist slammed into his stomach. Diver curled over on himself, retching, and Conrad took him by the collar and hauled back for a second blow.

But his sudden, violent attack had kicked Fury out of her shock. She leapt at the one-eyed man, fear and concern washed away in a torrent of anger. She was taller, but he outweighed her by two stone or more. It made no difference, not to Fury. She smashed a shoulder into his ribs and sent him sprawling into one of the worktables. The heavy bench skipped across the floor and random coils of metal spilled off it. "Don't fucking touch him!" she shrieked, hands up in tight fists.

Wheezing, Conrad dragged himself back to his feet. "I... tried," he gasped. His hand went to his torso, thick fingers kneading his side. "It's too late now. Say goodbye to your brother."

Weaver's grief-stricken moan made the hairs on Fury's neck stand on end. She whirled back to face Diver, now on his knees, clutching his belly. From the punch, she told herself. Nothing else. He'd be fine – just like Eleazar!

"Diver..."

He looked up at her, his face twisted with pain, his eyes wide with terror. "Fury!" he gasped, and then he doubled over, shivering. He began to retch again, violently.

"Get it out of your system." She dropped down beside him, her hand on his back. "I'm here, it's alright. It'll pass. I promise."

"Damnable fool," muttered Conrad. "If he survives, it will be a miracle."

"Oh, don't be so pessimistic, boss," spoke Tully lightly. "He might be tougher than he looks."

"Shut up, all of you," Fury hissed. She glared at Weaver who'd stumbled closer and gone to his own knees, mirroring Diver. "And quit your infernal moaning!"

He obeyed, swallowing hard. "It doesn't seem so bad. Maybe–"

Diver screamed. So loud, Fury fell back on her heels. The scream went on and on until a spasm rippled through him and laid him out. He seized, arms and legs going rigid. His jaw locked closed, so hard Fury feared he might have cracked his teeth. She scrambled back to him, tried to gather him close. His arms flailed wildly, knocking her in the cheek, the mouth.

She tasted blood but refused to let him go. A strange, hoarse keening emerged from him. His eyes went glassy. Then he was choking, white froth bursting from his mouth.

"What is happening?" Fury cried, horrified. All she could think about was how her father had died in the last Scourge to befall Koine. The seizures, the foaming mouth. All from a ghoul attack. It happened every so often. Punishment for sins, for blasphemy against the Creator Eternal and His Angelic army. Whole villages decimated by the Angelic Curse, a tenth of their populations transformed into Burnt Ghouls. Grayson Barret had helped repel an incursion, but he'd been mauled. Such wounds became necrotizing. And those afflicted died in horrible pain, frightening to watch, impossible to heal.

Was this a curse? She wanted to shake her brother, to scream at him. Why had he dabbled with Angelic magic? They knew the cost!

Abruptly, Diver's symptoms took a strange turn. Where her father had rotted before her eyes, skin sloughing off, flesh growing putrid, suddenly golden light shone through Diver's clothes. His skin and eyes gleamed with it. Rippling, coruscating. Heat poured from him. He ripped away from her, rolling onto his hands and knees. For a moment, he seemed almost to have control of himself again. Spittle and bloody foam dripped from his sealed lips, pooling on the floor beneath him. A convulsion wracked his slim frame and he heaved. His mouth opened wide: strings of bile splattered to the ground.

Another great heaving and he began to vomit. Great gobs of undigested food splattered to the ground. It looked like chunks of flesh, dark red and deep blue. Glistening, thick and meaty. More chunks worked up his gullet and out his mouth. Where was it coming from? They'd been starving!

Then it stopped, leaving Diver shaking. Relieved, Fury moved closer to her panting, trembling brother. Surely he would have expelled the Mithran. Was it over?

But her relief was short-lived. Groaning, Diver collapsed. Sweat sprang out on his upper lip and forehead, and he seized again. It released him, and he sagged like a limp rag. Another fit gripped him, twisting him violently. His mouth opened in a silent scream. His heels drummed on the ground, his back a bow against the floor. Fury tried to grab him, to hold him, but his skin was flaming hot. She screamed for him, her heart breaking, tears burning tracks down her face.

Her brother, her baby brother was dying.

Screaming woke him from a dream. A pleasant dream. He'd been flying. He knew it wasn't real, but he felt like it could be. Any other noise and he might have stayed hidden in his dreams. Slept right through it. But he recognized the screamer: Fury. Fury was screaming. So, Eleazar left his dream and opened his eyes.

He should have stayed asleep.

Diver lay writhing – he had a good view from his facedown position on his sickbed. Well, sick table – and Fury was shrieking like a tea kettle. The space around him held others, mostly silent. Watching, waiting. Seeing how Diver was convulsing, Eleazar could guess what they were waiting for. It should have alarmed him, to see his friend in such agony, but he could feel the call of the Mithran coursing through the boy. Despite how it looked, the holy substance was in fact *not* killing him. But change was never easy. Transformation especially so.

Gracefully, he rose, feeling stronger and more whole than he had since he'd fallen from Splendour. There was a heaviness at his shoulders, not pain as he half expected, but not entirely comfortable. With a twitch, he settled the metal bones against his back. He noted the hunks of meat scattered about the floor with a distasteful wrinkle of his nose. Leviathan flesh. He would know it anywhere, in any form, but especially this. The delicate wafers, the appetizing loaves smelling of good, baked bread, and the heartier bannocks were illusions. Manna was meat and gristle and fat. It was good that Diver had expelled so much of it. If he hadn't, the Mithran most certainly would have killed him.

"Fury. Stop screaming."

Her breath hitched in her chest at his gentle words and her screams stopped. She stared up at him mournfully as he approached.

"I – I – couldn't stop him–"

"Hush." He bent down and laid a finger against her lips. "I'm here now. I have him."

She swallowed and moved aside so he could gather Diver into his arms. His skin was fire. Excellent. He sat on the floor and held the boy between his legs, against his chest, whispering into his ear. "Don't fight the Mithran. Embrace the pain. Let it fill you. The sooner you give in, the easier it will be."

Diver convulsed, nearly tearing himself free, but Eleazar was strong. A keening slid from him and his eyes rolled back, showing white.

"It is everywhere now. Feel the flames burning away the old you, every bit of you, transforming your very essence. It is rebirth, Diver."

Diver shuddered violently, then stilled. The golden light rippling down his body slowed, grew steady. Vibrant. The Mithran was a living thing, combining with Diver's very essence. Eleazar knew its power, knew why the humans couldn't use it as the Angelus did. That creature Tully had been correct: the manna prevented it. But if what Diver and Fury had said about their upbringing was true, then Diver had only recently touched the forbidden fruit. Their mother had known the truth.

And now I understand why the Gullan were shattered and dispersed. Now I understand their unforgivable sin. How had they known our secrets?

Diver's eyes settled back in place, staring up at Eleazar in wonder. The trust within his grey gaze made Eleazar's heart stutter. He did not deserve such trust. He laid a hand on Diver's forehead, using his Charisma to further soothe the Mithran coursing through him. Now that it had become bound within Diver, the gods' metal reacted to his touch, cooling and settling like a hound beneath its master's sure hand.

Diver lay weak and stunned in Eleazar's arms. His fever was gone, his eyes clear. "The gods' metal found you worthy, my child," he intoned pompously, obfuscating for the sake of the company they unwillingly kept. "It is a miracle. Granted by the Luminous One."

"Impossible," said Conrad. He was leaning against a nearby table, holding his midsection for some reason. "Most men who try to eat the Mithran die in horrible agony or come out disfigured, maimed, only to die days later. Even miniscule amounts leave the user scarred for life. I should know!" He touched his glittering scar. "I saw him. He was like all the others. He was dying!" He turned to Eleazar. "What did you do to him? How did you save him?"

Eleazar shook his head. "I did nothing. Diver was found worthy! He is my treasured acolyte. Of course he was worthy."

"Thank the gods. Oh, Diver, you lucky, lucky fool!" Fury hugged her brother. "Don't ever do anything so stupid again!"

"I... can't make that promise." Diver's voice was raw. He cleared his throat. "I had to know," he added simply.

Sudden cackling filled the thick air. "He survived it! I told you. I told you all." Tully was capering about nearby, exceedingly pleased. "Oh, the things we'll do!" They swung a startled Ellis into an impromptu jig. The others shifted uncomfortably, glancing at the little engineer pensively.

"I have so many plans, so many," Tully continued, voice dropping to a mutter. "The Mithran can be *dissolved...*"

They scampered to their drafting table and began rifling through the papers. A pencil appeared in their hands, and they started scribbling madly, ignoring everyone else on the factory floor.

Conrad turned a dour gaze on Eleazar. "I don't know how the boy is still alive, but I doubt it has anything to do with 'worth'. Until we understand more, I don't want any of my people experimenting like this. That goes for you, too, missy."

Fury lifted her chin, her expression dark. "I have no desire to go through what my brother just did. But if I change my mind, you can't stop me. I guarantee it."

"Huh, I guess you like charging into everything like a raging bull!"

"Not everything," she countered, scowling. "Just violent jackasses."

He grunted, and the ghost of a smile tugged at his lips. "Well, you answer to this violent jackass, now, I'm afraid. Your brother already pledged your loyalty to me."

"My brother doesn't speak for me."

"Fury," Eleazar murmured, discomfited. He'd rather Fury didn't force these people to put her back in a cell. She had to see these were the only allies they were likely to find. "I pledged my loyalty to them, too. So…"

Her gaze skewered him. "So, I have to go along with all of this?" She swept a vicious glare over the room. "I'm supposed to trust these people after everything they've done?"

Ellis stepped forward; her hands raised placatingly. "I get your anger, but you've got to understand. The whole of Trin is out for your heads. It's a wonder you made it this long. Really, Fury, you have no place else to go." She tried a tentative smile. "Can't we be friends?"

"Lovely start to a friendship," Fury snarled. "Getting bashed over the head."

The former Akkadian captain winced at her comment. He was standing forlornly beside the table where Eleazar had been lying sick and shivering not long ago, casting wretched glances at Diver. Eleazar caught the longing look in his eye, and he pulled Diver closer.

"Weaver only tapped you for my sake," Ellis said hastily. "Trust me, we're all on the same side. Aren't we, Conrad? Joseph? We just – we had to be sure about... him."

Eleazar smiled humorlessly when her dark eyes shifted to him and away again. At least she had the grace to look embarrassed. Fury traded a look with him, and he could see Ellis's words were starting to sway her. At least enough that she would no longer be outwardly hostile. As for him, he wasn't willing to give much more than that, either. They might be rebuilding his wings, but the memory of that web, and the currents of searing pain dropping him like a stone, was too fresh.

"Make no mistake; we are not friends."

Diver's voice was no longer raspy, but he lay limply in Eleazar's arms, his head pressed against the angel's bare chest as if it cost too much to lift it. "We will never be friends," he said, his voice surprisingly strong. "But we *will* work together."

Weaver stared at him, then ran a hand through his disheveled locks and looked aside, jaw rigid.

"Hush, Diver," Fury soothed, brushing hair from his brow with gentle fingers. "You've been through the wringer. Save your strength."

Eleazar felt a shudder pass through Diver. For a moment, his brown skin shimmered with a coppery radiance. He started to rise. Eleazar and Fury helped him to his feet. He should have been unsteady. Instead, Diver rolled his shoulders and shook himself as if knocking invisible dust from his skin. There might have been a sparkle in the dim, acrid air.

Diver turned gleaming eyes on them. "Don't worry, Fury. I am strong." A wondrous smile stretched across his face. "My strength is boundless!"

Beyond them, bent over their drafting table, Tully started to laugh. Low and gleeful. As if they'd just received the greatest gift.

CHAPTER TWENTY-SEVEN

Conrad's compound was a collection of abandoned stables, makeshift dormitories, the partially reignited forge, and several other outbuildings contained within high fences of wood and iron and barbed wire. A substantial training ground sat at its center: All sorts of men and women used it on a daily basis, drilling with rifle, bayonet, and buck knife. Located in a maze of abandoned factories deep within Trin, the compound was well camouflaged from the outside. Secrecy was of utmost importance to the disparate group of revolutionaries, and although the three newcomers had been given free rein within it, they were also "encouraged" not to venture outside the walls.

Yet, somehow, it didn't feel like a prison, not like Vogel's manor. Here, they seemed part of something greater. Something beyond their own struggles to find answers or a way home for Eleazar. It wasn't an easy transition, though. After those first nightmare days, they settled in among Conrad's people as best they could. Tired of sleeping rough on the factory floor, they'd claimed an empty carriage house near the stables, dusty with disuse but with glass-paned windows and high ceilings. Together, Fury and Diver managed to convert it into a homely enough space. Each of them had their own room, and their own bed. It was a retreat, a safe place to escape from the nest of strangers who stared at Eleazar with morbid curiosity or outright hostility. He wasn't welcomed among these people quite as readily as two atheist-scum angel killers.

Diver recovered quickly from his ordeal, though Fury kept a close eye on him, watching for any signs of illness, physical or mental. He began to work with the other "soldiers" in Conrad's nascent army, lending his military training to the rabble who followed the one-eyed revolutionary. They lacked discipline, he lamented, and there was no true military hierarchy despite the number of deserters in their ranks. Or perhaps because of it. Still, there was an eager gleam in his eyes when he spoke of "whipping them into shape", and Fury had no doubt he would accomplish it.

A framework of gleaming "bones" slowly grew from Eleazar's back. The welding and the hammering caused him excruciating pain and vast amounts of energy, as he had to expend Charisma throughout the process, but he never failed to endure the torture rack day in and day out. At first, Fury tried to bear witness but watching him suffer had been too much. When his cries and groans turned into full-throated screams, or his teeth crunched through yet another of the dowels they wedged in this mouth, she would stumble out, dizzy and sick, feeling like a coward.

Later, stealing moments alone together in their new house, she would do what she could to ease his pain, dosing him with the pearls of Mithran and massaging his tense muscles. While she fussed over him she would talk about her childhood to take his mind from the heat and sounds and smells of the forge, and the likely failure of this whole undertaking. It was easy to speak of her better memories. Her mother had been harsh at times, strict and rigid, but she'd also been loving. And proud. So very proud of her. Grayson Barrett had been a doting father. His loss was a hole in her heart, but she was happy to talk about him. She brushed over his death, not wanting to remind Eleazar of the damage the Angelus did to humankind on a regular basis.

She talked about sweet, little Diver, so adventurous as a boy, but soft-hearted and a little naïve. Cynicism, the cruelty of war and the banality of army life had broken him, but Fury was certain those qualities remained somewhere in his lean killer's body. Behind his sharp, grey eyes lay hope and wonder still. The Mithran had made Diver bright with strength and confidence. He'd wanted to ingest more of it, but Fury refused, arguing they had so little remaining, they had to save it for healing Eleazar. In truth, she was saving it for herself. It tempted her, the shining little pearls of Mithran, but fear held her back. She would take it, perhaps, but only when the time was right.

"And what of love, Fury?" Eleazar asked her one late afternoon as they lay entwined together in his bed, his new "bones" now tucked flat to his back. "Did you know love in your little hamlet?"

She snuggled closer to him, running a hand down his torso, her fingers tracing the outline of his impressive muscles. "Oh, there was a boy, once. He did love me, I imagine, and I loved him. As one does, when young. Deeply, fanatically. Stupidly." She sighed, remembering that burly, fair-haired boy from her village who'd teased her as a child, then chased her when she grew tall and curvy. They had talked of marriage, she and Ben. And then... war had come.

"And what happened to your love?" he asked, trying to sound light and unbothered. And failing. She kissed his golden skin. There was no cause for him to be jealous. Ben was a shadow compared to Eleazar.

"I begged him to marry me. They wouldn't take him if he had a new wife." The memory no longer stung, but at the time she'd thought her life destroyed. Eleazar ran his fingers down her arm, and she shivered. "He refused. Luckily, he managed to get wounded in his very first firefight."

"So, he came home to you?"

She shook her head. "He fell in love with the woman who nursed him back to health. I think he lives in South Gardenshire. He's a farmer now."

"Hmm. No doubt his wife is fat and his children ugly."

She giggled like a gossipy teen before ending their conversation with eager hands and lips. They had so little time left – the Hallow Tithe was fast approaching – so she would take advantage of every moment alone with him.

What she didn't tell Eleazar, what she couldn't confess, was her secret dream of the two of them married and happy on some little farm in Koine. She would gladly be the fat wife tending to their ugly children, Eleazar tall and strong beside her. Without that golden frame of false bones spidering from his back. A man, just an ordinary man. Her man. Her husband.

A silly dream. Never to come true…

"Why do you weep, my sweet Fury?"

"It's nothing, Lee. We just… we have so little time…"

"Then we'd best make good use of it." He kissed away her tears and brought her to life with his touch, and in that moment she forgot her dreams and fears and everything but him.

Unfortunately, their brief moments together grew even more infrequent when work began on the final stage of Eleazar's wings. Adding feathers to the framework had proven problematic. Tully had suggested a different design, one of overlapping metal or even alloy-enhanced fabric, but Eleazar had adamantly refused. His wings would look like true wings. They would bear feathers, not metal plates. Finally, one of the artisans, a woman of exceptional skill and in-depth knowledge of bird anatomy, had begun creating molds for die casting. She soon produced a vast quantity of Mithran-alloy feathers to recreate his true wings. The bear-like engineer, Rory, had a unique touch welding them to the frame. It would be his masterpiece, he'd declared excitedly.

Eleazar was eager to proceed, perhaps imagining a set of glorious golden wings, glittering feathers carrying him aloft. They would be magnificent, Fury had no doubt, and she tucked away her dreams of Eleazar the man, knowing this was what he wanted more than anything.

More than he wanted her...

The work continued. Heat and hammers layered the exquisite feathers of his ever-growing wings, but it was a slow, hot, painful process. Perhaps less agonizing than building the "bones" but more tedious and exhausting for Eleazar. He grew peevish during and after the sessions, chasing Fury away with sharp words.

She tried not to take it personally. By now, she was all too familiar with Eleazar's tendencies to lash out when frustrated. Still, she found herself near tears more times than she ever had in her life. She'd never been a particularly weepy woman, so it came as quite a shock. Rather than give in to her sadness, however, she took to joining Diver on the training ground, practicing with her weapon of choice, the leviathan skin, as well as rifle and bayonet. It was easy to hide her tears while she crawled through mud and stabbed at straw-filled targets with her combat knife. Training for war supposedly. And she had to scoff at this, as well. At the audacity of these people to think they could fight angels as they fought men.

Yet I'm willing to believe one Angelus can take down all of Splendour. Madness...

Fury frowned. She was beginning to use that word a lot. A desperate mantra against the insanity of her life.

"We could use that look in a fight," spoke a gruff voice from behind her. Fury stiffened. She'd been enjoying a quick rest near the stables, observing the other fighters while she caught her breath. The day was warm for this time of year, one of those rare days which fooled you into thinking winter had ended. The tiniest hint of green had appeared at the edges of the training ground. Tomorrow it would most likely be under a bed of snow. And she would be glad to see it. When snow blanketed the ground, the war beyond Trin tended to reach a stalemate. All sides hunkered down to wait out the heavy snow and freezing cold. The occasional skirmish erupted here and there like the one they'd seen from the train, but for the most part, the combatants took a moment to breathe and regroup while in the deepest depths of winter. Come spring, the world would be at war once more. And so would they.

The search for them continued city-wide, but Conrad's compound was well-concealed in a particularly labyrinthine part of Trin, and the regulators didn't like trudging through snow any more than soldiers did. But when the Celestial Gate opened and the Tithing ships arrived, Conrad and his people would attack. She'd seen the stacked boxes full of rifles which crowded empty stalls in the stables. They had horses, too, and vehicles. And ammunition, including shells for big guns though she'd seen no sign of such weapons. She'd thought it a formidable collection, until Diver had disabused her of the notion.

"Maybe we can handle a skirmish, even a fight against a company or two. But the Angelus?" He'd shrugged, full of doom though his eyes gleamed with eagerness. "We need better weapons than this. Weapons that can hit them in the air. Big guns firing shrapnel rounds will tear right through the Angelus, but only if they fly close enough."

He'd sounded excited about the possibility. Morbidly so.

Conrad eased out of the shadowy interior of the stables, smoking a thin cigar. Ellis followed behind him like a faithful watchdog and threw her a friendly smile. She and Weaver seemed to be Conrad's personal guards, though currently the ex-captain was wrestling with Diver on the field. The others had gathered around them in a circle to enjoy the show. The animosity between the two was obvious, yet somehow, they couldn't seem to stay away from each other. Fury knew her brother well enough to know his loathing hid deep hurt; he'd liked Weaver before his betrayal. As for Weaver, he was just an ass.

Speaking of asses...

Conrad blew smoke toward her, and she waved it away disdainfully. "You could scare off a whole battalion with that face," he intoned mildly. She scowled at his insult, which only made him laugh. "I meant it as a compliment, missy. Your gaze is fierce, is all. Not ugly." He waggled his brows. "Not ugly at all."

"Thanks," she muttered, turning away from him to watch the combatants. Diver had Weaver in a grapple, bending the man's torso beneath him, forcing him closer and closer to the earth. Shirtless in the unseasonable warmth, sweat glistened on their bare skin as they both fought for better holds. She hissed as Weaver slithered out from beneath Diver and took the upper hand. But Diver had been ready for the move. His back foot shifted, and he flipped his opponent into the mud, landing on top of him like a spider. The crowd cheered when Weaver tapped the ground in submission.

"Your brother fights like a tiger," Conrad commented. "Weaver's a master of the martial arts. I've never seen him lose so consistently."

Ellis chuckled slyly at his words. "Joseph is a bit distracted these days. You know how he gets around pretty men."

Conrad echoed her laughter, surprising Fury. He didn't seem bothered by her comment. Diver had never hidden his preferences but he'd suffered for it in Green Hollow. Maybe things were different in the city? Perhaps neutral Trin was neutral for many things. It softened her attitude a bit toward the grim place.

"How goes the transformation?" he asked her after a moment. "Has the Angelus much hope he'll be able to fly again?"

It seemed a casual question, but she knew how deadly serious he was. They were spending resources they could hardly afford on Eleazar. So far, nearly all their Mithran was going toward his wings, but for a supply of the pure stuff Tully was using for their own secret project. The strange little engineer had demanded Eleazar's help with it, though their hatred for the Angelus was obvious. He'd obliged them reluctantly and had yet to tell

Fury what Tully was doing. It disturbed him, whatever it was. Tully also spent an inordinate amount of time studying Diver's transformation since he'd taken the Mithran, measuring every little change, remarking with uncontained glee at each increase in strength and toughness. That bastard had some plan for her brother, and she didn't like it one bit.

"I have no doubt Eleazar will achieve his goal," she answered primly. "But much of it depends on the skill of your people. Their work seems adequate, so far. Thanks to Eleazar, of course."

"Of course…"

She caught the growl of anger in his simple reply and smirked. He was sensitive about the talents of his people. She leaned against the post holding up the stable's sunshade. "I hope Eleazar, and my formidable glare, aren't all the weapons in your armory. My brother seems to think your revolution lacks the necessary arsenal to stage an effective assault. What good are all your plans without the equipment to back it up? Even with all your smuggling, your Mithran supply runs low."

"The Mithran problem will be resolved soon enough. There are plans in place. Don't you worry about it."

"I can't help but worry, Mr Conrad. We've risked everything to join you." Never mind that they'd had no choice. "I'd hate to have joined a revolution that's failed before it's even started."

Ellis was scowling at her by this point, though Conrad seemed unfazed. He took a final drag at the stub of his cigar then let it fall to the earth. Slowly, deliberately, he ground it under his heel. "You think this," and he waved to encompass the entirety of his compound, "is all we have? You think this is the whole of our operation?" He chuckled softly and clasped his hands behind his back. "I'm glad," he said. "That means it's working." He rocked on his heels a moment then started to wander away from her, whistling.

"Ass," Fury murmured. She straightened and flung the end of her scarf around her neck. "I don't know how you stand him," she said to Ellis who still stood in the shade with her.

"Yeah, he can be a bit much," she admitted. She fixed Fury with her dark gaze, suddenly serious. "But I owe him my life. He and Star. They showed up out of nowhere when I was knee-deep in ghouls. The Angelus sent a Scourge against the Akkadians while we had the Koine forces in a rout. I don't know why, no one knows why they do it. Just to fuck with us, I imagine. My company was spared, but the rest of our forces were turned into monsters. We were the closest warm bodies, the nearest hot flesh. They fell on us like crazed beasts. Burnt and fanged and vicious. Until there was only me and a few of my fellows left. Then there was only me."

Fury held still, mesmerized. Ellis stared into the distance, her eyes seeing horrors Fury could only imagine. She knew firsthand how horrid the ghouls were, but even she had never been faced with a host alone and surrounded.

Suddenly, Ellis's expression brightened. Her eyes crinkled. "And then there they were, out of nowhere. Star with her scoped rifle, picking off ghouls like she was at the fair, and Conrad with a machine gun on the back of a lorry, mowing down whole ranks of the creatures." She shook her head, looped braids swaying. "They'd been my comrades a moment before, but I cheered to see them slaughtered. That's what the Angelus do to us, you know. They make us turn on each other."

Fury had to look away. There was no defending the Angelus. She wanted to say Eleazar was different, but even he insisted he really wasn't. And yet, he wanted to be better, he truly did. That had to count for something.

"Star saved you that day – the Akkadian war hero?"

Ellis faced her, studying her for a moment before nodding. Perhaps she was remembering that day before the city gates when Star had been captured. They most likely would have made it through unmolested if Eleazar hadn't interfered. Apparently, the traveling show had been a very successful operation for some time. Recruiting deserters and disillusioned soldiers all across Avernus, running weapons and Mithran into the city, spreading revolutionary propaganda.

"Star and Conrad gave me a new life, a life of honor and freedom. And a cause to fight for. There's many like us. In the armies, on both sides. Brought together by hope for a better world. Just waiting for our moment to act. For a sign..." Ellis sighed and lifted a hand to brush her cheek. Fury shivered at her touch, wondering at the look on her face. "I owe them everything, sweet pea. Just you remember that."

CHAPTER TWENTY-EIGHT

Diver peeled himself off his sweaty companion, his breath quick and his heart thumping violently. His head was spinning, and he rolled onto his back. The straw pricked him through the blanket, bits clung to his filthy skin. The sand from the stable bedding seemed to get everywhere. A fine film of it coated him. He'd have to soak for an hour just to get clean, and even that wouldn't be enough. Because of the man lying next to him, lately he always felt dirty.

He hadn't meant to fall into bed with Joseph Weaver. Frankly, he felt sometimes like he hated the man. But the attraction between them was undeniable. Wrestling bouts did nothing to diminish it, either. Quite the opposite.

Still, what had finally driven him to seek out the ex-captain less than a week after they'd arrived, had been discovering Fury and Eleazar together. The sounds seeping from behind Eleazar's closed bedroom door had been obvious and he'd fled their shared home, sick to his stomach and broken-hearted. Not long after, he'd ambushed Joseph in a dark hallway, angry and jealous and hurt. Weaver had responded eagerly to his violent urgency.

After that first rendezvous, with the taste of Joseph's semen still on his lips, Diver had vowed it would never happen again. But seeing Fury and Eleazar together every day, watching their bond grow even as they tried to hide it was too much. He kept going back to Weaver. Just to feel *something*.

The pounding in his chest eased as he relaxed in post-coital bliss, and he was tempted to settle back against his partner, close his eyes and sleep. But that wasn't how things were between them. This time was no different than any of their other encounters. It meant nothing. So, instead, Diver rolled to his feet and hitched up his trousers.

"You always run away," remarked Weaver. Lying naked and spent on the woolen horse blanket, he propped himself up on one elbow. "We don't have to be afraid, Diver. Conrad makes sure of it."

Diver paused with his belt half buckled. "I've never been afraid of who I am," he said icily. He frowned, remembering what it had cost him over the years. Some men weren't strong enough to face such malice day in and day out. And he'd always had Fury on his side. He felt a surge of sympathy. The Akkadians hunted men like them. Men whose only crime was loving other men. The Koine weren't exactly open-minded, but at least they hadn't declared it a crime punishable by death. "Is that why you joined the Iron Corps? To keep your secret safe? Being in such an elite troop must have kept you protected, yeah?"

Weaver's expression grew guarded, and he flopped onto his back. A horse whickered softly from the next stable, its velvet nose whiffling at the bars between them. Diver was tempted to go to the curious mare and stroke her glossy coat, but instead he held himself very still. Waiting. He wanted an explanation for why Joseph Weaver had joined the brutal, violent, merciless Iron Corps. A good one.

"I had a choice," he said at last, so softly Diver had to strain to hear him. The mare gave a friendly whinny and nearly drowned out his next words. "Join the Iron Corps or kill myself." He grinned at Diver; his teeth bared cadaverously. "He thought death would be more honorable, but I chose to live instead. Yet another insult in his mind."

"Who...?"

"My father. He's a field marshal with the Seventh Army. He felt the Iron Corps would be the right place for someone like me, seeing as how they are all degenerate psychopaths. My 'affliction' would have to be concealed, of course, but I could find a place among their ranks." His green eyes wandered back to Diver, heavy with pain. "I didn't know what I'd be getting into. I swear. The minute Conrad gave me an out, I took it."

Schooling his face to blankness, Diver stooped to retrieve his shirt. He wasn't sure what to think, but he felt that surge of sympathy again. It bordered on pity. Other, more complex emotions fought together within him, leaving him shaken. He had tried so hard to keep hating Weaver even as he sought him out day after day. The hate was loosening its hold, and he didn't like it one bit.

Weaver sat up, reaching for his own clothes. Spots of color stained his cheeks, and he kept his eyes downcast. Shame? Embarrassment? Or merely hurt feelings?

This is getting too complicated...

A flash of gold outside the stall's barred window caught his eye. The training field was empty this late in the day. The troops were in the dining hall. It was always the perfect time of day to seek out Weaver for their clandestine meetings. Diver didn't want anyone catching them together. Especially the tall, golden-haired god striding out from the foundry across the way.

Diver watched Eleazar glide across the muddy field, his metallic wings sparkling even under an overcast sky. The Mithran called to him; it was in his blood now, too, a part of him as surely as it was a part of the Angelus. A bright wave rolled through him. Behind him, he heard Weaver gasp softly.

"You *shine*. Like you're made of copper and sunlight."

Diver ignored him, his body and soul aching at the sight of his angel. Next to Eleazar, Weaver was a shadow, a silly diversion. Outside, standing beneath a cloudy sky, his face turned upward, tears shimmering on his cheeks, was the man who possessed his heart. He could almost feel Eleazar's longing, his desire to launch skyward. To fly. His wings, so beautiful and finally complete after days of intense work, shivered open. Slowly, painfully. Nothing like he remembered when Eleazar had a true wing.

"What a waste."

Diver jerked. Weaver was standing right behind him, so close he could feel his body heat. The man settled gentle hands on his shoulders, kneading his rigid muscles.

"We shouldn't have spent so much on that useless project," Weaver said. His breath stroked Diver's neck, making gooseflesh rise. "He'll never fly, Creator take him. What a waste of Mithran."

"Get your fucking hands off me." Diver shrugged violently, knocking Weaver's hands away. He gripped the bars of the window so he wouldn't punch Weaver in the face and glared back at him. His lover stood with his hands raised, a shocked look on his face. "He will fly. Never doubt it!"

The shock faded, his eyes narrowing. "He won't ever love you, you know. He dallies with your sister. We've all seen how they look at each other. You're wasting your time chasing him, just as we've wasted our time trying to make him fly again!"

"Shut up. You don't know what you're talking about. Eleazar isn't – he's more than all of us. He is a god fallen to our world."

Weaver smirked, but his arrogance couldn't completely hide the hurt in his gaze. "He is an Angelus," he said harshly. "Never mistake him for human, kid."

"Don't call me 'kid'!" Diver wrenched his hands from the bars and turned on Weaver. "I can tear you apart and you know it. Watch your tone with me."

"Ah, yes, a little taste of Mithran and you think you're a god, too." He stepped closer, ignoring Diver's threatening posture even though he was naked and vulnerable. His eyes gleamed. "Go ahead and tear me apart. I won't even fight you." The gleam resolved into a shimmer of tears. "I'm here, right in front of you, and all you see is *him*."

"He is everything," Diver hissed. "And you are nothing."

Tears spilled down Weaver's cheeks, though his expression remained stone. "Good enough to fuck, though, right?" There was a crack in that stone. "Is that all I am to you? A good *fuck*?"

The straw-covered floor seemed to shift beneath him. Diver knew he had merely to reach out to Weaver, to touch him softly, to speak kindly, and everything would change between them. But his heart was full of wings and soft feathers. Dreams of sky and sunlight. So...

"Yes. It's all you'll ever be."

The stone shattered. Weaver's face grew ugly, and his breath hitched in his throat. Sobs, he was sobbing. Diver recoiled, shocked. Even more shocked by the regret he felt for causing him such pain. Suddenly, Weaver came at him, clutching wildly. Diver didn't even try to fend him off. He stood rigidly as the weeping man kissed him, teeth cutting his lips. Lust roared through him, and he gave into Weaver's violent advances with abandon. This was a battle he would always lose.

"I'll take it," Weaver gasped, his hands buried in Diver's hair, his body cleaved to his. Together, they tumbled into the straw and muck.

The cool air outside the foundry bathed Eleazar's sweaty skin. He'd needed a break from all the ideas, plans, sketches, and disappointment within the building. The boisterous debate about his very essence. Metal and fire and strange contraptions haunted his dreams. The noise alone was enough to drive him mad. He burned with frustration. His wings were complete, had been for days, yet they still felt awkward and alien. Where was the magic? Why was the Mithran so intractable?

Today, and not for the first time, Tully had suggested handholds on the ersatz wings. Their little revolution employed gliders all the time, apparently. Rudimentary flying machines which were laughable next to a drachen. Eleazar had scowled and nearly tossed the little engineer into the nearest furnace.

What good would it do him, these handholds? He would have to leap from a height, his flights short and pointless. He refused to do something so disgraceful. He needed to be able to move as he had, to fight and fly, dive and attack.

The magic lurked within the alloy; he could feel it. What would it take for his blood to flow through these metal wings as it pumped through his living flesh?

The pain he'd suffered these last few weeks seemed pointless. His artificial wings were useless. And the Celestial Gate was moving ever closer. Spring announced its imminent arrival in the slow greening around the training ground, the warm scents in the air, the deepening blue of the sky.

Physically, he felt stronger than he ever had. The Mithran he'd consumed had made him strong, as it had Diver. Unfortunately, his metal wings wouldn't respond to him. The bones closest to his flesh hummed and throbbed as he expected, but the farther from his body the wings extended, the less alive they seemed. He could move them, barely, and at the very least fold them tight to his back, but beyond such simple movements, they may as well be made of pure steel.

Anchored by his dead wings, Eleazar stood in the yard between the barracks and the forge and wept, his head tipped back, steel clouds heavy overhead. Here, even on a cloudy day, the world pulsed with life. He longed to feel such life pulsing through his new wings.

The wind picked up and the clash and discordant jangle of his false feathers offended his ears. With great effort he managed to open them somewhat, catching the stiff breeze. A cacophony of chiming erupted. It took all his strength to hold his wings open; the idea of executing a downward thrust to launch himself made him sweat.

Scowling, Eleazar tucked his wings closed. It took nearly as much effort as it had to open them. He looked up into the sky once more. The clouds had thinned, and patches of blue shone through. His heart nearly broke with longing. He had his wings back, wings built of the gods' metal, but something was wrong. Was the skill of his human allies lacking? He touched the intricate feathers. They shimmered and gleamed wherever his fingers went, responding to him as all Mithran responded to the Angelus. The detail and artistry was exquisite. No, it wasn't the humans who'd failed in this endeavor.

If I cannot fly, I will have to remove them. The thought came unbidden and turned his stomach cold. He didn't want to go back to being a half-angel. Worse, a man. No matter that he now lived among the wingless humans. He felt crippled without wings. Not human, but less than human. Even these false wings, strangely heavy as they were, had restored a balance he didn't know he'd lost. There had to be a way for the Mithran to come alive as it should.

Why couldn't he *fly*?

It's me. It's my blood which is too weak, not the Mithran.

Eleazar dashed the tears from his eyes and settled his gaze on the distant smokestacks. Here was a vision which didn't make his heart ache. He imagined the black smog would be difficult to breathe; he wondered if his people had felt ill after flying over the city during their search for him. Those tall brick stacks would have provided convenient perches as they swept the city. His scowl deepened. He hoped their lungs had turned black breathing in such filth.

He peered more closely at the distant forest of brick and mortar. Those things had to be a hundred feet high. Higher. Almost as high as the Crystal Cliffs of Lower Splendour, where he and his friends had played games as boys. Diving and swooping on updrafts and air currents. It had been a challenge to see how long you could dive, wings folded against your back while the ground grew closer and closer. And at the last moment, the brave Angelus would spread his wings and soar, fear and excitement pounding through his body, wings burning with the effort. Pumping hot and fierce with blood from a wildly beating heart.

Blood pumping, wings alive with magic and power...

He stared hard at those smokestacks. Thinking. They were high enough a fall might kill him. After all, there were no convenient trees here to catch him. No soft body of water to absorb his momentum.

So...

What if he jumped from those smokestacks?

Would fear awaken the Mithran? Would fear drive his blood pumping through his metal wings? Would his heart beat hard enough and fast enough to bring the Mithran to life?

It was an intriguing idea. What else would force the blood he needed through his artificial appendages? If that indeed was the problem...

It might be he would never fly. It might be the Mithran couldn't be used in this way, but he suspected they just needed to unlock the secret.

Would he finally be able to fly if he leapt into the void? Or would he find himself splattered across the ground?

The idea gripped him. He turned slowly, his heart hammering, back toward the foundry. He considered the men and women within. Tully and Rory and Harris and the others, all talented engineers and artists. But would any of them risk what they had wrought by helping him fling himself off a towering smokestack?

He turned again, the earth churning beneath his boots. The ground had thawed. Winter was nearly gone. The First Season Tithe approached rapidly. A stone rolling toward him.

His gaze found the small house he shared with Fury and Diver. Fury would have dinner ready. She trained as hard as her brother, but the war effort barely interested her. Eleazar knew deep in his heart she would be happy to flee this place. Happy to return to her woods, to freedom. No, Fury would not help him with this. She would refuse to let him jump.

A smaller turn and he stared toward the stables stretching along one side of the compound. Immediately, he felt Diver's presence somewhere within them. The boy's Mithran-infused soul called to him. Yes, Diver made the most sense. His was a reckless spirit.

Sudden eagerness filled him, and he strode toward the stables. Diver was clever, resourceful. If he put forth his idea, he was certain Diver would have a plan. Maybe he wouldn't have to splatter on the ground if his wings failed. After all, he sought the skies not the grave...

When he came upon Diver at last, it wasn't how he'd expected to find him. On his knees in a dirty stall, the unpleasant Akkadian captain crouched behind him, pale skin gleaming in the dim light. For a moment, he could only stare, his emotions roiling unpleasantly. The redheaded man was vile and base, not worthy to touch his treasured acolyte. His hands twitched and anger filled him. A single blow would break the man's neck. He could flay him alive in a flash. Blood splattering, anointing his acolyte. Purifying him after this... this desecration.

Mine.

The word growled through his mind, loud and vicious, startling him out of his growing rage. The voice was one he didn't recognize anymore. An old way of thinking. Full of cruelty and greed. Diver did not belong to him. Besides, hadn't he chosen Fury? This was not Splendour, where all the pinioned and human slaves belonged to him.

"Diver," he said flatly, keeping his terrible emotions tucked deep inside.

At the sound of his voice, the two men scrambled apart, Diver gasping and his companion cursing as he dragged at a tattered blanket to cover them. Red-faced, his dark hair mussed, and his mouth gaping, Diver stared at Eleazar in dismay. His jaw worked but nothing of sense emerged. Weaver wrapped an arm around him protectively, but Diver jerked away as if his touch burned.

"L – L – Lee," he managed to stammer. "I–"

"I need your help, acolyte," Eleazar interrupted. "Attend me."

"Yes, Eleazar, of course. Uh, just give me a minute…"

Sparing him any further embarrassment, Eleazar retreated. Behind him, faintly, he heard Diver mutter, "Shit," in a voice heavy with regret.

CHAPTER TWENTY-NINE

It was a pleasant day, warm and clear. After a week of rainy skies, Fury's spirits rose to see the sun again. Unfortunately, the Celestial Gate hung in the sky closer than ever, impossible to ignore as it moved toward the Tithing Ground of Trin. Her eyes kept rising to it as she crossed the training yard, empty due to the muddy conditions.

Today, Conrad's soldiers were scattered throughout the city, spreading propaganda against the Angelus, gathering allies, distributing weapons to those already sworn to the cause. It was all carefully done. Not every human felt the Angelus were oppressive overlords. Many believed they were benevolent immortals and sought their favor. What better way to garner favor than reveal traitors?

The compound felt strangely empty without the fighters in the yard. Not that Fury minded. Being surrounded by so many souls living together, eating together, training together day in and day out was starting to get on her nerves. She was planning an escape. Just in case. She had asked Ellis if there was a way of avoiding the regulators and leaving Trin. The ex-soldier had given her only vague reassurances, and a promise to show her "possibilities" at some undetermined future date. Frustrating, to say the least. Unfortunately, her companions seemed committed to the cause.

Lately, after a bout of awkwardness between the two she didn't quite understand – was it about her and Eleazar?

She'd thought Diver had accepted them – Diver and Eleazar had suddenly become confidants. Disappearing together after dinnertime and returning long after dark, leaving her to wonder what in the Abyss was going on. Neither would give her a satisfying answer, only referring vaguely to some side project of Tully's. Maybe it had to do with the sketch she'd seen on Tully's desk: A boiler suit of sorts, but one with wings, along with a detailed drawing of strange canisters to go on its back. She couldn't make any sense of the formulas scribbled in the margins, but she had a guess as to what it all meant.

Flying men. Sheer madness.

But what could be done without more Mithran?

Lately, the lack of the gods' metal had been a constant complaint among the engineers and artisans. Tully especially. There was grumbling. Once Eleazar was out of sight, the whispers began, the doubt and the resentment. Why had they wasted all their Mithran on an earthbound Angelus?

Those grumblings had encouraged her to put together a few go-bags, just in case. It brought back unpleasant memories of when they'd left home, but she persisted. Better to be safe, she'd decided. If you needed to run, it was good to be ready. This time, hopefully, they wouldn't leave a flaming wreck behind them.

Fat chance.

By lunchtime, neither Diver nor Eleazar had returned to the house, but she'd let another hour pass before going to look for them. Now, crossing the yard, her feet leading her automatically to the forge, she began to feel a growing unease. She paused at the door to the reclaimed factory, throwing one last glance behind her. A few stragglers wandered about the compound on errands. She spotted Weaver coming out of the stables across the way, his red hair flaming in the sun, his brow furrowed with annoyance, both hands bunching into fists, his eyes searching.

Briefly, their eyes met. For a moment, it seemed like he might call out to her. Then, abruptly, he stomped off toward the barracks. She had no doubt who he was looking for. Had he already searched the factory? But… if Diver wasn't there, where could he be?

Gone. It made no sense, but she knew it with bone-deep certainty. And if Diver was gone, she had no doubt Eleazar had gone with him. Why? *Why?*

She knew one person who might have answers for her.

"Where are they?"

The little engineer looked up from their drafting table, a dark frown on their face. "The girl," they said, adjusting their ever-present googles. "She seeks answers from me. Finally. I've been waiting."

"Waiting?" Fury blinked, unsettled by those outsized eyes peering at her. "For me? For what? Never mind. I don't have time for your weird little quirks, engineer. Tell me where my brother and the Angelus have gone off to. What sort of trouble are they in?"

"That's not the question I desire," they said, flipping through the stack of drawings before them. They landed on the one they wanted, apparently, for they slammed a hand down on the page and made a noise of satisfaction. "You wear their skin but know nothing about them. Why, furious child? Did your mother fail to educate you?"

"My mother left us," she said harshly, not wanting to be drawn down this tangent when it was Diver and Eleazar she needed to find. She had no desire to ask this person any more questions than necessary. Unwillingly, her eyes fell on the page. It looked like a schematic drawing of an animal, with measurements and side views and close-up details. Of dragonfly wings. Of shimmering scales rendered in full color – a bright blue. A long, lean body with a curling tail hooked beneath it. A broad head with big eyes and a strange mouth full of something besides teeth.

Baleen...

The word came to her, unfamiliar, but she knew it was what filled the creature's mouth. Long vertical plates of shimmering Mithran in its most basic form – a pearly rose rather than pure gold. Used to scoop and filter the dust of the Kosmos. She grew dizzy. How did she know this?

"The leviathans have called to our people for generations," Tully said, speaking softly, reverently. "Tell me they don't call you, too. Or is your Gullan blood too weak to hear?"

So, Diver had been right. Tully was Gullan. They'd both been wondering, Diver far more certain than she had been. It disturbed her in ways she didn't understand. She felt... exposed. Judged.

Automatically, her hand rose to grip the end of her scarf. "I don't know what you mean," she said, temporizing. She knew exactly what they meant. The dreams. "Blood is blood, nothing more. My mother was Gullan. Maybe she heard them. I've only ever had vague dreams. Nothing real."

Tully's bug eyes narrowed. "Good, yes. It starts with dreams. The lamentations."

Lamentations. Fury swayed, caught in a vision. *Creatures crying in the vastness of a harsh, too-bright world. Roaming freely, seeking the nebulae while avoiding the Hunt. But it was not their home...*

It is a prison. They are trapped. Dying slowly over millennia. Their cries tear my heart–

Fury squeezed her eyes shut, a strange keening echoing in her ears. No. She didn't have time for this! She blinked away sharp tears and reached for the drawings, slamming the pages closed.

"Where are they?" she croaked. "I know you've set them on a dangerous path. I see how you look at Eleazar!"

Tully leaned back, regarding her. "I did nothing to set them on this path, only aided them when asked. And it is no more dangerous than what we all must do. They go to do what is necessary, child, to push boundaries and limits, to ascend to the next level. As you should, Fury."

Fury yanked at her scarf. Angry. "So, you do know where they are. Tell me!"

Tully scowled. "When did you grow so timid?" they asked, voice full of castigation.

"No one has ever called me 'timid'." Fury scoffed. "They wouldn't dare."

"Oh, my child, I see right through you. You are frightened of your own shadow."

A sick feeling roiled Fury's stomach. How could Tully know that? She'd tried so hard to appear fearless. "You don't know me–"

"Why haven't you taken the Mithran as your brother did?"

The question stopped her cold. The pearls of Mithran she carried in her pocket suddenly seemed as heavy as boulders.

"You are pure. I can sense it. You have never eaten manna. Your mother did that much right."

"I – I don't want to take it. I don't see why–"

"Ah, Fury, I had such hopes for you." Tully spun on their tall stool and hopped down. "Perhaps I put too much on you, thinking you were the strong one. Your brother – he always seemed so frail. So weak compared to you. Who knew he had a soul of steel?" They laughed lightly, wryly. "Not steel, now, I suppose, but Mithran. Do you want to see what we've been working on?"

The change of subject left Fury reeling. She was trying to make sense of what Tully was saying. The odd engineer spoke as if they'd known her and Diver a long, long time. Which was madness...

Oh, Creator, not that word again.

"Look, Fury, look at what we have wrought." Tully pulled back a curtain, revealing a wooden rack. A boiler suit hung from it, or what looked like a boiler suit. Buckles and metal rivets marred the heavy canvas, along with strange piping. But the most amazing thing about it was the framework stretching from the shoulders of the suit, spread across the rack to either side, fabric taunt between gleaming struts. Like the wings of a bat.

If bat wings shone with gold.

"What?" was all she managed to say. But she knew what she was looking at. The drawing she'd seen. Now come to life. A flying suit.

"It is a prototype," Tully continued ecstatically. "Diver helped me with the design. He could have been an engineer, I think, if his parents hadn't failed him so miserably. But now he's meant for a greater purpose. The first soldier in our newest corps! He will lead us all into battle against the drachen. And if today goes well, your angel might be of some use beyond helping us with the Mithran." They reached out a hand to stroke the suit. "It will be glorious!"

Fury was horrified. "You aren't strapping Diver into that thing. I won't allow it—"

"*Stop fighting destiny*!" Tully shrieked. They turned on her, ripping the goggles from their face and tossing them aside. "By the Luminous One, you were meant for grander things!"

...*meant for grander things*...

Fury stared into Tully's grey eyes, fierce and angry and pleading all at once, her limbs numb with shock. No longer distorted by those thick goggles, the resemblance was uncanny. She recognized those eyes.

They were Diver's eyes.

He had always looked like *her*. Slight and slim, a great beauty with lovely brown skin.

It couldn't be. Fury gripped the edge of the drafting table and found herself staring at the drawing of the leviathans again. The pages falling open in an invisible breeze. They knew the leviathans in great detail, and Tully had spoken of the Luminous One, too. That was not a human curse. The Luminous One, the inscrutable god of the Angelus.

Only someone who'd spent time in Splendour would use such an oath...

Reeling, afraid she might fall, Fury clung to the drafting table. "How?" she said faintly, facing Tully once more. She wanted to vomit. "How is this possible? How are you here?"

Tully's expression softened. Lines carved their – no, her – dark face. Age and pain and experience. A lifetime's worth. Her body was transformed, no soft curves or rounded limbs as Fury remembered, just angles and hardness. Only her eyes remained unchanged.

"I am not here, my little angel," her mother said sadly. "Tuilelaith Cree is dead."

There was a roaring in her ears. Deafening. She couldn't see, couldn't feel.

Somehow, Fury found herself in the corridor leading out of the forge, ignoring the faint, yet insistent, demands for her to stay. She didn't recognize her mother's new, wretched voice. It was a stranger's voice. She couldn't face this, not alone. She needed one thing, only one thing could ground her, save her.

Diver. I must find Diver…

"Fury! There you are. I've been looking everywhere for you."

Fury looked up, blinking against the brightness of the late afternoon sun. Ellis was approaching her, her expression serious, almost urgent.

"You wanted to find a way out of the city, yeah?" she asked when she was closer. "Well, I think I've found–"

"Diver," Fury gasped. Ellis was reassuringly solid, tall and strong and capable. Exactly what she needed. "I have to find Diver. Can you take me to him?"

Her brow furrowing, Ellis stared down at her. "I think so. I might know where to find him, but we'll have to go into the city."

"Please, just take me to him. Thank you, Ellis. Thank you."

"No." A grimace twisted her features briefly, but she took Fury by the arm and started toward the stables. "Don't thank me for this, sweet pea."

CHAPTER THIRTY

The wind tugged at Eleazar's cloak. He clung to the bricks, fearing the garment's wild shifting might pull him from the tower. His fingers gouged the crumbling mortar, his toes braced against a limestone ridge. He should have lost the cloak, but even though the sun was low in the sky, the gold of his Mithran wings might have caught the light and drawn unwelcome attention.

He'd been too afraid to wait until nightfall. He couldn't jump into darkness. It would be like the Black Silence all over again, and he feared his heart might not be able to handle *that* much terror. No, he had to see the ground.

Eleazar pressed close to the rough brick wall, waiting for the wind to die. Several feet below him, Diver hugged the smokestack, moving laboriously. His progress was painstaking compared to Eleazar's, but far better than an average man's due to the Mithran. The ground lay a dizzying height away; a patchy, weed-filled lot before an abandoned factory. The lonely place appeared desolate and vacant, and any eyes would be illicit ones. Perfect. Even with a reward involved, such types were unlikely to alert the city regulators. Few among Trin's underground trusted the regulators to follow through on their promises.

The planning for this endeavor seemed ridiculously optimistic to him now as he inched up the sheer tower. The harness Tully had built was tighter than he remembered, cutting into his chest and shoulders and groin, and the heavy rubber ropes coiled around his torso threatened to drag him from the tower with every stiff gust. The day was warm and sweat poured from him, but every time he stopped to rest, the chill wind dried the moisture on his skin and gave him some relief. He was grateful for the metal bands spanning the tower at regular intervals; they were easier to grip than the bricks. Once, a ladder had been attached to the smokestack, but it had rusted away.

Finally, Eleazar reached the top. His hands gripped the edge, and he hoisted himself up. The smokestack was so large the edge of the opening was wide enough for him to sit comfortably while he waited for Diver. The human reached him a few moments later.

"By the… Creator," Diver gasped, lying on his belly atop the concrete ledge. He held onto it as if he gripped a lover. Eleazar scowled at the unbidden comparison, his mind flashing to images he had no wish to recall. "I thought I was dead… a few times. The wind…"

Eleazar leaned forward. "I hope we're high enough." He looked up and to the east where another smokestack rose into the sky, its tip brushing against the silver underbelly of a passing cloud. "Perhaps we should have chosen that one?"

Diver's eyes were squeezed shut. "This one is plenty high. Climbing up it has already scared me to death. I imagine jumping off will give you the fright you need."

"I suppose so. Are you ready?"

"Give me a second, please."

Eleazar drew off his cloak, casting it aside. It fluttered down from the tower, riding the wind like some strange, broad-winged bird. He could retrieve it when he landed safely.

Oh, Luminous One, protect me…

Laboriously, he stretched the Mithran wings. Soon, hopefully, he'd feel blood course through his false feathers and alloyed bones. A single step from this tall tower would launch him into the air. A single step and he would be on the path to vengeance at last.

Or possibly dead. His heart had been calm, thumping regularly, softly, but suddenly it came to life in stuttering violence. He drew a sharp breath, tingles drawing patterns on his skin.

It was strange to feel fear. He'd soared through open space without a single qualm; he'd dived straight toward the earth feeling only excitement and exhilaration. He'd fallen through the Black Silence and survived! How could this puny smokestack terrify him so?

I can't fly, that's why. Not yet. Eleazar took a deep breath. Good. This was good. He needed the fear, no matter that it made his balls shrivel and his stomach churn. His blood was pumping hard and fast. The Mithran grew lighter. He moved his wings, shifting his feathers so they lay flat. The movement felt natural. The thumping in his chest quickened. Exhilaration joined his fear. This was what he'd hoped. It would work.

"It will work," Diver said softly.

Eleazar turned to him. For days, they had worked together to execute this plan. Eleazar's plan. And during those days, Diver had shunned the ex-captain. The unworthy one. He'd been a devoted acolyte once more, and it had pleased Eleazar more than he could say. Abruptly, Eleazar pulled him into an embrace, squeezing fiercely. He hadn't said goodbye to Fury, and sharp regret filled him. What if…?

"It will work," Diver repeated, his mouth muffled by Eleazar's shoulder. He broke free and turned away to get into position. Throat aching, Eleazar checked his harness once again, and made sure the rubberized ropes were firmly attached to it. Tully had assured him the ropes would work to keep him from dashing to the earth should he fail to fly. But Tully's obvious disdain for him kept Eleazar's fear alive.

"Are you ready?" Diver called to him from his position near one of the slim spikes of metal jutting from the top of the smokestack. He'd wrapped the rubber cords tightly around the spike, then coiled a few lengths around his forearms. He held the ends firmly in his fists, his boots braced against the inside rim of the smokestack.

Slowly, he tipped his body back over the yawning darkness as a counterbalance in anticipation of Eleazar's weight. If Eleazar managed to fly, Diver would use the long knife in his belt to slice through the ropes and set him free. It would be dangerous, and there was a risk Eleazar would be caught in the coils and tumble from the sky even if he was able to fly. But the greater risk of smashing headlong into the ground had outweighed it.

"As ready as I'll ever be. Stand fast, Diver."

"You're the diver today," he said, grinning.

The light dimmed as a cloud passed over the sun. Eleazar looked up, squinting against the bright blue sky. Longing filled him. He'd never wanted anything more in that moment than to fly. Not even vengeance came close.

The cloud passed and the sunlight bathed him. Eleazar looked down, his vision sparkling with white spots. The ground seemed farther away than before; he had a long way to fall before he would need his wings. He raised his arms, spreading them wide as if to embrace the world, flexed his knees, and jumped.

Ash men crowded the streets of Trin. Released from their daily grind by shrill whistles and glowering overseers, they trudged home or gathered at the corner taverns. Lines of carts stood ready along the clogged thoroughfares, offering grilled meats, fried manna and hot cider for a coin or two. After so long in the compound, the noise and smells and people overwhelmed Fury. Even on horseback, they had to shoulder through at a walk, careful not to trample anyone, especially the many children. They were like rats, small and quick and filthy. Fury felt inclined to pity them until she saw a group of them corner a man in an alley, divest him of his satchel, and leave him bleeding and dazed on the ground.

"This city is a cesspool," she muttered bitterly. She stood up in her stirrups, hoping to spot her brother among the crowds.

Once she found Diver, she'd be able to think again. The two of them could figure out what to do about Mother.

Mother. It felt like a dream. She had wanted to find her mother so desperately. To see her, to talk to her, to ask her what had happened to her. But given the chance, she had run. She didn't even understand why.

From the moment she'd learned Tuilelaith had been sent with the Hallow Tithe, she'd been certain her mother was still alive. That not even years of brutal Angelic treatment could break Tuilelaith Cree. But she had been broken. She was dead by her own admission. No, Tully's admission. Only Tully remained. They, not her. And she wasn't so sure she wanted to talk to whomever Tully was. The mad little engineer.

Fury settled back into her saddle. "Are you sure you know where to find him? Or are you just stalling? I'm sure your orders are to distract me," she added scornfully.

Ellis gave her a look, her features screwed into a knot. "I told you it wouldn't be easy. Enjoy the ride, Fury. We'll be there soon enough."

The way ahead opened. Ellis guided her mount through a gap, kicking it into a trot. Relieved to pick up the pace, Fury matched her. She had no clue where they were going, so she had no choice but to stick with Ellis. The Naveen woman wasn't going nearly fast enough for her. Diver and Eleazar were doing something dangerous. Tully had given her only the barest shreds of a clue, but Tully was not to be trusted. Mother had always had her own agenda.

Mother.

You are meant for grander things, my little angel.

Where was Ellis taking her? The farther they went into Trin, the more nervous she became. Could she really trust this woman who'd already betrayed her once? Her true loyalty was to Conrad and their cause, not to her. Silently, she cursed her naïveté.

Can't we be friends?

Fury ground her teeth. She had seemed so sincere.

I owe them everything, sweet pea...

"Ellis," she said, moving her horse abreast of hers. They'd turned onto a quieter street. Too quiet. Suspicion leaked around her desperate need to find Diver. "Ellis," she repeated when the woman didn't answer. "Do you know how Conrad is going to get more Mithran?"

Ellis shrugged, looking uncomfortable. She glanced at her, but just as quickly looked away. Fury's unease grew, and she settled a hand near her hip, more precisely near the pistol hidden in her waistband. "He said he had a plan in place. Does it have anything to do with what Diver and Eleazar are up to?"

"He has his ways." Ellis shifted in her saddle. Her horse snorted and sidestepped, reflecting its rider's discomfort. "Conrad only tells me what I need to know. Who am I to question him?"

"You just do what he tells you, then? Whatever he orders."

"I do. I told you. I owe him my life; I'd do anything for him." She looked at her, her dark eyes pained. "Have you no understanding of loyalty?"

"A true leader doesn't require blind loyalty. You should be able to question his decisions!"

Ellis looked ahead, her chin raised and her shoulders stiff. "I don't question what is necessary for our cause, Fury. Right and wrong have no place in our world. We do what must be done, regardless of the cost."

Fury's heart sank. Ellis was a true believer, not to be swayed by mere words. Creator, she'd been a fool! And now she was lost in this strange city, alone and at the mercy of someone she should never have trusted. Nevertheless, she shifted in her saddle, clamping hard with her knees. Her mount blew a questioning whicker, silky skin shivering. Fury readied herself.

They had entered a small square suspiciously empty of people. Here, suddenly, was silence in a city which knew constant noise. The façade of a temple stared blank-faced at them, black eyes for windows in the ash-stained limestone.

Fury held her breath, trying hard to slow her pounding heart. The shadows seemed to hold a hidden multitude. Smoothly, Ellis reached over and grasped her horse's bridle. Fury jerked her reins and dug in her heels. The beast obdurately ignored her but for an aggrieved whinny and a stamped foot.

"Quit yanking at his head," Ellis admonished. "I trained him. He won't move until I let him."

"Why, Ellis?" she demanded. "What is this?"

"I am sorry, Fury." She looked at her, shadows lying across her dark face. "I had no choice. We had no choice. Our cause–"

Fury moaned low in her throat. Her hands released the useless reins, and she considered flinging herself off the horse and making a run for it. Or grabbing her pistol and putting a hole in Ellis. It wasn't too late–

The shadows came to life. Dark figures emerged from hidden places among the buildings, from the temple, figures dressed in the dreaded black of the city regulators. *Fuck.* Her pistol would only get her shot at this point.

One of them approached. "Is it her?" the regulator asked, peering up at Fury. "Yes, I recognize her. Good. Even your dear leader knows not to cross the governor."

"Do you have the Night Witch?" Ellis demanded. Fury's horse tugged against her hold, but Ellis yanked him still.

"As we agreed." The regulator gestured and more men emerged from the temple. This time, a woman walked with them. She was tall and thin, her clothing tattered and dirty, her blonde hair matted in long, thick ropes, but Fury recognized her. She even knew her name. Star Fletcher. The actress at the gates. The one Eleazar had apprehended and given over to Vogel. The one to whom Ellis owed her life.

She understood. She was being traded. Given to Vogel, and by extension, the Angelus soon to arrive. She sat stiffly, unable to formulate a coherent thought. All her bravado, all her fake bravery crumbled to dust. Soon, she would be at the mercy of Captain Pace. She'd be lucky if he only killed her.

"Star!" Ellis cried joyfully. "Are you alright? Have they hurt you?"

"I am well, Ellis," the woman said. She tossed Fury a glance, almost dismissive. "Let's get this over with, shall we? I'm eager to get home."

Ellis nodded, and her smile bent into a frown as she turned back to the regulator. "What about the rest of it?" she snarled. "When does it arrive?"

"Your ersatz leader should be receiving the shipment as we speak. The Angelus were… quite generous for this gift you've given them." The regulator drew his pistol and waved it toward Fury. "Come now, atheist. Don't make this more difficult than it has to be. Your judgment is at hand."

Ellis's fingers tightened convulsively, and her shoulders bunched. She glanced at her guiltily. "Don't fight them," she said in a low, harsh voice. "It will only make things worse."

"They'll kill me," she said, her voice a squeak. "Please, Ellis, don't do this…"

"I told you; I've no choice." She pulled the horse forward so she could whisper in Fury's ear. "They won't harm you, not yet. They wanted Eleazar, but Conrad wouldn't give him up. You were the next best thing. Stay alive, Fury."

Without another word, she kicked their mounts forward and handed the bridle to the constable. Fury sat like a wooden doll atop her horse, unable to move, unable to react. Men surrounded her and dragged her from the saddle, divesting her of her weapon with cold efficiency. She remained limp and unresisting, following Ellis's advice even though her heart ached at the betrayal. She didn't want to give these men an excuse to use their batons.

Someone approached her with manacles, and she knew the minute they were locked in place, she was done. She screamed at herself to fight. To do something, anything! If it were Diver or Eleazar in harm's way, she never would have hesitated. But for herself? Alone like this, she felt helpless.

Timid.

Why haven't you taken the Mithran?

One last hope.

Fury lunged backward, startling her captors. She tore from their grasp and fell to the ground, rolling like a madwoman, one hand snaking to her pocket and the treasure hidden there. Something hard thudded against her back, and again, but she barely felt the blows. Her desperate fingers closed around the precious pearls even as hands tore at her and a baton cracked her across the shoulders, her flailing arm, her unprotected kidneys.

She curled into a ball and stuffed the Mithran into her mouth. How many pearls were left? More than Diver had taken. Many more. She swallowed hard before another blow made her gasp in pain. A second blow caught her in the back of the head and spots of white appeared in her vision. All strength left her, but it didn't matter. She knew escape was impossible; she'd only ever had one goal.

And as someone clapped the dreaded manacles on her wrists, Fury felt her heartbeat quicken. Finally, she'd found the courage to take the gods' metal.

Too late. Far too late.

CHAPTER THIRTY-ONE

Eleazar dropped like a stone, the wind wailing in his ears. His heart thundered to challenge the scream of air, and the rush of blood was a welcome sensation. Fear and excitement pulsed through his veins, powerful and strong. Strong enough? He opened his eyes, tears blinded him immediately, but he blinked them away. His vision cleared and he watched the oncoming rush of the dark, dark earth with rising horror.

Good, good. Feel the fear, let it burn through you...

His blood was pumping hot and fast. Pushing through his veins, surging faster and faster as the ground filled his vision. What had seemed so far away, so small and distant, grew at a rapid rate. A small cluster of shrubs went from green blobs to branches. The red smudge of an outbuilding's roof became terra-cotta tiles. The details were frighteningly clear far too suddenly.

It was time. Now or never.

Eleazar flexed his muscles and pinched his shoulder blades to feel the remnants of his natural wings, connected so cruelly to his newly made metal ones. He could feel the blood pulsing up through the muscles. For once it seemed he could feel the very tips of the metal feathers dragging in the rushing wind. Heart pounding as hard as it could without bursting, Eleazar opened his wings as wide as they would go, pushing with all his might. They moved with reluctant slowness, but they moved. The bronzed feathers caught the wind and he felt himself slow ever slightly. His heart leapt wildly at the sensation.

Please, please, for Splendour's sake...

The tiles overlapped in precise rows but for a gaping hole near the peak of the roof, a hole growing ever larger. The outbuilding was as big as the barracks in Conrad's compound and the shrubs were trees with branches reaching toward him like skeletal fingers.

Using all the strength in his body, all the power of his will, Eleazar spread his wings–

Just as he reached the end of his ropes. Literally.

Wings spread, Eleazar was wrenched upward, flying weightless for a brief, ecstatic moment.

Desperately, he tried to beat his metal wings as he would his own true wings. But he might as well have tried to fly with wooden boards attached to his back. The false wings caught the air, true, and slowed his descent, even let him glide as the rubber ropes keeping him from crashing to the earth grew slack and he began to fall again.

He tried to straighten, to catch an updraft and at least manage a short flight, but he was dragged toward the smokestack by the heavy rubberized ropes. He was bouncing from the ends of them like a helpless doll.

The metal edges of his false feathers slashed into one of the ropes. He grabbed at it, trying to disentangle his wing, any pretense of flying abandoned. Fear gripped him as he swung in an arc. The smokestack–

He slammed into the bricks. Hard. He'd felt so weightless, he hadn't realized how fast he was moving until he hit the smokestack. The breath left him in a painful *whoosh*, and he bounced, flying outward in another reeling arc. His wing was still caught in the rope, the razor edge of the forged Mithran fraying the thick, heavy cable. Fear turned to panic. The cable was splitting. Would one rope hold his weight?

He wanted to shout for Diver, but he couldn't catch his breath before he crashed into the smokestack again. It was a miracle he hadn't dragged Diver from the top of the stack.

The stray thought skittered through his mind and then the rope gave way, and he was dangling by one suddenly very frail-seeming cord. It stretched to impossible thinness even as he clutched at it, desperate to keep it from his sharp wings, now tangled and as useless as they'd ever been. He would have laughed out loud at the irony of the situation if he'd had a breath to spare. His new wings were going to drag him to the earth like golden anchors.

The second cable snapped with abrupt suddenness.

He was falling again, the wind screaming in his ears, and he realized with a sinking heart that all the fear in the world wasn't going to bring his Mithran wings to life.

Diver used the remnants of the rubber ropes for a mad, sliding plummet down the tower.

His heart choking him, he raced to the long, low outbuilding where he'd seen Eleazar crash through the red-tile roof. His fingers tore at the wooden doors, sending chips of old paint and splinters flying. An iron chain and rusted padlock held them closed, but they were hanging on ancient, weathered hinges which yielded to his Mithran-enhanced strength. One door crashed free, raising a cloud of dust and debris. He coughed violently and spat dirt from his mouth then leapt over the broken door and entered the dark interior.

Blinded, he paused and coughed again, clearing the dust from his throat and lungs. Beams of light filtered down through the shattered ceiling, alive with scintillating dust motes. A large pile of debris lay illuminated and there were glimpses of gold among the wreckage.

"Eleazar!" he cried, bounding toward the pile in two great leaps. He tore at the wood and tiles, flinging them aside. "Eleazar!"

A moan emerged from the wreckage. Diver doubled his efforts.

Movement. The flashes of gold resolved into feathers, became wings. The light from above revealed the wings were whole, still beautiful, and entirely undamaged. The Mithran alloy was amazingly resilient. But what of the man attached?

More tearing at tiles and broken wood and finally Diver found an arm, a shoulder. He gripped Eleazar's flesh, feeling for broken bones as he knocked away more dust and debris. The curve of Eleazar's cheek shone from the mess, a tracery of blood fanned across it, making Diver's heart leap. He took a firmer hold of Eleazar's arm and pulled. Resistance. Then the wreckage gave up its prize and Eleazar slid free.

His eyes were closed, but not in repose. Rather they were squeezed tight against the rubble which had covered him. Diver dragged him to a clear space on the dusty floor. Eleazar's feathers chimed musically, but he lay limp in Diver's grip.

Heart racing, Diver scrambled to kneel close beside his head, smoothing golden hair from his scrunched brow. "Are you injured?" he cried desperately. "Are you hurt? Eleazar!"

Eleazar grimaced deeply, his eyes still screwed shut. "Stop shouting."

Diver clapped his lips closed and sagged in relief. He was alive, at least, but maybe in shock. Maybe he couldn't feel his injuries?

Eleazar opened his eyes. Pure agony rested in their blue depths. He stared at the shattered ceiling and lay unmoving.

"The ropes," Diver said anxiously. Eleazar's pain was not physical. It was much deeper. "They tangled in your wings. Tully didn't position them correctly. They didn't plan it right. It wasn't your fault. You might have been able to fly if not for the ropes!"

"No," Eleazar croaked. Slowly, he sat up, his movements stiff. His fingers plucked at his harness. "Get this off me."

Diver obeyed, slicing through the canvas straps with his knife. He tugged the harness loose and tossed it aside, vaguely disturbed by how meekly Eleazar sat while he yanked it away.

Eleazar's arm rose, reaching for him blindly, his eyes fixed on nothing. Diver grasped his hand and helped him climb to his feet, forced to jam a shoulder under his arm to keep the Angelus upright.

Eleazar's primaries scraped the ground like knives. "It wasn't the ropes," he said, his voice empty. "It was me. I failed."

"This time. It was just one test. We can try again. Try a higher smokestack, better ropes. Maybe you need more time, more Mithran!"

"We don't have more time. The Gate will open any day now, and I am helpless."

Eleazar's arm tightened around his shoulders, drawing him closer. A shudder wracked his tall frame, and he hunched over, breath gasping from him. The gasps turned to hitching sobs and his knees buckled beneath him. Diver kept him from falling. Barely. The steel and Mithran wings dragged at his friend. A dreadful thought entered his mind: If the wings didn't grant Eleazar flight, what good were they? He couldn't help but shudder. To see him pinioned *again*...

"You won't be helpless, Eleazar," Diver said, more harshly than he intended. Suddenly, he felt very, very angry. Strength roared through him, and he forced Eleazar to stand tall and face him. He grasped him by the shoulders. Stared into his deep blue eyes. "We will be there. Your faithful acolytes! You won't need to fly to face your enemies, to fight Pace or your brother, or whoever comes for us. Fury and I will be your wings. Together, by our might and our ingenuity, we will bring them crashing down to you!"

The compound was in an uproar when Diver and Eleazar limped home. The engineers, smiths and artisans crowded the muddy training ground, swarming a large canvas-covered pallet. Lights blazed around the perimeter, remarkably bright given their desire for concealment. Whatever was happening seemed important enough to bend the rules. Fury was nowhere to be seen, and Diver left to go find her while Eleazar pushed his way through the clamoring men to see what had caused such a ruckus.

Conrad was lording over the pallet, his arms crossed over his brawny chest and his chin up in smug satisfaction. Joseph Weaver stood at his back rather than Ellis. Not particularly odd. But the redheaded ex-captain's eyes were wide and his lips bloodless. He was staring straight ahead at nothing and had barely glanced at Diver. Usually, Weaver couldn't keep his eyes off the boy. Eleazar's hackles rose. Where was Ellis? His thoughts immediately jumped to Fury. The large, dark woman often shadowed her. Fury didn't seem to mind, but Eleazar had never liked it.

"Ah, Angelus!" Conrad's gleeful greeting distracted Eleazar from his dark thoughts. The one-eyed man waved him forward. "Let the Angelus through, you bloody loons. I told you I'd hold to my promise! Come, see what I've brought you."

Eleazar knew before Conrad lifted a corner of the canvas and tossed it back. Mithran. And not a few errant trinkets, but bricks upon bricks of pure rose-gold gods' metal. It made his heart pound. There was enough Mithran to make wings for a hundred men.

Beautiful, heavy, useless wings...

The Mithran glittered in the electric lights, a thousand colors lurking within the golden ingots. He reached out and touched it: A shimmer of energy passed along his wings and for a brief moment they felt alive. Startled, he stepped back and shifted his wings without thought, as he would have when they'd been true flesh and blood and feathers. They responded and then settled into cold, dead lumps tucked against his back.

"Where did you get this much Mithran?" Such a quantity meant hundreds of slaughtered leviathans. Thousands. Harvested over decades. It was barely a drop in the pool of Angelic reserves, but it was probably more Mithran than had ever reached Avernus. How in the name of the Luminous One had Conrad attained so much of it?

"The hows and wheres don't matter," Conrad temporized, shrugging carelessly. "Don't question my methods, Eleazar, just enjoy the results. Let's just say I did what I had to do."

Which was no answer at all, but Eleazar was having trouble working up an argument in the presence of so much sacred Mithran. Surely, he would be able to achieve flight with this much magic at his disposal. He would swallow pearls of it until he flew or he burst. It would be agonizing, even for him, but he would pay any price to reach the skies again. *Any* price.

Conrad clapped his hands, then rubbed them together avariciously. "Come on, you sloths, get this windfall into the foundry, even if you have to work all night. Quit standing around gawking and be of some use."

Conrad's gravelly voice cracked out further profanity-laden commands, sending his people into a flurry of activity. Only Weaver didn't leap to obey; he stood rigidly, his hand on his sidearm as if expecting an attack.

Briefly, Weaver glanced toward Eleazar. Their eyes met, but Weaver's bounced away like it hurt to look at him. His head dropped, and he stared intently at the ground. Eleazar sneered, his unease returning.

Where was Ellis?

Again, he searched for the errant bodyguard, a thread of disquiet wending its way through his belly. It made no sense that the absence of one woman would fill him with such foreboding, but it wasn't just *one* woman who was absent.

Fury.

He and Diver had been gone most of the day, and it was well past sunset. They'd expected her to be pacing anxiously, ready to pounce on them when they returned. Both of them had been braced to face her rage.

"You!" Eleazar strode toward Weaver, dodging the engineers and artisans who had begun the arduous process of carrying the ingots into the workroom. Wheelbarrows and a sledge appeared to aid in the task. The pile of Mithran began to shrink steadily. "Where is Ellis?"

"How should I know?" Weaver stood his ground, glaring back at him, but his hand tightened on his pistol. "I'm not her commander. She goes where she likes."

"You lie." Eleazar flared his nostrils. "I can smell when humans lie. You reek of sweat and sourness. Deceit and betrayal. What do you know, boy? What have you treacherous creatures done now?"

Somehow, Weaver's face grew whiter still. His arrogant demeanor vanished. "I didn't know anything about it, I swear. Tell Diver, I would never–"

"*Where is Fury*?!"

The enraged shriek blasted through the courtyard, bringing all activity to a standstill. Eleazar spun away from Weaver; he'd been about to scream the same thing, and someone had beaten him to it. The engineer, Tully, stalked from the foundry building straight toward the pile of Mithran, or more precisely, Conrad. They moved like a prowling lion, head lowered, hands curled into claws, their short, silver hair bristling.

On top of the pallet, a brick of Mithran in his hand, Conrad blinked his one eye but showed no other signs of distress. "Tully." He spoke lightly, as if glad to see them. "Can you believe it? The Mithran we need is ours at last!"

"Answer the question, Conrad," Eleazar said darkly. His wings had lifted from his shoulders, seemingly of their own accord. The thread of disquiet turned to suspicion.

"What? Fury? How should I know where she is?"

Tully had by now reached the pile of ingots, and they stabbed an accusing finger up at him. "She left with Ellis hours ago and neither has returned. What did you do, Conrad?"

Gone. Fury was gone. Suspicion gave way to dread. Eleazar felt unsettled, almost dizzy. "Where is she?" Eleazar growled, coming to stand beside Tully. For once, the little engineer didn't move away from him.

"Calm yourselves," Conrad said blandly, handing his ingot to a waiting blacksmith. The man, Harris, took it reluctantly, his gaze shifting between Conrad and Tully and Eleazar as if he were surrounded by growling dogs. "Ellis must be showing her around the city. Fury wanted to know the ins and outs of Trin. She's been pestering Ellis for days."

"Do you think I'm a fool?" Tully hissed. Suddenly, they regarded the pile of Mithran as if just noticing it. "You got your Mithran."

"Our Mithran, Tully. Ours! Don't you understand? Now, you can start mass producing the flight suits. You can make your 'miracle' rockets! You said you figured out the secret. Now you have the Mithran you need. I got it for you. Everything is falling into place, don't you see? They won't know what hit them!" He shifted focus to Eleazar. "And you, Angelus, with this much Mithran, surely you'll be able to fly."

Eleazar couldn't think about flying, could barely think at all. Something wasn't right. Not just Fury's absence. A violent rage rippled through his belly, terror chasing after, but it was distant. A thick fog had engulfed him, edged with horror. The Mithran. There was so much of it. Too much. The Angelus would never allow so much gods' metal loose in the human world...

"What did it cost, you monster?" Tully was shaking with emotion. Rage.

Conrad ignored them, moving to pick up another ingot. "Nothing I wasn't willing to pay. Trust me; it will be worth it."

Tully's face grew red. They raised clenched fists. "If they harm a hair on her head, I will kill you. Do you hear me, Conrad? I will drive a blade through your heart!"

"What the fuck, Tully? Have you lost your entire mind?" Conrad jumped down from the pallet, looming over the smaller engineer menacingly. "You threaten me to my face, among my people? For what? A stranger! What is she to you?"

"She is *everything*, you fucking bastard!"

Their shout reverberated around the courtyard. Half the engineers and artisans cringed, while others went about their work without pause. The Mithran shifted faster and faster. Blurring in Eleazar's vision. He swayed. It was getting harder and harder to think. He wanted to strike Conrad, but he was trapped in agony. His head pounded. His heart raced.

Suddenly, he understood. Sheer terror gripped him.

Shoving past Conrad, knocking Tully onto their ass in the process, he staggered to the pile of ingots.

"It's a trap," he gasped, tearing at the ingots, seeking the one causing him such physical distress. "Clear the compound! Now!"

"What are you talking about, Angelus?" Conrad demanded, reaching for him as if he intended to stop his frantic digging. An ingot nearly caught him in the chest, and he yelped as he jumped aside. "Have you lost your mind, too!"

Eleazar's hand grasped the ingot he sought. A shock of energy jolted up his arm, nearly as bad as the so-called "electricity" which had incapacitated him. But he was ready for it. He snatched the brick free, his teeth gritted.

Whoever had delivered the Mithran had hidden a destabilized brick within it, the gaseous essence contained only by a thin veneer of the gods' metal. Compressed in such a small space, it would be as powerful as a drachen engine. The casing would only hold it for so long. This one bar was enough to cause a chain reaction. This much Mithran to fuel it would blast Conrad's entire compound into pieces – and not a little of the city surrounding them.

His mind emptied of thought. Driven by fear and self-preservation, Eleazar tucked the ingot against his chest and bolted for the center of the training field. He had to get it away from the rest of the gods' metal!

"Clear the compound!" he shouted again. "Everyone to the streets! Now!"

He had no idea if anyone obeyed him. Heat poured from the ingot, scorching his skin. He had mere seconds. There would be no getting it out of the compound, but hopefully he could minimize the damage. He stopped and spun, the ingot in one hand, and at the apex of his turn he flung the deadly missile into the sky like a discus. It was a bright streak in the night sky, oddly beautiful, rising high above the stables.

Breath scraping in and out of his throat, his heart thundering, Eleazar turned and flung himself to the earth.

A heartbeat. Dirt in his nose and mouth. Sweat in his eyes. A blinding flash–

CHAPTER THIRTY-TWO

Fury was nowhere to be found. Not in the dormitory. Not in the foundry. Not in their little house. Not in the stables. Where in the Abyss could she have gone?

Ellis was gone, too. A few inquiries proved as much. Perhaps they were somewhere together? Somewhere outside the compound? He was aware (his sister thought she'd been so clever about hiding it) that Fury wanted a way out of Trin. An escape plan if all this went to shit. A distinct likelihood. Unfortunately, the Naveen woman had been more than happy to indulge Fury's fantasies. It should have made him relieved, knowing they were together. But the sudden appearance of a massive cache of Mithran the exact moment his sister had vanished was too much of a coincidence for his peace of mind. And as much as Ellis might like Fury, her loyalty was to Conrad and the Cause.

His increasingly frantic search took him back to the stables. Two horses were absent. *Damn it*. The stable hands wouldn't give him any answers beyond vague denials and confused recollections.

Frustrated, Diver was about to start breaking things when the sound of hoofbeats echoed on the cobblestones outside.

Relieved, Diver dashed to a door he rarely utilized. An alley ran alongside the back wall of the stables, cramped and filthy. From the outside, the stables looked like an abandoned building with boarded-up windows, peeling paint and crumbling brick.

Only those who knew about the compound would bother to travel down the trash-strewn alley. He slid open the battered old door on tracks well-greased and silent, his relief turning to anger, ready to give Fury a piece of his mind for frightening him so badly.

Two riders picked their way down the alley. The rising moon illuminated them. One was unmistakably Ellis with her dark skin, flowing braids and broad frame. Her shoulders were slumped. Diver sought the second rider.

It was not Fury. The rider was female, but there the resemblance ended. Slight and blonde and far too pale. His stomach fell to his boots. He clutched the edge of the door for balance. He knew her: The Mithran smuggler, the one imprisoned in Vogel's dungeon. He'd watched her get dragged away the day he, Eleazar and Fury had arrived in Trin. Never to be seen again.

Star Fletcher, war heroine. Suddenly returned to her people while his sister had gone missing.

Panic drove him down the alley at a run. His mad dash startled Ellis's horse, sending it into a squealing sidestep. The woman, Star, pulled her horse onto its heels, scowling at his sudden appearance. Diver leapt at Ellis, grabbing her by the jacket and dragging her from her dancing horse. The beast whinnied, half-reared and clattered hastily to the door Diver had left open, seeking the safety of the stables.

Diver manhandled the musclebound woman with ease where before she would have clobbered him. He barely reached her chin, after all. But the Mithran granted him unnatural strength and he took full advantage of it.

"Where is she?" Diver said, shaking her, his voice rising to a shriek. "Where is my sister!"

Her eyes red-rimmed, Ellis sagged in his grip, and suddenly he was holding her up rather than accosting her. She couldn't meet Diver's gaze.

"Gone," she croaked. Tears filled those red, red eyes. "I'm sorry. I had no choice…"

"Where?" Diver asked, unable to form more coherent questions. His rage was turning to panic. "Is she–?"

"She lives." Tears leaked from her eyes and cut tracks through the dust on her face. "For now. He wants to draw out the Angelus."

Diver didn't need to ask who she meant. His grip on Ellis eased; the woman had no fight in her, and her utter capitulation stole some of Diver's violent rage. "Vogel," he said. "He's going to give her to Pace, isn't he?"

Ellis managed a nod and closed her eyes. Pain creased her face, aging her by decades. It was honest pain. Ellis had liked Fury, maybe even more than liked, but she would have done as Conrad ordered.

"Creator damn you, Ellis! She trusted you; she *liked* you! How could you betray her like this? Even for Conrad? Is there no line you won't cross for him?"

"No, there isn't. I tried to warn her, I did, but there was no stopping this. Strike me dead if you must. I deserve it."

Diver groaned, deeply tempted to do what Ellis wanted. Instead, he released her. "I don't have to kill you," he snarled. "Eleazar will do it for me."

Her lips pinched grey at the edges. "I won't blame him if he does," she said. "I imagine he'll want to kill all of us."

Of that, Diver had no doubt. For a moment, despite the Mithran roaring through his veins, he felt helpless. Lost. All the jealousy he'd been feeling toward Fury suddenly seemed absurd. She was all he had in the world, all he'd ever had. His sister, his best friend. She'd done everything in her power to keep him safe and he'd always taken her for granted. And now she was in the hands of their enemies. Doomed.

"No." The word scraped from him, razor-edged. "We'll get her back. We'll raid Vogel's palace, kill anyone in our way. We'll burn all of Trin to the ground! I'll put a bullet in the governor's brain myself. I'll–"

"You'll do nothing," spoke a high, firm voice. The rescued woman stood behind them, holding her horse. He'd forgotten all about her. Her face was shadowed in the dark alley, but her sharp chin was lifted. "Years of planning are coming to a head. The fate of one woman mustn't derail everything we've done. Not you, not even your pet Angelus," and the sneer was obvious in her tone, "will be allowed to destroy our work. Revolution is coming. It requires sacrifice."

"Not my sister!" Diver turned on her, fists raised, shaking with anger. "And the Creator Eternal Himself couldn't keep Eleazar from trying to save her. I don't know who you are in all of this, but I guarantee you know nothing of our will and–"

A flash and a deafening explosion obliterated whatever else Diver was going to say as the world around them erupted.

A tremor shivered through the carpeted hallway of Vogel's palace. Slight and fleeting. Fury felt the vibration against the soles of her feet as she was marched down the hall toward Vogel's office where, ages ago, she'd watched Eleazar speak with Captain Pace in a crystal ball. Her guards didn't seem to notice anything amiss. At the end of the hall the wide, ornate doors to Vogel's chamber swung open and the governor himself appeared, looking darkly pleased.

"What exquisite timing!" He beckoned them forward vigorously. "Come, come, hurry along. You must see it for yourself."

The guards took her by the arms and hustled her forward. She was tempted to drag her feet, but she was already having trouble thinking clearly. There was a strange burning in her muscles and a terrible cramping in her belly. She'd expected pain, and it wasn't nearly as bad as she'd feared. Perhaps Mother had been right about the manna.

Tully, Tully, Tully...

It was hard thinking about her mother without withering regret. She'd run from the ghost of Tuilelaith Cree and now wanted nothing more than to talk with her – or them, whichever her mother preferred – to ask her what and why and how. The Mithran hadn't transformed her, not yet. She could only wait and hope. But the vision of that flying suit obsessed her. She understood one thing with vivid clarity: That suit was meant for her.

You were meant for grander things, my little angel...

Was she meant to fly?

The Mithran burned. She burned...

Her guards dragged her across the threshold into Vogel's office. The governor took her by the chin, frowning as he examined her, peering into her eyes – squinted painfully though the light was low – and sweeping his narrowed gaze over her burning cheeks, her sweating brow.

"What's wrong with her?" he demanded. "I told you she wasn't to be harmed."

"And she hasn't been, sir," one of them responded, daring to sound slightly indignant.

"Is she sick, then?"

"I don't know, Lord Governor. Perhaps? People live like rats in some parts of the city. There's no telling what she might have picked up."

Vogel hmphed doubtfully and released Fury's chin. "Do you understand where you are?" he said to her, loud enough to make her wince. "What's happening to you, yes?"

"I understand I am a prisoner," she said. She felt distant from what was happening, but she understood it all too well. "That you mean to hand me over to the Angelus when they arrive."

"Ah, good, you do understand. I always suspected you were the smart one. Creator knows Eleazar Starson is naught but a fool."

Turning his back on her, Vogel went to the grand bay windows behind his desk. He opened the lead-paned glass to the night air. The city lay beyond, lit by gas lamps and electric lights, it spread out below them like a field of stars. A full moon hung in the sky above and the night seemed nearly as bright as day. Vogel turned to her again, triumphant. He crooked his finger, beckoning.

Fury shuffled forward in her chains and joined him at the window. The breeze was cool and fresh, and in spite of her situation Fury felt rejuvenated by the rush of wind on her face. It carried the scent of green, open spaces, blooming flowers, and rich, dark soil. The tall, cramped brick and mortar buildings were made lovely by the darkness, though the burning of coal fires and the great belching of the iron horses lay a smoky haze over the city. For a moment, she noticed nothing amiss, and then she saw. Her heart gave a lurch.

A thick tower of black smoke churned from a distant portion of the city, limned by moonlight. For the first time since she'd started to feel the Mithran at work, she felt something besides pain. Fear crawled through her. Something terrible had happened. This wasn't smoke from a factory forge, or someone's coal stove. Out there, something was burning. Fiercely.

"It was such a simple plan."

Vogel spoke from beside her, right in her ear, making her start. His hot breath struck her cheek, reeking of leeks and sourness.

"Conrad couldn't resist such a bounty of Mithran, you see. Captain Pace knew this, as he knew who among his kind benefited from the illicit trade. It hadn't really bothered him, until now. But he knew an exiled Angelus might have use for the stuff, so he had to put a stop to it. He has dealt with his own people. All pinioned, as is their way." He chuckled softly. "And they call us barbarians. Though I suppose it's no different than lopping off the hand of a thief."

Flashes erupted within the column of billowing smoke. Explosions. She remembered the stash of artillery in the stables and felt faint.

"Of course, we've tried to draw him out. But even his wife wasn't a big enough prize. Though we didn't mind tossing her into the bargain. She's been nothing but a nuisance in our cells. Fomenting unrest and encouraging resistance." He sighed. "The idea of revolution is a disease."

Wife? Of course. It made sense Star was Conrad's wife. They'd been working as a team for some time now. Both would have wanted more than her mere freedom. Thus, a stash of Mithran had been offered. She wondered how much they'd gotten and felt a surge of hope to think of Eleazar with access to so much of the magical substance.

Perhaps Vogel and Pace had made a terrible blunder?

The tower of red-bellied smoke told her otherwise.

"How?" she asked numbly.

"Mithran can be incredibly volatile with certain manipulation, you see. Oh, yes, I know. I was surprised as you. Apparently, the Angelus have been using it to blast our world apart for generations, stealing mountaintops and the sort as they steal our bounty. Not that we were aware, mind you. Avernus is vast. But Pace had to let me in on the little secret to initiate his plan or I would never have agreed to it. Why give them so much of the gods' metal when they have an Angelus to manipulate it? Insanity. But if all those revolutionaries and their stockpile of weapons was destroyed along with the Mithran, what was there to lose?"

"How do you know your plan succeeded? You don't know anything. It could be a coincidence—"

Vogel's full-throated laugh rang out into the soft spring night. "Do you know how long I've been searching for his hideout?" He stabbed a finger toward the column of smoke. "There it is, plain as day. And my men are on their way to deal with any potential survivors."

"It won't be so easy to kill Eleazar," she said, adding silently, or Diver, "even if he was caught in the blast. He's an Angelus. He fell from Heaven and lived."

Vogel shrugged, unconcerned. "It wasn't our goal to kill Eleazar," he said reasonably. "Captain Pace wants him alive. And that's where you come in, my dear."

"He'll come before the Gate opens, I promise you. Captain Pace will be leagues away…"

Her disparaging words died in her throat as a shadow passed in front of the moon. Then another and another. Fury felt a thread of cold through her belly. It numbed her burning limbs. Reluctantly, she looked up, searching the dark skies for more shadows. There. And there. Gold traced the swollen bellies of a dozen drachen, descending slowly from a churning maelstrom of spiraling silver.

The Gate had opened.

CHAPTER THIRTY-THREE

The air seared his lungs. Diver coughed violently and was dragged back to consciousness. His head rang with thunder, almost drowning out the roar of flames. What had happened to him? Heat scratched at his legs like the claws of a ravenous beast. He lurched but was unable to rise. Something had him pinned face down against the ground.

Someone groaned wretchedly. Diver managed to lift his head enough to turn it. The air was full of cinders and ash, and a darkness broken only by the glow of fire coming from somewhere behind him, inching closer he knew from the heat ripping at his trousers. The blonde woman lay close to him, a dark bulk on top of her. Ellis, he realized with a shock. Blood crowned her brow and her eyes stared at him. Empty. She had shielded the other woman.

A flash to rival the sun. A deep boom tearing the world apart...

Panic broke through his muddled thoughts. He couldn't move. Could barely breathe. The thing pinning him was monstrous. He craned his head to try and see it. It was a mound of darkness silhouetted against the flames. Something hot and sticky dripped from it onto him, soaking through his clothes. Blood. It was a horse, he realized dimly. A dead horse. Blasted apart. It had saved him from the brunt of the explosion but now left him helpless to escape the flames.

NoNoNoNO!

He began to struggle. He would not die trapped like a bug!

Panicked, agonized screams drifted from the shattered stables. Unfortunate beasts trapped in the wreckage. The screams cut through him, and he panted for breath, fighting against rising terror. He couldn't move, couldn't breathe. Every breath seared his lungs like a dreaded gas attack. And he was trapped–

Trapped in a huddle of clawing, screaming men, mouths foaming, eyes streaming tears; flesh seared and blackening wherever the horrid yellow poison touched–

Diver thrashed and clawed at the cobblestones, dragging himself inch by inch from beneath the dead horse, fighting to escape, visions assaulting him. His fingernails broke on the slick stones. His breath wheezed from him, half sobs, half keening screams. He would not die like this!

Faintly, he heard someone calling his name.

More deafening rending cracks and shrieks erupted behind him. Diver squeezed his eyes shut, waiting for more crushing debris. Waiting for the end. And then, unexpectedly, the weight of the shattered animal vanished, lifted away as if by the hand of the Eternal. It crashed into the alley some distance from him with a sickening splat. Free at last, Diver scrambled to his knees, his feet, then beat frantically at his smoldering trousers. Coughing wracked him, and for an endless moment he was bent over, gagging and retching.

"Diver! Diver! Thank the Creator!"

Hands grabbed him, dragging him into an embrace. Shaken, singed, Diver clung to Weaver. Free. He was free. Cinders rained down around them. A smoking hole had been blown through the stables. The entire western end of the structure was obliterated. Fire burned steadily, a strange, white-hot conflagration creeping along, practically *eating* the wooden building.

And standing behind Weaver, between them and the destruction, stood his savior, hands covered in gore, golden wings extended in a sheltering expanse, eyes lit by an unholy glow to rival the unnatural fire behind him.

"Eleazar..."

Eleazar's bright eyes shifted from him to the still form on the ground nearby. "Ellis," he growled. He slipped past them and reached for her fire-blackened jacket.

"Don't hurt her!" Weaver shouted, breaking away from Diver and reaching toward Eleazar. As if he could stop the Angelus...

"It's too late," Diver said, keeping a grip on Weaver's arm. "She's dead."

"What? No! Let go of me—"

Eleazar had rolled her over at this point, and it was clear by her clouded gaze and limp stillness that she no longer lived. He stared down at her grimly, then his eyes shifted to the still-living woman who'd been beneath the ex-soldier. "You," he said, his voice full of dark menace.

"She can't be dead!" Weaver fell beside his friend, shaking her hard then checking beneath her chin for a pulse. His pale face went white, and his shoulders sagged. "You were always the tough one," he said softly. "Nothing could touch you. Oh, gods. Ellis..."

The other woman, Star, lay dazed at Eleazar's feet. She looked back at the Angelus as if he were a snake poised to strike.

"Conrad traded Fury for *her*," Diver said, his voice hard as nails, "and a pile of Mithran."

Eleazar reached down and picked her up by her ragged, smoke-stained shirtfront. She clutched his wrist as he hoisted her to her feet, whimpering. Who knew what injuries she'd sustained? Diver's Mithran-enhanced body – and Star's unfortunate horse – had saved him from any real damage. But any pity he might have felt for her vanished when she opened her mouth.

"Think carefully, Angelus," she gasped. "You don't know what's at stake! I must be with Conrad and our army when the time comes. I'm their inspiration, their shining Star!"

"You think quite highly of yourself," he responded.

"She's not lying," Weaver said. He climbed to his feet, his eyes still on his fallen friend. "Many of my comrades would die for her."

"Then she'll make an excellent bargaining chip." Eleazar shoved Star toward Weaver, who managed to catch her before she stumbled and fell. "She's your responsibility now. If you wish to prove your loyalty to us, you'll keep her in hand."

Weaver made no objection. He threw a glance at Diver, bright spots appearing on his cheeks, and took Star firmly by the arm. Diver wondered what sort of bargain Weaver had made with Eleazar. He'd very obviously chosen a side if there were sides to choose in all of this.

His eyes switched back to the burning stables. Heat poured from the conflagration; it showed no sign of stopping. Soon, the entire stable would be ablaze. There was no way they would be able to go back into the compound that way, and the debris from the blast had choked the narrow, dead-end alley.

"We have to get out of here," he exclaimed abruptly. "The fire will..."

"The storeroom," Weaver finished for him. "Shit. All that ammunition!"

"They'll be fighting the flames from the inside," Star said, oddly confident considering her predicament. "We have a protocol. They won't burn us out!"

"No man can stop that fire," Eleazar said, equally as sure. Star opened her mouth but quickly shut it at his withering look.

"Then we really do have to find a way out of here," Diver reiterated. He coughed convulsively as the smoke thickened. Embers rained like stars from the dark sky. Weaver pulled a handkerchief from his pocket and passed it to him, adding with not a little panic, "When the flames reach the ammunition, we'll be blown to the Abyss!"

"We can go through the stables," Star spoke up, each word emerging with reluctance. When the others looked at her in disbelief, she raised her soot-blackened chin. "We have protocols. Quick escape is one of our contingency plans. There is a way out if we can reach it."

Weaver's tragic expression brightened. "She's right! The tunnels. There's a trapdoor." His brow furrowed again as he took in the destruction nearest them. The roof had caved in, and the wood structure still burned, although with red-gold flames rather than the bright incendiary light consuming the rest of the building. "It might be buried..."

"Then we'll unbury it." Eleazar's wings reflected the fire hypnotically as he turned toward the stables. "Diver. Aid me. The Mithran in your blood will shield you better than the others. You, Weaver, point me in the right direction."

The escape route in question was indeed buried beneath flaming rubble. Eleazar tore through it like a bear tearing through scrub. Diver joined him, though less enthusiastically. He felt the heat. It scorched his skin, leaving blisters, but almost immediately, the injuries healed. Soon, Diver felt strength and confidence infuse him. He attacked the rubble, ignoring his pain. The terror of being trapped receded.

The other two felt the flames far differently. He could hear Weaver struggling to breathe, and Star cowered behind him, coughing incessantly as they moved closer to the promised trap door. But Star was the first to lunge forward and kick away burning straw to reveal an iron ring embedded in the floorboards. Using a scrap of her burned and tattered jacket, she gripped the ring and tugged hard. A section of the floor lifted.

With burning debris dropping around them and smoke choking the air, Star descended into the darkness down a ladder attached to a rough-hewn stone wall. Diver urged Weaver after her and motioned for Eleazar to go next.

The Angelus shook his head. "You next," he ordered with a fierce glare. "I'll not lose you today, too."

"We'll get her back," Diver said. "By the Creator Eternal and your Luminous One, I swear it!"

"I know. There is no other option I will accept."

Diver dropped into the tunnel and waited until Eleazar had gone through the trapdoor. The Angelus pulled it closed. And just in time. A distant boom rattled the stone walls of the tunnel. Dust rained from the ceiling. With a glance at each other in the deep gloom, they turned and bolted down the tunnel chased by hell itself.

They took her to the Tithing Ground to meet the arriving ships, Vogel giddy with the chance to hand her over to Captain Pace. He must have borne the brunt of Pace's displeasure after their escape at the Winter Tithe, for he took every opportunity to abuse her on the way. Tripping her, dragging her by her chains, lifting her by her hair to get her back on her feet, giving her several kicks ostensibly to keep her moving. His rage and bitterness towards her couldn't have been any clearer. She'd been the one who'd stabbed and shot Pace, but he had suffered for it. It pleased her immensely.

He and his guards dragged her to a stop beneath the royal flagship in the bright glare of a dozen spotlights. Two dark, winged shapes descended. Fury stared up at the approaching Angelus, her heart clattering. Tingles traced her skin; she felt aglow from within. The pain had passed, and a lightness had entered her bones. She was no longer afraid.

The two Angelus were ordinary ones, if any Angelus could be called ordinary, plumaged in soft browns and yellows, their skin nearly as dark as her own. In spite of herself and her long-held beliefs, she felt a reluctant awe in their presence. Perhaps they weren't immortal, or divine, but they were extraordinary. Unworldly. And she was only human.

Am I? Am I still only human?

"Good riddance," Vogel muttered when he handed her over to them. "I hope you get everything you deserve, foul woman."

"You as well, Lord Governor." She grinned at him as the angels hoisted her into the air. When they had reached a height, she spat, aiming carefully. Vogel's curses drifted up to her and she laughed to see him swipe at his hair in disgust. She always had been a crack shot!

She was unsurprised to find a greeting party when her escorts deposited her on the drachen's sanded deck. She'd expected Captain Pace, of course, and he was there, towering over the others, looking as fierce as ever. An ugly, twisting scar marred his neck. She smiled. He scowled darkly, death a promise in his black eyes.

Lamps illuminated the deck of the ship, but they were not electric lights, or even gas lanterns. They gleamed strangely, a soft phosphorescence swimming with blues and greens. Cold horror shuddered up her spine, and she knew with sudden certainty those lamps were eyes.

They call to me in lamentations. Songs of death and suffering...

She reached up to grasp one end of her scarf, seeking comfort in its presence. They had not taken it from her, thankfully. Its dark indigo sheen had been dulled by dust and grime, so it seemed unremarkable.

"This is the one?" spoke a male angel among the audience. He was shorter than Pace, but no less impressive. Lithe where Pace was bulky, he wore a fine, long jacket of deep purple velvet in an antique cut with matching hose rather than trousers. Lace spilled from his cuffs and collar, shining with golden thread. The colors complemented the deep emerald wings peeking above his broad shoulders, startlingly beautiful. His long, curling sable hair reflected the green of his feathers. She had never seen him before, and she'd never gotten a clear description from Eleazar, but she knew who he was immediately. The high cheekbones and straight nose, the piercing eyes (purple, rather than blue) and the arrogant tilt of his head gave him away.

Rastaphar Mikalson, the brother who had betrayed Eleazar.

Standing beside him, one slim hand resting delicately on Rast's velvet-clad arm was a female angel. The first she'd ever seen. And this was no ordinary female. She was tall and slender, nearly as tall as Fury, her skin milk-white and smooth as an unblemished peach. A fall of midnight-black hair spilled over her shoulders nearly to her waist, straight and silky. The feathers of her wings matched her hair, their blackness made deeper by the simple gown of white linen she wore which skimmed her perfect figure in a manner both seductive and innocent.

By comparison, Fury felt like a drowned rat just plucked from the sewer, for she knew this woman, too, as she knew Rast: Maurissa. Eleazar's betrothed.

He never loved her, she reminded herself fiercely. *She betrayed him! With his own brother. This is the treacherous bitch who shot him.*

So why did she feel a deep, burning envy for this graceful, gorgeous angel?

There were others with these three, but Fury gave them no notice. Hatred burned in her heart. Maurissa raised an arched eyebrow, perfectly shaped and groomed, noticing her seething regard. The hint of a smile touched her ruby lips. As if she couldn't believe Fury had dared to look at her, much less judge her.

"This is the woman who almost struck you dead, Captain Pace?" There was amusement in Rast's voice. He seemed nearly on the verge of laughter. "I must say, I was expecting someone much more impressive. Some warrior-woman like they grow in Naveen. Though I suppose she is rather tall and broad. Still, what a disappointment."

"You should be embarrassed, Pace," Maurissa added in a lilting drawl. Damn it all, even her voice was beautiful. Fury felt her face crunch into a scowl. Laughter rang from the female angel. "Oh, my, she is rather frightening to look upon."

Pace stiffened. His gaze grew darker if that were possible. He looked away from Fury, though, as if now she was beneath his contempt. "You have no experience dealing with the scum of the Below, Your Highness, my lady. They are far more treacherous than you can imagine. But that is my duty and my burden, and I accept it willingly. Not just the Silence must separate our people from these... beasts."

Rast gave a slow nod, his eyes on Fury. "And we are grateful for your service, Captain, never doubt it. I was merely surprised to see that the woman who almost took you from us is so... ordinary."

He said "ordinary" like it was a deadly disease. Fury lifted her chin; she did indeed feel ordinary surrounded by these winged and ethereal creatures. But it warmed her heart to know they were vulnerable, that they bled like humans, died like humans. These immortal angels were merely men – and women – with wings. It was the Mithran which granted them power. She could feel it in her own blood and bones and muscles. Like a drug granting invincibility.

You are not invincible. Tread carefully...

"And you say Eleazar will come for her?" Maurissa asked incredulously. She moved across the deck, her steps small and as delicate as the rest of her. "Like some dog in heat? Or a rutting pig?" Her lips twitched and her eyes sparkled with amusement. Keeping her distance, she circled Fury, appraising her. "I suppose losing one's wings does things to an Angelus. He's obviously lost what little mind he had left."

Fury bristled, rage choking her. "How dare you!" she hissed. She turned with the circling woman, keeping her in her sights. Her shackles seemed lighter now, almost insubstantial. "You shot him – poisoned him! He fell through the Black Silence, through nothing less than death! He fell all the way to my world and yet he lived. Then your poison tried to kill him. I had to cut off his wing to save his life. But, again, he lived. I imagine half of you lot would have died of despair!"

Maurissa waved a hand, clearly unimpressed. Fury's rage burned hotter.

"You will never know what we went through to reach Trin, to reach the Tithing Ground. Eleazar saved us, saved our lives more than once, and we saved him. Me and my brother. We passed through the Abyss to return him to his people and his own mother turned on him! And for what? For surviving and daring to be less than perfect! You think you all are perfect? You are the twisted ones! You are the broken ones. In heart and soul and mind, you are deformed. Worse than any Burnt Ghoul! You are not fit to step foot on Avernus. You are the beasts, not us! And Eleazar, your prince and your future king, is a god compared to all of you together!"

Wide-eyed, Maurissa stared at her until her tirade had finished, then she burst out laughing. She put a slim hand over her mouth, her eyes dancing, her slender frame shivering with jocularity. Finally, she managed to gasp out a few words. "Eleazar? A god?" She blinked tears from her eyes and smoothed her dress though there wasn't a single wrinkle in its perfect layers. "You don't know him at all, do you?"

Fury's cheeks burned. She clenched her teeth, unable to understand the joke. As if this... creature knew Eleazar better than she did. She gripped the chains of her shackles. The metal links were hot against her palms.

Rast motioned Maurissa back to his side and she glided to him obediently, still chuckling softly and shaking her head. "I see Eleazar has been on his best behavior during his little excursion among your kind. I suppose he did what he had to for survival's sake. Our lost prince is a much different sort in Splendour."

"Oh, yes," Maurissa added, her voice a deep purr. "Your noble god is a scoundrel and a sybarite, famous among our people only for his debauchery. His tastes are rather perverted. Our kind would never consider lying with your kind, but that never bothered Eleazar. He made his rounds among the nethermost brothels in Lower Splendour, fornicating with humans and pinioned. No creature was beneath him. Or should I say, all creatures were beneath him?"

She emitted another silvery peal of laughter, and Fury snapped her shackles like brittle twine. Before the laughter could die on Maurissa's lips, Fury had lunged at her, hands out to choke the life from the Angelus.

CHAPTER THIRTY-FOUR

"It's here, I can see the way out," Weaver said, stumbling along the last stretch of dank tunnel to reach a tepid pool of light. He stood within it, head tipped back, blinking against the pale sunlight leaking from an iron grate in the ceiling. "I don't know where we are, though. I got lost about ten turns ago."

"As long as we don't exit on the Grand Promenade, I think we'll be alright to leave the tunnels," Diver said, coming to stand beside him. He spotted a ladder against the wall, wooden and rickety. A way up.

"Nowhere in Trin is safe for us," Star interjected tiredly. She had led them through the tunnels for the most part. They'd had to stop a few times when she'd lapsed into a daze, still suffering ill effects from the blast, but her directions had led them here. "Not on the streets," she clarified from where she sat slumped against the damp wall, shivering. The constant wet had left them all chilled, but for Eleazar. "I told you before, and I'll tell you again, we must go to the Factory. Conrad will give you all shelter. I promise. He'll give you anything if you bring me back to him."

"Given that there has never been a mention of this so-called 'Factory' before, I find your insistence uncompelling." Eleazar emerged from the darkness of the tunnel, and the sad, dim light suddenly seemed a brilliant radiance. His warmth bathed them all, and even Star closed her eyes, her wan face relaxing in his glow.

"And where do you want to go, Angelus?" Weaver asked sarcastically. He put himself between Diver and Eleazar to Diver's annoyance, acting with inappropriate possessiveness. "To the governor's palace?"

Considering that was exactly where he'd said he wanted to go, Eleazar scowled at him. "You don't need to come with us if you're afraid. I don't need any cowards along."

"Cowards." Weaver scoffed. He rolled his eyes and turned his back on Eleazar. "Are you with him on this?" he demanded of Diver. "Flying off to commit suicide? Or are you going to be the sensible one and find yourself an army first?"

"What army?" Diver said, equally mocking. "For all we know, Conrad and the others have all been blown to bits."

"You don't believe that…"

Diver's lips thinned. He didn't want to believe it, but he'd witnessed the destruction firsthand. What other conclusion could be drawn? He returned to his main motivation, logic be damned. "We have to get my sister back."

"Tearing into Vogel's palace won't get her back," Star said, grimacing as she tried to shift into a more comfortable position. "The Celestial Gate was due to open last night. Which was several hours ago, judging by the angle of the light. He would have delivered her to the Angelus as soon as he could."

Her words drove an icy spike of fear through his heart. "You don't know for certain!"

"You are a dead woman if that is true," added Eleazar, trampling on the heels of Diver's outburst. "Pace will kill her for humiliating him!"

"No. He won't," she insisted calmly, remarkably brave in the face of Eleazar's threat. "The other one won't let him. From what I understand, he is the one who wants to draw you out. Not the captain of the Tithing ship."

"What 'other one'?" Diver demanded, confused.

She shook her head. "I wasn't exactly privy to all their plans. But I heard enough. Some bigwig has come for this spring's Hallow Tithe, and he wants 'Eleazar the Fallen' to be more than banished, if you get my drift."

Eleazar was silent, frowning fiercely, his gaze turned inward. "Rast."

"Rast?" Diver exclaimed. "Your Creator-cursed brother? He's here?"

Eleazar didn't respond, seemingly lost in thought. Trapped by memories of his betrayal, perhaps? His fall from Splendour, his banishment. Diver tried to read his face, but it was closed. And dark, very, very dark.

At last, his expression cleared. He focused on Star. "Where is this *Factory*?"

She smiled, her soot-blackened face triumphant. "So that's the way it is," she said. "I know your kind well, Angelus, and you don't disappoint. What's love compared to the chance for vengeance, eh?"

From the outside, the so-called Factory was less than impressive. The brick and limestone building listed dangerously and looked ready to tumble with the first stiff breeze. There was no smoke emanating from it, just thin wisps rising from the surrounding shacks which Trin's poorest souls had cobbled together from bricks, broken timbers and discarded tin shingles. All the glass windows had been broken out or scavenged and not a single light glimmered in its interior.

"The Factory is concealed within an old munitions plant," Star had explained before they'd left the tunnels. "The Koine company who built it moved their operations closer to the front a few years ago. It devastated this whole portion of the city. But, progress, you know?

"The walls of our lair are two feet thick. Plaster and wood and tin plating. And most of it is underground. There are tunnels that bring in coal and metal from almost a mile away. Closely guarded. Unfortunately, I can't get us to one of those tunnels without being spotted by the regulators. This is like going through the front door, really, and a bit iffy. Hopefully, someone will ask questions before shooting."

By the time they actually reached the hidden Factory, Star had long since succumbed to exhaustion and pain. Diver was carrying her, her weight nothing to him whereas Weaver had been struggling. Eleazar had not wished to take up the burden; he wasn't sure if he could be trusted not to squeeze her to death. So it was Weaver who led them through the doors hanging from rusted hinges into the gloomy, abandoned factory. Piles of dirt and debris littered the floor, and rats scampered into deeper hiding, disturbed by the intrusion, tiny claws clicking on the wood.

Eleazar scowled at the unprepossessing sight, wondering if Star had led them into a trap. It seemed unlikely. The woman didn't appear to have a death wish. After a quick inspection, he spotted the solid, iron door on an inner wall leading deeper into the factory. It was well hidden, tucked behind rusted scrap metal and rotted timbers, but Eleazar's eyes were sharp as an eagle's. A jagged, hard scent coated his nostrils. Iron and oil, and molten steel. And underlying it all, the sweet aroma of Mithran.

Eleazar felt a swelling of relief, recalling how quickly the engineers and artisans had been moving the pallet of Mithran into the foundry before he'd discovered the trap. Saving it would have been their priority after the explosion over the stables. *Protocols,* Star had claimed. These humans were remarkably efficient.

"So this is where you've been hiding the bulk of your operations," Diver said as Weaver moved a collection of timbers that looked like a pile of debris but was a clever shield. Moving it revealed the iron door fully. It was solid but pockmarked and streaked with soot and dirt as if it was yet another ruined part of the abandoned factory.

Weaver grinned. "We have an entire production line. And an annealing furnace. Molds, forges, everything we need to build armaments."

"How is this place not spewing smoke?"

"We pump the smoke out through underground pipes."

"Through all those hovels," Diver said, his brow furrowed thoughtfully. "Clever. Though I'd be happier if we'd known about this place a month ago. You called us allies, then kept your true operations a secret."

Weaver shrugged. "The fewer people who know all the inner workings of our organization means fewer people who can spill. Too many humans think the Angelus are infallible immortal gods, and even those who know the truth like things to remain the way they are. Conrad is cautious for damn good reasons."

"Conrad's so-called caution failed him," Eleazar said angrily. "He fell for an obvious trap with the Mithran, driven by short-sighted avarice. His greed might have cost him his life, too. Even if he survived the explosion, I guarantee he won't survive me if anything happens to Fury. None of you will."

As his ire rose, he shook his wings, a habit so ingrained and natural he did it without conscious thought. A simple trick of intimidation, fluffing one's feathers to appear larger, more threatening. He'd continued to do it even when he'd had no wings at all, only mutilated stumps.

The song which swept through the dank, broken husk of a factory sounded like wind chimes caught in a pleasant summer breeze. His wings had moved; his feathers had rustled. The sound and motion startled Eleazar. He fell still, his anger blowing away in a rush, replaced by quiet wonder. Desperate hope.

I must fly. Rast has Fury on a drachen. How else will I reach her? Dear Luminous One, please...

"Try not to kill us all yet," Weaver said wryly. "We might still be of some use to you. And to Fury," he added, throwing Diver a sympathetic glance before he rapped out an elaborate knock on the iron door.

The last few beats echoed into silence while all of them held an expectant breath.

Finally, there was a deep clang and the screech of metal against metal. Slowly, the door swung inward. The darkness beyond was impenetrable. A series of ominous clicks and clacks sounded from the void. Eleazar stepped in front of Weaver, his wings spread wide. His heart thumped with fear and excitement. His wings almost felt alive!

"Come any closer and you'll eat a bullet."

"Fire and it will be the last thing you do," Eleazar warned, his wings shivering. "I am Eleazar the Fallen! Tell Conrad I am here for him."

There were a few urgent whispers, and a flurry of footsteps. Behind him Weaver swore softly. "That'll bring him running," the ex-captain muttered.

"If he's still alive, he will come." Eleazar watched the void. Waiting. "What good is all that Mithran without an Angelus?"

They didn't wait long. In a matter of moments, Conrad's haggard face appeared from the darkness, his eye narrowed suspiciously. It widened at the sight of Eleazar, his jaw dropping. "It *is* you." The carbine tucked at his waist belied his breathless words. It was trained on Eleazar, its muzzle steady in the watery light.

"This is how you welcome me?" Eleazar demanded. "After what you did? Be glad I've come in peace, you odious little man. I have every right to tear you limb from limb."

The carbine trembled ever so slightly, then dropped. "Do it," he said, face pale. "If you must. I am merely a cog in this great machine we've assembled. Without me, the fight goes on, but without you, it's doomed before it starts." He scowled and his words turned bitter. "Tully made it abundantly clear to me. The Mithran is useless without you!"

"Conrad... stop being so dramatic. Why do you think I brought him here?"

A look of disbelief slackened his features. "Star?" he whispered, tears gathering in his eyes. "Is that really you, sweetheart?"

She emerged from the darkness, walking carefully, her arms clutched around her midsection. Her face was white beneath the dirt and Diver shadowed her as if he expected her to fall at any moment.

"It's me," she said softly.

"Thank the Creator! I was so afraid. Even after he promised. I – I thought Vogel would deliver your corpse!" He started toward her, but hesitated to push past Eleazar, looking at him as if he wasn't quite sure if it was safe. It wasn't a foregone conclusion.

"Be glad I need your army," Eleazar said to him, his voice soft with menace. "As far as I'm concerned your entire *machine* exists to help me save her."

"Angelus." Star laid a gentle hand on Eleazar's rigid arm, her dark eyes turned toward him placatingly. "We'll do whatever we can to save her. I promise you. I swear to the Creator Eternal. I swear to whatever you may hold most holy. I – I would never let an innocent be sacrificed for my sake."

Her words, so sincere and genuine, made Eleazar understand how she might inspire others. Unwillingly, he felt himself being swayed...

"Maybe not for your sake," he said gruffly, seeing through her charm. She rivaled the Angelus, this one! "But what would you sacrifice for your *cause*?"

Her open expression vanished. She eyed him shrewdly. "Conrad. Show the Angelus what we have wrought here. Make him a believer." She lifted her hand from his arm and her gaze turned fierce. "Revolution cannot be stopped. Not even by the gods..."

The abandoned munitions plant was dug into the earth itself, reinforced with beams and brick walls. The equipment left behind by the defunct ammunitions manufacturer had been repurposed for their use. The thump and clang of machinery was deafening. Men worked in the dim glow of coal fire and molten metal, shadowy figures against the flame and white heat.

Upon entering the hidden lair, women in plain, gray dresses with their hair pinned beneath scarves came and took away Star, pale and exhausted after her brief rally. Conrad screeched orders which they listened to gravely. The oldest of them gave a sharp nod but seemed unruffled by his harsh manner. Healers. Their demeanor reminded Eleazar of Fury when she'd tended to his injuries. The memory made his heart contract.

Rast has her. Soon, he'll dangle her like a tempting piece of fruit...

Once Star was taken care of, Conrad led them through the forges and beyond to the final production room. With a broad sweep of his arm and a satisfied smirk, he directed their gazes toward row upon row of rifles. Shining black muzzles with gleaming wooden stocks. Breech-loading and repeating. New and bright, freshly oiled. Hundreds of them, maybe thousands. Eleazar felt an upsurge of hope. He'd thought their stockpiles destroyed. Conrad was a cunning little bastard.

"The Angelus might be caught unaware, but they will adapt," Eleazar warned. "Don't underestimate their speed and strength. They will figure out your weapons' ranges faster than you can imagine."

"The rifles are mostly for *human* enemies, Angelus." Conrad strode down the line of weapons resting on wooden racks and reached another door into yet another room. Did this lair stretch on for miles? This one held weapons Eleazar had never seen before. Large metal contraptions with long barrels as thick as his wrists, painted a dull green and set on iron wheels. They looked like the ancient cannons he'd read about in the scrolls, but these were smaller and sleeker.

Diver gave a low whistle. "Anti-infantry field guns," he murmured. He scampered among the stockpile, exclaiming over each new discovery. He lifted the lid from a large wooden box, one of many. "High velocity shrapnel shells." Another row of weapons lay beyond the boxes. "Machine guns, too, you son of a bitch! I knew you were holding out on us! Damn. Now this is an arsenal!"

"We've been smuggling weapons for months, and scavenging artillery pieces from the battlefield, abandoned unwillingly and sometimes intentionally. We have plants in the army loyal to our cause."

"Which army?" Diver asked, frowning.

"Koine, Akkadian, Naveen, Veran, you name it. There are many of us, all ready to act once we strike the first blow. All joined by a single cause: to prove the Angelus aren't the immortal gods we were taught to worship. That they keep us at war with each other so we don't unite against them. But people will finally understand we can fight back. That this is our world!"

"They will merely move out of range," Eleazar countered, ignoring his impassioned speech. He cared little about this "revolution", he just wanted Fury back. And if he killed Pace and Rast in the process, even better. "They will stay safe within their drachens, and then what?"

Conrad grinned. "Our attack hinges on surprise, and Angelic arrogance. They will come for their Hallow Tithe. They depend on it. They will descend into range of our machine guns, unaware of what awaits. With your help, Angelus, we'll have Mithran-laced ammunition ready and waiting. They won't know what hit them!"

The glee in Conrad's voice made him queasy, and he could imagine all too well the devastation of such enhanced bullets against his brethren. And Conrad was right: Angelic arrogance was their greatest weakness. The Angelus would never expect the humans to attack them, not at the Hallow Tithe. They would do things as they've always done them. Sure in their arrogance that nothing human could harm them.

Rast will expect me to be alone, too, after Conrad's betrayal. Weak and desperate...

He struggled to keep his hope in check. It wouldn't do to fall into their own trap of over-confidence. And the Angelus had one weapon in their arsenal all humans feared.

"You're forgetting the Angelic Curse," he said darkly. "The drachen for the Hallow Tithe don't usually carry such weapons, but with my brother here, there can be no guarantees."

His words took a little of the starch from Conrad. A look of unease settled on his face even as he waved off Eleazar's concern. "They would never unleash the Scourge at a Tithing Ground," he said, far too blithely in Eleazar's opinion. "Not in Trin of all places. This city feeds them, keeps their war engine running. They might punish Trin, but they won't destroy her!"

Eleazar exchanged a skeptical glance with Diver, but there was no diminishing Conrad's confidence. Or his exuberance.

"Don't be too worried, Angelus. We're ready for anything, believe me. Now, our true goal – besides killing as many of them as we can – is to take out a drachen. Not just any drachen, either. We want to bring down the royal flagship."

Practically rubbing his hands together, he led them through the munition stores and pushed open yet another heavy wooden door bound with iron bands, revealing a workspace brightly lit with electric lights. The walls were whitewashed plaster, and the room was empty but for a row of wooden racks holding limp boiler suits.

Diver's gasp startled Eleazar, and then he noticed it, too. The boiler suits bore frameworks sprouting from their backs, shaped like wings but without the Mithran-woven fabric like the one Tully had made at the compound. Reflexively, he twitched his wings and was rewarded with a satisfying jingle of metal on metal. The ersatz wings crowding this space would never ring in such beautiful tones. They would look more like bat wings than bird wings when the fabric was stretched over the rigid frames.

His initial shock retreated before a visceral disgust at the ugliness of these... apparitions.

"What is this?" he demanded, his lips curling with distaste.

Diver pushed ahead of Eleazar and rushed to one of the hideous costumes, reaching for it with a tentative hand.

"Flying suits," he said, his voice soft with awe. "I thought Tully only had the single prototype. The bastard was building them all along. Out of sight."

"The skies have always belonged to the Angelus," Conrad said, looking upon the hideous suits with triumph gleaming in his eye. "It is the one thing they never let us forget. Bringing down one of their flying ships would be a symbolic victory great enough to put fire in people's souls! Even fear of the Scourge won't be able to keep us tame after that."

Diver spun around, his nostrils flared and his eyes bright. "These suits aren't complete, not without the Mithran wings and fuel canisters. Where's Tully?"

Conrad turned to Eleazar, challenging and triumphant. "Tully has been waiting for you, preparing as best they can without your unique... radiance. With these suits, we can hit the Angelus where they live! We can hit Pace's ship—"

"Fury will be on that ship," Eleazar said sharply. "You'll do nothing until we retrieve her, understand?"

Conrad's eye appraised him, narrowing at his useless wings, his expression hard. "And how will you retrieve her, Angelus?"

He opened his mouth but couldn't speak. Hopelessness threatened to drag him into the Abyss—

"I'll do it."

Diver. He had one of the boiler suits in his grip. Golden light swirled in his grey eyes. "She's my sister," he said simply. "Now, where the hell is Tully? I want to fly!"

CHAPTER THIRTY-FIVE

From the roof of the Factory, Diver observed the darkened slums below and tried to quell the nervous roiling of his stomach. There were no streetlights here, only small trash fires lit for warmth. This was the poorest part of Trin and want was rampant. Homes no better than shacks, beggars on the corners, streets more mud than brick. Though manna was abundant in Trin, here it was scarce. The people here held no value to the greater city. They were more nuisance than citizen. Conrad's revolutionaries provided for them as best they could, seeing potential loyalists among the rabble. Hot soup of mostly broth and vegetable scraps, day-old bread scavenged from the trash of bakeries in better parts of the city, milk on the verge of spoiling, coarse manna only fit for the dogs of the wealthy. Still, the gratitude of the locals kept them safe.

Diver tugged at his gloves, hoping that gratitude would extend to flying men. It wouldn't do to have the city regulators alerted. Once the fuel canisters had been finished, with Eleazar's help, Diver had volunteered for this test flight, eagerly strapping himself into the completed prototype. Since he'd seen Tully's drawings, he'd known this suit was for him. He could feel the Mithran laced in its wings, calling to him. Unlike Eleazar's impractically feathered contraptions, these sleek appendages felt light on his back. Perhaps Tully should have insisted on this more practical design for Eleazar?

No. Eleazar had been adamant. He would never abase himself by wearing such ugly wings…

And he would most likely never fly again for his arrogance.

It didn't matter. Diver would be the one to fly, and Eleazar was hardly useless…

Tully had practically crowed to see them both alive and well, giving him a fierce hug with their bony arms before dragging Eleazar to the waiting Mithran. For two days, the fallen Angelus had lit up the Factory with his Charisma, allowing the engineers, craftsmen, munition workers, and a bevy of seamstresses to work with the gods' metal. Production on Mithran-laced shells and bullets replaced all other munitions. A Trin factory, even one hidden underground, had a capacity to produce literal tons of explosives, and the stockpile of gleaming ammunition grew exponentially. The wings for the flying suits were churned out with remarkable alacrity on electric sewing machines then stretched across the waiting frames by eager craftsmen. And Tully, working in their workroom with Mithran charmed by Eleazar, finished a dozen sets of their "miracle" rockets as if the Creator Eternal Itself was lending a hand.

"Are we ready?" Diver asked, growing impatient.

"Almost."

He felt Weaver adjust the fastenings on his suit and straighten the wings sprouting from his back. A weight followed, dragging at his shoulders. The rockets of Mithran fuel. He held his breath, listening to the snap of connectors being engaged. Thin wires of a Mithran-copper alloy attached the rockets to the toggle switch nestled in the palm of his heavy leather gloves. He had only to move his thumb to control ignition. The wings would respond to his movement once he was aloft. In theory. The flight suit was essentially a rocket-propelled glider, enhanced with the magic of Mithran. All the volunteers for their new Aerial Corps had experience with fixed-wing gliders, a rudimentary flying machine the Angelus barely noticed in their lofty heights. As soon as Diver completed a successful test flight the others would fly, taking advantage of the night to practice. There was only a dozen or so of them, unfortunately. But it would have to do.

And if he crashed, or exploded in midair, their battle against the Angelic drachen would be far harder, if not impossible. Though there was no convincing Conrad to wait. The plans were in place, the battle had to proceed. They would get no better chance than at the Spring Tithe which gave them almost a week to prepare – Pace had apparently jumped the gun and arrived far earlier than usual in his eagerness for revenge. The Tithe had yet to arrive in full. They might be unable to achieve their symbolic victory if the suits failed, but they'd leave undeniable carnage in their wake. The gauntlet would be thrown...

"I should be the one doing the test," Weaver muttered as he once again checked over Diver's flight suit. "I've flown glider missions a time or two. And these rockets aren't much different than some flamethrowers I've used. I have experience controlling the burn."

"Not a chance. I get to fly first." Weaver was on one knee, checking the straps on his boots and Diver gave him a condescending pat on the head. "If I live, you can go next."

Weaver grabbed his wrist, yanking his hand to the side. He stared up at him, practically glaring. "You'd better live," he said, his voice rough.

"Don't be so grim, my boys." Tully emerged from the shadows, coming to join them at the edge of the roof. They clapped Diver on the shoulder, beaming at him through their thick goggles. There were burns on Tully's face from the compound explosion, but overall, the engineer had escaped with relatively minor injuries. They were the most eager to engage the Angelus, their anger about Fury (inexplicably) matching Diver's own. "The suit will fly, and Diver will fly it. He will lead us into glorious battle. Imagine it! A Gullan boy! It will be fitting. My people will finally have their revenge."

Diver frowned. "I don't care to avenge an entire civilization," he said. "I just want my sister back. And I want justice for Eleazar."

Tully's gleeful mood vanished in a scowl. "Still under his spell, I see. Don't you understand how the Angelus trick us? They *make* us love them. I, too, felt the compulsion from their dreadful Charisma. I lost a lifetime! Only after I grew immune to it could I escape them and return home! Broken and wounded, half-dead from the stress of living in 'perfect' Splendour."

Diver blinked, shocked by this revelation. He hadn't known much about Tully's life, only that they were Gullan and they despised the Angelus. But, who among the Gullan wouldn't hate the Angelus? His own mother had infected their entire family with her hatred.

"You were in Splendour?" he asked, suddenly eager to hear more even if he wasn't sure he wanted to know everything. Obviously, Tully had suffered greatly. But thoughts of his mother reminded him why he and Fury were even in this situation in the first place. By helping Eleazar, they'd wanted, no, *hoped*, to find her. Or at least find out what had happened to her.

"Did you know any other humans there?" he demanded. "Any other Gullan?"

They stared at him for a moment, their expression inscrutable. "No. I was the only one."

A surge of disappointment filled him. He turned away, his eyes blurring. Had she died on a drachen? Had she never reached Splendour at all? Or were humans kept away from each other in that cold, cold heaven?

It didn't matter. He tightened the straps on his harness, making sure the rockets on his back were secure. Only Fury mattered.

"Never mind," he said harshly. "I'm as ready as I'll ever be. Let's get this thing fired up."

A grim-faced Weaver handed him the suit's helmet – a modified version of Diver's gas mask. He hated it. It felt claustrophobic to have his head encased in canvas and leather and his sight distorted by thick glass lenses. He held it in his hands, breathing deeply for a moment or two, building up his courage. Before he could change his mind, he lifted it over his head and settled it into place. Weaver's worried gaze met his through the lenses.

"Come back to me in one piece," he said firmly.

"Stand clear," was Diver's muffled response. Weaver nodded and stepped aside, moving behind him to stand with Tully.

Taking a step toward the edge of the roof, Diver tightened his grip on the ignition control, careful not to flip the switch yet. It would spark the charge in the twin rockets and supposedly propel him into the air – or incinerate him in a spectacular blast of compressed Mithran.

"The Mithran is under great pressure. It will burn long and hot, but we need to be able to control the burn if we want to maintain flight." Tully had gone into great detail explaining air pressure and combustion and thrust, but most of it had gone right over Diver's head.

"Remember," Tully called to him from where they and Weaver had retreated toward the stairwell. "You only have about thirty minutes of fuel for this run, and only if you use it judiciously. Don't get carried away. Control the burn!"

With that reassuring bit of advice, Diver stepped to the edge of the roof, his heart pounding. Had Eleazar felt this rush of terror standing on the edge of the smokestack? At least he'd actually flown before and knew what to expect. Diver swallowed. Hard. He flipped the ignition switch.

Heat and noise erupted behind him. Diver was pushed upward; his feet left the roof, and he flailed a moment before he stiffened his legs and straightened out. He was launching upward into the night sky, his blood rushing, his sight blurred. His breath came in short, panicked gasps. He became aware of a high whistling shriek. The wind. He controlled his breathing, and his goggles cleared enough to let him see silvered clouds streaking past him. He felt like a bullet shot from a gun and couldn't think beyond the fact that bullets shot into the sky always came down.

Control the burn, control the burn…

He was going too fast, far too fast. The heat against his legs seemed about to light him on fire! With a wiggle of his thumb, he eased off the burn. Immediately, the intense heat faded and he felt himself decelerate. Shock made him gasp and flail his legs, breaking his smooth trajectory. Had he eased back too much? The streaking clouds slowed to towering mountains penning him in on all sides. The beauty of it captured his attention. He held his breath, suspended in time. Instinctively, he twitched his shoulders, tipping his wings as he began to fall, his terror leaving him in the rush of air flowing over him and under him. The Mithran wings felt alive! They held the wind in a shimmering embrace, holding him up.

A laugh of pure joy burst from him. The sensation was intoxicating. He was flying!

The rockets still burned. He could no longer hear the wild roaring, but he could still feel the heat along the backs of his legs. The reinforced canvas was protecting his skin, and the heat was a welcome contrast to the frigid air of the upper atmosphere. Carefully, he dipped his wings to the left and felt a wild thrill as he slid to the side. He turned the other way. Again, he was rewarded with a remarkable responsiveness. Growing ever more confident, he adjusted the toggle on the ignition. The corresponding thrust pushed him forward and he tilted his wings to catch the air just so–

He soared upward in a climbing curve, shouting at the rush of it. He tried a new maneuver, turning in a tight spiral, playing with the burn of his rockets and the tilt of his Mithran-enhanced wings. He gritted his teeth, changing direction fast, then wrestled himself back into a clean soar.

It worked! By the Creator Eternal, it worked!

The initial excitement and terror diminished somewhat as Diver grew used to controlling the intricacies of the flight suit. A sudden sense of urgency gripped him. The others would have to begin practicing now, tonight. The Hallow Tithe was less than a week away. They had to be ready!

Lost in thought and planning, Diver turned and began to spiral lower. He had to return to the roof. Time had lost all meaning up here in the vast sky, but some deep instinct told him to return to safety. The red clouds had darkened to an ominous purple which made him think more time had passed than he'd realized. The roof of the factory seemed terribly far away, a small patch of black. Small fires winked at him from the surrounding city. A new fire flared to life on top of the factory. A beacon to guide him.

Diver toggled the ignition further closed, hoping to conserve his fuel supply. The Mithran wings rippled in the stiff wind. The roof grew larger beneath him, a welcoming landing surface, but it seemed miles away.

His fuel gave out halfway to the roof, and Diver rode the wind in disturbing silence but for his rushing blood and labored breathing. He could make out Weaver waving him in next to a steel drum with a fire dancing from it, Tully a small, still shadow beside him.

Diver focused on the flames, making adjustments with his wings to steer himself in for a landing. When he was over the roof, he lowered his legs. He was moving far more quickly than he wished, but there was nothing to be done for it now. One foot touched the tar paper, and then the other and he was running across the roof, his wings dragging him into the air a few more times. He took a nosedive, sliding uncontrollably until he crashed to a stop against the steel drum, his whole body shuddering with relief and exertion. The searing heat from the trash fire sent him scrabbling back a few feet. Hands grabbed him. Weaver. He heard wild, ecstatic laughter.

Diver gripped his lover's arms. His legs shook. He ripped off his helmet and threw it to the ground. The cool night air bathed his sweat-covered face, and he was glad to be on solid footing again. The flight had been exhilarating but the landing...

"We'll have to work on your landings," Weaver said.

Diver nodded, not quite able to speak yet. Tully's crowing quieted, though they let out a few more excited exclamations as they checked Diver's suit.

"They held, by the Luminous One," they cried, tapping at the empty tanks, and running their hands along the wires. They straightened out the Mithran wings, muttering to themselves. Sounding eminently satisfied. Diver staggered as the little engineer swung him around and embraced him enthusiastically. "We're ready! We are ready to storm the heavens!"

CHAPTER THIRTY-SIX

"It is time to bait the trap, little worm."

Fury lifted her head, her face aflame and the taste of blood in her mouth. A shadow fell over her, shielding her briefly from the bright sun. Pace. Come for her at last.

They'd kept her lashed to the mizzenmast for days, deprived of food and comfort, given only a dribble of water and the occasional use of a bucket. Quite the luxury, really. She licked her lips, cracked and bleeding from thirst and the dry, frigid air. The beating she'd endured after daring to attack one of them seemed a light punishment compared to this seemingly endless torment. The Mithran in her blood and bones burned as hot as ever, taunting her. She was supposed to be *strong*.

After breaking her shackles, it had seemed an easy thing to throttle Maurissa, to silence her tittering for all eternity. She'd been denied such satisfaction. Brute strength was no match for the speed and agility of an Angelus. She cursed her foolishness. How often had she witnessed Eleazar defy the laws of gravity and physics? Even with one wing, even with no wings, he was a lethal weapon.

The raven-winged angel had evaded her attack with ease. Gliding out of reach, dodging her fists, until some other Angelus had struck Fury in the head, sending her crashing to the deck, stunned and gasping. In that moment, as blows rained on her, she was almost relieved. If they killed her, perhaps Eleazar wouldn't be drawn into their trap.

Alas, they did not kill her. Sense prevailed and she was tied to the ship's mast, bleeding and broken. A single memory saved her from succumbing to her wounds, from giving up entirely: Eyes, a deep, stunning blue, widening in a brief flash of sheer terror as her fingernails scraped a pale, porcelain neck, leaving bright scratch marks. It not only kept her alive while her Mithran-enhanced bones and flesh slowly knitted together, but the memory also kept a smile on her face and a hope in her heart. An Angelus, glorious and strong, had *feared* her.

"She seems well enough, in spite of everything," Rast said from somewhere. She couldn't quite manage to clear her sun-tortured vision. "A tough creature, this human." He made a noise. "Though she reeks like death."

Her bonds loosened. Fury hissed as blood rushed back into her deprived limbs. It was all she could focus on so miserable was the pain. She did what she could to shake feeling back into her feet and legs, her hands and arms, stumbling along like a drunk. Pace had her bicep in his iron grip and gave no care to whether she walked or was dragged. On her other side was Rast. Today he was dressed in fine black velvet again, but of a more practical cut. Trousers instead of hose, tall boots instead of slippers. A scaled cuirass covered his torso, and with a start, she recognized it as leviathan skin. It was green to match his wings, and the scales were large and oval.

From a nymph, came an unbidden thought. Her lip curled in disgust.

"I will be glad to finally end this debacle," Rast said peevishly, tossing a glance towards Pace and ignoring her. "Your simple plan has devolved into chaos. Why you couldn't have finished Eleazar when you had the chance is beyond my comprehension."

"He carries the blood of an ancient line. He is a descendant of the Luminous One. Clipping his wings was all I could do to him, as well you know. And banishment is as good as death for an Angelus."

"Is it?" Sarcasm dripped from his words. "Is it, Pace? Then explain to me what we're doing here, exactly? In the stinking Below!"

Pace brooded. His grip on Fury tightened and he shook her. "It was the atheists," he hissed. "They took us by surprise. Eleazar let them think more of themselves, let them think they could touch us! They are the ones who got him mixed up with these so-called revolutionaries. We'll have to root them all out and punish Trin for this blasphemy lest it spread."

"Yes, we will." And Rast's voice was oily smooth again. "You'll get your wish. I promise. After they deliver the Tithe, Trin will face justice. And the Archons will deal with Eleazar once and for all. Perhaps, in the end, this will be for the best. All our missteps are merely opportunity, yes?"

Pace nodded, seemingly mollified. "This world has been left to its own devices for far too long," he said darkly. "The Beasts have reached a level of advancement which cannot stand. We must reduce the population to a more manageable level if we wish to maintain our control. I've been arguing for it for decades now. You were the only one who listened, my prince."

The conversation ended when they reached a set of stairs, and Pace dragged Fury up to a higher deck. The brisk wind struck her in the face, making her tremble violently. Her breath fogged in ragged streams and the cold stung her nostrils. The warmth from the two angels kept the worst of it at bay, but she shrank from them, unwilling to bask in their unnatural radiance. They'd spoken of "reducing the population" as if it were a task to be dealt with before dinnertime. It didn't really surprise her. These were the same creatures who'd destroyed her people, after all, for some perceived slight.

No, it was more than that. It was fear.

Bright eyes widened in terror...

Fury regained her footing on the stairs. She lunged upright, walking beside Pace rather than letting him drag her. Pace threw her an irritated look as she drew even with him so that it seemed they were walking as equals, but Fury smiled at him pleasantly and lifted her chin. She would not let these demons terrorize her.

"You won't win," she said softly as he led her to the ship's aft deck, where a great crystal globe sat atop a rose-colored marble pillar rising from the smooth planking. "When he comes for me, he'll destroy you all."

A low grunt slipped from Pace, a sound of disdainful amusement. "A pinioned angel is no threat to me or my fleet," he said. "Keep telling yourself whatever you need to, woman. It has been days, and there is no sign of Eleazar. But... I suppose even an atheist must believe in something sometime."

"He will come."

Behind them, Rast chuckled. "I'm starting to see why Eleazar likes this one so much. He always did love his faithful pets."

Pace took her to the globe. It matched the one in Vogel's office – except for being twice its size. Colors swirled in the crystal's strange depths. Greens and blues and flashes of pink. The colors drew her in until she felt like she was falling into them. Head reeling, she tore her eyes from it and focused on the clouds moving slowly across the bow of the ship. Towering, glorious clouds of white and silver and gunmetal gray, in a sky so deep blue it was almost purple. Her breath snagged in her throat. Despite her situation, she couldn't help but be awed by the beauty and majesty around her. If she lived, she'd never forget the sight.

"Maintain your dignity, human," Pace grumbled to her, keeping his grip on her arm. "He will see your bruises and battered face, and then we will see if he truly cares about you."

Rast came to stand before them, placing himself at the orb. He raised his hands to either side of it, his palms facing the crystal. The orb glowed with an inner fire, the colors spinning. Rast spoke, his voice reverberating around them, around the ship, amplified and strengthened. It sounded...

It sounded like the voice of the Creator.

"People of Trin! We have come to root out a criminal among you, to scour the city for an apostate and a malefactor. Cast from Splendour for his offenses and made mortal by the power of righteousness, the Angelus known as Eleazar continues to foment rebellion, to flaunt his evil tendencies and threaten all your souls with his corruption. This woman before you is his concubine and succubus. She has blasphemed against us, against the Creator Eternal! For that, her punishment is death."

The word "death" echoed and thrummed inside Fury's head. It was hardly a surprise. Why else perform this charade? They couldn't just kill her outright, not if they wanted Eleazar. If he thought he had a chance to save her...

She would be bait, but also a leash on his aggressions. Fury ground her teeth in frustration. It would be better for Eleazar if they killed her now.

Rast continued, "Those harboring Eleazar the Fallen will suffer the same fate! All citizens who aid our endeavor shall be rewarded. Come the morning of the Spring Tithe, one hundred citizens from each ghetto will bear witness to this traitor's execution. Choose your representatives wisely! Only those of sound mind and able body, pure of heart and full of devotion will be welcomed on the Tithing Ground. Only those who reflect the righteousness of Trin! It will be a great honor, a renewal of our sacred covenant. Chosen Ones, the blood of these traitors will wash you clean!"

The final word echoed from the clouds then all was silence. Fury's ears rang. Rast turned to her, a supercilious smile on his handsome face. His resemblance to Eleazar turned her stomach.

"Enjoy your final days, human, and be glad only death awaits you on the morning of the Spring Tithe. Those who attend your execution will not be so fortunate."

"What do you mean?" she demanded, even as dread filled her. There was only one weapon the Angelus used against humans. The fear of it alone had kept the people in line for centuries: The Scourge. He had to be bluffing!

"You know exactly what he means," Pace said, he took her by the arm and forced her back down the steps to the lower deck.

"No! Please! You can't do this! Dear Creator, in a city this size, this densely populated – the carnage will be incomprehensible!"

"Well, of course, my dear," Rast said pleasantly. "That's the point."

The search for Eleazar the Fallen began in earnest soon after the Angelus' grim visage faded from the clouds. Fear seized the already shaken city – how often did their immortal overlords speak to them directly? Only in the direst of circumstances. Dark shapes descended from the sky, seeding more terror. These were not gangs of foreign men with cannon and guns come to level their city, kill their children and rape their women. The creatures descending on their city were gods. The holiest of creatures, their masters and overlords. Relentless. Merciless. Every corner of Trin would be scoured...

Many of Trin's citizens were less than thrilled to be subjected to an Angelic hunt. But those that put up resistance met swift, brutal ends. Sabers, clubs and even pistols did nothing to slow the Angelus. A man could raise a fist in threat or even manage to level his pistol at the creature come to tear apart his home but that was as far as he got. One moment, he was a man, a whole and breathing person, and the next he was a limp ragdoll of flesh and bone and blood.

While the citizens of Trin were being terrorized, the Hallow Tithe began arriving from all corners of Avernus. By train and ship, by wagon and lorry, by mule and cart. Each country's shipment had an escort of soldiers as was custom. Men who'd been trying to kill each other marched in orderly fashion alongside their home country's offering. Stripped of weapons, they could do no more than glare at their enemies. Black-jacketed regulators stood watch over all of it, their standard carbines more than sufficient to keep the peace. The soldiers were not allowed on the Tithing Field but would spend the day of the Spring Tithe in Trin's many public houses, brothels and taverns, waiting for their orders to return to the front.

Hearing the reports coming in from their spies and whisper network – they were closely monitoring all activity in Trin, Angelic and human – Diver couldn't help but recall his own brief time on Tithing duty. He'd followed his orders, mostly, but sneaking onto the Field to see the Angelus' famed drachen had seemed a great lark at the time. A boyish fantasy fulfilled. Of course, it had ended in disaster and gotten him a week in the stockade. Unfortunately, his second adventure to the Tithing Field had been even less enjoyable. At least this time, he would be flying *over* the field. Perhaps he would have better luck?

Things weren't off to an auspicious start. Rast's pronouncement, though expected, had sent the rebellion into even deeper hiding. The regulators in charge of the search for Eleazar had suddenly gained an eager competence with grim Angelus towering over them, kicking in doors and scouring neighborhoods they usually avoided. With so much activity spread far and wide, they'd had no choice but to go underground. Literally.

"We anticipated this," Conrad was insisting yet again as he strode back and forth along the packed tunnel. "They were always going to tear the city apart. Our plans haven't changed. Not a bit."

There was some grumbling at his speech, but no outright complaints. The tunnel was dark and cold and cramped. Nervous excitement hung like a thick fog, the heightened emotions palpable. They were going into battle, some for the first time. Fear was unavoidable. The hardened soldiers among the revolutionaries remained calm, almost fatalistic. Better to believe you were dead already, a few joked idly. Such grim attitudes rarely calmed the greenies.

"Every army in Trin right now has our people in their ranks. They will help us infiltrate the Tithe, put our weapons in place." Conrad grinned as he turned on his heel and stalked back down the line of rebels. "And that's not all. The Angelus handed us a gift by demanding citizens bear witness to this so-called execution. Gives us even more opportunity to seed the field with our people!"

This brought a few quiet cheers from the line. Diver shot Weaver a glance. The redhead was nodding, once again fully behind Conrad. They sat near the sledge with their flight suits layered atop it, fuel canisters tucked around them. He itched to fly again. The test runs had been quite successful this past week. The Mithran-enhanced suits responded to their human pilots remarkably well. The mix of magic and technology was transformative even for those who weren't full of Mithran like himself. Each volunteer was as eager to take to the skies as he was.

They had decided the newly minted Aerial Corps would carry blades, not guns. Slim, razor-sharp weapons forged from the Mithran-steel alloy. Rifles had proven unwieldy. The kick alone sent flyers wheeling unexpectedly. Luckily, no one had ended up accidentally shot before they nixed that plan. A dozen sabers had been easy enough to forge. They were standard issue for field officers. Eleazar had assured them the alloy would slice right through angel wings, too. And given the sweat on his upper lip at the statement, they all had believed him.

Despite himself – his main focus was going after Fury – Diver felt an excitement about the upcoming battle he hadn't anticipated. He felt like they had a real chance of not only rescuing Fury but also striking a blow against the Angelus. It was a far different feeling than he'd had going into combat before, that bitter terror and hopelessness. Now, he felt purpose and that most dangerous of all feelings. Hope.

Earlier, seeing Fury's bruised and battered face cast upon the clouds, her eyes glazed and unfocused, hearing her death sentence broadcast throughout all of Trin, he'd been filled with terror and dread. Rescuing her had seemed impossible in that moment. The very gods had her prisoner. Held her fate in their hands. But the swiftness with which Conrad and his revolutionaries had responded to the pronouncement, the eagerness underlying every action and reaction, the absolute confidence in their plan: It had assuaged his doubts, his fears. By the Creator, they could win!

"We will win," he whispered.

"What was that?"

"Nothing." He stared at Weaver for a moment, studying his face. The fine brows and pointed chin. The easy smirk. His stomach flipped. He hadn't wanted to care, but *fuck*... he did. Would Joseph survive this? Would either of them?

"It'll be alright," Weaver said, his gaze soft in the flickering lights. They'd wired the warren of tunnels with electricity, but it was unreliable. Good enough for the moment. They wouldn't be here long. "We'll save your sister. You and me, yeah?"

Diver opened his mouth to speak when a sudden warmth filled the tunnel. Sighs whispered among the revolutionaries, a sense of calm followed the warmth. A sense of awe. All eyes turned toward two new arrivals: A tall man with golden hair which gleamed in the electric light with a haloed radiance, and a woman dressed in a formal military uniform heavy with gold braid and glittering medals. They almost seemed like a couple, standing shoulder to shoulder in the dim tunnel, radiating confidence. Eleazar's wings were lifted from his shoulders, catching and reflecting the light. Diver's breath caught in his throat. Eleazar found him, locked gazes. For a moment, no one else existed.

"The royal drachen is descending," Star proclaimed, her voice carrying up and down the tunnel. "And the Tithe is arriving from all corners of Avernus. The time draws near. Are we ready?" She raised her arms, spreading them wide. Her red lips broadened with a radiant smile. "Are we ready for a new world, my friends?"

A cheer of agreement answered her. People straightened, stood at attention. Excitement rippled through the tunnel. Her hand clenched into a fist and she punched the sky. "To victory! For Avernus! For humanity!"

Amidst the revelry, Diver held Eleazar's gaze and mouthed two words: "For Fury."

Eleazar nodded gravely, his eyes blazing. His wings shuddered, feathers bristling before lying flat again. Diver's heart broke at the look on his face. As much as it was needed, hope was a dangerous emotion.

CHAPTER THIRTY-SEVEN

Inexorably, the morning of the Spring Tithe approached. Above the Tithing Field, the drachen began to shift. Smaller cargo ships descended to the ramps. Larger ships armed with fantastical golden horns escorted the Tithing ships, a new and startling occurrence. Those great curving horns bore a disturbing darkness within them, a deep malevolence that struck terror in the hearts of Trin's citizens. The threat of the Angelic Curse had subdued many an unruly population in the past. But surely it wasn't necessary in great and loyal Trin? Why such a show of strength from their immortal masters? Could it be…?

Perhaps the talk of rebellion bore some truth?

Speculation ran rampant as the ghettos gathered their Chosen for the Tithing Field, spurred by Conrad's people. The Angelus were worried. Wasn't it obvious? The rebellion was real. Resistance was encouraged. Whispers drifted like smoke: What true god knew *fear*?

More than words moved among the citizens. Weapons passed from hand to hand. The precious field pieces they'd managed to gather were hidden among the carts and lorries delivering the Tithe. Boxes of ammunition, rifles, hand bombs, and machine guns were concealed in grain deliveries, stuffed in barrels of pickles and stored in empty wine casks. Rebel soldiers – dressed in homespun and cheap, factory-made clothing – secreted themselves among the deliveries, posing as herders, drivers, and escorts. Regulators ordered to keep the peace were knifed in dark alleys and replaced by loyal revolutionaries. And even among the Chosen, those faithful, righteous souls, were armed and ready fighters.

When the sun dawned on the morning of the Spring Tithe, all was in place but the final piece of the puzzle. As the Angelus prepared to receive their Hallow Tithe and the Chosen stood in neat ranks beneath the drachen, awaiting the honor of witnessing an execution, a dozen, strange hump-backed figures crawled from the sewers of Trin.

The so-called Aerial Corps wouldn't launch until their target appeared, and they wouldn't attack until it was safe. Until *she* was safe. Diver had sworn it to Eleazar, and he'd had no choice but to trust his word. After all, Eleazar had no say in that part of the plan. A flightless Angelus was worse than useless.

Concealed in a cart with one of the big guns Conrad had scavenged, Eleazar the Fallen crouched beneath a shroud of canvas with a group of eager gunners and cursed his brother. No one had searched the Tithing goods, but for a cursory glance to sort the vehicles into appropriate categories. Perhaps Governor Vogel and his people believed Conrad's revolution had been destroyed in a violent conflagration? That there was no one left to strike at the immortal Angelus? They had scoured the city, after all, and found no sign of rebels, and only the whisperings of rebellion. Nor had there been any sign of a fallen Angelus. Despite the effort Rast had spent hunting him the last week or so, Eleazar suspected it had been only for show. Rast wanted him here, wanted him to reveal himself in a reckless manner.

Fury's face rose once more in his memory, battered, bleeding. Her eyes blank. His teeth ground together. He would repay his brother every cut and bruise tenfold. He had sworn as much to Diver before they'd parted ways. Each had their role to play in this battle, though separating hadn't been easy. It didn't seem right not to have Diver beside him. With Fury gone, too, he'd never felt so vulnerable.

"You will lead the fight from the ground," Diver had told him, skirting the unfortunate reality of his useless wings. "I will snatch Fury from the ship as soon as I get sight of her. They must reveal her to tempt you, right?"

Eleazar had nodded, having no doubt about that. Rast would make a spectacle of her death before they collected the Hallow Tithe.

"Conrad seems certain of his plans," he'd replied gruffly, his hatred for the man tucked away for the moment. "Now that we've begun to mobilize, I have hope in them, too. Fly high and fast, Diver. I'm counting on you to bring Fury back to us."

"On my life, Lee..."

They had embraced one last time. Diver in his flight suit and Eleazar dressed in a soldier's uniform, looking more human than ever despite the golden wings folded on his back. Weaver watched them surreptitiously from a short distance away, outfitted in his own shiny new flight suit. The ex-captain had immediately volunteered to follow Diver into the battle in the sky, and Eleazar had to grudgingly admire the man's courage.

He caught his eye and sent a silent plea: *Protect Diver.* Weaver seemed to understand; he gave Eleazar a slow nod.

Eleazar's rage and fear burned hot and cold as he peered up at Pace's flagship, a great gilded bulk directly over the center of the Tithing Field. He was holding *his* ship several leagues aloft. Well out of range of human rifles. Pace was no fool. They would have to take the fight to him. To the flagship.

Fury was there, he felt it in his bones. He strained forward, waiting, watching. The breathing of the others in the canvas-covered cart scratched against his eardrums. He felt like a wire stretched too tight. His wings had never felt so alive; he was aware of them even more than he'd been aware of his natural wings. They seemed to have a life of their own, a desire to launch and fly at last. He hadn't wanted to say anything to Diver, to give him false hope.

A thrill of fear and doubt shuddered through his bones, but he ruthlessly suppressed it. He would fly. He had to.

There was activity on the flagship as the sun rose higher, the morning bright and warm. Eleazar doubted many of the humans on the field had the vision to see the crew suddenly climbing the rigging in a purposeful commotion, but they saw the red sails open suddenly and catch the wind. The ship began to turn in a slow, lazy spiral, dropping through the clouds, growing larger and larger. Eleazar tensed, his hand bunching the heavy canvas over his head as if it were delicate silk. What was Pace up to? It was too much to hope that he'd land the ship.

A trumpet blast sounded across the Tithing Field, followed by another and another until the sound rolled like an avalanche. For an endless moment the blaring horns obliterated all other sounds then abruptly ceased.

A disembodied voice rang out overhead. "Show yourself, Eleazar! I know you're out there lurking in the shadows. You were ever the coward, dear brother!"

Rage rolled through him at the sound of his brother's voice. It took all his self-control to keep from flinging back the heavy canvas and launching himself into the sky.

That and the deep, debilitating fear he wouldn't be able to fly at all.

"Come out, Eleazar! Will you try and save your human whore? Does she mean nothing to you?"

And then across the sky appeared Fury's face, Rast beside her with a savage grin. He had a blade to her throat. On the foredeck of Pace's ship appeared two tiny figures: Eleazar knew it was Fury and his brother. They stood at a gap in the railing. His gaze bounced from those two forms to the immense projections against the clouds. They had appeared so quickly. Was Diver even in place? His muscles tensed, and his wings rustled with a sound like bells. The soldiers in the cart with him gasped and shuffled for their weapons.

"Well, dear brother, I have just one thing to say to you." He paused, his gaze menacing. His blade tipped up Fury's chin. She seemed dazed, her eyes unfocused and distant. What had they done to her? Suddenly, Rast looked directly into his eyes, or seemed to. The knife moved with lightning swiftness, striking across Fury's throat. In the same motion, Rast spun Fury and sent her backward through the gap in the ship's railing. "Catch."

CHAPTER THIRTY-EIGHT

She was falling.

And choking. Choking on blood...

Pain and fear lurked on the edges of awareness, but primarily Fury felt... joy.

She wasn't falling, she was flying.

Mithran filled her. A shining substance, light in her veins. She closed her eyes against the stinging cold wind and spread her arms. The ends of her scarf, the rest of it wrapped securely around her torso, snapped in the violent wash of air. She imagined they were wings sprouting from her back, and it felt right. This was where she'd always belonged, in the sky, in the brilliant blue sky. Soaring like an angel. Nothing could touch her. Nothing could harm her.

Before, not so long ago, she'd thought she was doomed.

Trapped in the hold of the drachen, beaten (even more fiercely than the first time) and terrified, all hope lost...

She'd tried to lose herself in sleep, perhaps never to wake, but it had been impossible. Agony kept her from any peace. Even with the pulse of Mithran surrounding her, she'd known only suffering. She had curled into herself on the hard planks, praying for death. The smooth wood beneath her cheek throbbed with power, taunting her. So much Mithran, so close to hand. Yet entirely out of reach. The pulse of it made her heart thrum. Her rushing blood seemed full of whispers: *Fury, Fury, Fury...*

The Mithran had called to her. Persistent in its demands: *Feed, Fury...*

On what? She asked herself in the dark of the hold. There was nothing–

Eat the ship.

Fury's eyes snapped open. Those words had been clear. Spoken into her mind. She held her breath, fighting against the constant pain. Had she imagined it?

Eat... the... ship...

She blinked. The darkened hold had grown as bright as day. The planks themselves gleamed in a tracery of gilding. She rolled laboriously onto her belly and pressed her lips against the floor. They tingled from the contact. Spurred by the sensation, she opened her mouth and ran her tongue across the slick wood. Heat shot through her, making her teeth ache and her mouth throb. She wrenched her head back and gave a weak cry at the rush of hurt that followed.

The pain will pass...

Yes. Pain was nothing. The heat from the Mithran felt good in this achingly cold prison. Tentatively, she lowered her head, her neck shaking with the effort. She kissed the wood, drawing a deep draught of air, breathing in the warmth of the Mithran. The power of it.

Eat the ship, Fury. Eat your fill.

She obeyed. Her mouth opened and she dragged her teeth across the planks, gouging the wood and drawing splinters. They pierced her gums and stabbed the roof of her mouth. She tasted blood and swallowed reflexively.

The heat, the blessed heat, rushed through her again. Stronger this time, better.

Fury, Fury, Fury...

Encouragement. The chant urged her on.

A choking, demented laugh rose from her gut. Blood sprayed onto the wooden planks, and she lapped it up like a dog. Her teeth, her strong white teeth raised on fresh fish and nuts and wild roots, tore into the Mithran-laced wood, finding purchase, rending and tearing. It became easier with each pass, the wood softened by her blood and spit. She lay her palms against the wood, pressed her body full length against the floor. Laughter grunted from her; she felt wild, maddened, strong.

They'd come for her just as she'd swallowed all that she could fit inside her. The bewildered guards had sworn, yanking her to her feet and wrenching one of her shoulders from the socket in the process. With barely a thought or even a wince of pain, she'd popped it back into place and sagged in their grip, forcing them to half carry, half drag her from the dark hold.

The two angels handled her gingerly after seeing what she'd done to the planking, casting glances at her and snarling when she returned their looks with a vacuous smile. They took her to the upper decks, and she blinked in the sudden, blinding sunlight. It seared her eyes, leaving blue imprints on the inside of her lids. But it didn't matter. The sun felt warm and welcoming after days in the dark, frigid hold.

I am not afraid. I am full of light.

Captain Pace, Rast and the treacherous bitch awaited her on the foredeck near the great, gleaming communication orb. So, the time had come. They would broadcast her execution to all of Trin. Her heart began to pound. The Mithran roared in response. She'd never felt stronger in her entire life. She stood straight, bearing herself like a soldier. She wore the leviathan skin as her mother had taught her. Armor against the world.

I am not afraid.

"Here she is, the lady of the hour," Rast said, smiling. His handsome face was alight with triumph and his purple eyes practically glowed.

"Let's get this over with," Maurissa said, a delicate frown on her perfect lips. She wore garments of pure black which hugged her tall slender frame like the sheath around a blade. Her unearthly beauty was washed out by the bright morning sun, and the irritated expression on her face made her ugly.

Fury stared. Here was the true Maurissa, faithless, cruel, arrogant. Her high, tight collar hid the scratches Fury had left on her neck. But they both knew they were there. Fury smiled at her and was satisfied to see red spots on her pale cheeks.

"Yes," Pace added briskly, barely giving Fury a glance. "We have much to accomplish today. Once Eleazar is dealt with, we can load the Tithe. Only after can we begin the Scourge. Else it will be pure chaos down there." He gave Rast a pointed look. "We cannot afford to lose this Tithe, your highness. The Archons will be displeased."

Rast's triumphant smile turned brittle. "If the Archons had recognized my right to the throne in the first place then none of this would be necessary."

"If you could have held Eleazar steady on the back of that nymph, none of this would have been necessary either," Maurissa interjected sweetly, plucking at imaginary dust on her sleeve.

His expression dark, Rast took Fury by the arm and hauled her to a gap in the railing. He turned her so they were facing the glowing orb, but not before she'd glanced over the edge to the green earth far, far below. It was like looking down on an anthill. People covered the Tithing Ground along with the usual tribute. Ah, yes, the honored few. The Chosen. Poor, sacrificial bastards. Was Eleazar down there? And Diver? Could they do anything to save her?

Or would she have to save herself?

The cold blade pressed against her flesh. Rast spoke, his voice loud in her ear, but she barely heard him. She raised her eyes to the blue, blue sky instead. It was calling to her–

Literally.

She could hear her name: *Fury. Fury.*

She gulped, stunned. Her eyes were drawn inexorably toward the Celestial Gate turning in lazy spirals above them. So close. Close enough to reach out and touch.

You are the light we will follow.

The voice, that voice again. She strained toward it. She was light. She was—

The sting of the blade was a kiss to her. And then she was flying.

"No!"

The word was a roar, sending ripples of fear and shock through the entire Tithing Ground, even as all eyes were fixated on the tiny figure plummeting from the sky.

Eleazar flung back the concealing canvas and leapt to the edge of the cart, his bare feet gripping the wood like talons. His compatriots reached for him, hissing warnings, calling him a fool, but he ignored them, brushing off their hands like bothersome insects. Rage and terror rolled through him, and he felt a burst of energy rush upward and outward to the ends of his wings.

His living, powerful wings.

So. This had been the key all along, not fear. Rage had brought his wings to life.

Fury.

With a gathering leap and a massive downward beat of his golden wings, Eleazar launched himself from the edge of the cart, breaking its axle and sending bandoliers and men tumbling into the mud. Like a hunting hawk, he arrowed toward the tiny, dark figure streaking toward the earth.

Diver's squad was scattered throughout the streets of Trin, slowly making their way to the Tithing Ground. They'd dropped their concealing cloaks the minute Rast's face had appeared in the clouds. No time for subterfuge. People scattered before these strange apparitions, screaming, sobbing. Diver supposed they looked like some demonic counterpart to the heavenly Angelus. They were moving under their own power, which wasn't easy in the claustrophobic flight suits but each of them had a limited supply of fuel and they had to save it for battle.

The plan of attack had been to gather at the cardinal points around the Tithing Field, and rise from all sides, focusing on the royal drachen. Hopefully an aerial offensive would both shock and overwhelm their enemy. How would the Angelus react to flying humans? Flying humans armed with razor-sharp Mithran-alloy blades, no less? The others could fight, but he was going for Fury first. Once she was secure, he would be free to use his sticky bombs against the flagship!

But before he could reach his designated location, Fury appeared in the clouds above, standing meekly beside Eleazar's shit brother, a knife pressed to her throat.

And all at once, Diver heard nothing but a roaring in his ears. The world turned red, and he hit his ignition switch, toggled wide for maximum burn.

His feet left the ground right as his sister tumbled over the golden-hulled ship and dropped toward the earth.

He screamed. The sweat burning his eyes could have been acid. The rockets roared on his back, heating his legs. He was burning too hot, too fast. He didn't care; it didn't matter.

He wasn't going to reach her in time.

Still screaming, he prayed to a Creator he didn't believe in to give him more speed, more power–

A streak of gold caught at the edge of his vision. Startled, his scream choked off. At the sight that met him, he slowed his burn, toggling the ignition almost closed.

His heart nearly burst. Eleazar had risen like some vengeful god. He was streaking toward Fury, a bolt of lightning in the clear, blue sky.

Heart thundering, panic and rage and fear mingling in his belly, Diver watched his friend fly for the first time and a savage joy filled him. He shouted in triumph: Eleazar would catch her!

Diver watched the golden bolt intersect Fury's plummeting form and gather her up. For a moment, the two hovered together, Fury securely in Eleazar's arms. His wings were held out like great golden sails then slowly, they began to descend in sweeping circles. Diver laughed in relief.

"Watch yourself!"

The warning cut his laughter short. Weaver flew past him, blade in hand. Above, angel upon angel leapt from the deck of the Royal Drachen and dove toward Eleazar and Fury. Diver lit up his rockets again and charged after them.

Below him, his volunteers rose on their strange bat wings: Only a dozen, but what a spectacular dozen! Tarps were ripped from the backs of wagons and lorries, revealing fixed machine guns and their precious artillery pieces. More weapons appeared among the Chosen, now arranging themselves into units, sweeping along innocent bystanders to get them out of the mix. Vogel's regulators milled about aimlessly, flummoxed. More Angelus poured from the smaller drachen, enraged at the audacity of the rebels. Not a few fighters quailed at the sight of those magnificent creatures streaking toward them, fierce raptors of inhuman speed and strength. But the bark of machine guns erupted in response. The screeching attack slammed against a spray of bullets.

The Angelus in all their immortal glory began to fall from the sky.

CHAPTER THIRTY-NINE

"Fury, Fury, I've got you."

"Eleazar..."

Her voice was faint. He risked a look at her neck and saw the wound wasn't as terrible as he'd feared. It appeared shallow: It hadn't nicked the artery beneath her ear or blood would be pumping from her. He held her close and angled his wings to hasten their descent. Pace and Rast had sent their minions chasing after them, and he couldn't fight with Fury in his arms. He had to get her somewhere safe.

The battle screams of the Angelus made his blood boil; he ached for vengeance, he ached for blood. The twang of bowstrings and the whir of arrows made him twist in the air. A few of the bolts struck his wings – and bounced off. It startled him. Mithran-enhanced arrows had struck him down before. His natural wings had no defense against the substance. Not so his new wings!

A grim smile twisted his lips. In trying to destroy him, they had only made him stronger.

Eleazar tucked his wings close and dropped into a dive. Far below, Conrad had made his move. His people were boiling out of every nook and crevice, rising from the Tithe and the Chosen, armed to the teeth with human guns. He found Conrad and Star in the huge lorry they'd commandeered, driving it straight through the Tithing Field. Regulators chased it, firing uselessly, aimlessly. Star was on one knee beside the field piece Conrad was manning, armed with a sniper rifle, dressed in her hero's uniform. She was firing and shouting encouragement to her fellow revolutionaries even as she picked off Vogel's regulators.

Shadows gathered over him, blocking the bright sun. He gritted his teeth and with a twist of his shoulder, he slipped sideways. Two angels screamed past him, one blue and one cardinal red. He twisted again, reversing his direction and a third foe rushed past, clad in brown and gold feathers.

This time he wasn't as lucky; the angel struck his primaries and sent him spinning. He was forced to spread his wings to get them under control and he lost the momentum of his dive. The spinning stopped, but suddenly they were a struggling goose beneath a bevy of hawks.

But then those hawks had their own troubles.

They'd attacked as a group, afraid of nothing and no one, much to their detriment. Chasing Eleazar had put them in range of human rifles.

Screams filled the sky. Eleazar watched in amazement as his all-powerful brethren began to swerve and fall, desperate to dodge projectiles they couldn't even see. Their bodies tumbling to the earth, crashing into carts and barrels of tribute. Many of the humans below were panicking, dashing aimlessly about while others moved with purpose. More deadly bullets strafed the sky.

Taking a chance, he went into another dive. Speed was his best hope. He angled for the edge of the Tithing Ground, where he could see Conrad's people setting up barricades. More of the city's regulators were emerging from the surrounding streets. They were attacking the revolutionaries, thinking they were after the Tithe, completely unprepared for what they were running into.

As he neared the barriers, he spotted Tully's silver hair among the others. He didn't care for the strange engineer, and Tully hated him. But... Tully had been enraged by Fury's kidnapping. She would be safe with them.

"Tully!" he shouted the moment his feet touched the ground. The engineer spun at his call and hurried over. "Are there any healers among your group? Fury needs help–"

"I'm fine, Lee."

Her voice was muffled against his chest, but it was strong. Fury lifted her head and gazed at him. Golden light swirled in her dark eyes. Her face glowed with vitality and the wound in her neck looked nearly healed. Startled, Eleazar set her on her feet. She smiled at him, holding onto his arms to steady herself. "Thank you for catching me."

Her eyes were glazed, distant. He searched her face, concerned. Had she been tortured? Was she in shock? Her hands gripped him firmly and her smile appeared genuine. Ecstatic, even.

And then he understood. "You took the Mithran."

Her smile broadened, and her eyes grew brighter. "Yes. The small bit I had, and more. It's in my bones, Lee. I am bound with light!"

"I see it." Tully drifted toward them. They seemed dazed, too. And nearly as ecstatic as Fury. "My Fury." Their hand lifted, shaking slightly, reaching for her. "You finally did it. Your fear is gone now, isn't it?"

Fury's expression dimmed momentarily. She stared at the goggled engineer, pulling back from their trembling fingers. "Yes. Mother," she replied to Eleazar's great shock.

"Then you understand what you must do now?" Their hand dropped, their eyes darting about like fish in a bowl, taking in the whole of her. Triumph laced their voice. "You wear the Talisman as I taught you. My good girl."

Fury frowned, one hand touching the leviathan skin girding her.

"Ah! I have something, something just for you, Fury. Wait here." Tully scurried away, disappearing among the crates and bales the others were dragging into barriers.

Eleazar felt Fury shudder and looked at her in concern. Her face looked more normal, thankfully, and he felt a surge of relief. He took her cheeks between his palms. "I thought I'd lost you."

"I thought I *was* lost," she said simply and laid a hand atop one of his. For a moment, they locked eyes and the world vanished. Then fear filled Fury's countenance.

"Where's Diver? Is he– Did he survive the blast?"

"You would have known if he hadn't," he said.

"Yes." Her gaze turned inward for a moment, and then she relaxed. "Yes. You're right."

"He's above us, Fury, fighting with his squadron."

She squinted against the bright sun. A gasp broke from her lips. Eleazar followed her gaze. A streak of black and gold zipped among the angels, moving with incredible speed and mobility. It made the Angelus appear like a confused flock of sparrows. More of those strange apparitions had risen to fight alongside Diver, but they weren't nearly as quick or capable.

Two of the suited men were struck down by one angel's sharp sword as Eleazar watched. The second disintegrated in a ball of flame, however, and took his attacker with him.

"Flying men," she murmured, astounded. "It wasn't madness after all. Do we... Do we have a chance?"

"A dozen humans in flight suits can't take down the entire fleet." Eleazar hissed as another of their soldiers went down in a ball of flame. He clenched his teeth. "They're going to all get slaughtered at this rate."

"Then you'd better hurry, Angelus." Fury spoke sharply, sounding far more like herself. "You know what you must do. Your bastard of a brother is waiting for you. You need to stop him. He's going to unleash a Scourge on those so-called Chosen! He means to destroy the entire city!"

"Of course he does," Eleazar growled, not surprised in the least. His brother was a cold-hearted demon!

Rast. Anger rippled through him. His desire for vengeance was as strong as ever, and now that Fury was safe he could claim it. He shook his wings, pleased at the glorious chiming.

He could fly, he could fight, he could *kill*. He glanced skyward, finding Pace's flagship surrounded by angels and a few suited men in vicious combat. The royal drachen was the pride of the fleet, a symbol of Angelic prowess. Conrad had been right about one thing: If they could bring it down, all of Splendour would tremble.

And if he removed Rast's head from his shoulders, he'd destroy a viper among the Angelus, too.

Despite the guns spitting at them, the Angelus attacked like the gods they pretended to be. Their gleaming swords were scythes mowing down human chaff. Their speed and strength allowed them to lay waste to vast swaths of the rebels on the ground. The rifles without Mithran ammunition did damage, but it took bullet upon bullet to take down one Angelus. Even then, the creature managed to kill a dozen in its death throes.

Diver reluctantly had to admire their courage. They flew right into danger without hesitation.

Although was it courage? Or arrogance?

He spared as little attention as possible to the horrors on the ground. Conrad and Star were doing their best to rally the troops, to keep their focus. This had been their plan all along: Mount an attack on the Tithing Ground. Kill the Angelic host and bring down a drachen to show the world the Angelus were not the infallible immortals they claimed to be. All the armies of the world would bear witness from Trin itself.

Diver and his unit had been tasked with attacking the flagship. Out of the reach of humans, seemingly, the ship itself had few defenses. Just the Angelus themselves! He and his men darted among them haphazardly, striking and withdrawing in the screaming roar of their rockets. Their blades were perfect for selective strikes. Even with little training and practice, the men were wielding those blades with remarkable precision. Rage and fear had given them preternatural instincts. The

Mithran seemed to feed on such extreme emotions, enhancing speed and strength in the human fliers.

Diver felt stronger and faster than anything alive. His enemies fell to his blades one after the other while he remained untouched. It was glorious, and horrible; he was home.

I belong here. Raining death...

An opening in the defenders and a boost to his rockets shot him above Pace's ship, and Diver targeted the rigging and the vast, battened red sails with his sharp-edged Mithran sword. He twisted and banked and was pleased to see more of his soldiers had followed his lead. The sails didn't keep the great ship afloat but damaging them limited its maneuverability. And great heavy sailcloth dropping onto the decks of the ship further confused and hampered her crew.

Two sailors launched from the foredeck armed with polearms, arrowing directly toward him. Their wings were dull sparrow brown. Diver landed on the upper yardarm of the main mast, toggling off his fuel and balancing on the balls of his feet. His breath was harsh and loud in his helmet, moisture was collecting on the inside of his goggles, and he yanked off the contraption. The fresh, cold air hit his damp skin, chilling him, but he drew in a deep, grateful breath. He didn't need the helmet anymore, not with the Mithran flowing through his veins. He tossed it aside and faced his enemies with a snarl.

Screeching, they broke in opposite directions, swooping in from left and right to attack him from both sides simultaneously.

Diver stepped off the yardarm and plummeted straight down toward the deck far, far below. The two angels barely avoided colliding with one another as their target vanished, one slamming into the yardarm and the other wrenching himself sideways at the last minute before chasing after Diver.

But he'd anticipated the move and fired his rockets halfway to the deck, shooting up past his enemy. He caught sight of the angel's startled face as they passed one another. His enemy hit the deck in a splatter of blood and feathers.

Unfortunately, the other angel had recovered from his unexpected collision with the yardarm and came at Diver as he rose. Diver twisted to avoid the sharp polearm, shifting his wings and firing his rockets for more speed. The angel was persistent and swift. It was all Diver could do to stay out of his reach, swooping and diving and banking, barely ahead of the thrusting polearm. The sharp blade caught him in the side, slicing through his suit and tracing a line of fire across his torso. He screamed through gritted teeth and dropped a dozen feet to avoid a follow-up blow.

A flash of bronze and gray streaked across his blurring vision. Weaver, he realized dimly, recognizing his colors as he struggled to regain control of his suit. The ex-captain sliced neatly through the angel's wing with his Mithran blade. The angel shrieked, and plummeted from the sky, still clutching his useless polearm. Diver rolled onto his back.

"Up!" he shouted, gesturing fiercely. Together they swooped higher, rising on rocket flames back toward the royal drachen. Barely touched apart from its slashed sails. Diver scowled, wind whipping tears from his eyes. They had to do some real damage.

He led Weaver past the port side of the ship, eyes searching the deck. The drachen were controlled by great orbs much like those used for communicating. He found the vast, glowing object near the back of the ship, behind the main mast. It was the heart of the drachen. Its power source, its control center. And there he stood: Pace. At the helm, hands over the glowing ball, standing tall and proud. Two more Angelus stood with him: Rast and an exceptionally beautiful female with night-black wings. A pool of calm amidst the chaos.

He grasped Weaver's arm and pulled him higher. Hidden in the clouds, he closed his toggle, letting the power of the Mithran coursing both through him and his flight suit keep them aloft.

"I'm going for the bridge," he told him, patting his midsection – and the collection of hand bombs he carried inside his suit. Their iron jackets covered a sticky core, perfect for slapping on armored lorries. "Gonna blow that orb! Lead the men against the others. Keep the Angelus off me, yeah?"

Eyes wide behind his goggles, Weaver clung to his arm, his wings trembling in the stiff wind. It was more Diver's power holding him up than his flight suit or the bat wings. He shook his head, and said something, but Diver couldn't hear him.

"Do it!" he screamed angrily. "It's a fucking order!"

And with that, he lifted his legs and planted his feet in the man's torso, sending him tumbling. He watched until Weaver regained control, then put him out of his mind for the task at hand.

Alive with purpose, Diver hit his ignition and dove straight for the bridge of the drachen far below.

CHAPTER FORTY

Diver felt amazingly calm as he fell toward his target. In one glorious explosion, he would rid the world of Eleazar's enemies. They would win the fight with this attack, too. Taking out the flagship of the almighty Angelus would send a message across the world. Even if the other drachen continued to fight, even if they managed to put down this rebellion, the seeds had been planted. Avernus would finally understand who their true enemy was. Others would rebel, refuse to gather the Hallow Tithe. The soldiers in the city would carry the news to their armies. The war might stutter, even halt, when humans realized they had a common enemy. A mortal enemy…

And the Angelus would learn to fear them.

The wind whistled past him. His eyes teared up and he blinked them clear. The orb was his target, but he kept an eye on Pace. If anyone could stop him, it would be the captain.

Pace, tall, imposing and stoically unconcerned by the battle raging around him, directed a bevy of Angelus with gestures and shouted commands. They were lifting horns from perches along the railing of the drachen. Horns of pure Mithran, wide at one end like strange cornucopia. He knew foul blackness lay inside them.

Diver's heart stuttered. Would they release the Scourge?

Rast and his female companion stood beside Pace. Supremely confident.

He dismissed them as quickly as he noticed them, all his attention on Pace.

He recognized his mistake when the female's level gaze rose to find him. She lifted the crossbow in her hands and targeted him with cool precision. His eyes shifted and suddenly all he could see was the deadly bolt aimed at him. His heart thundered. He held a hand bomb in one hand: He had only to slam into the orb, even if he was skewered like a pigeon on a spit–

She loosed, and wings of gold deflected the missile meant for him.

Diver slammed into his would-be redeemer at top speed. The world spun in a tangle of golden wings, red sails and bright blue sky. The impact knocked him from his course, and he let loose a stream of silent curses as his plans crumbled to nothing and he and Eleazar smashed into the decking far beyond the control orb.

The revolutionaries were holding off the city regulators, their makeshift barriers blocking the narrow streets feeding into the Tithing Ground. This was far beyond what the regulators were used to. Policing a subdued populace was a far cry from fighting armed resistors. The unrest had bled into their ranks, too, through Star and Conrad's relentless propaganda campaign. In some divisions, the regulators fought amongst themselves.

In Tully's small pocket of resistance, spirits were high. The fighting was intense, but it was with fellow humans not the preternatural Angelus. There was even a sense they might *win*.

Having never been swept up in the fever of revolution, Fury watched the skies instead. Nearby, men and women cut down black-jacketed regulators with unrelenting rifle fire. The cries of the wounded, the shrieks of the dying, all of it was distant. She was single-minded in her desire: Her battle was in the sky. With her brother. And with her angel...

He had launched mere moments before, and she could see the flash of his wings up high in the turmoil, fighting his brethren. She tracked his movements as well as she could until the bulk of a drachen blocked her line of sight. A frustrated moan slid between her clenched teeth. She strained toward the heavens. What good was her strength, her newfound power, without a way to fly?

"Here! I'm here, Fury. Look what I have!"

Fury turned, distracted. Tully held a bundle of shimmering fabric, bright gilded wings folded atop it. The wings looked more like Eleazar's than the batlike wings of the flight suits. Tully shook out the suit: it was obvious this one was lighter and thinner than the others.

"What is it? Why does it look so different?"

Tully whipped off their thick goggles, their grey eyes studying her sharply. Assessing. All the vague, semi-mad vacuousness had fallen from their expression. "I made it for you. It is spun from Mithran. Beyond compare." They laid it on a nearby crate, spreading the wings to either side, and began to undo the fastenings. "It had to be of a fine weave. The Talisman is to be worn over it. With this, you will lead them home."

"What in the Creator's name are you talking about?" Fury ground her teeth, finally feeling something besides urgency. She glared at her mother, for once seeing the woman she remembered in the lines of their face and the fierceness in their eyes. Anger roared through her. Years' worth. She grabbed Tully's arm and wrenched them around. "Make sense for once! Diver is up there. Fighting all alone! Do you care at all about him? About your son!" Her vision grew blurred. Tears stung like acid. "Did you ever care about any of us?" she shrieked. "Your children? Your husband? All you had to do was keep your mouth shut! All you had to do was stay with us and be safe!"

"Fury, my little Fury, there you are…"

"Shut up! You don't know me; you don't know us! All you ever cared about was your vendetta. Your hatred destroyed us! *Killed* us!"

She was screaming in her mother's face, lost in her rage and grief and resentment. All the things she'd wanted to say for years spewing from her like vomit—

Then suddenly she was face down in the dirt, a knee in her back and her arm twisted painfully.

"Calm down."

The firm order quieted her immediately. Her sobs hitched into silence. Years had passed, but she recognized this tone in her mother's voice. It brooked no disobedience.

Tully spoke. The chatter of machine guns a backdrop to their words: "I was taken away too soon, and it is my greatest regret. My greatest failing. Your training had barely begun, your path not set, and I knew Grayson didn't fully understand what was necessary. He was a good man, your father, but he was soft and you were his favorite. He wanted you to have an easy life."

Hearing her father maligned, Fury struggled briefly, but Tully was an immovable weight atop her. A sharp pain in her arm settled her. Her mother continued.

"I don't blame him. I'm the one who let myself be captured. My arrogance was my undoing, thinking I could speak my mind, be open about my heritage. For that, I apologize, Fury."

"Just for that?" Fury growled. Another twist and her chin ground into the dirt.

"Listen to me! We don't have time for your childish resentments. Nothing you have suffered compares to what I have endured, believe me. The Angelus broke me. I was their plaything, their *pet*. A Gullan woman, blessed of the ancient leviathans. We are bound in ways the Angelus cannot understand, and it *enrages* them."

Fury lay still, enthralled despite herself. *They speak to me, sing to me. They are in my dreams...*

"Humans don't last long in Splendour. But I lasted. If only out of pure spite! Finally, my tormentor grew bored of me, and I managed to escape on a Tithing ship. I took my chance and made a leap of faith."

"You survived," Fury said, giving them a small concession. "You survived all of it."

"No," Tully said grimly. "*Tuilelaith* did not survive. Conrad found that broken carcass and somehow put a human back together again. I am Tully now, and my Gullan blood is sullied by the manna I was force-fed in Splendour. You are my last hope! You are the key, Fury, do you understand?"

She didn't. Not at all. She gathered herself, ready to use her newfound strength to toss her mother off her.

But Tully's next words stopped her cold: "It was no accident the Angelus fell at your feet, Fury."

"What?"

"The leviathans marked him and sent him to you. He was a useful tool; none of this would have been possible without him. I suppose I owe him that, at least. He led you to me and gave us the Mithran. Eleazar the Fallen!" They laughed. "From his dust, you will rise!"

The decking shattered like glass, and they crashed into the bowels of the drachen. Stunned by the impact, Eleazar lay in a tangled heap. Sunlight streamed down from the gaping hole in the decking, illuminating clouds of drifting dust. Nearby, Diver shifted in the wreckage, moaning. Relief shivered through him. Since leaving Fury's side, he'd had only one goal: Find Diver. And when he'd seen his acolyte – his *friend* – in a suicidal dive toward the royal drachen, he'd done everything in his power to reach him in time.

"Diver." Eleazar struggled to right himself and untangle his golden wings. The metal feathers clashed and rang. "Get up! They'll be on us–"

A shadow fell across him, and he looked up to find a figure perched on the edge of the shattered deck, emerald wings spread wide, and one arm drawn back. He held a javelin, its sharp point made of Mithran. Rast.

He would know his brother's wings anywhere.

"This time, you have nowhere to run, brother!"

Rast drew back his arm, his powerful muscles bunching. Even through the smoke and dust, his eyes gleamed with murderous glee. Desperately, Eleazar heaved at the wreckage pinning him in place, knowing it was futile.

The javelin flew. Unstoppable – just as Diver threw himself across Eleazar's chest.

The impact of Rast's weapon shook Eleazar, but he was untouched. A low, guttural cry sprang from Diver's lips. The javelin shivered in his back; he lay sprawled atop Eleazar, shielding him from what would have been a fatal strike to his heart. Shocked, Eleazar stared in horror at the shuddering javelin protruding from his friend's back.

Above them, Rast cursed and dropped into the hold, straddling the trapped duo. A scream tore from Diver as Rast grasped the javelin. Eleazar shouted in impotent rage. Teeth bared, Rast worked at the javelin, but seemed unable to complete the killing thrust. More curses burst from him, and he yanked the weapon free. Diver's jet pack came away, impaled on the razor-sharp barbs. The furious angel reached for it, annoyance clouding his triumphant expression.

On top of him, Diver lifted his head and gave Eleazar a sickly grin, his eyes jerking toward the ignition switch gripped in his fist. Pain etched his features – the javelin had pierced him along with the jet pack – but his eyes shone with glee. He toggled the switch.

Flames blasted from the damaged jet pack as the fuel ignited, launching Rast skyward. The tubes connecting the pack to Diver's suit snapped, spraying fuel in a wild undulation. The liquid spewed across the wrecked hold, combusting and igniting in blue-white brilliance.

CHAPTER FORTY-ONE

Rast was roaring. Shrieking. Then silence.

Around them, flames ate gleefully at the hold. Eleazar lifted himself from beside a struggling Diver. "We have to get to the orb–"

"Must I do everything?"

Eleazar wrenched around. Maurissa stood on the deck above them, unbothered by the smoke and chaos. She held a crossbow, one he recognized, now aimed at his heart. "Submit quietly, Eleazar. For the sake of Splendour. For the sake of these *humans* you seem to love. These beasts."

"I will not submit peacefully to my demise," he snapped back, quietly gathering himself, one hand holding onto Diver. If he could launch, then maybe–

"Demise? We aren't going to *kill* you," she said with feigned shock. "Why go to all this trouble just to kill you? We need you to return to Splendour, my dear prince. The Archons demand your abdication. Else they won't let Rastaphar rule in your place. You must name him as your rightful heir."

"Abdicate?" Eleazar blinked, his shock not in the least faked. His free hand tightened into a fist. So, now he understood this farce. The Archons were nothing if not traditionalists. His mother might have banished him, but the council would want the line of succession secured lest it throw all of Splendour into internecine war. They desired peace at all cost in Splendour. "And why by the Luminous

One would I do that? Especially since Rast is most likely charred to ash!"

"Do you think your brother so easily killed? His strength puts yours to shame." Her eyes slipped toward something on the deck behind her. "He'll need but a moment to recover."

He scowled. He should have known it would take more than a little explosion to kill Rast.

"Do you care nothing for your home, Eleazar?" she demanded. "Have you become a Beast of the Below in truth? Do your duty for once! Did you ever truly believe you were worthy to sit upon the Great Throne of Honour?" She scoffed, the crossbow dipping. "Return to Splendour with us and we will give you a palace. Would that appease you? You will have everything you need to return to your depraved existence."

The blood drained from Eleazar's face. Deep in his heart, he felt a tug. To return to Splendour, to his life of ease and frivolity... would it be so terrible?

Maurissa smiled a terrible smile. "You can even keep your little pets."

"Hey."

Her dark eyes narrowed, shifting toward Diver, obviously miffed to be addressed by a human. Diver was grinning, his gaze pinned on the black-winged Angelus. "Catch," he hissed.

He lobbed something toward her with an underhand throw. It looked like a ball of iron.

Eleazar saw Maurissa's face scrunch with confusion even as she caught it with one hand. Diver was already turning, arms over his head, tucking himself small. And Eleazar was turning with him, wings extended, shielding his friend from what he knew was coming–

The concussion rattled his wings, sending them into an oddly beautiful song. Maurissa's shriek only added to the music. The blast reverberated through the hold, blowing out the flames eating at the Mithran-laced wood.

His ears rang from the explosion. It seemed to take forever until he could hear again. Pace was screaming orders, loud but purposeful. He heard a terrible roar, filled with hysterical rage.

And underneath it all, an ominous hum that made his innards twist.

"We have to get out of here," he said. A dazed Diver let him gather him into his arms and Eleazar leapt skyward for the opening in the deck.

He didn't fly far; his head still rang from the hand bomb and Diver in his heavy flight suit was dead weight in his arms. He managed to get to the aft deck before having to land. Smoke blocked the view behind him, but he could just make out someone crouched on the deck, wings extended, hands clawing at a pile of tattered black feathers...

Maurissa. Emerald wings sheltered what was left of her. Rast's roars were terrible to hear.

Beyond them, launching into the open sky from a dozen drachen, were scores of Angelus armed with golden horns.

Pace had unleashed the Scourge.

"Eleazar is not a pawn in all of this," Fury cried, shaking out her numb arm. Her mother had released her, finally. Her head was reeling. The bugle of horns, deep and ominous, sounded in the distance. A strange noise amidst the thunder of guns. "I refuse to believe that!"

"I don't care." Tully jerked their chin toward the flight suit. "Put it on," they ordered in that voice Fury had no choice but to obey. When had she ever said "no" to her mother?

Still, she hesitated, allowing herself one small resistance, staring at the suit as if it might rise and attack her.

Fury, Fury, Fury...

Whispers urged her forward. She did what she was told.

The suit fit perfectly. It wrapped her from head to toe in

shining gold and black, reminding her briefly of the garb Maurissa had worn.

With great ceremony, Tully wrapped the leviathan skin around her torso, crisscrossing it over her shoulders and tying it off at her waist. The dark indigo scales caught the sunlight in fiery streaks. Fury craned her neck to see the wings. Though delicate seeming, they bore razor-sharp edges. They looked more like *real* wings. Like Eleazar's wings.

Was it true? What Tully had said about Eleazar?

Fury grimaced. Did it matter? It didn't change all they had endured together. It didn't change her feelings for him.

"I fly for Eleazar," she said impulsively.

Tully's expression scrunched but she said nothing and focused on helping Fury into a pair of sleek leather gloves. Unbidden, a memory flashed in her head of Tuilelaith putting mittens on her hands when she was a child. The bitter cold of Koine winters couldn't stop Fury from playing in the snow, and her mother always insisted she dress warmly. Her face had been just as grim and serious back then, too. She felt a surge of emotion. Once upon a time, her mother had loved her.

"Now, one last thing," Tully said briskly. "The power source."

Fury shook off her memories. Shoved them to the very back of her mind like the useless clutter they were. Sudden eagerness wiped everything else away. She thumbed the toggle switch attached to one glove, careful not to flip it. Yet. Tully had moved behind her, settling heavy tanks on her back.

She hissed as something pricked her. There seemed to be tiny needles along the inside of the rockets, and she shifted. "Something's poking me," she complained, arching her back. "I don't think it's on correct–"

Tully pushed against the tanks, there was a click and then a sudden pressure between her shoulder blades. Abruptly, those tiny needles stabbed into her spine from her neck to her lower back, punching deep. Fury shrieked and leapt away from Tully, her back on fire. She twisted to face them, outraged.

"What did you do?" Desperately, she tried to tear away the leviathan skin and get to the suit, but Tully grabbed her wrists and forced her hands away, shockingly strong.

"Don't," they warned, eyes fierce. "Give it a moment; let the needles settle into your flesh. If you rip them out now, the damage might be irreparable."

"Damage?" Fury cried, trying to pull free of Tully's tight grip. "You stuck needles in me?!"

"Blood is necessary, Fury. Stand. Still!"

Her mother's command thundered in her ears. She gasped in a great draught of air and stopped fighting. Hot tears leaked down her cold cheeks, but the pain along her back was fading. The burning turned to an intense warmth like sunlight soaking into her skin. Her heart pumped fast, and a throbbing echo rolled down her back. A lightness filled her. She drew herself up and flexed her shoulder blades. Her wings *opened*.

Triumph transformed her mother's face. For a moment, she was Tuilelaith Cree once more, as beautiful as Fury recalled.

"I couldn't do this for Diver," they said. "He managed to ingest the Mithran, but his blood is sullied by manna. Not as bad as mine, of course. Still, too much of the gods' metal might kill him. When I thought you lost, I feared all hope was lost with you. But look at you now! *Look* at you! Alight with power, ready to fulfill your destiny."

Fury wrenched herself free. "I'm not here to fulfill any *destiny*." All the emotion, that brief, small warmth she'd felt toward her mother vanished. "I only care about Diver and Lee! I don't give a fuck about you! I don't give a fuck about being Gullan, or the Creator-cursed beasts floating around Splendour. Find someone else to fulfill your vendetta."

Tully merely stared at her. "True to your name," they murmured. "You'll do what you must, Fury."

Fury stepped back, shaking with anger. She wanted away from Tully, away from her memories. Years of pain and grief and loss would never be healed by this person.

A sudden swelling of screams rose above the noise of combat. A thousand voices raised in horror. Even Tully startled to hear it, whirling toward the terrible sound.

"What is happening?" Fury's voice shook. Combat still raged, thumping and barking, but this was something else.

They couldn't see much in their barricaded position. The Tithing Field was blocked by wagons and a pile of debris. A low, chest-numbing hum sounded beneath the screaming. It made her teeth ache. She shook her head, overwhelmed by the strange droning.

Horns. It sounds like a thousand horns playing one deep disturbing note!

"Oh, Luminous One, spare me!" Tully said, their voice ragged with terror. "Oh, no, no, no! Fly, Fury! You must fly now!"

"What? What is it?"

But Tully wasn't listening. They shoved her hard, back toward a clear space behind the barricades. The line of defense against the regulators was breaking. Fury could see the men and women falling back, running from something, eyes raised toward the sky.

A black rain was falling. Fury froze, unable to take her eyes from it.

"Launch!" Tully screamed at her.

Fury couldn't move. They would all be turned! Their army would be obliterated–

Tully grabbed her hand and toggled open the ignition switch.

The rockets on her back blasted her off the ground as the rain swept over the barricades, over the unfortunate revolutionaries. Over–

"Mother!"

Fury screamed, but it was too late. She was in the sky, flying fast, as the Angelic Curse drowned her mother in blackness.

CHAPTER FORTY-TWO

"Eleazar!"

Rast roared his name. He'd risen from the ruin of his lover, his fine clothes charred, but his wings wide and undamaged, gleaming with power. It shone from his fierce, angry face. Charisma. Not to charm or persuade but to destroy.

Eleazar knew in that moment his brother had never intended to take him alive no matter what Maurissa might have thought. Rage scorched through him, igniting his own wells of Charisma. Strength followed; he felt renewed.

Deep inside, he knew it wouldn't last. He had to make it count.

He glanced behind him to where he'd settled Diver. Scorched and wounded, his acolyte leaned against a pile of rigging, his legs sprawled and his wings a broken tangle on his back. He gave Eleazar a ragged grin, panting like a weary dog.

"Don't fret about me." Diver pulled his jacket aside, revealing a final hand bomb. This one had a handle and its round head glistened with a greasy substance. "I have my mission to complete."

Filled to the brim with murderous Charisma, Eleazar could only nod. There was no room for worry or fear. No space for love or affection. He turned his back on Diver and answered his brother's challenge, rising on wings of steel and Mithran.

* * *

Diver stripped off his flight suit, leaving it in a pile on the deck, smoking and bloodstained. Already, he could feel strength returning to his limbs despite the beating he'd taken. The wound on his back was nothing more than a scratch. He lifted his arm and rolled his shoulder, pleased to have full range of motion. Once again, the Mithran was proving vital to his survival. How much could he endure with the magical substance in his veins?

Best not to find out...

Battle raged beyond the railings of the ship on the ground far below, but the deck of the great drachen was relatively calm. Black smoke poured from the blasted open hold, but the fire had died. Too bad. He'd hoped it would spread and take out the entire ship. He sighed. Nothing was ever easy.

High above him, Eleazar and Rast spun and clashed like two falcons, coming together and breaking apart in a hypnotic dance. Diver's teeth locked in a grimace. Even with the Mithran roaring through him, he was trapped without a functioning flight suit.

He wasn't entirely helpless, however. His hand went to his midsection. To the sticky bomb. He had to get to the control orb.

He edged along the railing of the ship, daring to peek over the side. The flagship had lost altitude – perhaps due to his aborted attack? – and he could see the battlefield in relief. He tried to ascertain who was winning on the Tithing Field, but a heavy fog rolled over the forces. He frowned. It was thick and gray and seemed to move with purpose. A seeking mist...

Ice crawled up his belly. Even from this height, he could hear the collective screams from a thousand throats. Scores of Angelus swept the field in formation. Foolish against the human guns. The bullets took their toll, but the Angelus stayed the course. They were playing golden horns. Beneath the screams, he heard the deep hum of the strange instruments. A low note announcing doom.

Shapes milled about in the strange fog. Blackened figures. Burnt...

A desperate noise slipped from him, a child's whimper.

Diver peeled himself away from the railing. He had a mission. Navigating the last few feet over the damaged decking – he had to leap over a hole to reach safety – took all his focus. On firm footing, he checked for enemies and saw none. The way to the vast control orb was clear. Not even Pace remained–

Something hard and heavy clamped down on the back of his neck. His feet left the deck. He reached back, clawing at the hand grasping him by the scruff, his legs flailing. For all his newfound strength, he was helpless to break free. His gut turned fully to ice; he knew who had him.

"Foul human. Disgusting little bug."

Diver went still, hanging limply in the giant Angelus' grip. Pace flew the short distance to the control orb, carrying Diver with him like a stray he'd found rummaging in his trash. He landed beside it in a great blast of wings and let Diver's feet touch the planking, though his gauntleted hand didn't budge from his neck. Panting in fear and exhilaration, Diver let his hand drift slowly toward his jacket. His heart thumped wildly. He was right where he needed to be.

The furious, hulking Angelus placed his free hand on the orb. It gleamed in response to his touch, and the ship shuddered beneath them. It began to rise. Was he trying to escape?

"Eleazar the Fallen!" The words boomed louder than thunder, the crystal taking his voice and amplifying it. Diver winced but took the opportunity to stuff his hand inside his coat. The feel of the sticky bomb slowed his racing heart. His sweaty palm closed around its handle. A hint of panic dried his mouth. Would it slip from his grip?

Focus, Diver. One chance...

Pace's disembodied voice filled the sky. "Eleazar the Fallen! Your revolution has failed. Your human allies will fall to the Scourge. Return to my drachen at once and perhaps you will save this one!" He shoved Diver forward. Suddenly, his face was broadcast across the clouds, bloody, dirt-streaked, eyes wide with panic and fear. "Surrender to me now, or I will crush this boy like the bug he is!"

Fury flew. Fast and high. The Mithran-fueled rockets propelled her, but she was beating her ersatz wings like a rising hawk. She had no helmet. Her hair whipped around her face, stinging her cheeks, lashing at her eyes. She barely noticed. For all that she'd strained to reach the sky, her gaze remained pinned on the ground. An unnatural fog had risen wherever the black rain had fallen, twisting around the people trying to run. Their screams reached her even over the roar of her rockets. They fell to the fog, only to rise burnt and ravenous. Any human spared the Scourge quickly became victim to hordes of newborn ghouls.

Her breath wheezed in and out of her hard-clenched teeth. Her mother's position had been overrun. Had Tully been transformed, or merely eaten? A panicked sob burst from her. She'd barely made it out herself. Thanks to her mother...

Make it count, Fury.

Painfully, she lifted her head, turning away from the horrors.

The horn-bearing Angelus had completed their ruinous run and were wheeling in the sky, preparing for another. Their wings glittered in the sunlight, a murderous rainbow. Her heart thrummed at the sight. Such glorious creatures. Deserving of worship–

She tore her eyes away, fighting back against the intense feelings of awe and wonder. It was Charisma manipulating her. That was why their wings glowed so fiercely.

Fortunately, those humans not taken by the black rain of the Scourge weren't swayed by the angels' charm offensive either. Buoyed by blood lust and rage, they fired shrapnel shells at the Angelus from their one remaining field piece and sprayed bullets from several fixed machine guns entrenched close to the center of the Tithing Ground. The fragmentation shells exploded among the low-flying Angelic formations, tearing through flesh and wings, breaking apart the wedge-shaped waves.

Their destructive symphony faltered.

Some of the machine guns were now aimed at the ravaging ghouls. They had to contain them, whatever it took, if the creatures reached the city...

Fury steeled herself against that horrid thought, refocusing her effort on reaching her own target. What was happening on the ground was out of her hands. Let those trained in warfare deal with it. Her place was with Diver, with Eleazar.

Mama, I'm sorry, so sorry...

Wind clawed tears from her eyes. She blinked them away with ferocious determination.

Pace's ship hovered above the thickest fighting. The largest of all the drachen, smoke rolled from its deck and one great red sail dragged over its railing. She increased her speed, arrowing toward the ship.

Bright golden wings appeared among the clouds. They rose from the royal drachen. Eleazar. Even amidst the battle fog, his Charisma gleamed brightest. It drew her like a lodestar.

Adjusting her wings and ignition, she started toward him–

A voice boomed around her, deafening. She pulled to a stop – her wings remarkably responsive. The words crashed atop her like mountains. They rattled her bones so hard she could barely make sense of them. She heard Eleazar's name. It was a threat, a demand for him to surrender. Fury shook her head, her ears ringing, and then Diver's terrified face was splashed across the clouds as hers had been what seemed a lifetime ago. Thick fingers were wrapped around his slender throat, Captain Pace a dark bulk behind him.

Eleazar might need her, but Diver needed her right now!

Lighting up her rockets, she made her choice.

* * *

Locked in deadly combat with his half-brother, Eleazar heard Pace's warning through a red fog of rage. He took no heed. The vision of Rast slicing through Fury's throat and tossing her casually from his ship replayed itself in his mind. Nothing mattered but wiping Rast from the face of Avernus. All of this was his fault! He'd cast Eleazar from Splendour, turned his own mother against him, and tried to murder his lover. Death was too good for him!

"You were my brother!" Eleazar screamed at him as they closed once more, grappling, tearing at each other, wings beating furiously. "I worshipped you!"

Rast's face was a blood-streaked rictus, his lips drawn back from his teeth. His clawed hands lunged for Eleazar's throat, leaving hot scratches on his skin. Eleazar hissed, struggling to break out of Rast's grip. His wings rang discordantly around them, then grew tangled with Rast's emerald feathers. Together, they dropped, the air whistling past them. They wheeled apart.

"You are nothing to me!" Rast cried. "A useless spawn! Unworthy of life, let alone the Throne!"

He swooped in close, lashing out with his bare feet at the last moment – his fine boots had been lost to the flames. Eleazar took a hard kick to the chest but ignored the pain and threw himself at his brother.

They fought savagely. More animal than Angelus. Brute strength against brute strength.

"Sooner a dog rule Splendour than you!" Rast growled, arms straining to keep Eleazar's hands from his throat.

Eleazar bared his teeth, and took his brother in a grapple, tangling around him like a snake. Hands behind his neck, he forced his head down. "The humans are your downfall, Rast, not me! They know the truth of us! They will never stop fighting!"

Twisting like an eel, Rast slithered free, leaving skin and blood behind. His great emerald wings beat at Eleazar, sending him flailing. Before he could recover, Rast was on him, hands at his throat again. Rast managed to take him by the neck.

"Then I will send a Scourge such as this world has never seen!" Rast's scowling visage swam in his vision.

The hands around his throat grew tighter, cutting off his breath. Eleazar wrenched at Rast's thick arms, amazed at his strength. He'd grown so used to fighting humans he'd forgotten how powerful the Angelus were. Especially Rast. He could not beat him. Even in his rage and bloodlust, Eleazar was a poor second to his brother, and his well of Charisma was running dry.

Ignoring his burning lungs, Eleazar beat at his brother like a madman. Rast had to be stopped. Better Splendour be drawn into a civil war than let him take the Great Throne of Honour. It would be a disaster for both their worlds. Eleazar had always known Rast possessed only disdain for humans. But… this was something else.

The Angelus needed the humans. Needed them to tame this vast world and deliver sustenance to Splendour. Rast was mad, a mad fool. He knew his brother would follow through on his threats, no matter the cost. Rast would crush this rebellion, and then he would crush the world.

Eleazar batted his wings frantically, trying to tear free from Rast's grip. The sharp Mithran feathers beat against him. Blood misted the air. His wings sliced Rast's clothes to ribbons then his skin beneath. Eleazar's vision was growing dark, but he fought on. He would not let Rast destroy the world.

Out of desperation, Eleazar lunged forward. It threw Rast off center, and, startled, he loosened his hold on Eleazar's neck. Enough for Eleazar to gulp a breath, and wrap his arms and legs around Rast. He poured all his remaining Charisma into his muscles. Rast growled and struggled but couldn't manage to get leverage in this awkward embrace.

"Fight me!" he shrieked. "You coward! Fight like an Angelus!"

"I'm done fighting." The words scraped from his damaged throat. Rast had nearly crushed his windpipe. Eleazar closed his wings, drawing them tight to his back. Weakened by their battle, some of his primaries tattered from the earlier blast, Rast alone couldn't hold them both aloft. His wings flapped uselessly, unable to counter their combined weight. He screeched and cursed him to the Abyss, trying desperately to break free. Eleazar held on, all his remaining Charisma throbbing through his limbs.

"Let's see if you bounce, brother," Eleazar hissed. "Yeah?"

Locked together, predator and prey, they fell.

The great, dark-winged captain holding Diver by the scruff tracked the brothers' fight, his face dark with anger. Dangling in Pace's grip, Diver couldn't see who had the upper hand. Thankfully, Pace's ploy had failed; Eleazar wasn't rushing back to save his acolyte.

Diver sent his Angelus a silent prayer, wondered briefly where Fury might be, then yanked out the sticky bomb. With a violent lunge, straining to the end of Pace's hold, he slapped it against the glowing orb. It clung like a burr. Surprised, Pace jerked him back, but not before Diver unraveled the pin.

Tossing Diver to the deck, Pace reached for the device, his eyes widening and his wings opening in alarm.

Diver grinned savagely, looking back over his shoulder as he scrambled away. The expression on Pace's face filled him with pleasure. It was terror. Pure terror.

Counting seconds in his head, Diver raced toward the railing. Better to fall than be blown to bits. Or so he figured. Pace had reacted quickly, but it wouldn't be fast enough.

He reached the railing and vaulted over it, but as his feet left the decking a wave of concussive force blasted into him, throwing him forward like a child's toy. Stunned, he rode the wave, fighting blackness as he flew through the sky.

Something latched onto his jacket, and then he really was flying. Diver gave a great gasp, his lungs filling with much-needed oxygen. Astonished, he craned his neck to see what had him.

"Weaver," he croaked. The ex-captain didn't seem to hear him. His helmeted visage pointed straight ahead as he flew at top speed away from the drachen. Diver could hear his breath sobbing in his chest, and the arms holding him aloft shook alarmingly. His head addled, Diver strained to look behind them, worried his ploy might have been in vain.

Pace was smeared all over the deck of the ship, blood and limbs and feathers plastered against the scorched planks.

And the massive control orb sparkled and spat, energy swirling in its depths like writhing serpents, churning faster and faster.

Faster, he wanted to urge. Would they be out of the blast zone? There was no way to know. All the ship's Mithran would explode in a chain reaction. Nothing could stop it. They would live or die by–

A winged figure appeared on the deck of the royal drachen, dropping from the sky, head turning frantically, gaze sweeping over the ship, most of which was obscured by smoke and flame. Someone from his squad? He wanted to shout a warning, but they would never hear him. Their flight suit was strange, almost glittering. Not made of canvas, but something else. A deep blue cloth wrapped their torso.

Leviathan skin, he realized just as his sister spotted him, the oval of her face turned upward. Fury gathered herself and leapt, her wings extended–

Gold. Like Eleazar's...

The deck split beneath her in a blossoming explosion. It caught her as she rose, light and heat enveloping her. She disappeared in that fatal bloom. Diver closed his eyes against the violent light and heard nothing but his own screams.

CHAPTER FORTY-THREE

The soft ground embraced Eleazar. He breathed in the smell of the earth and felt no fear. When he'd first fallen to Avernus, the scent of dirt and living things had been overwhelming. Now, it reminded him of his time in the woods with Fury and Diver. Compared to all they'd endured since, it was a happy memory. A time of peace before the chaos. The spongy earth held him gently, like a cradle. He lay spread-eagled, sunlight bathing his face. It was so bright. He closed his eyes. He was so tired...

The good smells of earth and grass vanished in a wash of blood and cordite, smoke and ash. Hot steel and burning Mithran. He gasped, dragging in a breath, his lungs aching and empty. His heart stuttered in his chest, pounding violently. It hurt but he embraced the pain, nearly certain it had stopped beating the same as his lungs had stopped breathing. Fighting panic, no longer comforted by the walls of earth surrounding him, he wrenched himself up, struggling to be free of this premature grave.

His wings gave him the most trouble, tangled as they were in the spongy soil – though he was beginning to understand the moist, springy earth most probably saved his life. Sense returned to him as he fought his way free. Memories of fighting, of falling. Of a white-hot explosion. He remembered his brother being torn away from him by the blast. And then... nothing.

Until waking up inside the earth...

The hole was deep. He had to scramble up the sides of the angel-shaped depression. He was too weary, and his wings were too dirt-logged, to even pretend to fly. Long, thick grass provided ready handholds to drag him the last few feet to freedom. Exhausted, he lay face down on the field. The thunder of guns sounded distant, but the shaking earth told him otherwise. A battle raged near. He coughed violently as smoke and dust blew over him. Tentatively, he pulled back his wings and lifted his head. The Tithing Field was a wasteland beyond him. Corpses, blackened and raw, lay scattered everywhere, riddled by bullets and shrapnel. Little more than chunks of flesh. Bile rose in his throat. They were Burnt Ghouls, yes, but they had been people.

Eleazar managed to get to his feet. There was no sign of Rast. Had his brother survived? Perhaps he lay somewhere buried as he had been? Or...

He searched the sky for the royal flagship. It no longer hovered over the center of the Tithing Field, but it wasn't hard to find. A great, flaming, smoking hulk rested on the field, and he recalled again that white-hot explosion.

"Diver did it," he whispered, pride swelling his chest only to turn to staggering grief. Sharp tears blinded him. Diver had sacrificed–

"Leeeeee!"

He spun at the feral shrieking. A man raced across the shattered terrain toward him, his face blackened with soot and his clothing scorched and tattered. A second man followed, wearing a flight suit stripped of its wings and wires, his bright hair shining in the sunlight. The red hair was a dead giveaway. Of all the humans wearing flight suits, only Joseph Weaver had hair that color. Which meant...

Eleazar crashed to his knees, weak with relief. A moment later, Diver engulfed him in a fierce embrace, weeping wildly on his shoulder. Gently, he held his friend, blinking away his own tears. "Diver," he said at last.

"Lee, Lee," Diver murmured through his sobbing, seemingly helpless to say anything else. He sounded so heartbroken.

"Shh, shh, it's alright. I'm alright. Diver, calm down. Please."

But Diver wouldn't be soothed. His wretched weeping continued. The sounds tearing from him were terrible to hear. Eleazar looked at Weaver, brow furrowing. The ex-captain stared at them, white-faced and stiff. "We have to move," he insisted, coming toward them, one hand reaching for Diver's shoulder. He lowered his voice, speaking gently. "It's not safe here, Diver. Please..."

Diver wrenched away from Weaver, even though the man hadn't touched him, burying his face against Eleazar's neck.

"He's in shock," Eleazar said to Weaver, a little sharply. "He thought I was dead. Give him a minute!"

Weaver ran a hand over his face. "He's not crying for you."

When Eleazar looked at him in confusion, he added grimly, "Fury was on that ship."

After the loss of the royal flagship, a great roar rose from the combatants on the ground. The battle seemed to be turning in their favor. The ghoul hordes had been corralled and were being devastated by a concentrated barrage. Those lucky enough to escape the Scourge had retreated to the safety of Conrad's defensive line. The terrible symphony of horns had ended; the Angelus returned to the drachens. Now those same ships seemed to be drifting aimlessly. Hope rose among the humans despite their losses.

Had they won?

"We've sent them running, I tell you!"

Conrad's jubilant voice grated against Diver's ears. He'd stopped sobbing, but his head was full of wool from the uncontrolled blubbering. Fury would be ashamed of him. Sitting like a useless lump while the fight still raged. But the idea of picking up a rifle made his belly hurt. What good was any of it now?

I'm all alone...

Eleazar had taken the news far better than he had. No weeping, no grieving. Just cold rage, and a strange burning hope that Fury still lived which Diver credited to deep denial. He'd witnessed firsthand Fury being consumed by a white-hot conflagration. Even if she had eaten a literal *ton* of Mithran, how could she have survived? No, his sister was gone, and he was alone in the world.

Cold mud seeped through his trouser bottoms. He sat on the churned-up ground, leaning against a pile of empty pallets while men and women shouted and fought and killed and died around him.

Conrad's ridiculous claim roused him a bit. Enough to peer into the sky and find the remaining drachen. They were hardly fleeing. Even as he watched, they began to come together in a loose formation. Who directed them now that Pace was gone? His neck still ached from the pressure of those cruel fingers. He was glad Pace was dead, but the cost, oh, the cost.

I was supposed to die in battle. Not Fury...

Nearby, Eleazar stalked a short path behind the embedded machine guns, casting his eyes toward the drachen. Of all of them, he had the best idea of what the Angelus might do. He'd lost track of his brother in the chaos, his vengeance stalled like a jammed pistol, and most likely searched the skies for a glint of emerald wings. His glowering presence took some of the starch out of Conrad's gleeful triumph, at least.

"Looks like they're forming up for an attack run," Weaver speculated, peering skyward. He and what remained of their short-lived Aerial Corps had gathered in the hastily built trenches – more shallow ditches with a wall of dirt than effective fortifications. Out of fuel, earthbound like the others, they'd removed their wings and empty rockets. Backup reserves had been located at Tully's position. And Tully was dead. Or turned, which was the same thing.

The other "soldiers" of the revolution, dressed in civilian garb and armed with shiny new rifles from the Factory, manned the makeshift battlements. Sweaty-palmed and breathless with fear, they held fire and let the precious field piece frag the hordes with high energy shells, only engaging when a few of the ghouls managed to get close.

"Do not underestimate Angelic terror," Eleazar warned darkly, eyeing the ships. "It is a powerful motivator. If they flee now, then all of Avernus will know they are weak. All of Splendour will be at risk. Without the Hallow Tithe, they will starve."

They. So, Eleazar was truly one of them, now? He looked at his Angelus, and the empty husk of his heart thumped. He was still the most glorious creature he'd ever seen. But... without Fury, what were they? Diver felt like a tripod with one leg kicked away. Teetering...

"Who's left to lead them?" Conrad demanded. "Pace is dead, and your brother is too, most likely. Their flagship has fallen; the rest are drachen sent to collect the Tithe, not warships. They should retreat, or we'll show them what's what."

Eleazar scowled at him. It seemed to be taking every bit of his will to restrain himself from striking the one-eyed revolutionary. It was apparent to everyone watching. Even Conrad took a step back. He muttered something foul and returned his attention to his artillery crews. His wife, Star, laid her keen regard on Eleazar. She wore a formal uniform, complete with braid and a row of medals, her "War Show" costume: The Hero of Radene, The Night Witch, Akkadia's shining Star, an inspiration as much as she was a commander.

"Is Captain Weaver correct?" she asked. "Are they going to attack?"

"They have no choice." His feelings toward Star weren't quite as bitter as they were toward Conrad, but he spoke to her reluctantly.

"It's suicide," Weaver interjected. "Those ships have no weapons. Any attacking Angelus will have to fly right into our guns."

"The Angelus won't leave the drachen, and those ships are made of Mithran. They will withstand your barrage."

"For a time maybe," Star said while she loaded the scoped rifle in her hands with a fresh magazine. Her legend as a sharpshooter had not been exaggerated. She'd been picking off any stray ghoul in range. Clean head shots. A mercy. "But every gun here is using Mithran-enhanced ammunition. Enough to rip them apart eventually."

Eleazar laughed. It was an ugly sound. "My brethren are slow learners, but they do learn. This time, they will stay in their ships where your bullets can't touch them. It will make their horns less effective, but they will keep coming. They won't stop until they rain destruction on all of us!"

Moving past her to the barricade, he spread his wings and leapt up the muddy slope. At the top, heedless of any danger, he waved an arm at the creatures massing against them. "They won't stop until every last one of you is like them!"

The burned humans screamed and groaned with one voice. Diver wanted to clap his hands over his ears. Weaver grabbed him by the arm and dragged him to his feet, ignoring his grunt of protest. "We need flamethrowers," he said, pulling Diver along with him to the battlement. "They're more effective than rifles at close range."

"There's a cache of flamethrowers down the line, Weaver," Star said to him, giving a jerk of her chin. Her face was pale; she had to know what was coming. "Arm as many as you can."

Weaver put his mouth close to Diver's ear. "Stay with Eleazar, no matter what, you understand me?"

Too tired and numb to speak, Diver could only nod and then Weaver was gone. His absence made Diver feel even more bereft. Perhaps he wasn't so dead inside as he'd thought? Rousing himself, he lifted his head. The Burnt Ghouls were easy to see from the top of the battlements. They swayed together in a thick stand, their strange moaning intensifying. The swaying quickened as if they were working up the courage to charge. A visceral fear made his belly knot, but other than that he was hard pressed to pull up any real feelings. Dying at the hands of a horde of Burnt Ghouls had once seemed the worst fate imaginable. Now...

I deserve a dishonorable death...

The shadows of the drachen passed over the amassed ghouls. The ships had formed a wedge and it pointed directly at their line of defense. As one, the charred folk looked up and grew still as if mesmerized by the golden underbellies of the drachen. A low, ominous hum filled the air. Terrible and familiar.

All up and down the line, men and women started to murmur, started to tremble, started to weep. By now, they all knew this horrible sound. This time, it came from the ships. This time, the Angelus would not expose themselves to gunfire.

"They learned the hard way. But they learned." Eleazar spoke grimly. Fatalistically.

The wedge of ships broke in four directions. A gasp of horror rose from the defenders. Two ships still swept toward them, dropping lower and lower, aiming for the line of machine guns and their remaining field piece, but the others flew toward the surrounding city. The dreaded horns appeared at the ship's gunnels, reduced to dozens instead of hundreds. But the awful noise grew in volume. A black rain began to fall across the field again, thin and haphazard, but it would be only a matter of time before it fell over the city.

And on the Tithing Field, with a deafening shriek, the last of the Burnt Ghouls swarmed.

Not to be last for long...

"Fire all guns!" Conrad screamed. "Blast them with everything we've got!"

"Target those ships!" Star cried to her section of the line. "Don't stop until they're dust!"

"The ships are staying out of range," one of Diver's people shouted, panicked. "Oh Creator, they're heading into Trin. The city... the whole city will be turned!"

The woman, a sturdy, unflappable soldier who'd taken out several Angelus with her Mithran blade, dropped to her knees, screaming in sheer horror. Her fear infected those around her. The guns fired steadily, but some soldiers abandoned their posts, fleeing. Their families were in the city...

"Don't break! Don't run!" Conrad's screams had grown hysterical. "Fucking cowards!"

"Keep firing!" Star scrambled to the top of the battlements. Her blonde hair blew loose in the wind as she lifted her rifle to her shoulder and fired at the oncoming hordes. Cool and calm. Those around her rallied at her courage and began to fire steadily. Ghouls fell in waves but more replaced them. Unstoppable.

The black rain drifted closer and closer. The horns sang incessantly.

They were dead. All of them. Diver looked at Eleazar just as the Angelus turned to him, doom sheeting down behind him. His face was pale, his eyes wide and horrified. The black rain wouldn't affect Eleazar. As for him...

Diver closed his eyes. He felt Eleazar grab his shirt, heard the metallic chime of his wings, but the rain was already falling around them even as he was lifted off his feet. It soaked through his scorched uniform, touched his skin. The sound of the guns stuttered to a halt. Replaced by screams.

CHAPTER FORTY-FOUR

Silence.

It was palpable. A force, not just an absence of sound.

Blackness surrounded her. There was no up, no down, no sideways. Not even the memory of light.

Nonetheless, Fury knew she was hurtling forward. Upward?

There was no air here. Some deep instinct had made her hold her breath and she knew better than to release it. Eleazar had warned her...

This was the Black Silence.

There had been an explosion. Right as she'd launched. It had lifted her, propelled her, tossed her impossibly high. Right through the Celestial Gate.

Her lungs hurt. A lot of her hurt. It was dreadfully cold. Her exposed hands were numb, her face frozen. Minor concerns. She had to breathe. Had to take in air. She would die. Die here in this impossible place!

Like a diver breaching the surface of a vast ocean, she burst into light. Her intake of air was a desperate wheeze. She gasped in the sweetness, feeling strength return to her limbs, and sense return to her oxygen-starved brain.

Her wings caught the wind, carrying her away from the swirling maelstrom. Back into the living world, somewhere full of light and air. She felt a surge of gratitude–

The pain she'd managed to ignore while struggling for breath returned with a vengeance. It was hard to pinpoint her injuries, there were so many of them. Her feet felt shredded, one arm hung uselessly, the other was red and blistered. Something warm and wet leaked from her ears, soaking into the leviathan skin she wore. Blood filled her mouth. She spat and strands of reddened saliva were carried away by the wind.

Fury coughed, and something rattled in her chest. *Fuck.* More coughing, and the rattle tore loose. Blood bubbled up her throat. She retched until she was wrung out. Weak, weary, she closed her eyes, letting the wind cradle her. This darkness wasn't so bad.

Suddenly, the wind swirled around her, tossing her about like a hummingbird in a tempest. She was too weak to scream. And then the empty sky was alive with creatures. Shimmering wings and shining scales caught the light and refracted it. Fury's eyes teared up in pain, but she couldn't look away. It was glorious. Something rose beneath her, a gargantuan creature at least as long as the drachen had been.

Trembling with relief, near the end of her strength, Fury settled onto the creature's vast back. The scales beneath her cheek were the same color as her mother's scarf.

Only the most ancient of leviathans darkened to such a deep indigo.

"I'm here," she whispered. The world was growing brighter. The dying always saw light at the end, didn't they? "I heard your song. Such... sadness. I'm sorry..."

Do not be sorry, Talisman Keeper. You have come to lead us home.

The voice. No longer whispering, urging, cajoling, but speaking clearly. There was such hope in it. She smiled weakly, torn by the irony. She was here, yes, but too wounded to be of any use.

A deep guilt invaded her. She'd eaten their bones for power. She wore their skin like a fancy dress. Yet when her mother had revealed her purpose – to free the leviathans from their prison – a purpose it had taken generations to fulfill, she had scoffed. She'd turned her back on her destiny. Now, she would die and there would be no one left to free them. The thought filled her with such sadness she began to cry.

Do not weep. You answered our call. You have brought the Talisman. Your light will lead us through the Black Silence.

"I... I can't," she choked out the words. How could they not understand how broken she was? Even with Mithran coursing through her body, the explosion had caused too much damage. This wasn't a slit throat. Her insides were paste. She tried to rise, tried to rally, but she had no strength. She sagged against the shining scales. "I'm too weak. I should have come when M —when Tully told me to. I am sorry. I've failed you all. Tully is... Tully—"

Sobs broke from her, sending agony throughout her broken body. She didn't care. She deserved it.

Ah. Tuilelaith Cree. Our faithful one. She was the last Talisman Keeper. One of the Blessed. The voice grew gentle. Kind. Forgiving. *Like you...*

"How are we blessed?" she asked bitterly. Even dazed and struggling for consciousness, she could feel the Mithran at work, but it was a slow and agonizing process. Could the gods' metal outrun death? "The Gullan are lost. Scourged..."

A mournful bellow erupted from the creature, it thrummed through Fury's bones. *So much has been lost. So many of my kind have been destroyed. Mind and body and soul. We are the last of our kind who remember. The final few Travelers.*

Fury was growing numb to the cold. Numb even to her pain. A strange warmth blossomed in her chest. "Travelers? I don't understand..."

Another mournful bellow and images flooded her mind. A vast expanse, not sky-blue, but star-spangled black. The deepest night sky. But it was an unending sky, infinite. Bright swirls of gaseous clouds pocked the velvet blanket, and from one such swirl streamed a shimmering line of leviathans. They undulated together, moving in synchrony. Like a school of fish navigating the ocean.

Once, we traveled the galaxy, skimming from nebula to nebula, seeking the energy of the cosmos. We feed on the dust of creation.

Bright swirls of cosmic dust dominated the star-washed blackness. The leviathans, the Travelers, speared through these nebulae, mouths open – mouths full of gleaming baleen – and scooped the shimmering substance into their maws.

But the galaxy is a vast and dangerous place, even for Travelers. Enemies abound...

Suddenly, a new nebula swirled into existence. It was glorious. A sweeping pool of light and dust, crimson and cobalt and viridian. The pod of celestial creatures shifted subtly, drawn to this newborn feeding ground.

We thought we had found a new home, a place of bounty, one which could sustain us for millennia. But it was a lie. A trap.

The leviathans entered the newly forming nebula, flying straight toward its bright heart, each following the beast before them, none understanding what was happening. One by one, they disappeared, snapping out of existence as if vaporized.

"What am I seeing?" Fury asked softly.

Our doom...

The space shifted around her, and Fury found herself back in Splendour, resting upon a deep, dark cloud bank. But this Splendour was different. The sky was stark white. It made her ill to look upon it. The leviathans had scattered, their graceful pod broken apart, lowing a grief-stricken song as they moved about aimlessly, seemingly blind. Here, they were bulky, clumsy. Vulnerable.

Vaguely human-shaped *things* appeared from the white and attacked the confused leviathans. Raw, red flesh shone through their blackened skin. Long-limbed and crooked, they had silver fangs too big for their wide, grinning mouths. Even as numb as she was, horror crawled through her belly at the sight. Ghouls. Not quite Burnt Ghouls, but frighteningly similar. Their fangs sank into leviathan flesh and their talons ripped through shimmering scales like knives through lace. Black blood boiled from the doomed leviathans while others fled deeper into the strange, stark place, leaving the pod to their fate.

One great and glorious creature, of the deepest indigo, managed to escape the bright, cold world. It crashed through a swirling vortex of blackness. A gateway. A portal. It could only lead to one place...

Fury blinked.

An image of a massive, broken, bloody form resting atop a great mountain flashed in her mind. The creature. It had reached Avernus. It lived, but barely. People, humans, surrounded it. Dark like her, on their knees, praying and weeping. They swayed together in unison. The creature was speaking to them, though Fury couldn't hear what it said.

She...

At the leviathan's direction, a man with a curved blade took a great swathe of her skin, flaying her alive. But this was not a trophy, not an act of cruelty. The leviathan hummed, imparting her directions to these people. Fury's people. The Gullan.

They wore the holy raiment. Kept the memories alive. The knowledge that the great Travelers were trapped in purgatory. They consumed her bones as she taught them, imbuing their entire people with deep, hidden power. They burned her flesh, her heart and organs, as was proper, sending her spirit skyward. The closest she would ever be to the stars. They collected her blood in urns, a most dangerous substance, a weapon to be used against their enemies.

A weapon unfortunately turned against them...

Fury witnessed the Scourge of her people, black rain turning them into Burnt Ghouls. Entire villages were destroyed, along with the holy raiment and urns of leviathan blood. Useless now to save them. Some tried, but they could not fight the army of winged Angelus descending upon them.

There were survivors. A blessed few. One raiment was saved and passed among them. Down generations as they scattered to the far reaches of Avernus. Her mother's scarf. The Talisman.

Fury blinked and she returned to the too-bright world. The leviathan's prison.

Our captors were creatures driven by instinct, by primitive hunger. Celestial beings like us, only twisted. They made this place to trap us, to feed upon us. But our flesh and blood was poison to them, and in their rage they flayed many of us. Our skin strengthened this prison, formed a firmament, making escape impossible. Eventually, they became so desperate for sustenance, they feasted on our bones. Unlike the humans, with only Mother to consume, these beings had an endless supply. It made them into gods.

The terrible slaughter faded from the stark sky, replaced by airy palaces floating on clouds and Mithran-laced flying mountains. Drachen drifted lazily between the beautiful Aeries and Angelus winged through the sky, glorious and supreme. But a darkness lay hidden within the beauty. A rot. Could the Angelus see it? It didn't seem likely. Though... hadn't Eleazar questioned the way of his world? Hadn't he been vilified for his questions, his doubts?

No wonder they cast you out, Lee. Questions lead to the truth...

Once again, she lay on the back of the massive leviathan, clear blue sky all around them. The winds had grown fiercer; they were descending rapidly. Toward what? But she knew: The Black Silence.

You will lead us through the darkness, Talisman Keeper. Our ancestor, the one who made it through the gateway, through the Black Silence, prepared the way. You wear her skin. She knew, even then, someone from the outside would have to come and free us. We thought Tuilelaith...

The depth of its sadness was an ocean.

But she had been tainted by our flesh. We had to wait. For the daughter. You were promised to us, Fury. I sense the power in your blood, stronger than any of your kind. You are full of light. You will lead us home. You have only to fly.

Fly? She couldn't even move. Fury moaned, her agony blazing, overwhelming her. Even lying flat, she felt dizzy. The cloud-studded sky swirled in her vision. She shifted, trying to work her wings open, but the best she managed was a flutter. She sobbed. "I can't. I can't fly!"

You must. Implacable. The command made her bones ache. The beast began to turn, to tilt. Its great head lowered, and its tail rose, its wings buzzing blindingly fast. She started to slide across its smooth indigo scales. Her heart pounded with fright. She slid faster. Toward empty air and a swirling black vortex.

If you cannot fly, then you must fall…

CHAPTER FORTY-FIVE

Eleazar had given every last bit of himself in the fight against Rast. It took more strength than he had left to lift Diver and carry him a short distance away from the line of death sweeping over the defenders. They crashed together in a world of chaos. Men and women ran headlong away from the front line, all pretense of fighting abandoned. The drachen followed slowly, dispensing the Angelic Curse from those dreadful horns. The song ceased abruptly, but the damage had been done. Half the remaining forces had been burned and the other half routed. Their machine guns sat abandoned in the shadow of two great drachen.

Shocked, Eleazar could barely fathom what had happened. How quickly things had turned. He held onto Diver, waiting for his friend to fall to the Curse. Eleazar would break his neck the minute his skin began to blacken–

"Lee, I can't breathe," Diver said, struggling against his hold. "Let me loose. I – I think I'm fine."

Eleazar pulled back. Black liquid streaked Diver's face, dripped from his hair and drenched his uniform, but he was unharmed. A miracle!

Diver swiped rain from his cheek, staring at the moisture on his fingertips. "The Mithran," he said. "It has to be the Mithran."

"Thank the Luminous One!"

But there was no time to be grateful. Eleazar staggered to his feet, yanking Diver along with him. They were hardly out of danger. The surviving Angelus would see Trin razed to the ground before letting word of their defeat reach the rest of Avernus.

Without Avernus, without the Hallow Tithe, Splendour will fall...

It took him a heartbeat to decide he didn't care.

"Lee!" The sound of excitement, of hope in Diver's voice stopped him when he was about to drag them into a run. Eleazar halted. Diver was on his knees, facing the drachen. His expression was radiant. "What is that?" he asked in an awed cry. He pointed a trembling hand skyward.

A light had appeared in the center of the Celestial Gate. As bright as a falling star. It streaked through the sky, leaving a long tail behind it. On this trajectory, it would land at the center of the Tithing Field. Eleazar stumbled a few steps, his wings snapping open. His breath sobbed in his chest.

Could it be?

Something else emerged from the Gate, following the light. Something enormous. Diver cried out, sounding ecstatic as an entire group of winged creatures burst forth from the swirling maelstrom. They moved through the sky in an undulating ballet, sheer wings buzzing madly. Eleazar fell to his knees, mirroring Diver's pose, struck dumb at the sight.

Leviathans. Leviathans had come to Avernus.

Alien creatures filled the sky above the Tithing Ground. Gargantuan, sleek beasts in blues and purples and indigo. The humans had no idea what they were. For all they knew, these gigantic winged and scaled creatures were there to eat them alive. It was hard to appreciate the doleful wisdom in their great eyes when one was fleeing hordes of Burnt Ghouls and the Angelic drachen unleashing waves of black rain on the edges of the city. The citizens of Trin assumed the leviathans were yet another doom descending on them. One more horrific monster to tear their world apart.

Until the leviathans began to tear the drachen apart...

Hulls made of Mithran splintered and burst beneath their onslaught. The great beasts smashed through the puny ships, using their thick, scaled bodies as battering rams. The Angelus managed to strike a few of the leviathans with massive harpoons, but even being impaled did not stop their destructive rampage. The largest of the creatures, a beast of the deepest indigo, did the most damage. Moving with ponderous grace, it crushed half the ships targeting the city, trumpeting its glee in a wild, triumphant song.

The screams and weeping of Trin's citizens stilled. A calm settled over the city. Where the shadow of the greatest leviathan passed, the people fell as one in deep reverence, foreheads touching the earth, their grateful tears watering the bricks.

Both Conrad and Star had been caught in the Angelus' final assault, along with most of the revolution's leadership. The field piece and the machine guns were lost, leaving men and women armed with rifles and flamethrowers against an advancing horde of their former comrades. The Aerial Corps still had their Mithran-alloy blades and they cut through ghouls like scythes through wheat.

The two drachen which had targeted the main line of defense had been smashed by a lone leviathan and had crashed into their own ghoulish army. Stunned Angelus fled the scene, unwilling or unable to fight, chasing after the single drachen which had survived the avenging leviathans, now rising hastily toward the Celestial Gate.

Eleazar kept one eye on the fleeing ship even as he tore through the ghouls like a fox in a chicken coop. He lost track of it when a surge of swarming ghouls took all his notice. Roaring, he spread his wings wide, a gleaming rallying point for the fighters. A new line of defense formed around him. This was no longer a war between humans and Angelus, but a battle for survival – and Eleazar was a living flame eating through the ghoul hordes.

Fighting alongside Eleazar, Diver screamed in angry defiance as he sliced through blackened flesh. Perhaps now he believed as Eleazar did that Fury was alive. His Mithran-enhanced strength gave him an advantage the other humans didn't possess. Only he was willing to throw himself *into* the ravenous hordes. Glad to have him at his back, Eleazar ripped Burnt Ghouls apart methodically, working through them with one goal in mind: The light. Reach the light...

That falling star had been Fury. She had fallen from Splendour, there was no other explanation. She had fallen through the Black Silence. And he hoped and he prayed to the Luminous One that she had survived as he had. He had to reach her, and only this army of Burnt Ghouls stood in his way. Exhausted and depleted, too weak to fly for more than a few feet, nevertheless, he could kill. And kill. And kill...

The tide began to turn when they neared the shattered remains of the royal drachen. The allies had managed to hold against the ghouls and now began to encircle the remaining creatures.

A new faction of fighters emerged from the west, from the direction of Vogel's palace. Led by a line of soldiers armed with flamethrowers, this group also contained not a few black-jacketed regulators. Perhaps allegiances had been muddied before, but now all humans were united against the hordes.

The two forces closed around the swarm of ghouls. The slaughter was intense. Heartrendingly so. These were their friends and comrades, lost to a curse. More than one fighter wept as they killed, but they never hesitated to strike the blow. To deliver mercy.

After a final frenzy of rifle fire, flames and singing blades, a heavy silence fell across the battlefield broken only by the harsh breathing of the survivors and the meek whimpering of the wounded. The smoke began to clear. Enough to see the skies above were empty. The leviathans were gone; the drachen too. Not a single Angelus flew in the deep blue sky.

Those humans left alive released a collective breath, too stunned and heartsick and broken to feel anything but relief. They had won, but the cost of victory had been a bitter one.

Covered in gore, and with no one left to kill, Eleazar stood in the shadow of the fallen drachen. The way was clear. He could go to her now. He hadn't seen where she had landed, not precisely, but he could feel her near.

Above them, the swirling darkness of the Celestial Gate began to shrink. To close.

He'd been so eager to go to her, but now he couldn't move. His heart seized in his chest then stuttered into a terrible pounding. Fear. It was fear.

"It was her," Diver said, his voice a croak. "Wasn't it?"

His friend knelt at his feet in the churned-up earth, his face gray with fatigue. His blade lay in the mud beside him, so crusted with blood and ash and gore it looked misshapen. He was staring at the smoking remnants of Pace's ship. He had to fear what they would find as much as Eleazar.

The remaining fighters reached their position, picking through the corpses, seeking ghouls to put down or wounded to rescue. A bedraggled Weaver appeared, leading a group of regulators who looked relieved to be alive. They deferred to the redheaded captain with meek compliance as he issued commands. The regulators were armed with the electrified sticks Eleazar remembered Conrad threatening him with. He scowled but understood. A good zap would bring down any recalcitrant Angelus.

A stifled sob tore from Diver when he laid eyes on Weaver. He scrambled up from the mud and threw himself at the man. Calmly, almost matter-of-factly, Weaver looked him over carefully then kissed him. Deeply, thoroughly.

For once, seeing the two of them together didn't cause Eleazar a surge of jealousy. He was glad for them, for Diver. When Weaver broke off the kiss and smiled down at Diver, his face was radiant. Eleazar felt a momentary hitch in his chest, but it passed quickly. Weaver found him and his expression turned savage.

"I have a gift for you, Eleazar," he said, grinning darkly. He moved away from Diver, but kept a firm hold of his lover's hand. For his part, Diver looked a little stunned.

Weaver turned and waved forward a knot of soldiers in boiler suits. These men and women weren't armed with flamethrowers, but more of those electrified sticks and slim, Mithran-alloy blades. The last few of Diver's ill-fated Aerial Corps. They had an unlikely prisoner in their midst. An Angelus, arms bound behind his back. A captured hawk. One with shimmering emerald wings.

"They found him unconscious behind our line," Weaver explained. "Buried in the mud. Thought you'd want to say hello to your brother. Or goodbye, I suppose."

Rast stared at Eleazar, his eyes bright and wild in his mud-streaked face, full of hatred and not a little fear. His muscles bulged and strained under his bonds, but he made no move to break free. Recalling the taste of electric sticks, Eleazar understood. Unwillingly, he felt a sliver of sympathy for his brother.

"We'll end him for you, Angelus," spoke up one of Rast's handlers, a soldier barely more than a boy. He raised his blade and placed it against Rast's throat. Mithran, Eleazar knew all too well, would part his tough Angelic skin like paper. The boy snarled. "Just like he did to Fury!"

Fury...

Suddenly, he wanted nothing more than to be away from this sad wretch of an Angelus. Briefly, Eleazar tried to call up the fires of vengeance, the white-hot rage which had returned the power of his wings, but he felt nothing but impatience. Fury lived. He knew it. Nothing else mattered. Not his revenge, not Rast, not his lost throne. He looked into Rast's amethyst eyes one last time and saw a hatred he no longer felt.

"Do what you want with him," he said tiredly, turning his back on his brother. "I don't care anymore."

Incoherent shrieks of rage followed him as he picked his way into the shattered drachen, but they flowed over him like water over stone. He heard someone following and knew it was Diver at his heels. Only one thing mattered.

Fury.

The sky had cleared. The maelstrom was a black smudge drifting away. No longer ominous. Certainly nothing to fear. She had survived the Silence. Twice. What more was there to fear in this great, wide world?

Fury had done her duty. Let her final sight be the clear blue sky...

She had fallen. All in the blink of an eye. A fleeting moment. Yet... eternal. Stars had been born and died as she fell. Galaxies rose and collapsed. Infinity bore witness to her fall. With bated breath. Time forgot Itself.

And then...

The Travelers, long absent from the stars, returned home at last.

The universe exhaled. She'd felt it through her bones, heard it with her soul. Something terribly wrong had been set right. The lamentations had become exultations. Joy beyond measure.

She had done her duty and now lay like a broken doll amidst the wreckage of Pace's ship. A warm breeze caressed her gently. Like breath. With it came a faint whispering of pain. Lying in wait. Shattered bones and agony. She wanted only oblivion—

No, Fee. Not yet. Open your eyes.

Fury started, her eyes flinging open. A whimper slid from her as pain wracked her body. Everything she had feared. But... no... this was a good pain, a healing pain.

"Papa?" she whispered. It had been Grayson's voice.

She did well, our little angel.

For a moment, she saw them. Her parents. Standing together, arm in arm, smiling down at her. As they had been. Young, whole, beloved.

Then the rubble shifted, voices rose in the distance. Calling her name. She blinked, and her mother and father were gone.

"She's here! I've found her!"

A golden warmth enveloped her. Long before his shadow fell across her face. Her angel. The only god she'd ever believed in. She bathed in his glory, felt renewed. The breeze caught at his feathers and their music filled her ears. He knelt beside her and gathered her into his arms, holding her close. Carefully, as if she might break.

She sighed, happy to bask in his warmth forever. But one concern roused her. "Diver?"

"He's—" Eleazar started to say, then Diver's voice broke in, "Fury! Fury, I'm here!"

She lifted a hand, reaching, and he was beside her, grasping it hard. Immense relief filled her, and she relaxed against Eleazar. Diver moved closer and laid his forehead against hers, sobbing gratefully. Eleazar shifted, his wings chiming as he raised them into a curving shelter, shielding the three of them.

"We have you," Eleazar whispered. "We have you, Fury. All is well."

The light was pure gold in the shelter of Eleazar's wings. Growing brighter as Fury grew stronger. She felt the power of the Mithran throbbing through her veins. She felt the wings on her back, each bone and feather. Alive with possibility. She had survived the Black Silence. Twice. Fury Barrett-Cree was no longer afraid. She would rise. She would fly again.

Oblivion would have to wait.

ACKNOWLEDGEMENTS

I owe a debt of gratitude to a lot of people: John Baker, agent extraordinaire at Bell LomaxMoreton, The Small God of Hype, without whom this book would never have been published. Gemma Creffield at Angry Robot books who took a chance (again!) on me and my crazy pitch. Simon Spanton, my amazing and talented editor who helped me make this book the best it could be. His guidance and insight were immeasurable. Andrew Hook, my most excellent copy editor. Alice Claire Coleman, the artist behind my amazing cover. Desola Coker, editor at Angry Robot who makes sure everything is running smoothly and I keep to my deadlines! The Transpatial Tavern, my fellow writers and friends who keep me sane and motivated. You know who you are! And to all my new agent-siblings, you guys are killing it!

I want to give a shoutout to my sister Michele Randall for being my biggest cheerleader. And last but definitely not least, a very special thanks to Robert Daley, my husband and support system, my best friend and favorite traveling companion. The man who serenades me with banjo music while I write.